# FARRAGAN'S RETREAT

BY THE SAME AUTHOR

 *Principato*

# TOM McHALE

*Farragan's Retreat*

NEW YORK / THE VIKING PRESS

First published in 1971 by The Viking Press, Inc.
625 Madison Avenue, New York, N.Y. 10022

Published simultaneously in Canada by
The Macmillan Company of Canada Limited

SBN 670-30846-3

Library of Congress catalog card number: 73-132861

Printed in U.S.A. by The Colonial Press Inc.

*To Dori*

# FARRAGAN'S RETREAT

# CHAPTER 1

## *The Killer Poses*

Farragan had absolutely no intention of murdering his son, Simon: fathers did not usually quash their own seed, after all, given the time and trouble it took to make it grow. Even if a substantial number of people thought Simon definitely needed quashing.

But it occasionally disturbed him that he so positively enjoyed fantasizing the killer poses. This August Sunday morning, between the Offertory and Communion of the Mass, he was into them again for perhaps the thirtieth time.

Pose one was doggedly simple. Farragan, with revolver already in hand, had only to pull the trigger after aiming point-blank at the victim's heart the instant the latter opened his apartment door in response to Farragan's knock. But of course there was one problem with pose one beyond the possibility of powder burns and the indictment of the victim's erupted blood on Farragan's too-close lapels. This was the fact that the victim was Simon—whom Farragan loved in essence but was compelled to despise in principle—and for this reason he guessed he might not be equal for the remainder of his life to his memory's recall of the victim's shock of recognition of his own father.

Happily, though, Farragan had no real intention of killing his son. Despite what other people thought best.

Pose two, coinciding with the ringing of bells to mark the offering of the wine, was an easy shot from a darkened back alley through an angled distance of twenty feet or so into Simon's second-floor bathroom. Easy, of course, provided Simon was compelled to use that convenience during the nighttime hours while Farragan might safely stalk him from the outside. But in a previous scouting trip to Montreal, Simon—justifiably narcissistic—had favored the place abundantly after dark, standing with razor or tweezers in hand before the mirror, with his head and shoulders completely exposed above the level of blacked-out window glass that still vaguely certified the outline of the remainder of his form beneath. This was the pose that Farragan hoped would come through: under the enlightened tutelage of his sister, Anna, he had become deadly with the .38 through intermediate distances, even with the weight of the silencer hanging on its nose. And there would be no problem of a moving target either.

"Lamb of God who takest away the sins of the world . . ."

Farragan prepared to go up to the altar for Communion. He rose from his seat and smiled automatically at the woman who admitted him to line though there was hardly a need for her to stop. At this hour of the morning the cathedral dwarfed its spare collection of worshipers.

Pose three was actually a multiplicity of poses. It had a central theme of moving target, and Farragan's problem was to get somehow close enough to equal the hoped-for accuracy of pose two but at the same time avoid the difficulty inherent in pose one. In two previous Montreal trips he had shared Simon's movements and

knew his son was often accustomed to pass before a near-by church
with three eternally darkened Gothic entrances on his way to and
from his apartment. Also alongside a small park, with three gates,
that was separated from the walk by a high row of hedge. One
point was fairly obvious, Farragan decided as he slid to his knees at
the altar railing: if it was to be pose three, in the area of Simon's
apartment, the liquidator needed to stay absolutely concealed. Someone might remember him from the last two trips he had made to
Canada.

In the moment before the bishop's scented hands placed the
wafer of host on his tongue, Farragan was still fantasizing: Jesus
Christ, mercy. I kill only for a just cause, O Lord, he consoled the
godhead. In the instant of the return of the prelate's hands to the ci-
borium, he decided that shooting Simon in the back was certainly
cricket, in light of what had happened to the boy's cousins, Malcolm and Edward. Really, after the letter of condolence the bastard
had written to Ho Chi Minh, he deserved no consideration at all.
Farragan gritted his teeth with the memory as he eased the host
down his throat.

Pose four—on the way back to his seat—was many-faceted
also. It was the arranged-meeting pose. Farragan had already
thought of renting an unobtrusive car, then telephoning Simon to
meet him in the outlying districts of Montreal, and shooting him as
he drove up to the spot. There was also the darkened hotel room
where Farragan might register under a fictitious name. And other
possibilities: it wearied the mind to liquidate the victim so many
times over. But were he really going to kill him, Simon would be
just as good as dead.

"Go, you are dismissed," said the bishop from the altar. Just
like that. Farragan remembered the Latin of the old rite: *Ite missa est.*
Something was gone from the Mass, he thought sadly, since they
wrote it up in the vernacular. The magic act of Transubstantiation

was harder to swallow when they proposed it in English. But then Farragan was not a Catholic for nothing. Reverently he blessed himself and exited toward the rear.

It was six-forty-five now, and the fountains in Logan Circle before the cathedral seemed to him already to flag in the face of the rising heat. Philadelphia enjoyed three blessings, Farragan's father had always said: two rivers, the Irish immigrations, and unenviable high percentages of humidity. In accordance with the old man's irony, then, another steam bath of a day was on its way. Farragan mopped at his brow, then cut through the line of cars waiting to bear worshipers away and crossed to the middle of the circle to stand anointed for a long moment in the spray that blew from the fountain jets. Behind him, the cathedral bells began suddenly to boom, and he turned to see an unexpected flight of pigeons burst out of the belfry and pivot and circle the spires once before they settled to earth in a cluster. Farragan was caused to think of Europe. The Saint-Sulpice in Paris, or the piazzas in Florence. But Philadelphia was not without possibilities either: for all his irony, the old man had never said it was not a beautiful city. For his part, Farragan loved it immensely, and it grieved him somehow that he had had so little time or reason to be in center city these past few years.

Ahead of him, at the end of the Franklin Parkway, was the hill-crowning hulk of the art museum beside the Schuylkill, and since he was not due at Anna's for target practice until eight o'clock, he decided to walk that far for exercise. Traffic in the parkway was light, and in the park itself he was suddenly conscious of a whole race of little old ladies walking their dogs. Widows, Farragan decided in an instant. Widows who lived as a result of careful planning in those high-rise apartments near Vine Street and survived the day from rising till the hour of sleep with an endless monologue of doggie talk. One, near by, spoke French to a silken-haired Afghan. Her tone was plaintive and keening. In response, the dog's eyes were rheumy and distended. It slumped to the ground before her with an audible sigh. Neither of the lovers had noticed Farragan's presence.

He walked on, then abruptly cut across the parkway toward the Rodin Museum. Three summers before, Farragan was returning home late one Sunday night from the shore when he saw two Negroes fornicating on the grass beside the museum. Only he had thought it was rape: the woman's arms and legs flailed up and down and the man rose and fell upon her so that, from his car, Farragan decided the woman was being beaten. Dumb hero, he had raced across the lawn shouting, "Leave that woman alone!"

"Get the fuck outta here, whitey," the man had warned, not missing a stroke in his incredible rhythm. His pants clung to the end of his legs, and his naked buttocks—like some cliché that Farragan could not precisely remember—glistened in the moonlight. Below him, the woman's arms had fallen leadenly to her side. She smiled sheepishly at her would-be protector.

"There's nothin' wrong. I'm not bein' attacked."

"She likes it," the man had said, his tone somewhat softer.

"Oh, I'm sorry. Forgive me. I didn't understand," Farragan had apologized. "Forgive me."

He had turned swiftly to retreat and banged into the hulk of the naked Thinker astride a block of stone. Behind him, the fornicator had laughed softly as Farragan limped to his car to flee to the safety of suburban Wynnewood.

Now, this morning, he searched in the grass for a remembrance: the imprint of the woman's buttocks or shoulder blades, perhaps. But there was only the green thickness of a well-watered August lawn. The image of that perfect copulation came to him instead, as it had many times before; but since it was Sunday, he permitted only a moment's enjoyment, then vehemently decried himself a voyeur: O God, what temptations do you let assail me that I should enjoy the vision of other peoples' fucking? He marched quietly off the lawn, neatly avoiding the Thinker this time, hastening toward the end of the parkway in his urgency to quiet the beginnings of erection that had stolen upon him.

At the art museum he climbed the long file of steps and stood panting for breath behind the balustrade at the top. The view was sufficient reward. Below, on the Schuylkill, a long shell eased away from one of the boathouses, and two girls in culottes waved like sirens at the receding rowers. There was a wistful quality to the scene, and Farragan suddenly hoped all the young men would return safely to the girls, their shell intact.

He watched another flight of pigeons tear off the Spring Garden Street bridge at the horn blast of a truck: they flew in a straight line this time, paralleling the river, then came to rest atop the Thirtieth Street Station. Beyond was the Penn campus, and the beginning of a rueful memory: Simon had lasted exactly three days at that place. Until he called home at two a.m. to tell Farragan he was on his way to New York to try Columbia for a late admission. He simply knew too many people at Penn to make it a viable experience.

Farragan had no idea what a viable experience was until four days later, when he caught up with him in Chicago, where Simon had persuaded that university to make room. For two days father and son had walked the city streets, gently arguing, and had three times gone to Marshall Field's for fancy and expensive ski equipment that Farragan guessed was never used anyhow, since Simon went to the Bahamas that Christmas, and the following one, if he remembered correctly.

Oh, but what a bastard that kid was! Where were all those skis and poles and thermal underwear now?

In the end, it was Brandeis that consented to graduate him, and Farragan—still grateful for that kindness—had sent off a check to the Alumni Club at Waltham only a few days before, vaguely wondering what kind of university it was anyhow. The brilliance of Simon's final transcript had been scant consolation: it ranged across the varicolored paper of four different universities in a period of five years. Five schools, if you counted Penn. Really, the only artfulness Simon possessed, in Farragan's opinion, was snowing admission committees. Beyond this, there had been but the din of rebellion and a frenzied renunciation of Farragan's beloved Church. The father pitied his son this loss: but there was nothing to be done for it. Simon simply failed to work on any team, God's notwithstanding.

Looking over the balustrade, Farragan saw the perfect analogy. A shell—perhaps the one that had pulled away from the boathouse —skimmed down the Schuylkill toward the museum like a water spider. Put Simon in that boat and he would make certain there would be no stopping in time to avoid going over the waterfall beneath the bridge. There could be no gentle tongue clucking over the folly of his fumbling either. Simon was hardly a fumbler. Putting boats over waterfalls had become his profession. It was partly for this reason he deserved to be killed, Farragan considered sadly, at the same time anxious himself to know when the shell would begin its turning.

But it was mostly because of what had happened to his two cousins and not at all to Simon that he deserved, in other people's estimation, to be killed. Farragan rekindled his anger, remembering how the argument went. Malcolm, who was Anna's only son and twenty-two years old, had come home in January from Viet Nam in a box that could not be opened. They had buried him in Wynnewood with all the pomp and patriotism the Farragans could provide, then hung desperately on the weekly letter from Da Nang from twenty-year-old Edward, who was their brother Jim's son.

In June, two days before the Army notification that Edward had been wounded in action and was being hospitalized, Simon had

fled to Canada. A week later, in the midst of their stoic grieving
over the loss of Edward's right arm, all the Farragans—Farragan
himself, his sister, Anna, and brothers Jim and Edmund—had received copies of the letter of condolence Simon had sent to Ho Chi
Minh.

And three weeks ago Edward was flown in from Viet Nam
and discharged. Farragan had gone to the airport with Jim and his
wife, Margaret, and Anna, also, to welcome his nephew home. The
reality of that pinned-up shirt sleeve—long anticipated—had, in the
end, proved unnerving. Farragan had covertly crossed himself out of
reverence, then felt the tears flash to his eyes. Margaret, the mother,
had fainted outright, and Anna had clung to Edward's neck, whim-
pering: Malcolm, Malcolm, my darling Malcolm. Jim, when he was
done ministering to his fainted wife, had saluted his son, then
reached with his left hand to shake Edward's with a convincing ease
that was by now a reflex from practicing the motion so often.

Christ, but the kid had been so damn gutsy, Farragan remembered, the tears flashing forth again. Worth a thousand Simons.
Twenty years old, he had played father to Anna, walking her out to
Jim's limousine with the one good arm left to him, and telling her
he had heard from a couple of Green Berets in Saigon how brave
Malcolm had been. In the car he had lent the arm to his mother and
kidded her away from her tears by warning her exactly how he
wanted his dinner steak done that evening. Then, inevitably, he had
asked after Simon.

The response was a universal silence. They were already a mile
from the terminal, and Farragan, positioned in one of the jump
seats, had heard in the quiet the soft hiss of suspension as the car
cornered through the airport circle. He prepared to speak, closing
his eyes for an instant before looking back at Edward.

"Simon is in Canada dodging the draft," Anna got the words
out first. There was none of the expected vehemence in her voice:

only a chilling matter of factness that was somehow worse than vehemence.

"You're kidding," Edward had said mutely, staring at Farragan. "That doesn't sound like Simon."

"Read this, Edward," Jim had directed from the driver's seat. He passed an envelope to Anna, who opened it for her nephew. Farragan recognized a much-thumbed copy of the Ho Chi Minh letter.

"The dirty motherfucker!" Edward had shrieked after finishing the page. He crumpled it into a ball and threw it at Farragan.

"That filthy fucking traitor! He's sorry, is he? Did Uncle Ho send Aunt Anna a letter of condolence for Malcolm? Did anybody get a letter of regret over the loss of my arm? Answer that one!"

But Farragan had been unable to respond. He had turned his head toward the outside, where Kelly's brickyard flashed by at seventy miles per hour, and wept and wept with shame.

It was less than a week later that Jim and Anna demanded the ultimate punishment of death for Simon the traitor. A kind of ritual killing, all things considered.

In response to their intensity, Farragan was the Farragan he despised most: frightened again in his late forties by their curious capacity for malevolence that he had been frightened of since childhood, and intimidated by their knowledge of his young mistress, Marie, that they might use to wreck his real marriage, he had pretended to agree. And further, complying with ritual, to serve as hit man. There was no other choice. Because it might still give him a chance to plead with Simon to leave for the vaster obscurity of Europe while brandishing the horrible weapon as proof, before Jim or Anna got to him. And if he be unsuccessful in persuading his son, at least a delay that he might blame on Simon's temporary absence from Montreal.

But there could be no second delay. For Jim and Anna, with their merciless efficiency, would find a way to have his corpse back in Philadelphia and buried in the name of the American Republic shortly thereafter. Unconvinced of his danger, Simon was, truly, just as good as dead.

# CHAPTER 2

# Let No Doves Enter This House

Farragan left the art museum, walking quickly southward toward Anna's house on Panama Street for his final session of target practice before the liquidation.

But at Market Street he forgot about his son for the moment and was suddenly preoccupied with the bareness of that thoroughfare. Off to his left, about seven blocks away, was the grotesqueness of City Hall. Not a single vehicle moved anywhere between. Where, he wondered, at this time of morning was the myriad collection of foreign sailors and American transients that infested the penny arcades and pornographic bookstalls along this street? A panhandler sidled up to him, feigning before making his pitch a neat jig of a dance that looked especially ludicrous because it was seven-forty-five of a Sunday morning. Farragan cut him short and handed him a quarter, thinking vaguely of sleazy hotels and mission breakfasts.

He escaped across Market, heedless of the light and the bum's benediction in the name of God, and passed before the antique shops and mini town houses that bolstered the restored colonial image of downtown Philadelphia. At Panama Street he turned into the real suggestion of two centuries before and knocked on the door of Anna's house. It was opened almost immediately by Mrs. Crow, his sister's companion-housekeeper. She spoke always with the breathless conspiracy of the old Irish, and Farragan prepared to mask his distaste.

"Good morning, Arthur."

"Good morning, Mrs. Crow. Is Anna up?"

"Yes, she's been waiting for you. She's in the garden having a little breakfast. How would you like your eggs?"

"Shirred, with a tiny piece of ham, perhaps."

"Very well. Arthur . . ."

"Yes, Mrs. Crow?"

"She's upset. Another boy who was in Viet Nam with Malcolm came to see her yesterday," flew at him in her voice for secrets.

"Why upset? The other boy was a great comfort to her, wasn't he? She made him stay for a week, if I remember correctly."

"This one was a dove, Arthur. He had two drinks, then took off his shirt to show us a shrapnel wound, and told us that wound and Malcolm's death were both for nothing. Anna threw the bastard out into the street, and by that time was so upset she had a few more drinks and went to bed."

Your loyalty is excessive, Crow, Farragan decided as he moved through the house toward the garden. Anna was an alcoholic. There was no euphemism for it. You probably helped her into bed last night when she could no longer stand. The wonder of it was that at fifty-five she always got herself back into some reasonable kind of condition the next day.

Anna was sitting in a morning coat at a table in the garden beside the eternally befogged igloo of her midget greenhouse. Farragan winced involuntarily at the sight of her: her gray hair fell long and lifeless to the level of her shoulders and deep pouches of atrabilious coloring clung beneath her eyes and made him think her liver might be on the way out. The eyes themselves were glazed and bloodshot.

"Look pretty bad, do I?" Anna asked him ruefully.

"I'm not accustomed to seeing you so early in the morning," he told her, taking a seat and pouring himself a cup of coffee.

"Nor many others, thank God. The greatest comfort to my old age is the five-p.m. Mass on Sundays. It gives me the whole day to pound myself back into shape."

"Why did you have to go off on such a toot anyhow?"

"You should have met that dove bastard that was here yesterday. I almost shot him. He had Malcolm's Christopher medal, the one the Army couldn't find when they sent his body home to me. This kid was a Puerto Rican, and when he gave me the medal, I grabbed him and kissed him, and Crow kissed him, and the three of us sat around crying in the parlor. Then we found out he was a dove. Malcolm's death was a goddam waste, he kept saying to me."

"What did you do?"

"I threw him out. Then I burned Malcolm's Christopher medal. To think that little Spic had been carrying it around with him this many months . . ."

"You ought to let those flowers outside the greenhouse to get a little air for the rest of the summer, Anna," he said. Peering inside, Farragan could just barely discern the sad blooms through the haze of humidity. They reminded him of some calcium-starved rats he had once seen in a medical laboratory.

"They're all right, Arthur. They may not look completely fantastic right now, but I'm the only one in the neighborhood who has fresh flowers during the winter months that don't come from a florist."

Farragan supposed that was enough justification for suppressing them during the summer, then. At the back of the narrow garden, geraniums—albeit temporary—grew lushly in the turgid Philadelphia atmosphere. A forest of dark-green ivy climbed the wall. Above was the huge studio window of J. Worthington Duffey's apartment. But the curtains were drawn, and blessedly, J. Worthington Duffey had not yet appeared.

Crow brought his breakfast and placed it silently before him. He could tell from the way the albumen clung to the side of the baking dish that the eggs were overdone. Farragan ate silently as Anna stood up before the control board of her greenhouse—a miasma of thermometers, barometers, switches, and dials that governed a welter of variables like temperature and humidity. In lieu of a dog or cat, like the widows in the park, she cooed at her flowers instead.

"How are Mama's little flowers today? Were any of you cold during the night?"

"Oh, Anna, I don't think they could have been cold at all," Crow said, gasping. "The temperature was turned way up last night."

"Oh, yes, but don't you know how cold it gets between two rivers on a summer night even, Crow?"

"Well, yes, you're right, Anna, about that."

Let them have their little game, Farragan thought, slicing through his ham. Crow needed the assertive strength of Anna, and after losing three husbands and an only son, Anna needed anything she might lay her hands on: thus her drinking and her captive flowers and her extreme righteousness about the morality of almost everything. Anna was a grand dragon in the War Vets Ladies' Auxiliary: together with Crow, her handmaiden, she plotted and prepared, then went off to yearly conventions, returning always after the skirmishes with a bust covering of new victory medals. More power to her then, he decided, as long as it kept her going.

In the next moment their brother Jim stepped out of the house into the garden. Farragan did not hear the bell ring and knew the front door was never left unlocked. Jim, then, had a key to Anna's house. Somehow, that knowledge disconcerted Farragan, who always had to knock at the door. They were too much a set of partners—Jim and Anna—in agreement on every decision that had to be made in the family business, and in total agreement long before Farragan had permitted himself to be persuaded about Malcolm's and Edward's sacrifice and Simon's cowardice in light of those sacrifices.

"Good morning, Anna. Good morning, Arthur. Hello, Crow."

Jim was jovial in excess, but Farragan saw the need. Crow, knowing nearly everything about Farragan family affairs, could not be permitted to know about Simon. Farragan joined in the façade-building and smiled and pumped his brother's hand.

"Well, it's certainly nice to see you all together on a fine Sunday morning," Crow said, a touch of the brogue creeping into her voice. "It's too bad your brother Edmund couldn't be here now. I'd cook you all a fine breakfast of pancakes and sausage."

"Oh, yes," Jim said indulgently. "It's a shame he couldn't be here. But his duties keep him so busy, don't you know?"

"God knows, yes. Runnin' that whole monastery by himself, the poor thing. You'd think they'd send him some help now."

No one spoke. Farragan stared mutely ahead, through Anna and her garden wall and all of Philadelphia, perhaps. It occurred to him for the first time that Crow just might not know that Edmund was one of the remaining five priests in his order. With the others all older—the next youngest, by at least ten years—Edmund was a cinch to become Father General of the Tirungians. What matter that he be the sole survivor and Father General to no purpose? For years, Jim had taken a fanatical pleasure in introducing his brother to friends, then turning aside to whisper that Edmund was up for the kingship. No one could dispute the fact: no one had ever heard of the Tirungians.

"It's just a shame about how overworked he is," Crow said.

"Yes," Jim agreed. "By the way, do you get the Sunday *Inquirer* delivered to the house, Anna?"

"No, I don't bother with it."

"Crow, would you be so kind as to go outside and get me one? You can take your time."

"I'll need some time, Jim, since I might have to go as far as Broad Street to find a newsstand."

"We trust you won't be running off with anybody you might meet on Market Street," Jim said, winking.

"Oh, you're just the most horrible man," she answered gaily, then accepted a dollar from Jim and prepared to leave.

"I'll be back as soon as I can, Anna," Crow called from the front hallway. When they heard the door close behind her, they rose with single impulse and went quickly into the house to the basement door. Downstairs, where anyone else would have settled for a den or rumpus room, was Anna's shooting gallery. Hidden in the police-infested center of Philadelphia, Farragan's sister lived in perpetual fear of being raped by a Negro. Wished for it, perhaps: Farragan was never able to make the distinction. But she prepared herself for any eventuality with daily target practice and had a permit to carry a revolver with her at all times. In the month's time since the decision had been made to wreak vengeance on Simon, it was Anna who had taught him to be the killer.

While he waited with Jim, their sister struggled into her coveralls behind them. When she was ready, and looking like a female defense-plant worker, she handed Farragan the revolver, then switched on the lights to illuminate the target figure astride an oval track at the far end of the basement. On three sides of the plaster-board man were thick styrofoam retaining walls to absorb slugs and collect richochets.

"Try fixed target at forty feet, Arthur," Anna instructed, suddenly springing to real life from the abyss of her hangover.

Farragan loaded the .38 and fired once at the man. A spurt of flame leapt from the nozzle of the silencer. The death hole appeared instantly near the middle of the chest, slightly to the left of the heart.

"You got that coon right where it counts, Arthur," Anna rasped out. Both she and Jim were smiling broadly now. The rhythm was beginning: to her, all the target figures were Negroes; to Jim—with a vestigial memory of the war still fiercely operative—they were Japs; Farragan saw only Simon, his son.

"How many Japs did you kill during the war, Arthur?" Jim asked the question slyly for perhaps the thousandth time, winking openly at Anna.

"One," Farragan hurled back. Jim was always trying to trip him up on this. He had killed one Japanese: in a moment of blind panic at meeting the man face to face on a small Pacific atoll that was supposed to have been cleared. Farragan had confessed the hit to his brother during the first drunk they had together after the war, and had been paying for it ever since. Jim, apparently, had killed many: Farragan's brother saw this as some index of superiority. Other men had ceased thinking about it the day after discharge.

"If you knew how to shoot like this then, you could have killed lots more," Jim said.

"I never saw any more."

"I'm saying *if* you had. . . ."

"Yes," Farragan agreed.

"Arthur, try moving target, walking," Anna said. She pressed a button and the target piece turned sideways to reveal another dimension of a man with a thirty-inch waist. Then the figure began moving along the oval track at walking speed. Farragan fired five times. Three wounds appeared between the hip and shoulder. The spent bullets were doubtless in the wall behind.

"That's not bad, Arthur," Anna said, going forward to chalk an X over each hit, "but you've gotten four hits a number of times in the past."

"If that fourth shell was meant for a fourth Jap, he would've nailed you by now," Jim said.

"There's only one of Simon," Farragan told him evenly.

"Try running target now." Anna pressed the control again and the man swept about the oval track. This was the worst for Farragan: the sense of urgency in the target's revolutions always unnerved him; its weaving and bobbing reminded him of a fat man driven by fear, and he had recently known nightmares in which he himself was the terror-ridden victim astride an oval track. He took a second revolver from his sister and fired twice, missing both times. Behind him, Jim and Anna groaned in unison. Desperate, Farragan rushed the figure and pumped three bullets into its head. When Anna brought the man to a halt, he emptied the remainder of the slugs into the plasterboard stomach. Then he lowered the gun: his hands were trembling and sweat rushed out of his pores.

In another moment Jim pinned his arms behind him, and Anna took away the revolver.

"Arthur, Arthur, for the love of God, I was only kidding about those Japs," his brother implored.

Anna wiped at his sweated face with a handkerchief. "It's a one-in-a-million situation, Arthur, but it has to be done. We can't take the chance of hiring anyone outside the family to do the job."

"Malcolm came home from the war in a coffin, Arthur," Jim said slowly, not releasing his brother's arms. "My Ed is having a bit of trouble swimming down at the shore this summer, since he has only one arm. This is a family of patriots, and it can't be expected therefore to be magnanimous enough to permit one of its own to sit scot free up there in Canada writing letters of condolence to Ho Chi Minh. Simon is getting what he needs. By Thursday night it'll all be over, and if we make every move the way we planned, no one will even have a suspicion it was one of his own family."

"He's as good as dead," Farragan told them. Jim released his arms.

"Good," Anna applauded. "Now let's go upstairs laughing, and if Crow is back, we'll joke with her for a few minutes, then you two can leave whenever you're ready."

Farragan's sister peeled off the coveralls, replaced the morning coat, then switched out the basement lights. They mounted the stairs and went quickly outside to the garden, taking up places around the breakfast table. Farragan poured himself a cup of cold coffee, raising it to his lips with a still trembling hand.

"What time tomorrow do you intend to leave for the monastery, Arthur?" Anna asked.

"Very early. The bus leaves the Greyhound terminal at six a.m."

"You make sure Edmund knows what he has to say, on the off-chance the police come around checking up on you," Jim warned him.

"He knows already."

"You can't have a better alibi than a priest's word, I guess," Anna said.

"Lucky we found an order to take him." Farragan dared to say the truth.

"He could have been a Jesuit," Jim retorted.

"Not for all the money in Philadelphia," Farragan said quietly. Then Crow came through the front door. Breathless, as ever, she handed the Sunday *Inquirer* over to Jim.

"God love you, Crow, you didn't have to run all the way," Jim said.

"I thought you'd all be bored sittin' around here with Anna feelin' as bad as she does."

"I feel much better now, Crow, thank you."

"I have to go," Farragan said abruptly. He was about to rise when he heard the rattle of curtains being drawn open on the massive studio window above the end of the garden. The others turned their heads away, a conditioned response, and Crow began gathering up dishes in furious preoccupation. But Farragan, fresh from the horror of having murdered his only son, was suddenly atremble with laughter, and he waved and nodded gratefully to the naked figure of J. Worthington Duffey standing in full view before them. J. Worthington Duffey was the archbishop's unmarried brother. Knowing who he was, Anna, Crow, and especially Jim had spent years trying to convince themselves there really was no naked man up there.

But to Farragan, on particular days, Duffey seemed like the only other sane person in the universe. For the two who sat beside him, shielding their eyes of a Sunday morning against the frankness of the exhibitionist's minuscule genitalia, were decidedly nuts. In desperation, since their proposal for Simon's assassination, Farragan had written daily pleading letters to his son about a removal to France or neutral Sweden, perhaps. But Simon had simply not believed it. As might be expected. In the same way, Farragan realized, that the police might be hard put to lay hands on evidence if ever he went to them with the story. . . .

"You shouldn't indulge him like that, Arthur," Anna snarled, breaking into his thoughts. "It's immoral the way Duffey goes around without any clothes."

Christ Jesus, Farragan thought, what the fuck was Duffey's nakedness compared to murder?

## CHAPTER 3

# *The Bus to Lahore*

Farragan's wife—doubtless in special communion with those once violated but now moldering women she sought constantly to have canonized—charged through the exact-change lane onto the Ben Franklin Bridge, pausing only an instant to flip a quarter into the yawning basket and not waiting for the green light to flash THANK YOU. She floored the accelerator and moved Farragan's Cadillac up the ascent, doing fifty miles per hour before reaching the summit, regardless of this fog-ridden early morning's posted fifteen. Below, on the Delaware, barges inched upstream toward Trenton, sounding mournful whistles all the way. On the bridge, Muriel Farragan flashed past frightened behemoths of trucks creeping across toward Philadelphia.

"It would be a shame to die today, Muriel," Farragan said quietly. "I've been looking forward to going on retreat for some time now."

"I know, Arthur. I know you've been anticipating these two

weeks. But I can see through fog. You should know that by now."

"Yes, but the pavement is wet. Think of the girls, Muriel. You're their mother. Think if we had an accident."

"We won't have an accident, Arthur," she said, clicking her teeth, then increasing speed and plunging onto the wide expanse of cobblestone at the Philadelphia end of the bridge, heedless of the Negro policeman who stood eerily in a blinking bath of yellow light, waving his arms and blowing his whistle at her to slow down.

"Arthur," she asked after a moment, "is Simon still alive? He's my son, too, but I haven't heard from him in such a long time."

"He's alive," Farragan said grimly.

"Where?"

"In Canada. In Montreal."

"That's where Saint Joseph's Shrine is, isn't it?"

"Yes."

"Is he making a pilgrimage, Arthur?"

"No, he's dodging the draft."

"Is that bad?"

"He's a traitor. It's very bad. Why do you ask?"

"I worry about him, Arthur. I never see him."

"That's because he's never around. Now, remember to get in touch with me if anything goes wrong down at the shore. If a bad storm warning comes up, get off the island with the girls and return to Philadelphia. It's almost hurricane season, you know. Is anyone coming down to stay with you?"

"Only Gina McFarland, Arthur. We're going to get the canonization drive rolling for Blessed Elizabetta La Voci."

"That's a new one, isn't it? She's not the same one whose village we visited in France last summer, is she?"

"No, Arthur, don't you remember? That was Blessed Françoise Le Bœuf. We seem to be banging into a blank wall with her, though. It seems best that we abandon that effort temporarily. Blessed Elizabetta La Voci has proven miracles to her credit."

"Where's her village?"

"In Italy, Arthur. Can't you tell by the name? Perhaps we can go there this fall."

"Perhaps. Why is she particularly deserving of sainthood?"

"She was only twenty, Arthur, and working one day in the fields near Turin when she was dragged into a tool shed and raped by a Communist who worked at the near-by Fiat plant. All the laborers who were outside the tool shed trying to save her heard her screaming, 'Dear Sweet Jesus, help your virgin daughter!' When he was through with her, the rapist strangled her."

Farragan peered through the windshield. Outside, on the skid row of Vine Street near the docks, bums, barely discerned, reeled along the sidewalk toward mission breakfasts, or leaned grotesquely on the sides of buildings.

Inside, Arthur Farragan—businessman of Philadelphia in the twentieth century, owner of two Cadillacs, two homes, safe money in Swiss banks, and a one-third share of a two-hundred-unit trucking line—listened to his wife, whose failed mind ranged freely through the dark and passionate villages of Europe looking for spoiled women to beatify. Somehow—and it disturbed him—the easy language of their Catholic cult made him only slightly uncomfortable.

"What happened when the rapist came out of the shed, Muriel?"

"Her brother killed him on the spot."

"Then what happened to her brother?"

"He was taken to Turin for trial but acquitted because of the particular nature of the crime."

"Oh, I see." But that was all he said. Minutes later, hurtling into a solid wall of fog that Farragan suspected was the environs of the Schuylkill, she made a screeching left turn and flew southward along Seventeenth Street, lurching from side to side in the streetcar tracks. In another moment she drew up beside the Greyhound terminal at Market.

"You *can* see through fog," Farragan agreed.

"I've told you so, Arthur." But it was true: since the prolonged and rugged birth of the twins five years before, when her mind had slipped away to be replaced by the rheumy eyes and her spiritual communion with violated women, her vision had become marvelously improved. Also her prowess in driving a car. Somehow, Farragan had come to trust them both implicitly.

"Arthur, don't forget to pray for Simon while you're on retreat. I'll pray for him also."

"Yes, do that," Farragan answered mutely. He turned, before opening the door, to regard his wife's profile: at forty-two, she seemed to him, incredibly, to have exactly the same ivory-smooth skin as on the day the Jesuit had first introduced them at Georgetown, some twenty-four years before. The straight black hair, long to the shoulders, had no sign of gray. The eyes, childlike in their wideness since the debacle of the twins, understated her age by ten years. Forgetting for the instant that he had not made love to her in five summers, he reached across and laid a soft hand on her cheek. Beneath his finger tips, her skin went taut with fright.

"Blessed Elizabetta La Voci, help me," she implored softly, terrified at the touch of her own husband.

Instantly Farragan withdrew, opening the door.

"Forgive me, Muriel. I'm so sorry," he told her, taking his two suitcases from the back seat. "I haven't done that in years."

"No, you've been good until now. I must get back to Beach Haven, Arthur."

Farragan closed the door, after placing the suitcases on the pavement, and the Cadillac set off in a lurch, making an illegal left turn onto Market. Sadly he watched it recede toward City Hall, trying to remember how many raped women Muriel had sponsored to the Pope in the past five years. Countless numbers, it seemed. Then he entered the terminal, marching through the transient-laden files of benches in the waiting room, and descending on the escalator to the bus platforms.

There, in the acrid stench of diesel fumes and the engine blasts of busses entering and leaving the terminal, his spirit heightened, Muriel blessedly forgotten. In a normal year—when he need not be concerned about the sacrifice of his son—this was always the beginning of the happiest time for Farragan. Dropping suddenly out of the accustomed fast stream of his life at an early-morning hour into the ancient prewar bus that bore him uncertainly out of Philadelphia to Edmund's Monastery of Saint Blaise in the Poconos was a yearly adventure that became dearer now as he advanced to real middle age. It was Farragan's bus to Lahore: a distant place of safety behind consuming ethereal mists. The name, taken from myth or a vestigial memory of some otherwise forgotten literature, may have existed in fact. But Farragan resisted learning its actual whereabouts and tempted no possibility that the romance be dissolved. Lahore was his private state of mind. Dedicated on the exterior to efficiency and cost-slicing in running of a truck line, besieged by the relentless demands of union representatives and others, he often—in the afternoon before it was late enough for a first drink—saw himself aboard that rickety conveyance approaching those ethereal mists. Today, many hours in advance of that drink, he searched for the bus with an acute thirst. Accordingly, it sat tired and listing in a bay between the beefy sleekness of two Greyhounds.

"Hello, Mr. Farragan. Welcome aboard."

"Hello, Feverer," Farragan said to the driver, the sadly disappointing part of the whole fantasy. He shook hands with the mountaineer who wore a red wool hunting cap in anticipation of a blazing August day. "How have you been?"

"Can't complain too much. I saw your brother, Father Edmund, a few days ago. He told me you was comin' upstate."

"How was Father Edmund?"

"Fat. He must've put himself on thirty pounds this last year. He's startin' to look like a goddam doughnut."

"He's almost fifty years old, Feverer." Farragan heard himself defending.

"That don't have anything to do with it. I'm sixty and I look like a rake. It's the fear that keeps him eatin' like that. As long as he can stoke it in, he don't have to think about livin' up there in that haunted monastery by hisself. He's been up there close on twenty years, you know. They ought to send him somebody to help him out and keep him company."

"That would certainly be desirable, Feverer. But there are only five priests in his order. They can't spare anyone."

"Well, that's a damn shame, Mr. Farragan. I've been meanin' to talk to you about this for some time now. They ought to close down that place and let him buddy up with another priest so he'd have somebody to talk to. He's about at the end of his rope now. We got up an honorary membership for him at the club down in the village so he can come by for a beer when he wants and have somebody to shoot the breeze with. Couple of the boys taught him to play pool. He's pretty good on the dart board, too."

"Edmund goes into a bar to drink?" Farragan asked. He guessed his tone was incredulous.

"Seven nights a week sometimes. Claims he can't get to sleep without it. That monastery is a hell of a place to have insomnia, I'll bet."

"You're certainly exaggerating this thing, Feverer. To begin with, he can't be drinking seven nights a week. There are Sunday Blue Laws in Pennsylvania."

"He knows the password."

"Oh, my God. But he's a priest. Doesn't anyone ever say anything to him when he comes in for a drink?"

"He don't wear his uniform, Mr. Farragan. We give him a pair of jeans and a huntin' jacket, and he wears that, so nobody besides the boys ever knows who he is."

"Thank God for the boys," Farragan said ruefully.

"They're a fine bunch of boys, all right."

By this time Farragan was installed in the first seat beside the door. Before him, the double-plate front windows were bordered with papier-mâché flowers and fringe, and two white plastic statues of Jesus clung to the glass on rubber suction cups. Vaguely Farragan recalled a bus on which he had once ridden in Spain. Otherwise, the fear that Edmund had been, or might become, loose-tongued about Simon in the Sportsman's Club in Somerton Pines grew apace. Sweet God, that was all the situation needed: a hundred Pennsylvania mountaineers willing and ready to testify in Philadelphia that the Farragans were out to do in one of their own clan. . . . He would have to straighten out Edmund's drinking problem quickly. Have Anna ship him out a color TV, perhaps.

"Arthur . . ."

Muriel stood unexpectedly at the door to the bus. Seeing her was a jolt. He considered already that she must be halfway returned to the shore by now. Feverer removed his hat.

"Arthur, do you think it would be all right to use the postage meter at the Zephyr terminal to send out the campaign literature for Blessed Elizabetta La Voci?"

"How much were you planning to send out?"

"About two thousand circulars."

"All of it in the United States?"

"No, Arthur, some to the friends of our movement in England, Ireland, France, and Italy. I know it might sound like a lot to you, but do you think you'll be able to confuse the Internal Revenue about it?"

"We'll work something out," Farragan said, surprised as always at the clarity of her failed mind on certain things. "Go ahead and use it."

"Thank you, Arthur." She touched him tentatively on his hand with two fingers—more of an advance than he had enjoyed from her in five years—then was gone, her high heels clacking across the downstairs waiting rooms toward the escalator.

"She looks kind of like an angel, I think," Feverer said. "I'd never expect a lady like that to have any business in a bus station just like anybody else."

"My wife has only rarely had any occasion to take a bus anywhere," Farragan said, though he was exalted by the judgment.

"You sure do see a lot of beautiful women in Philadelphia, Mr. Farragan. Who's Blessed Lizabeth Voci?"

"Someone that was raped and strangled that my wife is interested in having made into a saint."

"Was she a relative?" Feverer asked, preparing to mourn.

"No, nothing like that. Just a little Italian girl who deserves a break."

"Well, I'm glad to hear she's not family. God knows you people got your hands full enough with Father Edmund as he is." Feverer said no more. He turned over the engine, whose four cylinders Farragan could hear banging and clanking in recognizable order, and eased out of the terminal into the fog. There were no other passengers. Farragan, constrained to silence by an agreement of twenty years before so that Feverer might better battle traffic, lay back and thought of driving through Lahore. Accommodating him, the bus swayed rhythmically to and fro: at Broad and Susquehanna he saw camels passing through the mist. Also at the Willow Grove turnoff that led out of the city.

Two hours later, in Bucks County and south of Easton, Pennsylvania, the bus boiled over for the first time. Feverer pulled to the side of the Delaware Canal. Farragan helped him haul the slimy water in tin cans to ease the overheating, then poured two quarts of sludge oil into the crank case while the other held a newspaper as a filter.

Later, when it boiled over for the second time in the Water Gap, it was the occasion for lunch. After Easton and the villages that surrounded it, Farragan was once again the only passenger. Feverer took down two box lunches that his wife had packed the night before from the rack above his head and removed two quarts of beer from a cooler. He handed one of each over to Farragan.

They sat on a grassy slope beside the Delaware facing the cliffs of the New Jersey shore. By now the sun was hot and had burned away the fog, and the grass was dry beneath them. Farragan devoured a chicken-salad sandwich and swigged beer from the bottle. Feverer talked of life and people and eventually got back to Edmund.

"I'm Dutch Reform and not one to be criticizin' another man's religion, but I can't figure out just what Father Edmund by hisself is doin' up in that place. A caretaker'd be just as good. He told me hisself he can't make a Mass unless somebody helps him, and there usually ain't anybody up there."

"It's the will of his superior that he stay there," Farragan lied, then shrugged his shoulders for Feverer's benefit to indicate that any means of release for the captive of Saint Blaise was beyond him. But Jesus, he thought, resting his eyes on the Jersey cliffs again, the Farragans had abused their brother Edmund. He sat atop that haunted mountain—on which Farragan would not have passed a night alone—no better than an alibi at this particular moment, and not even worth that if the nightly drinking at the Sportsman's Club loosened him up too much.

At forty-seven, Edmund was the wish fulfillment of their parents, neither of whom had had the misfortune to live long enough to see what they had wrought: the family priest in a cage. The Farragans had needed a cleric to complete the pillars of their dynasty and sent detective priests out to find an order compatible with the recognized limited intelligence of Edmund. The Tirungians, with eleven priests, the healthy endowment of several rich and pitying Catholic old ladies, and four mountaintop *palazzos* spread variously throughout the East and intended to be fashionable retreat houses, had made a place for him.

At fifteen, perhaps before puberty in the case of their Edmund, he had been shipped off to their seminary to be hammered into a cleric. Endowed somehow with the power to say Mass and absolve sins, he had become the Farragans' very own minister and absolver. He had weepingly given the last rites to both their parents and been celebrant both times at the Solemn Requiem Masses in the cathedral that saw them into the ground. He had baptized all the Farragan offspring of Jim, Anna, and Farragan himself, churched their women, and shyly given benediction at family banquet-orgies.

Recently his chanting had also seen Malcolm safely into Eternity. And in a comforting blaze of incense and holy water, he had presumed Edward's amputated arm (elsewhere disposed of) into the family plot, lest it wander alone and fitful through the Afterlife.

But Farragan loved the simple Edmund: though, like the pragmatic Feverer, he also pitied him. Edmund had failed to become the great cathedral preacher of Jim's and Anna's ambition, and now his life's purpose came directly out of Philadelphia. When the question of relinquishing the Monastery of Saint Blaise had come up some years before on the death of one of the Catholic widows, it was Jim and Anna who had tightened their belts to keep Edmund in a job. Saint Blaise was a Farragan subsidy, then. Never once, even at the exhortation of Farragan himself, had they taken Edmund's incredible loneliness into consideration.

And what a loneliness it was: waiting on the weekly phone calls from his brothers and sister, the twice-yearly visits of the Father General of his order, and holidays like Christmas and Easter and one week in June when he might come down off the mountaintop and join his family in Philadelphia or at the shore. Otherwise, he waited these days like a man obsessed for any possible response to the ads for retreatants he had begun placing in some of the Catholic periodicals. But results had been disappointing. One man, a Baptist, had stayed two full days then made off with a silver chalice given Edmund by their mother. The police were still unable to find him.

By now he had drunk most of his beer. Feverer, beside him, had already drifted off to sleep. Farragan spread his coat and lay back on the grass, staring through the slight shifting of leaves above at the intense blue sky and the orb of sun that hung in it. He was caused to think happily of his father: after the war, when that old man handed a healthy Zephyr Motor Freight over to his children, he retired to his acres on Wynnewood and, weather permitting, spun out the end of his days drinking beer from quarts and sleeping it off in a specially preserved uncut section of lawn behind the house. This, while his wife screeched and hissed from an upstairs window and assailed him for being shanty Irish to the marrow, though she was secretly relieved at the immense distance in either direction to their nearest neighbors' homes. In the end the old man prevailed, and Farragan the son envied him the luxury of guzzling beer and passing out on the turf with the knowledge that at that stage of his life very little had been placed in jeopardy by his incaution. He had gone back, as the old people said.

How Farragan longed to go back!

But it was too early to peel off the veneer: there was still

Simon to be made safe, and Edmund to be shored up before he fell apart completely, and Muriel and the girls to be protected. Impulsively, Farragan rose to fight off his fuzzy-headedness.

He shrugged out of his clothes behind a bush and descended to the river, where he waded in naked. The water was clear and deep, and there was no appreciable current so near the shore line. Farragan swam a hundred yards upstream, then floated slowly down again on his back. A man and woman went past in a small cabin cruiser and saluted his nakedness with their drinks. In time he returned to the bank, shook himself dry, and dressed. Feverer was still asleep and snoring. Farragan shook him to wake him.

"I was havin' a dream," Feverer said on sitting up.

"What were you dreaming about?" Farragan asked.

"Do you think Father Edmund ever thinks about havin' a woman sometimes?"

"I've never considered the possibility. Edmund is a priest."

"Yeah, but he's still a man. If I was him, I would've come down off that hill long ago and found me a woman."

"He's trained not to think about it, Feverer."

"He's still cherry."

"What do you mean?"

"A virgin. He told me so hisself one night down at the club when we had a few drinks together."

"Let's hope so. He's a priest, after all."

"That don't seem like a proper thing for a man to wish his brother, Mr. Farragan. I always wished my brothers would get as much as they could stand."

"Your brothers weren't priests, Feverer."

"No, it's like I told you before, we're Dutch Reform. One of my brothers is a preacher, though. I wished him a lot just like anybody else, and he got a lot, I guess. He has ten kids."

"Unfortunately, I'm not in a position to wish my brother a lot, because he wasn't meant to have a lot," Farragan joked, trying to mask his growing exasperation.

"Well, that's a damn shame, Mr. Farragan. I've been haulin' you up to Saint Blaise twice a year for nearly twenty years now. It's time I spoke my piece. Your family done wrong cuttin' off his balls and stickin' him up on that hill like that. He was a good horse twenty years back. Now he's got eyes like a rat because of the fear, and he chews his fingernails like a kid. I asked him why he wanted to be a priest if this was all it got him, and he told me your mother wanted him to be one, and that's why he is one. How do you like that?"

Farragan might have wept for Edmund's admission. Also because of Feverer: he lived in dread of meeting salt-of-the-earth types like the bus driver because he had no defenses against them. Jim, his brother, would have knocked him down on the spot, then conveniently reshaped the truth for distribution to the people he played golf with or invited to parties in his home.

"I think we'd better go, Feverer. Your bus ought to be cooled down by now. Father Edmund is expecting me today before dark."

By his silence, Feverer showed he understood. They pulled away from the river bank and traveled over the twisting Pinchot roads of the Depression days from hamlet to hamlet until they came to the top of a hill and saw Saint Blaise in the distance. It was the very beginning of sunset, and Farragan was reminded by the monastery of mad Ludwig's castle he had once visited in Bavaria. He thought to enjoy the sight while he could: later, in full darkness, it would be vastly more sinister and menacing.

"There's music comin' from up there, Mr. Farragan," Feverer said. He halted the bus. An unrecognized Gregorian chant floated over the hills. It surprised Farragan that the public-address system, installed in the days when Saint Blaise was meant to be a posh retreat house, still worked.

"I wonder why he's playing that chant," Farragan mused out loud.

"Atmosphere, probably. He's got two guys up there on retreat with him."

"What two guys?" Farragan asked, suddenly apprehensive, and cursing the possibility of someone's messing up the carefully prepared-for alibi.

"An old guy whose daughter turned into a hooker and a young artistic one with a beard who's thinkin' about turnin' Catholic. I took them up from Easton yesterday. They must've thought I worked there, because they told me everything about themselves on the way up."

"Oh, shit," Farragan mumbled. But that was all he said. He handed Feverer a twenty-dollar bill and told him to keep the change. At the entrance to Saint Blaise he swung his bags to the ground and waved to the old man, forgiving him, as the bus rolled off. Then he started up the hill in rhythm to the sweet voices of monks, anxious to see what the two alibi wreckers looked like.

# CHAPTER 4

## *Tiger in a Cage*

At the top of the hill Farragan paused for a moment beside the ornate and rusting gates of the compound to regard the main building of Saint Blaise. The second and third stories and the four corner towers of the monstrosity had been closed off to save on heating costs—and Edmund's sanity, as well—and now, at sunset, tattered curtains flopped outward through the broken windowpanes. For Farragan's purposes, they suggested ecclesiastic spirits coming awake for the monastery's night shift, and as always he saw—or thought he saw—movements behind the blood-red stain on the glass. While he rested, the record on the P.A. system came to an end and was replaced, after the resounding click of another disc dropping onto the turntable, by the recognizable "Pavane for a Dead Infanta."

He walked along the gravel driveway toward the main entrance, where Edmund's Land Rover—a gift from Anna and Jim—was parked. The massive entry door was open and flies buzzed in and out of the house. Edmund's mongrel of a watch dog raised his head to look dumbly at Farragan for a moment, then fell back to dozing.

Inside, he wandered through the thickly carpeted and paneled reception rooms with half-burned logs in each of their fireplaces, and listened for Edmund. Dust rose in diminutive clouds from every tread on the rug, and he realized for the first time in his years of visiting that the house must be wired for sound inside also, since the melancholic "Pavane" was only slightly less distinct than outside. At the end of the third room in the series he dropped his bags on a faded couch and opened the bronze double doors to the long hallway leading to the chapel.

"I beseech you, dear Christians, to remember the admonition of our Lord Jesus . . ."

Edmund was preaching from the altar.

A stupendous joy arose in Farragan that his brother was finally being put to some real use. He crept farther into the hallway and saw Edmund pacing savagely about the front of the chapel behind the altar railing, banishing devils, and raising the dust from the carpeting as Farragan himself had done with each footfall. Above his head, the sanctuary lamp burned, as ever. This year, in accordance with Feverer's testimony, Edmund, in his Jesuit-style cassock, had a girth like Friar Tuck.

Before the preacher, in the first pew that had been covered with a bed sheet to guard against the dust, sat a wizened, hunchbacked old man, and a thin, dark-haired younger one that Farragan could tell from behind wore a beard. Edmund caught sight of his brother while raising a chubby fist to demonstrate the wrath of God: the arm fell meekly to his side.

"Arthur, I didn't think you'd be here until later tonight," the preacher said, clearly embarrassed.

"We had only two boilovers this time, Edmund. Go on with your sermon and don't let me disturb you."

"Oh, that's all right, Arthur. I was just finishing anyhow."

"But you only just started," protested the younger man. He turned in dismay to Farragan, and the latter saw he had great neurotic eyes, full of spiritual or other anguish, like an El Greco saint. A finely trimmed beard clung to the outer rim of his face.

"I could listen to more, too, Father," the old one said.

"Perhaps later. I'm tired now." Edmund yawned elaborately. When he withdrew his hand, Farragan saw sadly that the ratty glint of fearfulness had returned to his eyes.

"I didn't know you had any retreatants this week, Edmund," his brother said.

"I found out at the last minute the gentlemen were coming up here. This is Mr. Farrow, Arthur," he introduced the El Greco youth. "This gentleman is Mr. Bowen. Mr. Bowen is seventy-one years old," he added, for no apparent reason.

"I'm Arthur Farragan, Father Edmund's brother."

"Are you intending to stay a long time, Mr. Farragan?" the younger asked.

"About two weeks."

"I'm staying at least that long myself."

"Mr. Farrow is in crisis," Edmund explained.

"Why's that, Edmund?"

"I've given myself two weeks to reach a final decision on whether or not to convert to Catholicism," Farrow said.

"Our religion was not intended for all men," Farragan heard himself say.

"The Church of Christ holds her arms out to all who need her, Arthur." Edmund rebuked him for the first time in his life. "It is we who take our faith so much for granted who naturally have little sympathy for another man's distress."

"I never take my faith for granted, Father," the old one spoke. "I live it each day as if I had been baptized only that morning. That's why it hit me so hard when I found out my daughter was a prostitute."

"How did you find out?" Farragan asked, already knowing part of the old man's story.

"Some guy wrote me a letter and didn't sign his name."

"Ow. It may all be a lie, you know, Mr. Bowen. Some character sending a poison-pen letter out."

"I showed her the letter, Mr. Farragan. She said it was true."

"That's terrible," said the El Greco youth. "It seems being a Catholic implies no kind of moral superiority, as I had hoped."

"What the hell were you expecting?" Farragan demanded. "A halo?" The instant he threw the barb, Farragan knew what it was that made him instinctively dislike the El Greco youth: his intensity—though elsewhere directed—reminded him of Simon's own. He followed up greedily on the attack. "Have you ever been in the service?"

"No. I was a conscientious objector."

"I knew it. It had to be something like that."

"Arthur, this isn't right," Edmund said. "This gentleman has come here in the midst of a crisis. I'm here to help him."

"Forgive me, Edmund. I didn't mean for this to happen," Farragan said, realizing that Edmund's ministry needed bolstering as much as Simon's defection needed to be deplored.

"Why don't we suspend now, and meet in an hour for dinner?" Edmund suggested. "How do you like your steak, Mr. Bowen? Mr. Farrow?"

"Well-done for me," said the old one, "and could you chop it up into little pieces?"

"Medium-rare for me," said the youth, stricken. He edged out of his pew toward the far aisle beside the wall so he would not have

to pass by Farragan, who stood in the main aisle. The old one hobbled out wordlessly with a cane.

"Let's go to the kitchen and fix dinner, Arthur, while the gentlemen get ready."

Farragan carried his bags along the hallway after the flowing-
jelly amble of Edmund and through the three baroque reception
rooms to the dining room, where fake-medieval heavy oaken tables
and benches had waited these twenty years for retreatants to fill
them. Crusader shields hung upon the walls. Above was a vaulted
oaken ceiling. One table, doubtless used by Edmund for his solitary
meals, was covered with a stained white tablecloth. Footprints led
through the dust from the kitchen.

They descended the circular stone staircase into one eccentric,
but indisputably wealthy, Catholic widow's concept of a kitchen in
a dungeon. Along the outer walls were darkened alcoves that held
clusters of deep freezes, upright refrigerators, stainless-steel sinks,
and vast expanses of rusting gas ranges that might have been adequate for the purposes of an army. At the back of each alcove facing
west, the rose tint of sunset came through barred windows. Those
to the east were a deep purple. As always, Farragan was disappointed by the lack of an entire community of monks roasting
meats and chanting over great fiery pits. The sudden thought of the
lonely Edmund waddling back and forth across this cavernous room
to fix his meals three times a day filled Farragan's eyes with tears.

"I'll put on the corn to cook and warm up the grill for the
steaks. I made the scalloped potatoes yesterday, so I'll only have to
heat them up a bit. Would you like a drink, Arthur?"

"Yes, I would."

"I have lots of beer, or some Scotch, Arthur."

"Scotch would be fine, Edmund."

Farragan's brother pressed a foot pedal that sprung open the
double doors to a huge refrigerator. Inside, six-packs of Budweiser,

sacramental wine, and fifths of Chivas Regal sat cooling all together. Edmund took out the Scotch and poured two tall glasses right up to the rim, neglecting to add any ice. At forty-seven, a fat-cheeked child, he looked to his brother for approval.

"Have you just begun drinking this year, Edmund?"

"It makes me sleep better, Arthur," he said. Farragan had drawn himself onto a work stool beside the rough-surfaced concrete table that doubtless had appealed to the Catholic widow as medieval. He sipped at the copious glass of Scotch but had no intention of finishing it. Edmund drained nearly half his glass with one gulp: the frightened, ratty eyes grew instantly distended and fibrous with blood. A new courage shone out of them. He licked his lips, then sighed appreciatively like a kid with a Coke on a hot afternoon. Farragan watched him hoist himself onto another work stool, his split-front cassock falling open. The crotch of his clerical pants was stained white. Sperm, probably, Farragan guessed.

"Feverer tells me you go down to the Sportsman's Club in Somerton Pines now and then, Edmund."

"Just a couple of nights a week, Arthur, to talk with some of the boys. I play pool and darts with them, too."

"Drink loosens the tongue, Edmund."

"I haven't said anything about Simon."

"What if you get drunk some night and let it slip? We'd all be in jail. You, too, since you're in on it."

Edmund looked about the kitchen dungeon, and Farragan believed that he almost smiled: the notion of being in jail with other prisoners may have been infinitely preferable to being at Saint Blaise by himself.

"I won't get that drunk, ever, Arthur. You'll never get in trouble because of me."

"I hope not, Edmund. The family has had trouble enough during the last half year. That would be the last straw."

Edmund drained his glass, then poured another cold one. After a long sip, he made his face look resolute.

"Arthur, I've decided I have something to say to you."

"What is it?"

"I don't approve of this business of killing Simon."

"Then why didn't you air your views at the family council when it was decided instead of making complications now? It's too late."

"It's not too late. The trouble with me is that I've always let Jim and Anna do all the thinking, and just gone along for the ride. . . ."

"The trouble with you is that you hadn't had a drink before we sat down to decide his fate that day," Farragan said, wondering how far away the El Greco youth and the old one were from this conversation.

"Stop treating me as if I were a fat alcoholic, will you, Arthur. I've done some thinking. I don't want Simon killed. He was good to me. He used to call me up once a week and talk to me about a half an hour no matter where he was. When I went up to Cape Cod last year for a week, I stayed five of those days with him at Brandeis College. We drank beer together every afternoon in a dark bar called Herbie's. Two nights we double-dated together. My girl's name was Mia. She still writes me every two weeks or so, Arthur."

"Sweet Mother of Jesus! What does it take to remind you that forty-seven-year-old priests don't go on double dates with their nephews?"

"Nobody knew I was a priest. Simon's too clever to spill the beans and embarrass everybody. Why don't you just forget about it, Arthur? Lots of boys have run away to Canada. I knew last year he was going to take off if he got his letter from the Army."

"You did? Why the hell didn't you say something?"

"What would you have done if you had known? March him down to the induction place with a gun and hand him over?"

"At that time maybe not. But now, since I can't look Jim or Anna straight in the face, you can be absolutely certain of it."

"You don't really want to kill him, Arthur. Why don't you admit that it's Jim and Anna you're trying to appease? It's those two I've been trying to appease for the last twenty years. It would be exciting to put something over on them for once. Let's warn Simon to lie low up there in Montreal. We can get up a phony death certificate and have a closed coffin full of rocks sent back to Philadelphia. I'll say the funeral Mass and we'll bury the rocks and nobody will ever be the wiser. Simon doesn't ever want to come back to the States, anyhow."

"Please remember something, you dumb fucker!" Farragan raged, inadvertently smashing his fist on the concrete table. "Not so long ago you read a funeral Mass over a coffin that was full of your nephew Malcolm and not of rocks. You also staged some kind of service for the spiritual repose of your nephew Edward's right arm. Are you going to dishonor both of them and your office as a priest by burying a pile of rocks so you'll have somebody to go drinking with next year at Herbie's bar, or introduce you to girls named Mia? Answer that one."

"I'm sorry, Arthur. I was only trying to offer you a way off Jim and Anna's hook."

"I'm not on Jim and Anna's hook. Try to understand that. Killing Simon is my own responsibility. He deserves it. Your very small part in all this is simply to say yes if the police ever get around to questioning my whereabouts for the next two weeks."

"You have a curious double standard when it comes to my priesthood, Arthur."

"That line comes straight out of Simon's mouth, Edmund. Aided by your own drinking, of course. What you're being asked to do for the sake of your family seems hardly as grievous as reading a Solemn Requiem Mass for a pile of rocks in the cathedral. Now, how about getting started on dinner. You've had enough cocktail hour for anybody."

"I think I understand, Arthur. I'll put the corn and potatoes on now. Please try to be pleasant to Mr. Farrow. He's not responsible for the fact that he's here during the week you need a story to cover your movements."

"Yes, you're right," Farragan conceded. "I'll try to be more civil to him." But that was mere diplomacy: what really pained Farragan was that he could not risk telling Edmund he was on a mission of mercy to Canada rather than one of vengeance. There was no trusting the priest's capacity for allegiance to Jim and Anna once the booze subsided.

Vaguely, on the outside of the kitchen dungeon, Farragan heard the sound of more monks that had evidently replaced the Ravel "Pavane." Edmund, weaving slightly, began placing the already husked corn into the boiling water. He opened the oven door and slid in a casserole of scalloped potatoes. Farragan, trembling slightly, reached the bottom of the glass he had not intended finishing. With a handkerchief he wiped away the trickle of blood from his hand where he had smashed it against the concrete table. Then he regarded his brother, who was vigorously salting the steaks beside the grill: from behind, the wrap-around expanse of Edmund's undulating cassock reminded him of a circus tent being buffeted by the winds. In a moment the priest returned to the table.

"Is Marie coming up as planned?" Edmund asked.

"Yes, on Wednesday morning. I'm to use her car to get back to Philadelphia to catch the plane for Montreal."

"She may have to stay several days in the guest house by herself until the two retreatants leave. I don't believe Mr. Farrow will stay as long as he says he will. I'll have him converted by Friday at the latest. But to be on the safe side you should delay your departure until they're gone. It wouldn't do to have them know you left for two days, then returned, especially if the police came snooping around for my alibi. You do have a whole two weeks, you know."

Ah, the wonder of drink, Farragan considered, watching Edmund's rheumy eyes: from rebellious idealist to logical conspirator in the space of minutes. The second wave of inebriation brought the fox out of its lair, then. Please God that it be a dependable pattern in the future.

"I'm supposed to kill Simon on Thursday, Edmund. I'm conditioned for it. I don't know if I can keep my hatred at such a pitch for as long as two weeks."

"It's a chance you'll have to take, Arthur, and I'd caution you to be wise about it. Anyhow, if it is to be two weeks, there are certain consolations. You'll have Marie to yourself for a longer period at any rate. Only you must be careful that the languor of your lovemaking doesn't undermine your determination to act on Simon."

"Yes, you're right about that. It doesn't bother you, Edmund, that Marie is my mistress?"

"We've talked about this before. You're not, in my opinion—even though you may consider you are—responsible for the traumatic shock Muriel suffered at the birth of the twins. Under such circumstances, the Church recognizes the real possibility for annulment."

Edmund paced back and forth across the cobbled floor now, his brow creased with the effort of argument, at last the great theologian of all the Farragans' wishing and dreaming. But what did he propose? Annulment? After the way Farragan loved his Muriel? The idea was out of the question. He loved Marie also, her youth and soft blond sleekness, the imperturbable calm. But of Muriel he had made a goddess, and had every time approached the marriage bed with the reverence of a suppliant. And now it was his fault, Farragan considered, that she gave way to sleep at night in a separate bedroom, after quieting the nameless daytime terrors of her mind with drugs, doubtless watched over by the spirit horde of violated and beatified women with whom she communed.

"Annulment is out of the question, Edmund. Besides, Marie is only twenty-three. I'm not going to kid myself that this will last forever. She deserves better, one of these days, than to get tied up with a man twice her age."

"Do you think you appreciate her more because she's so young compared to yourself?"

"How do you mean, Edmund?"

"Well, I mean her youthfulness. Her skin must be very soft and her mind open to all the new ideas you could propose to her. It must be exciting for you to teach her all the forms of sexual experimentation you've learned in the years of your marriage."

"Yes. How soon are we to eat, Edmund?"

By his long sigh and the sudden droop of his shoulders, Farragan's brother capitulated. "I'll put the steaks on to broil now, Arthur. Perhaps you might take out the bread and condiments to the table?"

Farragan picked up the items from a sideboard and carried them up the stairs to the vaulted dining room. Edmund bore close watching, he decided, as he lit the great candles at either end of the table they were to use. After rebellious idealist, logical conspirator, and grave theologian, the booze had released a horny tiger in its turn. All in all, it was inevitable, he supposed, and a proper justice for the clan Farragan that normally calm waters were being disturbed during this particular week.

At dinner, though, Farragan felt somewhat consoled: starch was at work combating the drink-fed exaltation, and Edmund gradually succumbed to being Edmund once more. The end of sunset blazed through the arches of stained-glass windows and, outside, an automatic timer went off and the huge bell in the tower beyond the guest house began to toll the Angelus. A boys' choir softly chanted an unfamiliar litany that Farragan knew only was in praise of the Virgin. The mood was peaceful and the two retreatants easily complied. The El Greco youth released an interminable sigh that told he had already given up the dialogue with Reason and passed through the filmy curtain into the Church. Edmund graciously scraped the kernels from an ear of corn for the old one, whose beatific face suggested he was enjoying some extraordinary vision, the like of his harlot daughter returned to the year of her First Communion dress.

At length, Farragan broke into the Dream: "What's on the agenda for tonight, Edmund?"

"Well, I really hadn't decided," the cleric answered uncertainly. "I thought we all might go down to the Sportsman's Club later for a little drink." He looked to El Greco and then the old man with a sly glint of promised pleasure in the ratty eyes. Farragan might have struck him for his corruption.

"But, Edmund, these gentlemen are on retreat."

"We were down at the Club last night, Mr. Farragan," El Greco told him. "I'm quite partial to it actually. It impresses me as an aspect of the Church in dissent. Catholicism is being revitalized, after all. Now the shepherd goes out to find his flock. In New York priests play guitars in coffee houses."

"But not in Philadelphia," Farragan said. "Edmund isn't in revolt. He enjoys his work."

"I also enjoy a little drink after a hard day," Edmund said. His two retreatants broke into peals of appreciative laughter. Farragan was mute: he saw there would be nothing short of an electrified fence to keep his brother from visiting Somerton Pines this night. He himself would have to go along to make sure Edmund kept his mouth shut.

"Are you going to preach after dinner, Father?" the old one asked.

"Well . . . I'm not sure. . . ."

"I'm going to unpack and then lie down for a while, Edmund," Farragan said. "I don't think I'll be able to hear your sermon tonight, much as I'd like to."

"Oh, that's too bad, Arthur," Edmund said with undisguised relief. "I was going to talk on the Decline of the Spirit. Well, let's all take our dinner plates into the kitchen and clean off the table. Then we three can go to the chapel."

In a row, the others followed Edmund across the room to the stairway. There, the old man turned and silently handed Farragan his plates and cutlery, indicating with a glance that the steps were too much to manage. On returning from the kitchen, Farragan carried his bags with him. He went quietly off to his cell to unpack while Edmund herded the others into the chapel.

In fifteen minutes, when he had finished, Farragan removed his shoes and stole into the hallway in stockinged feet, creeping toward the sound of Edmund afire with his preaching. He peeked around the corner as before. The retreat master, his face white and sweated with the intensity of his particular anguish, beseeched his two charges with open arms, "What doth it profit a man to gain the whole world and lose the gift of his immortal soul?"

El Greco nodded effusively in agreement and the old man clacked his teeth sadly. But Farragan at the doorway was all apprehension: at forty-seven, Edmund the Timid had evoked from a bottle a Jekyll-Hyde kind of magic that permitted him a temporary respite from being Edmund the Timid. He shot pool with the boys down at the Club and preached wisdom to the multitudes as long as they included no members of his own family. But this was only a symptom of how dangerous he had become. If he truly disapproved of the murder of Simon and was loose-tongued and opinionated every time he got near a drink, then Edmund was in trouble with Jim and Anna. Weary of complications before he had actually spared his first victim, Farragan the executioner imagined a great unwinding spiral of cover-up deaths in the offing.

# CHAPTER 5

## At the Sportsman's Club

At ten o'clock they piled into Edmund's Land Rover and rumbled down the hill to the Sportsman's Club in Somerton Pines.

There were nine cars in the lot before the neon-lit log building, and, on disembarking, Farragan counted Wallace-for-President stickers on the bumpers of seven of them. For the instant he was caused to think of their drivers at the terminal. Jim and Anna had been on the lookout for such stickers in the employees' parking lot for weeks now, only none had turned up so far. But then, at least forty per cent of their drivers were Negroes: that certainly made for a bit of caution in any of the remaining whites who might have caught the far-right-wing bug of the Wallace variety. Muted violence was not unknown at Zephyr Motors. Drivers, black and white, had been suspended for trying to kill each other in arguments over favored runs. Twice during labor disputes Farragan had had the windshield of his Cadillac bashed in.

Edmund entered the club first, clad in the gift blue jeans and hunting jacket and followed by El Greco, old Bowen, and Farragan. The place was a single large rectangular room, brilliantly lighted, with a zoo of bear, deer, moose, and bobcat staring down from the chinked walls on all sides. Pike, trout, and pickerel, mounted on lengths of polished wood, hung suspended from the ceiling rafters like party decorations and turned slow circles in the rush of air from a huge window fan. Farragan saw that a severe dichotomy presided here: all the men, some twenty of them, clung to the bar, while their women sat in booths along the opposite wall. Between them, in presumably neutral territory, was an area of dance floor and a pool table. Heads swung away from the bar to scrutinize them, then smiled broadly at the sight of Farragan's brother.

"I'm hot for a game of eight-ball," Edmund shouted to no one in particular, clapping his hands together.

"Let me at the bastard. I'm gonna run his ass around that table tonight," promised a giant of a man who reminded Farragan of one of their mechanics whom he had once seen remove a tire from a wheel rim with his bare hands. The contender tumbled off his stool. "Where's your quarter, Edmund baby?"

"Right here, Charlie, and it's good American coin all the way through." Edmund pulled a quarter from his pocket and slapped it down hard on the edge of the pool table. From the moment he had entered the door, his accent had changed to a nasal twang like that of his opponent, Farragan noticed.

"He beat everyone he played last night," the old one told Farragan excitedly. The El Greco youth concurred. They sat down at a table near the door, and the bartender was on them almost immediately. Farragan ordered a Scotch and water, then changed to bourbon since there was no Scotch. El Greco required a glass of muscatel; the old one asked for blackberry brandy and soda. A tall glass of beer had miraculously appeared at the pool table for Edmund.

Farragan's brother broke the rack and ran three low balls in succession, splitting the air with cries and huzzas as the killer spirit rose. After each hit he passed the high sign to Farragan, and the latter responded dutifully in kind. The contender sank what looked like the 12-ball in a corner, then missed an inexplicable 10-ball bank shot to one side pocket, when it appeared to Farragan he might have nudged it into its opposite. While the other played, Edmund danced and shuffled against the wall in his excitement. A second beer appeared miraculously again to replace the empty glass of the first, and Farragan felt his stomach contract: for what guarantee was there, really, that Edmund could be kept from shooting off his mouth about Simon after as few as three of those beers? Across the room, his brother drained the glass to the halfway mark, then set it on a window sill, where he began tapping the windowpanes with his finger tips against the clusters of moths that clung to the outside.

In his turn, Edmund sank the 3-ball in the side, then scratched. His opponent missed every shot thereafter. Twenty-five minutes later, when Farragan was finishing his second bourbon, his brother dispensed with the 8-ball after calling the pocket no fewer than six times.

"He's a better man than me," the contender said. He shuffled back to his bar stool, shaking his head sadly, and, despite Edmund, something inside Farragan responded happily to the notion that the bigger they are, the harder they fall. Up front, his brother was calling for more action. A spindly sixtyish mountaineer who might have been Feverer's sibling slid from his place and neatly flipped a quarter onto the felt. A henna-haired, buxom woman in an orchid dress followed after him, carrying the man's drink. Obviously prompted, old Bowen broke silence for the first time.

"I suppose this is the kind of bar my daughter goes into," he said to Farragan's elbow. Indecipherable country-and-western blared out of a juke box behind them, making it difficult to hear.

"I certainly don't think she could stand to make any money in this bar. These people don't look all of that well off," Farrow commented. "Do you, Mr. Farragan?"

"No, this isn't the right kind of bar if you're in it for money," Farragan said. "But then, it's not for money alone that girls go into prostitution, you know."

"I know that," Bowen said. "A doctor told me that. It just makes me think I put something bad into her since she turned out the way she did."

"It may have been your wife," Farragan said, an earnest believer, since Simon, in the possibility of dubious genetic contributions.

"She was a saint, my wife. I worshiped her. Nothing bad could have come from her."

"You never can tell," said the El Greco youth. But that was all he said. Edmund was now pitted against the henna-haired woman, who had taken over the man's game. She bent low over the table, laughing giddily at each miss, the orchid-covered expanse of her buttocks or the wealth of her breasts eliciting constant comment from the bar. For an instant some notion of chivalry rose angrily in Farragan, then quickly declined: this was not his kind of pub, after all. Nor the woman his kind of woman.

In fifteen minutes Edmund sank the 8-ball, after seven pocket calls this time. The woman slinked off, generous in defeat. Farragan's brother bounced the cue stick on its end so that the tip shot upward and touched the ceiling. He snatched it deftly from the air on the way down and pointed to Farragan. "Come on, Arthur, you play with me now."

"I haven't played pool in fifteen years, Edmund. It'd be a massacre, really. Why don't you shoot with somebody who would be more of a challenge for you?"

"Oh, go on, play with him," five or six people from the bar urged simultaneously.

"There's no need to worry," the man who had just opposed Edmund assured him. "Nobody ever gets heckled here if they're not an expert."

"That should comfort my ego," Farragan said. He walked over to the table and lay down his quarter on the rim. Edmund broke the rack. Within five minutes Farragan, nonplayer, had run a rapid five balls off the felt. When he looked up for the first time in the exultation of his re-beginner's luck, he saw the tortured mien of Edmund the Ancient and Intimidated. The sporting brotherhood had all quietly left the bar and now ranged about the table, eying Farragan narrowly. He looked at the one who had first played against Edmund: the man slowly shook his head no.

Farragan missed all subsequent shots. When Edmund took his quarter after eight pocket calls this time, Farragan guessed sadly that his brother was bearing away a trophy that equaled some vindication for all their life together. He returned to his seat while Edmund challenged the bar to a dart game. In minutes, uninvited, the big one pulled up a chair beside Farragan.

"You did right lettin' him win," the man said.

"I thought he was a champ," Farragan said.

"He's pretty bad. But he can beat anybody, I guess, if the other fellow isn't botherin' to hit anything."

"Is that usually the case?"

"Pretty much. We thought we had a sure honest loser in you when you said you didn't play in so many years. But even you was too good."

"How long has this been going on?"

"About a year now. Edmund's a good guy, but he was losin'

his marbles up on that hill. Of course he's pickin' up a lot of bad
slang and rustic habits here with the boys in Somerton Pines.
Curses a bit more than his family might appreciate. People tell me
they're rich Republicans down in Philadelphia, but then they don't
seem to do a hell of a lot for him besides leave him here to vegetate.
They haven't got too much cause to be mad if something does get
changed about him."

"I'm his brother," Farragan said—apologetically, he believed.
But at the same time he was now tempted to consider the possibility that no one in Somerton Pines thought enough of Edmund's
sanity to view the story of Simon's impending assassination as credible. He also wanted to mention that he had never voted for a Republican in his life.

"Are you the one whose boy got killed in Viet Nam?"

"Yes," Farragan lied instantly.

"Well, I sure am sorry. I'm ashamed to be sittin' next to you
in that case. My own boy is AWOL in Sweden right now."

"You're kidding. . . ."

"No, sorry to say, I'm not kiddin'. He was stationed in Ger-
many and took off with some rabid intellectuals and asked for asylum in Sweden because of the war."

"What are you going to do about him?" He hoped he didn't
sound too righteous.

"Nothin' much I can do, I guess. If he ever gets back here I'll
pound his ass a few times, then stick him up on a tractor seat. He's
a good boy and never been too far outside these mountains before
he went into the Army, and I guess that's the trouble. He'd be a
pushover for them rabid intellectuals. It's them that ought to be
shot."

"Yes," Farragan said softly, thinking that was exactly what he
was supposed to be in the process of doing.

He looked up, at a nudge from the man, to see Edmund winking broadly at him in open conspiracy. He was playing darts with the henna-haired woman, who was obviously tipsy by now. Her first throw landed far out of center. Edmund's next, compensating, missed the board completely and hung shuddering in the wall.

"He's a real gentleman, Edmund is," the man said to Farragan. "Viola's the only one he actually can beat playin' darts, so he always lets her win."

"Seems like a vicious circle," the El Greco youth said.

"Yes, it's something like that, all right," the man agreed, not without a touch of weariness, Farragan thought.

In time Viola had won her game. Farragan watched his brother drain another beer as if it were water. By now, the redness of his face was appalling: streams of sweat ran down the furrows and creases, and the graying hair was matted to his head. Farragan became apprehensive lest Edmund suffer a coronary. Beside him, the mountain man seemed to read his thoughts. "He won't never take that huntin' jacket off. He just about lives in it, I think. Cripes, it's about ninety degrees outside there now, I'll bet."

"All that beer he's drinking can't be helping matters any," Farragan said ruefully.

"That beer'll bust his bladder before it does his heart. It's special one-point stuff the bartender keeps handy just for Edmund so he can make it up the hill when he leaves here nights. It's the dancin' might do him in yet. Wait'll you see him when he starts. You'll think he was gonna explode."

"Edmund dances, too?"

"Mostly with Viola there. She's a good sport. They kid around quite a bit."

"Father Edmund is very congenial," the El Greco youth said.

"Yep. He's certainly not what you'd imagine a priest to be like," the big one said. "Knows how to talk up a blue streak in the vernacular, if you know what I mean."

"Priests aren't the way they used to be in the old days," old Bowen said sadly. "The Church is really changing."

"Yes," Farragan agreed. But too quickly for his purposes: in lieu of Gregorian chant, Edmund seemed to best prefer country-and-western. He finished another beer, then plunked a quarter in the juke box. Nasal voices sang instantly of love, and Farragan thought miserably of his beach house—a whole world away—where he might at this moment be listening to the softness of Mantovani, sipping Scotch, and remembering Muriel as she had been before the darkness overcome her. Ahead of him, with the seedy, orchid-clad Viola, his brother the priest moved cheek to cheek about the limited dancing area at the pace of a fast fox trot from before the war, nodding and winking to Farragan. Dance done, he took one of four heavyset women from a table beyond the bar and waltzed with her. Huge, with a girth nearly as large as Edmund's, she lay her head unsmilingly with a long sigh on his shoulder. In accordance, Edmund slowed down the pace.

"Edmund is the greatest thing ever happened to this bar," the man beside Farragan spoke. "He dances with all the women and gets them off our backs. If any of you guys wants to dance with them women, there's nobody's husband gonna take offense."

"I'd like to dance," El Greco pronounced. He drained his muscatel and stood up to solicit Viola. The old one complained that dancing winded him too much. Farragan had no desire to waltz with any of the three remaining women, each of whom seemed to weigh more than he himself did. Silently he watched his brother trading knowing glances with El Greco, who was considering coming into the faith. Both women had their eyes tightly shut.

One incredible Charleston later, Edmund swept over to the table excitedly. "Arthur, where's Marie?"

"In Philadelphia, Edmund."

"Arthur, let's call her up and sing love songs over the phone."

"No, don't be absurd."

"Why not, Arthur? Don't be so stuffy. She'd enjoy it."

"No, she wouldn't enjoy it for one thing. And for another, you're a priest. Please try to remember that fact."

"A priest . . . a priest . . . ," Edmund chanted, swinging his head from side to side in a rhythm of despair. "I'm a priest. . . ." Then Farragan realized that he had caught sight of himself and hunting jacket in the blue-tinted bar mirror. "I'm a man also." His brother thumped his chest fiercely. "I can beat everybody in pool and darts, and I drink more beer every night than anybody in here. The women like to dance with me, too. Right, Charlie?"

"Right, Edmund," the man agreed.

"The answer is still no, Edmund," Farragan said.

"Why not? Marie has a good sense of humor. Better than yours, obviously."

"I don't want anybody making a joke out of her. She wasn't raised in the finest Catholic boarding schools here and in Europe to have middle-aged men calling her up at midnight to serenade her."

"Cut the crap, Arthur. Was she raised in the finest Catholic schools to be your mistress the month after she graduated?"

Oh, impossible! Impossible! Farragan lamented. The haunting dream of his adult lifetime come true: to be trapped in the inner core of a barroom brawl among people that were not his kind. All about him the faces ranged sweating and amused, waiting expectantly on his reply.

"You son of a bitch, Edmund! How dare you?"

"I'm forty-seven. I never serenaded a woman in my whole life."

"You weren't meant to! Why can't you get that straight? Think of Mother, Edmund! Think what she'd say if she knew." Farragan was pitching low.

"You talk of Mother, Arthur? If Mother really knew how it's

been for the last twenty years, she would have sent up a woman for me."

"Oh, my God," Farragan moaned, not knowing from where he might next attack. The big man beside him grabbed his shoulder and sat him down again. "There don't seem to be anything wrong with callin' up a girl to sing to her a little bit, Arthur."

"She's my ward," Farragan said, livid with anger. "She's not the kind of girl you call up from a bar for the purpose of serenading."

"Is she a Republican girl, Arthur? It might do her some good to loosen up a bit," the big one said.

"No. I don't know what her politics are. She's off on a vacation anyhow."

"In the same place as Simon?" Edmund questioned evenly. "That city must be bursting with leftist Americans."

He stood above his brother, leering boozily down at him with the certainty that Farragan was about to move to the phone and ask for long distance. Behind him in the juke box, more nasal voices sang ironically of love. In the main, the faces that watched them were by now perplexed.

"All right, I'll call Marie for you, Edmund," Farragan said. "But she might not be at home."

"Call her and see," the big one urged. "Come on, boys," he called to the surrounding faces. With a single impulse, they sprang from their stools and clustered about the wall telephone. Farragan got the long-distance operator on the line. As he prayed for no response from Marie at the other end, Edmund gave directions about the first song to be sung. It was "Rose Marie." Everyone apparently remembered the words or had simply never stopped singing them. Farragan listened miserably as Marie's soft voice answered the operator. He deposited ninety cents from a pile of change made readily available. Privately he pictured her lying in bed in the flowered green night gown he himself had given her.

"I'm sorry for what's about to happen," Farragan said.

"What's about to happen?"

"You're about to be serenaded by Edmund and his friends."

"How romantic. Are they all priests?"

"Not exactly. They're sportsmen."

"Put them on, Arthur."

Farragan held the receiver out to the chorus, and, on a three count from Edmund, they began to sing:

"Sweet Rose Marie, I love you,
I'm always thinking of you. . . ."

From far off in Philadelphia, Farragan heard his woman laughing with delight. In minutes, when "Rose Marie" was finished, Marie began calling his name: "Arthur, Arthur . . ."

"What is it, Marie?"

"Tell Edmund to sing a solo for me."

"You want him to do that? Edmund," he said to his brother, disbelieving her words, "Marie wants you to sing a solo."

"I'll sing 'Maria' for you, Marie," Edmund said taking the phone. Farragan, who had never heard his brother sing before tonight except in the service of the liturgy, was surprised to find he was a pure tenor. He also wondered how Edmund the Priest had come to know the words that he sang into the bar mirror with earnest facial accompaniment. Marie's judgment came through in an instant. "That's beautiful, Edmund. It's really beautiful."

When he was finished, Edmund spoke into the receiver. "Are you coming up to stay with me, Marie? Yes? On Wednesday? Good, I'll expect you. I hope you didn't mind the boys and myself calling you up? Arthur seemed to think you'd be upset. Do you want to say hello to the rest of the boys?"

·

Evidently she did. Farragan stood mutely by as the Somerton Pines brotherhood lined up like giddy children to say hello one after another. In his turn, El Greco explained he was on retreat with Father Edmund and asked what age Marie was. Old Bowen told her he was seventy-one and warned her to avoid the pitfalls that had trapped his own daughter. Farragan took the phone from him. "Treasure that advice forever," he said. "Mr. Bowen is talking about the kind of girl who enjoys having a bar room full of men call her up in the middle of the night to sing to her."

"Any girl would, dear Farragan. Do you think I'll be able to see you for a few moments alone up there, what with so many men waiting on the sight of me?"

"We'll work something out," Farragan said, restored. "Now I have to take Edmund home since he promised, among other things, to say Mass for us tomorrow."

"Stop patronizing me, Arthur," Farragan's brother said suddenly, the serenader's elation gone from his face.

"Good-by, Marie. I'll see you Wednesday."

"I want to talk with Marie," Edmund said insistently. He reached for the receiver as Farragan hung it back on its cradle.

"Why didn't you let me speak with Marie, Arthur?"

"I'm leaving, Edmund. This has gone far enough. I'll start walking back. Please be good enough to stop for me if I'm still on the road when you're ready to leave. Will someone put the right change in the phone when the operator calls back for the overtime?"

Farragan handed his fistful of change to the big man named Charlie. He started out the door, and old Bowen hobbled behind him. On the front porch, just as he was about to descend the steps, Edmund caught up with him.

"Arthur!"

Farragan turned in response to the urgency in the voice and

ran straight into the great chubby fist of Edmund. He reeled from
the porch into the dust and looked up in astonishment to see his
brother leap upon him and begin pounding his head with his fists.
Vainly, Farragan tried to get off a single punch at Edmund's face. In
seconds two of the club members pulled Edmund to his feet.

"Edmund, what the hell's got into you? You can't go around
hittin' people with all that weight behind you. You could've broke
his jaw, and he's your own brother," the woman named Viola said.

"He wouldn't let me talk with Marie," Edmund shouted,
trying to break loose from the two men.

"Why the hell should he, Edmund? It's his girl friend. And
you're supposed to be a priest."

"I'm tired of being a priest," Edmund raged, tears filling his
eyes. "I'm forty-seven years old and I've never been to bed with a
woman. I've never slept with anybody in the same bed in my whole
life."

"Cheer up, Edmund," Viola said, patting his stomach with the
flat of her hand. "In a couple more years you'll be over the hill and
it won't matter anyhow. You just have to hold out until then."

"Oh, Jesus, shut her up," Farragan said. Now in a sitting position, he was thinking he might shoot her if only he had a gun.
Blood flowed from his nose and a cut above his eyebrow. He
touched a hand to his upper lip and found it was already swelling.

"What right does he have to tell me to shut up?" Viola asked
her audience.

"Keep quiet, Viola," the big one named Charlie told her. He
pulled Farragan to his feet and handed him a handkerchief. "This
man's boy got killed in Viet Nam."

"Oh, dear." There was a universal sympathy for Farragan from
the club members, their women, El Greco, and old Bowen. Farragan
looked warily to his brother for the truth, but Edmund only blub-
bered pathetically about the lack of women in his life.

"You'd better take him up to the monastery now, Arthur," big Charlie told him. "You know how to drive that Rover?"

"Yes."

"Put Edmund inside, boys, and let's call it a night."

Unresisting, Edmund was led to the door of the Land Rover and put inside by the two men. El Greco helped the old one through the driver's door into the back seat, then clambered in himself. Still patting at his wounds with the handkerchief, Farragan started up the engine. Charlie came to the door to speak to him before he drove off. "If you need any help up there, Arthur, telephone the Sportsman's and we'll send somebody up. And if I don't see you again, I sure am sorry about your boy gettin' it in Viet Nam."

"Thank you for your help," Farragan said, wishing for the moment that Charlie's boy had gotten it in Viet Nam. You wretched bastard! he wanted to shout; but the man was simply too big. Instead, he started out across the lot onto the highway and saw in the rearview mirror the sportsmen and their women standing together in the glow of red neon light, being washed over by the clouds of dust he left behind. The woman named Viola waved after them.

"Is Father Edmund all right, Mr. Farragan?" the El Greco youth dared to ask after they rounded a bend in the highway out of sight of the club.

"I think Father Edmund is a bit worn out and needs rest. He's been at his job a long time. Perhaps it would be best if you and Mr. Bowen left tomorrow. He really isn't in any condition to conduct a retreat."

"I'm all right, Arthur," Edmund said through a layer of phlegm. "There's no reason for the gentlemen to leave."

"I think you're a little too overwrought to continue. The gentlemen can come back another time."

"They stay. I won't hear any more argument," Edmund said stonily. "Mr. Farrow needs help with his conversion. Mr. Bowen's daughter must be prayed for."

Farragan was mute, and frankly amazed, gritting his teeth against the new wave of rage that overcame him. They bumped off the highway onto the heaving asphalt of the road that wound upward to Saint Blaise. In moments Edmund spoke again. This time his voice was hollow, the phlegm coating removed.

"Arthur, I just figured out how I got to be the unredeemable mess I am."

"You're not any kind of unredeemable mess, Edmund. You're just tired."

"No, I am a mess, Arthur."

"How's that?"

"It's because of our goddam mother that I'm like you see me."

"What did you say?" Farragan asked, turning his head to stare in disbelief at his brother in the middle of rounding a curve.

"It's because of our goddam, sweet old Irish mother that I'm such a mess today."

Automatically, Farragan slapped his brother across the face with the back of his hand. "Don't you ever say a thing like that, Edmund! Don't you ever dare insult our dear mother! She was a saint! Jim and Anna would kill you for that if they knew!"

Behind them, the two retreatants cringed in their seats.

Edmund began crying again. And as he shot the Land Rover through the monastery gates, Farragan found it in him to cry also. But only because of his continuing duplicity. Mother was a convenient yardstick for keeping the likes of Edmund in line. But he wished to Christ he could make up his own mind whether he loved the old lady or not. To her husband she had conceded about as much time in their marriage as it took to conceive the lot of her children. Otherwise nothing until the day he was buried, when they could not drag her away for hours from weeping and clawing at the earth of his grave. And so it went, hot and cold, with Farragan himself: an unsolvable problem.

Before them, Saint Blaise sat huge and ghostly in the moonlight. But for the first time ever in all the nighttime approaches he had made to the rotting *palazzo,* Farragan was not concerned enough to fear the ecclesiastic spirits that haunted within.

# CHAPTER 6

# The Funeral Supper

Farragan could not sleep that night for having doubts about his sainted mother.

He stood in his tiny cell, grasping at the bars of its single window and staring out over the expanse of rippling high grass to the one-armed Jesus statue that was alternately phosphorescent and nearly invisible as a full moon slid in and out of its cloud cover. Secretly his self-vision of a modern-day ascetic out of Philadelphia was pleasing, and he reveled in calling this his special night of spiritual torment. But the dull pain of his jaw where Edmund had punched him occasionally grew sharp and reminded him of the reality: the case for their mother's excellence needed bolstering. Accordingly, Farragan gave it a try and thought gloatingly of her burial.

When the old lady died six years before there were one hundred and twelve cars in her funeral cortege. Of this number Farragan was absolutely certain, since he had stood beside her grave on that day of leave-taking with Jim and Edmund and Anna and counted the vehicles as they left the cemetery.

Of the one hundred and twelve, Anna, the infinitely precise, had later revealed at the funeral supper, ninety-seven were black. Thirty-one were limousines, and there were twelve station wagons. Three Zephyr Motor Freight stake trucks wrapped in black bunting had borne the tons of flowers that were later heaped on her covered grave. No one, thanks be to God, had been so irreverent as to drive with the top down, though there had been eight convertibles.

This night, six years removed, those one hundred and twelve cars were comforting evidence in the case for their mother. But on the terrible day itself they had been only scant consolation. And afterward, in Jim's home, the catered funeral supper that was intended to ease the pain turned instead into a complete disaster. There, Farragan, a man just turned forty on that hot August day, had stared incredulously past his mound of gravy-coated food that might have done better service for a lumber camp in the middle of winter at a kind of pagan rite that appealed to him vaguely as having a necessary counterpart somewhere in the Russian literature. Gogol perhaps, for at least half the guests in the room were his mother's own variety of dead souls: the ancient ones from the ghettos in Kensington and Frankfort that she had always summoned out of the walls to swell the numbers at any family gathering. Now they alternately ate and cried and praised her memory and downed glasses of wine in a single draught and wiped the sweat from their faces with huge handkerchiefs. Beside him, Muriel, pregnant then with the twins, had complained of feeling faint. He turned to see that her face was incredibly pale and sweated also between the dark curtains of her hair, and hastened her out of the room. In the band's intermission while the players ate like the death revelers at a corner table, an undistinguishable Requiem had begun mounting out of Jim's stereo equipment.

"Your family is really a wretched establishment, Arthur," Muriel had told him unexpectedly but flatly when they were both seated on a long couch in another room that was appreciably cooler. For his part, Farragan resisted the urge to slide to his knees and beg her not to be too strongly opinionated about anything during pregnancy lest it somehow leave its mark on his yet unborn.

"It's just their way, Muriel," he said instead. "Our mother is dead. All those people were her friends. It's only their way of mourning."

"They weren't her friends, Arthur. They were only movie extras for every occasion she felt compelled to stage a family extravaganza. Otherwise they were never about. I've seen them to a man at all your tribe's weddings, funerals, and christenings since we were married. They're the very same ones who came to our wedding years ago in Georgetown, aren't they?"

"Yes," Farragan said wearily, "the same ones, or some like them. Please don't excite yourself, Muriel."

"Tell me something truthfully, Arthur, since your mother is finally gone and it won't matter any more: did she really hire a train to bring them all down that day?"

The Requiem drifted feebly in from the other room, punctuated by the clank of silverware and an occasional muted sob. Farragan sat heavily against the back of the couch.

"No, Muriel, she didn't hire a train."

"I knew it! I knew it all the time!" She had leaped to her feet and stalked about the thick carpeting on black heels with an intensity unlike anything Farragan had ever seen in the sixteen years of their marriage. "Oh, to find that out after all this time! It nearly drove us mad. My own mother went to her grave after ten years of trying to learn the answer. The railroad wouldn't give out the information, and the station porters all swore they had carried the luggage of a wedding party but couldn't remember what train they'd come from. They'd all suddenly just appeared. Tell me, Arthur, how did she get those people down to Washington?"

"By truck."

"By truck? Oh, my God, how pathetic! We were duped!"

Tears had rushed to his cheeks then, but more from the habit of sentimentality than outrage. His mother had been buried that day, after all. "Pathetic, Muriel? You call it pathetic? Just because my poor, dear mother wanted me to go into my marriage on an equal footing? We didn't have a horse farm in Virginia. It was your mother who got the whole thing going by dropping a guest list with two hundred and fifty names on it into our laps."

"You'll have to excuse that failing, Arthur. It was only a defense maneuver. We were petrified. Mother's head was still reeling from the sight of that brassy hundred-cylinder Dusenberg your old lady used to drive to the grocery store. I seem to remember that someone once lost his eyesight from the reflection."

"Muriel," Farragan said, "we can't be talking like this about her on the very day she was laid away."

"I can, Arthur. Now, for the first time in eighteen years I'm able to say it: your mother was a goddam, A-number-one bitch! And if I didn't think your brother and sister would strangle me on the spot, I'd go back into that orgy and tell everybody how I felt!"

By then he was on his knees in the deep carpeting, still crying and clutching her waist and leaning his ear against her stomach to hear the ticking of the embryo. "She wanted my wedding to be perfect, Muriel. She knew how I worshiped you. It was her way of showing you how much she thought of you."

"Oh, cut it out, Arthur. It was her way of showing my mother who was boss. Nothing more. I'm just glad she's dead now and won't be the first one into the maternity ward to plant a big, wet kiss on my face the minute after the baby is born."

"Muriel, for Christ's sake," he wailed, weeping anew, "they buried her today. . . ."

"Good riddance. I'm going home now, Arthur. You stay with

your family, and by all means don't stop crying. They'll love you all the more for it."

He had followed after her to the outside, helping her into one of the rented limousines and giving the driver directions in a tear-choked voice.

"She only wanted my wedding to be perfect, Muriel," he repeated as the car eased out of the drive.

"Nuts! One-upmanship, that's all it was," came the fading reply. But that was all. Farragan had trekked back to the house and into the room they had just left and sat down opposite a mirror this time, the better to enjoy his cry. He loosened his tie for comfort and pondered the enigma of his mother, about whom Muriel, his goddess-wife, had kept a guarded silence these many years. But, as always, when he came to recount the details of his wedding, he could barely contain his mirth beneath the overlay of tears: it was truly his preferred memory of the old lady.

On that day she had collected her dead souls—packing them like sardines or gypsies into five covered trucks—and left Philadelphia for Washington at four a.m. Then, in a pioneer era before the advent of superhighways and with trucks already old before the war and not yet able to be replaced from a lack of priority, Farragan, after two hours of delay, was faced with the real prospect of being married in a strange church before two hundred and fifty O'Haras of Virginia and no help at all from his distant and beloved Philadelphia. This, until the reading of the Gospel, when the place shook from the tread of many hundreds of feet and the vacant side of the church filled up in minutes. Farragan, joyous, had turned once to receive the high sign and a wink from his mother, then winced involuntarily as she called across the aisle to Muriel's mother in a voice louder than the priest who had been engaged in the singing of the liturgy, "We're sorry to be late. There was a derailment on the line somewhere ahead of us."

Afterward, his union with Muriel sanctified, his mother had backed him into a corner at the reception to tell him breathlessly how a drive shaft had snapped on one of the trucks in the Maryland farm country, and how it had to be towed at half speed and still stuffed with wedding guests into Washington by one of the other vehicles that had three times boiled over from the effort. But except for that inconvenience and the delay it had fathered, her elaborate and formally drawn plan that included a floor diagram of Union Station and a signal whistle that she wore about her neck, had gone off without a hitch. They had drawn up to one side of the train station, walked through to the other, where the busses she had chartered were waiting for the travelers, then come straight on to the church.

"If one person gets drunk, Mother, then everybody will know you didn't come by train," Farragan had told her in panic, frightened out of his wits by the possibility of the secret's being disclosed to his new in-laws, since even he himself had thought she was coming by train.

"Nobody's going to get drunk, Arthur. If they do, they ride back to Philadelphia this evening at the end of a tow chain. They've all been forewarned," she said, scanning the heads of her people, who had already achieved integration with the O'Haras and spoke with party politeness of race horses, Harry Truman, and the vicariousness of train travel.

In the end, at five in the afternoon, she had given two short blasts on her whistle and herded the dead souls onto their busses for the return, via Union Station, to their trucks, leaving Farragan to his new wife and in-laws and the immense romantic vision of five loads of Philadelphians lumbering triumphantly home silhouetted against the fiery Maryland sunset. . . .

At the funeral meal, in the other room, the band had begun playing again and the strains of "Mother Machree" drifted out toward Farragan. He stood up, weeping as much from the humor of her one-upmanship on that day as from sorrow, and returned to his plate. There, Jim was sobbing between gorgings of mashed potatoes. He wiped his lips and leaned across the table to kiss his brother on the forehead. "Cry your heart out, Arthur. Get out the pain," he had said, blowing his nose violently. "God knows you were her favorite. You'll miss each other the most."

There were more than two hundred people at the meal, and in the next instant Farragan believed he saw every one of them eye him mournfully and nod in agreement with Jim over their food. Exalted, he had returned in that moment to the primacy of his childhood, the rivalry of siblings finally resolved at the age of forty. In testimony, Anna had left her seat and come to kiss him on his youthful cheek, as had Mike Mailey, her third husband, who had gotten along with the old lady like another son. From his place, Edmund had given a silent benediction, and many in the room had crossed themselves.

Somehow prompted, the band had begun again to play "Mother Machree," and from the wave of sniffling and muffled sobs that swept the huge room, Farragan realized angrily that many another mother was being called back from the dead. To his mind there was not sufficient space for all of them, and he had thought seriously of rising to exhort the band to silence. But, blessedly, old Barnes had saved the day: or at least for a time he had brought them all back to the worship of the one, true Mother.

"Stop that music!" he had ordered, standing at his place. The low rumble of a shock of reawakening traveled the room, and Farragan had looked up first into the darkening face of his brother Jim. Barnes was an ancient alcoholic with a red lightbulb of a nose who had begun working for their father forty years before, in the time of the construction company, and then was spinning out the end of his days in the terminal repair shop, putting back together the spewed innards of truck transmissions with incredible skill. Uninvited, he had come dressed in a tuxedo to Jim's home after the cemetery and taken a seat at the funeral meal to eat and drink and weep over their mother. At the time, Farragan remembered, someone—Jim or Anna—had simply decided it was easier to set another place than ask him to leave. But their largesse had deflated the instant he shuffled into the center of the room demanding everyone's attention. Jim had half risen from his chair, a scowl on his face, and reproached the old man. "What do you want, Barnes? What is it?"

"I have a story to tell, Jimmie, about your mama, Mrs. Farragan, which you don't know about yourself. And I can tell it now 'cause she's dead and not around to be tellin' me somethin' like, 'Stop squealin', Billy Barnes, just 'cause I did a little charity for you once upon a time.' "

"Oh, God bless his heart!" Anna had cried, and Jim and Farragan himself, full of instant regret over his annoyance, had pummeled their eyes with handkerchiefs.

"You think your mama was the best woman that ever lived, Jim and Arthur and Anna and Father Edmund. But she was even better than that. She came over from the Auld Sod with less money in her pocket than a poor nigger woman, and she became a great lady and rich as the dickens. But she never forgot them she started off the race with. You Farragan children don't much remember when your daddy owned the construction company. But I remember 'cause that's when I first met your mama. She come round one day when I was climbin' up a ladder with a hod of bricks and stood there watchin' me for a time. Ah, but she was a pretty girl. She had the red hair then, and honest-to-goodness green eyes, and her head was covered with a black shawl. Then she said in her funny little accent, 'How are ya feelin' today, Billy Barnes?'

" 'I feel good, ma'am,' I said.

"And she said, 'How's your wife, Billy Barnes?'

"And I said, 'She's good too, ma'am.'

"And she said, 'How's your little boy, Alfred, and your little girl, Cynthia?'

"And I said, 'They're fine too, ma'am.'

" 'You doin' much drinkin' these days, Billy Barnes?' she asked me real quick and sneaky like that.

" 'I'm doin' some,' I told her.

" 'You better ease off, Billy Barnes, or you're goin' to be in a worse hell 'cause of the drink than you are now,' she told me.

" 'Yes ma'am, that sure is good advice,' I said, and after that I never touched a drop until the weekends," Barnes had said so unctuously that Farragan, despite the ever nearness of tears, had roared with laughter like the others. Inspired, the old man had unleashed his real theatrical presence.

"But she was more than a boss for me. She was a friend to this poor drinkin' man you see before you, and never had any prejudice about the fact that I took a black woman for my wife. One time I remember I had a bit too much and was movin' roughly along Spruce Street downtown, when this big cop stopped me and started givin' me the razz. Just then Mrs. Farragan pulled up to the curb in her Dusenberg car and said to that cop, 'He's a friend of mine, officer. Please help him into the car.'

"And that cop said, 'This bum's a friend of yours?' and he got a real funny look on his big red face.

"And your mama said, 'You heard what I said, pal,' just like that, 'cause she wasn't afraid of anybody, not even a cop.

"Then one second later that cop was helpin' me into that Dusenberg like I was the King of Philadelphia, and your mama pulled away from that curb and I said to that fat cop, 'You keep up the good work now. Hear?' "

Alone in the middle of the floor, old Barnes had nearly split his sides with laughter, Farragan remembered. But only a doubtful ripple had spread about the room: the police commissioner was there. The warning look had come onto Jim's face again, and, seeing it, Barnes had instantly resorted to serious reminiscing.

"But it's 'cause of my son, Alfred, that I remember your mama best. You don't know about him, Jim or Arthur, but he died years ago from the kidney disease. But not before your mama put him in the hospital and paid with her own money for two operations to help cure him. I just bet that great lady never did tell you about that, did she? No, 'cause that's how she was. She never was needin' to brag about her charity like some people," Barnes had suddenly choked out, the tears rushing to his eyes. He had stood a long moment before the death revelers, his bulbous nose snapping back and forth. Everywhere in the room handkerchiefs had flashed forth to liquid eyes. Across from Farragan, Jim, his brother, had pushed aside his plate and lay down his head on crossed arms, moaning into the tablecloth. Impulsively, Farragan had reached across to comfortingly pat the bald spot.

"She was so good. She was so good. She was the Virgin Mary herself!" Barnes had shouted. "I have to tell you the rest. Your mama visited my Alfred at the hospital nearly every day for months, and sat and talked with him. She even went into the operatin' room, dressed in a little white coat, and held his hand for courage and patted his head durin' both them operations, when the doctors was cuttin' him up right beside her and their instruments and their hands was covered with his mulatto blood. But your mama just kept right on smilin' with bravery. You knew your mother was brave, but did you know she was that brave, Anna?" Barnes had asked.

"Oh no, Billy Barnes. I didn't know. Nobody knew. Oh God, she was a saint!" Anna had shrieked, and many others had echoed her judgment.

"But wait, Anna darling! Wait! You've got to hear about the funeral," Barnes had sobbed. "I've got to tell you 'cause I'm goin' to die soon and the truth must be known. Alfred died, and your mama came to the funeral at the nigger church and held my wife's black head against her breast all through the service, cryin' and sayin' her rosary. And when it was over, and that old black folks' hearse wouldn't start, we put that poor boy's coffin in the back of your mama's Dusenberg and she drove me and my wife and our dead Alfred to the cemetery. When we got there, the three of us put his coffin on a dolly and put it in that hole. And since I dug it myself, I had to fill it in, and your mama said, 'Who's goin' to cover Alfred up, Billy Barnes?'

"And I said, 'There isn't anybody but me, Mrs. Farragan. I'm goin' to get a shovel now.'

"And she said, 'Bring one for me, Billy Barnes, and I'll help you.'

"And when I came back, your mama had rolled up her sleeves and taken off her shoes and stockin's and put her purse aside and helped me fill in that hole.

"You all know her from the cocktail party and the country club," Barnes had said, sweeping an arm about the room, "but you don't know her like I did. That great, rich woman from the Philadelphia suburbs with a Dusenberg car and a mink coat and diamond rings standin' in the heat in the nigger cemetery helpin' to fill in a poor man's grave. Can you imagine anyone but a livin' saint doin' that?" the old man had sobbingly demanded.

Then, Farragan recalled, Theresa Ginty, a mammoth-busted crony of their mother's, had flung herself forward on the table in her grief and collapsed it, hot gravies and vegetables flying onto the knees of some twenty weeping people. But the event was almost unnoticed. Jim had sprung up from his place to hold old Barnes tightly against his chest and kiss the wispy fibers of his hair. He called for a chair and sat the ancient down, and slowly fed him some brandy to revive him, then left him with the bottle for good measure. It had taken Barnes a full five minutes of bottomless weeping to bring himself under control. All about him, the pain of loss had gushed from the supper guests in deluges of tears. Jim had retired to a long couch in one corner of the room, prostrate with his grief. Anna, alternately shrieking and moaning, had held Edmund's head in her arms. Farragan himself, frankly embarrassed by the memory, had soaked through the cloth of her mourning dress from bawling directly onto her shoulder.

Then Barnes had risen to continue his narrative.

"She was your mother, Farragan children, and sometimes maybe you took her for granted, like children will. But she loved you all. She came sometimes as much as twice a week down into my transmission pit. That great lady came into my dirty, filthy work place and sat on her special covered chair, and asked me how I was doin', and how my children were doin', and then she talked to me about her children. She said Jim was a great American patriot 'cause he killed many Japanese durin' the war. And Stephen, your poor dead brother, he was a great patriot too, 'cause he had died fightin' them Nazis in France. And Anna, your mama always said you was the most beautiful girl, and that you never lacked men who was anxious to court you and marry up with you. And Father Edmund she used to say was a holy man 'cause he was a priest. But Arthur was the baby, and she always loved him the best, not 'cause he was any better than the others, but 'cause he was the youngest.

"And the last time she came to see me, which was the day she died, she told me that Arthur was her special conspirator. And I said to her, 'What do you mean, Jedda Farragan?'

"And she said that he was the conspirator with her in her secret life.

"And I said, 'What kind of secret life are you talkin' about?'

"But right then is when your mama got sick. She sat in her chair and her eyes started rollin' around, and her head was bobbin' from side to side and she kept sayin', 'Ah, aaah, aaah,' like that. And after she said, 'Aaah,' a couple more times, she said, 'Secret life . . . Arthur . . . secret life . . . Arthur.'

"And I said, 'Yes, Jedda, what secret life? You get it out and you'll feel better instead of storin' it up inside you where it's just waitin' like now to bust out from guilt!'

"But then she fell on the dirty floor and started rollin' around, and I picked her up and put her back on the chair and said, 'Get it out! Get it out, Jedda Farragan, and you'll return to bein' normal again!'

"But she never did get it out. She sat there tryin' for about fifteen minutes, but the guilt inside was a devil too big to pass through her mouth, and finally she peed in her pants from the effort and fell into a deep swoon. That's when I went to call the nurse to tell her to bring some of them smellin' salts, but she never did tell me what was her secret life."

Inevitably, it was Jim, Farragan remembered, who came first out of his shock at the tale Barnes had been telling. He stood up from the couch of his grief to advance slowly toward the old boozer, his face the color of a blast-furnace door, his eyes and the veins of his neck bulging with fury. And when she understood an instant later, Anna had gotten out of her seat so abruptly that Edmund, pining in her lap by now, had been dumped ingloriously on the floor.

In the second before Jim was first able to break the silence, Farragan recalled that no one had actually known where their mother had had the stroke, beyond the morgue attendant's cursorily given information that it was in a truck bay at the terminal. The dark, unaccountable stains in her hair had been grease from the transmission pit, then. Mechanically, clearing the floor for some aspect of a barroom brawl to come, Farragan had risen from his place and edged back from the center of the action.

"You nigger-loving bastard!" Jim had raged. "Our mother was

taking a stroke for fifteen minutes and you just stood there and didn't do anything?"

"I didn't know it was a stroke, Jim," Barnes had begged, walking backward away from his accuser. Farragan's brother had suddenly lumbered out of his place with the shambling gait of a rhino and caught up with the old one at the French windows, where he threw Barnes through the narrow-glass-and-wooden frame of one corner portion. Then, heedless of a door knob, he charged the center frame that would not give way in three or four onslaughts, cutting his hands and face on the shattered glass. Outside, Barnes had sprung nimbly to his feet and raced across the terrace to the driveway to hide behind the wide flanks of Jim's Lincoln only moments before Anna had whipped out her revolver to fire six wild shots into the opposite side of that car. When the barrel was empty she had flung the gun after the bullets for good measure and then was wrestled to the floor by her husband, Mike Mailey.

During this night of spiritual torment six years later, Farragan could still recall with absolute awe that it had taken ten big men to pin Jim to the floor lest he commit murder on the outside. This, until the heart attack had come that put Farragan's oldest brother in the hospital for two months afterward.

And for years after that incredible day—even until now—it still concerned Farragan that he might somehow have been a little more demonstrative at the time. But the truth of it, as always, was that he was eternally filled with reservations about the old lady: and obviously, in the case of old Barnes, she had been at it again. The occasional proper instincts of a fiend; more facets than a diamond; more angles than the span of a prism. If reincarnation were indeed possible, he could not for a moment imagine enough combinations for the form of her return.

# CHAPTER 7

## The Reluctant Warrior

Outside his cell, the moon passed through a long, cloudless expanse, and Farragan could clearly see the silvery herd of deer that edged out of the pines to poke timid heads through the openings in the monastery fence. Inside, he released his grip on the window bars and found his palms covered with the rust of years of neglect. They were also sweating from the agony of reliving the day of the funeral supper, and he hastened to the tiny sink to wash them.

The horror of that ceremonial meal, he decided while scrubbing up, was that it was only the beginning of a familiar memory trail. There were more of the old lady's exploits, and worse, until things hit an unquestionable rock-bottom low when the shade of their dead brother Stephen hove into view. How she came to be such a universally acknowledged saint of a mother was something Farragan could never fathom.

In the days following their mother's burial, Farragan remembered, both he and Edmund had taken shifts waiting outside Jim's hospital room for news of his condition. When he was finally admitted, he found Jim slightly propped up in bed at the center of converging arcs of light from two scented candles that burned on either side of him in an otherwise darkened room.

"What secret life?" Jim had asked in a husky whisper as his brother bent low over him.

"Nothing you don't already know about," Farragan had assured him. "She used to sneak off to the old churches up in Kensington and Frankfort to pray, and often took me with her. But that's the only conspiracy I was ever involved in."

"I thought that was it. It couldn't have been anything else."

"That's all I know of, Jim."

"Then that's it. Fire Barnes. I'm liable to go berserk if I ever see him again."

"It's been taken care of. He's leaving Philadelphia today to live with his sister in Savannah," Farragan lied.

"Good. This town isn't big enough for the two of us," Jim had said. But mutedly. Almost instantly the sleep of peace overtook him and his brother had quietly gotten up to leave. In truth, only the day before, Barnes had quit, and Farragan, cautioning him never to return, nor reveal what he knew about their brother Stephen that Jim and Anna and Edmund did not, had taken pains to make certain the old man's retirement plan would go through before schedule. There had been no mention of Savannah.

But it hardly mattered. With Barnes bought off, and Jim fervently convinced of his mother's sanctity because he had never really been unconvinced, and Anna off on a bender that would cause her to forget whatever the gnawing doubts had been, Farragan found it easier again to bear the burden of knowledge about their mother's "secret life," as Barnes had termed it, and the colossal hidden fact about Stephen that it was also his sad lot to know.

That day, he had left the hospital and impulsively driven into center city and then up to Girard Avenue, where he turned off to follow the keyboard slashes of white sunlight beneath the Elevated into Frankfort. There, in the place of his mother's favorite Church of Saint Colum Major, was a broken-glass-strewn vacant lot waiting for urban development to put up a project building. Mystified as always at the memory, Farragan recalled the days when she had sneaked off here to do her earnest praying. In those late twenties, and Depression thirties, she had had the good sense—or perhaps the kindness—to leave her car downtown and use the El to get back to her homeland. Once returned, she changed costume in the row house of her crony, Theresa Ginty, and excited again the shabby, beleagured fulfillment of what Farragan came to recognize in later years were her real aspirations. Then off, with himself as her companion, to the dark, old churches like Colum Major and the company of other women with frayed coats and shawls drawn over their heads.

Stretching out on the narrow bed of his cell, Farragan grew instantly sweetened at the memory: there, among the pungent and ever-present odor of incense, in the blackness broken by large banks of votive candles that seemed to multiply with the deepening of the Depression, Farragan the Child swam in the comforting lilt of rarely heard Gaelic:

> *Go mbeannuighthe dhuit a Mhuire*
> *ata lan de gracta, ta an Tiarna id . . .*

While others asked for clothing or money, he believed his mother's fervent prayers were for simplicity. Later, satiated after hours of continuous rosaries, she went dispensing sly envelopes of aid in the cabbage-fouled homes of people she had left behind but was never able to give up.

And it was to these same people that she went also for her

once-monthly drunk, Farragan learned when he returned home unexpectedly one weekend from prep school and went off to the ghetto to find her: a fact that was unknown by any other member of their family except his father, although it had been going on since the first days of their marriage. This, doubtless, was the secret life that Barnes had been on the verge of finding out about before the stroke overpowered the old lady.

Her drunk was a regular two-day caper in the Shamrock Bar of her crony Ginty's brother, and it was later slept off in Theresa's house. After the first time that he bungled in upon her exploit, Farragan began to recognize the signs: the irritability and restlessness that grew apace as the twenty-eight-day parch drew to its close. Then she was gone for her visit to the old people, away from her staid and restrictive home of new wealth, where she constantly guarded her language and never touched a drop.

It was to that same favored bar that she took Farragan some nights before his wedding for their first and only drink together. In the paid-for privacy of a back room, she had let down her gray hair full length to her shoulders and begun instantly weeping for no reason that her son could understand. Beside her, Theresa Ginty alternately downed shot glasses of bourbon and sobbed, with her head resting on the great crossed hams of her arms. Then, newly returned from the Army and reinstated at Georgetown, he heard the somehow unsurprising news that the patriarchy of the Farragans was, in truth, a façade.

"It was me who got him goin' in the construction business, Arthur," she told him, the brogue rushing back to her voice. "Your old man was a lazy swine and would've been content to go on bein' a bricklayer and Saturday-night drunk for the rest of his life if I hadn't gotten him that loan for the equipment. Thanks be to God, the guy died and there was no one left to collect what was owed him, or we might still be livin' up here in Frankford. But then I was pretty sure old Hollaran wasn't goin' to see too many more sunrises when I put the tap on him." She had winked slyly.

"You've always been a good mother to us. You'd lie and steal and beg to keep us in food and clothing if you had to," Farragan the Son had exalted her, for the drink was already up to that level.

"Don't think for one moment that I haven't, Arthur. I've done all of those things you've suggested. And more. It was me who told your old man to grab up those trucks when the company went bad from mismanagement, and me who finagled contracts during the Depression when others couldn't even put gas in their tanks. All I can say is that it's damn lucky the war came along and made him rich despite himself. My strength was givin' out around forty-one from keepin' that man on his feet."

"Nobody could've done a better job than you, Mother."

"I've raised you all the best I knew how, and placed all of you somewhere in life. You're the last and you're goin' to marry a pretty decent girl in a few days, and after I know you're set I can just roll over and die."

"Sweet Jesus, Jedda," her friend Ginty had said, "don't die after all the good you've done in life."

"I want to die. I want to die after what I've done to poor Stephen. That's the sin I'm drinkin' for now."

"You didn't do anything to Stephen, Mother," Farragan said, hoping to console her, "except make him face up to his duty and not permit him to dodge the draft. It's a sad enough thing, but it's not really your fault his number came up over there in Normandy."

"Aw, Arthur, you're a wonderful boy just back from the Army and about to get married," his mother had said. "But you don't know the half of that story about Stephen. And if you did, you'd probably strangle me for what I've done."

"He got what he needed, Jedda," Ginty said. "You couldn't have one like that hangin' round the house after the war was over."

"No, I guess you couldn't at that." But that was all. In minutes, Farragan, sensing that the supreme honor of this journey to the inner sanctum was ended, complained of tiredness and left the two women to their hallowed task of self-relief, considering it more than gently ironic that three days hence, at his own wedding, his mother might in no way be prevailed upon to take a drink. But that suggestion of some kind of hypocrisy was minimal, compared with the possibilities she had unearthed about Stephen.

In the early days of the war, when Jim and Anna's first husband had rushed off to enlist, Stephen had waited nervously beneath the disapproving glance of their mother for his draft notice. When it finally did come, he ran away and could not be found for two weeks. This, until the day Farragan was in the terminal office with his parents, when Barnes came by to tell them he thought someone was living in one of the abandoned trucks that sat rotting in a field beyond the parking-lot fence. At five o'clock, when most of their employees had left, three Farragans and the trusted Barnes had hastened out into the knee-high grass. There his mother had snagged and torn her stockings on the low-lying clumps of thorn. But it had hardly mattered: she had rushed up to the side of the old van and pounded on it with her fists. "Stephen Farragan, you come out of there this instant!"

For a long moment there had been nothing, then a muted sobbing that told the four they had their man. Farragan's father and Barnes had opened the back doors of the van to reveal Stephen cringing in a corner, wrapped in a blanket and weeping. His face had been gaunt and bearded, the eyes two frightened lights in its midst. The smell, Farragan recalled, had been appalling: the mixed odor of feces and unwashed body, discarded food tins, and the mildew decay of the van itself. Farragan's mother had clambered inside first, pulling Stephen to his feet.

"I don't want to go, Mother," Stephen had pleaded. "I'm afraid to go."

"You must go. I won't have everyone asking me for the length of this war why you didn't go and what's wrong with you."

"You must go," Farragan's father had said in keeping with the level of his logic. "Do you want Hitler here in Philadelphia, Stephen? Do you want those Nazis molesting your mother and sister?"

But Stephen had only cried hopelessly. He was led off with his blanket still clutched about his shoulders, and taken home for two days of quick rehabilitation. On the morning of the third he was driven to the induction center by their mother alone. He was killed on the Normandy beachhead in 1944.

But that drink with his mother before his wedding had been the first of any suggestion that she had sent Stephen to his death. The others, Jim, Anna, Edmund, and Farragan himself, who was a short time later in the service, had considered only that she sent him to do his duty. What greater service for one's country? In the main, it was the same argument they had used in forcing the decision to liquidate Simon a short month before, though by that time Farragan alone knew the true version of Stephen's story.

"Mother would have killed Stephen herself if he had really refused to go, Arthur. She was a tremendous patriot, and if she were alive right now she'd tell you to gun down Simon rather than let him shirk his duty the way he's doing up there in Canada," Anna had told Farragan when she sought him out at the shore with Jim and Edmund a few days after the one-armed Edward had returned from Viet Nam.

That day, Farragan—not unlike the noble Achilles, in his own estimation—had left his house and gone to sit naked and brooding and stung by a driven sand in the dunes near by. From the distance, he had seen them marching toward him, disparate and illusory like the folk of Fellini films, bobbing on the extended surface mirage like camels or elephants or whatever else might be fantasized on the edge of a desert come down to meet the sea. For the confrontation Edmund had donned his Jesuit cassock, which hung far behind him in the wind. Jim was dressed in his summer-weight suit of mourning, neither black nor gray exactly, but some subtle flavor of expensive sorrowing in between, and, as Farragan watched, twice ran back to retrieve the straw hat which blew off his head. Anna, encased in a dark suit and heaving down into the wind so that the wide expanse of her sun hat was forced flatly onto her hair, carried her high heels in one hand and hugged a highly reflective object of glass and metal to her breast that Farragan assumed wearily was their mother's coffin picture.

For his own part, Farragan's instinct was to flee, for two of that group were as loathsome to him as anyone he knew. He had looked south, beyond the dunes and across the bay, and could just discern the crass towers of Atlantic City shimmering in the heat. The distance, foreshortened, had the look of only yards, and he thought of stepping nimbly across the waters, though it was more than fifty miles, and over the relentless pine forests and onto the boardwalk, where he might lose his three trackers in the crowd. Instead, he had struggled back into his bathing suit and gone out to meet them, then invited them behind a large dune that gave cover from the wind.

There—with Jim and Anna sitting on a single bleached and rotting log and Edmund squatting down and staring resolutely out to sea because he had been ordered not to betray their solid front—had occurred, Farragan remembered, the most preposterous family council ever.

"Thank God, Mother's not alive to see us here now," Jim had begun savagely.

"Oh, I don't know," Farragan had said, trying for a laugh, "she had an occasional use for humor. The notion of our sitting down to a family council behind a sand pile in a summer gale with most of it blowing down our necks might have seemed pretty amusing to her."

"Cut the crap, Arthur! You know what I'm talking about," Jim had shouted above the wind.

"Yes," Farragan had responded softly, nodding contritely. But that was all. Within ten minutes, each of the three proponents of Simon's assassination had given his oration: Jim, as eldest and titular head of the family and father of a one-armed veteran; Edmund, still facing out to sea the better to control his stutterings, as family moralist in residence, veneered over with the sanctity of the priesthood to boot (despite himself, Farragan might have knocked him on his ass for that masquerade); then lastly, Anna, seeking her own variety of restitution for her dead son, Malcolm. For emphasis—like the gilding of the simple lily of her argument—she had finally produced the gold-framed coffin picture of their mother.

Instantly, Farragan had stifled his horror over their proposition beneath an outburst of proper theatrics: for patriotism, for idealism, for the most primitive emotions in the American breast. So much so that, by the stunned looks on their three faces, he thought for a terrifying moment that he had overplayed and tipped his hand and made them certain that any trip he took to Canada with a concealed weapon would be to warn Simon of his danger rather than to dispose of him in a kind of ritual killing.

But, in fact, they were merely shocked at his instant acceptance, and, when they recovered, comforted him with the assurance that he might parcel out his burden of personal guilt onto the apparently willing shoulders of the other three in the event that he was apprehended. It would be the Farragans' own crime of passion then, worthy of no more punishment (split four ways) than the legendary Sicilian taking revenge for his wife's adultery.

Later, he recalled, pretending to be subdued and compliant, he

had held up the coffin picture—the family icon of the Farragano-
vitch if there was one—to the sun for a long moment, then solemnly kissed the glass facing and handed it back to Anna. Silently,
the three had stood, and retreated from behind the dune into the
gale's windstream, their clothes and hats blowing before them now
as they receded toward their car.

When he was sure they were far enough away and not likely
to return, Farragan had sat down and given way to a convulsive
trembling that he finally cured by retching into the sand, thinking
it incredible all the while that, six years after her death, their
mother was still so completely omnipresent and available for use as
a precedent.

But, Christ, if the others only knew how little the precedent
she had set had to do with patriotism.

# CHAPTER 8

# Behold the Beloved Son

Despite everything, Farragan believed he still loved his handsome (though now long-haired with an ill-trimmed mustache) and unquestionably brilliant son, who was in the habit of doing the exact opposite of what he was told almost since birth. The father, therefore, had always played an elaborate psychological game, disdaining the strap and recognizing early that to better one's head on the rocks of Simon's opposition was indeed to invite a cracked head. At fourteen, Simon, a devout agnostic, was confirmed by a bishop in their parish church because Farragan had affected to forbid him from participating in such a superstitious rite. He had taken the proper girl to his prep-school prom, his father remembered, because it had been suggested (Farragan, you bastard!) that she came from a family of imprecise background: nigger maybe, though the word had sounded unconvincing to Farragan himself.

For the chance to show him off to their country-club friends in a Sunday round of golf, it was necessary a week in advance to begin

simultaneously debunking country clubs, golf, and the institution of
the American middle class until the message reached the unaccountable portion of his brain that returned negative responses. Then
they would be on the links with two other middle-aged men at ten
a.m., after Mass and a congenial family breakfast, with Simon gra-
cious and shooting in the low eighties and Farragan playing a worse
game than usual because he was so intent on controlling the bound-
lessness of his pride in his son's game.

Often Muriel, before the hard birth of the twins, came by in
the late afternoon for a drink, and the three would stay to dinner
with friends on the club terrace as the fiery sunset melded into darkness. Then Farragan—a man become a god from sitting between his
wife of fabled beauty and presence and his whole university of a son
who lectured rather than spoke so that men in their forties and
fifties put down their forks to better hang on his every word—could
only keep silent and survive the tear-inducing tightness of his chest
that he always assumed came from having too much of a good
thing. This, until they were home again.

Then Simon would become alternately enraged or depressed
about the ritual he had spent the whole day participating in, and vil-
ify Farragan for his continued attachment to country clubs, golf, and
the institution of the American middle class. But the father was little affected by this. Only filled with a kind of wonder: for despite
his intelligence, Simon was still something of a chump. Prone to
forgo the old logic every time. Dangle the carrot of converse
suggestion before him and he went for it impulsively to break the
string and fling that vegetable back. For Farragan it had become a
safe rule at hand and, until the events of last summer, he had
known precisely years in advance how he was going to induce
Simon to be married in the Church—the next big hurdle in Farragan's estimation—whenever the time drew near for that happy
event.

But Simon had stopped snatching at Farragan's calculated carrots on July Fourth the summer before.

That weekend, Simon, finishing up at his third university and preparing to transfer to Brandeis, had deigned to visit with them at the shore for a few days. When he drove up in front of the house, Farragan, returning from the beach, realized sadly that the new Pontiac convertible he had joyfully given his son for his twenty-first birthday three months before, had probably not been washed since then. Even more sadly, he saw that Rollins, Simon's lanky, long-haired, usually bovine-smelling roommate was along for the trip. Rollins came from a moneyed WASP family that had already disowned him. He had picked up with Simon at Chicago and kept pace with his transfers from school to school these three years.

Farragan had rushed up to kiss his son on the forehead, as always, then shook hands facetiously with Rollins, whose odor this time was like pungent modeling clay. Between them, on the front seat, they had but a single small overnight bag of clothing to last four days. The rest of the car—the well of the back seat and the trunk—was filled with boxes. Simon explained that they contained antiwar protest literature for delivery in Philadelphia and Baltimore that he proposed they carry into the house for safekeeping.

"I don't think you'd better do that," Farragan had said. "Your Aunt Anna will be down later today to stay the weekend. She's liable to go berserk if she gets to read any of that stuff. Put your car in the garage for a couple of days and I'll lock the door. It should be all right there."

But, please God, Farragan had thought, trying then to control his anxiety, let us have four days of surf-washed safety. Anna at least was family, and the worst she might do was label the paperwork subversive and return to Philadelphia in a huff. But who knew about the rest of the world? Farragan, hidden safely in its base, was turning slowly with the growing monolith of the national conscience against the war. But Simon, the beloved son, was miles ahead out in front in his commitment to the peace. And he disdained the function of what Farragan would have called practicality. With his forthrightness and idealistic honesty and the superb madness in him that passed for courage, he was perfectly capable of driving up to the front door of an American Legion convention and walking inside, barefooted, long-haired, and mustached, to begin handing out his literature along the aisles. Dear Christ, but Farragan had enjoyed nightmares over the possibility of reaction to his peace-loving son! In that instant, leaning against the sun-warmed flanks of the Pontiac, he might have hugged Simon to his breast, begging him to forsake honesty, his passion for democracy, his hatred of war, and his smelly hippie traveling companion, Rollins (who even now was raising eyebrows on his neighbors' porches), and come live the acceptable life of a surf bum near his father at the shore until whatever was wrong in the America that Farragan no longer understood righted itself.

But no, that was an impossible consideration: Simon must be about his own thing until he reformed the world or wearily settled for being wise and compromising instead. Farragan could not hold him at gunpoint on the Jersey beaches for his own protection indefinitely. As an alternative, thinking of Anna's propensity for snooping, he proposed that they raise the convertible's top and windows and lock the doors. "There are birds nesting in the garage that have crapped up the upholstery on your mother's and my own car."

Later, failing in his delicate hint to Rollins that he might enjoy a shower after his long trip from Massachusetts, he at least got them to take a swim with him so that by the time they returned to the house and were seated with Muriel on the wind-blown sun deck for a drink, Rollins' modeling-clay odor of before had dissolved into the more compatible freshness of sea water. Only a thick crust of salt clung beneath his eyebrows, and his hair was stiff and matted and long to his shoulders, and when Anna had arrived later—nervous as usual from her sleepless concern over Malcolm in Viet Nam and further irritated by the crush of traffic coming down from the city—she had started in on Rollins and Simon before she was halfway through her second drink.

"Why the hell don't you two guys get a haircut and clean up a bit?" she had said, the arteries flashing in her cheeks beneath the putty of her make-up in a sure testimony that her mood had gone foul.

"I look this way because it's the way I want to look, obviously, Mrs. Mailey," Rollins had said flatly.

"My own son's fighting for his country and living in a trench in Viet Nam, and I'll bet in all the time he's been there he hasn't smelled as bad as you do now."

"One is expected to keep vigorously clean in the military, Mrs. Mailey."

"Cut the 'Mrs. Mailey' crap with me, Rollins. Where did you find this lad anyhow, Simon? You used to be a nice clean-cut boy when you were in prep school. But now look at you. Your father made a mistake not sending you to the Jesuits. They'd straighten you out and trim that hair of yours in no time flat."

"The Jesuits aren't the answer to what this is all about, Anna." Farragan had tried soothing. "They're having their hands full right now like the rest of the schools. It's a universal problem."

"Universal, my eye. Malcolm went to the Jesuits. He always brought nice boys home from school for weekends. They looked right and smelled right and were going to be doctors and lawyers or politicians. What are you going to be in life, Mister Rollins?"

"I'm going to go to law school, Mrs. Mailey."

"You aren't going to get past the admissions interview with that mop of girl's hair hanging to the middle of your back. When it's time to go, you call me. It'll be my pleasure to take you to my

son's barber, then treat you to a two-hundred-dollar suit so the
dean'll think you're one of them for the time being."

"Ram it up your ass, Aunt Anna," Simon had snapped. "Nobody wants to be clothed with the profits of some of those hauling
contracts Zephyr Motor Freight has with the military."

"They don't, don't they? I'd be the last one to remind you,
dear nephew, but those dirty profits pay for, among other things,
that flashy convertible your idealism didn't force you to send back,
and the two to three hundred dollars a month you run up on your
gas-company credit card from traveling all over this vast and beautiful country of ours. Not to mention that overly generous check your
father gives you every month for living expenses."

"We accepted the car and the use of the credit card, Mrs.
Mailey," Rollins told her coldly, "because it helps us beat the Establishment at its own game. With it, we can travel to coordinate with
other antiwar protest groups, and it's convenient for hauling literature around for distribution. Right now we've got about fifteen
boxes of pamphlets to be handed out in Baltimore and Philadelphia
downstairs in the garage."

"What! You've got a carload of that subversive shit in this
house while my Malcolm is over in Viet Nam?" In the next instant
she threw what was left of her drink toward Rollins, spilling most
of it on Muriel instead. She raced with surprising agility across the
intervening space and slapped Simon's face with a fury that made
Farragan recoil from the suggestion of pain. In another moment he
had risen to pin his sister's arms behind her back. Muriel, doubly
wide-eyed with fright, had fled from the deck into the house and
closed the door behind her. Farragan had managed to maneuver
Anna—who compensated for the loss of her arms by spitting into
Simon's hair—toward the staircase that led down to the beach.

"Anna! Anna! For God's sake, stop it or you'll have a heart attack!" he had screamed into her ear, grateful that by that time it was

full darkness and his neighbors would have to be wearing infrared glasses to know what was going on. Halfway down the steps he released her. She had kicked off her shoes and rushed the rest of the way onto the sand, crossing the beach with long furious strides to stand in the feathering edge of the surf in her stockinged feet as if to cool her anger. By the time he drew up beside her, she had already lit a cigarette and was crying bitter tears.

"It's all your fault, Arthur. I could see this coming since he was in prep school. You should have taken a strap to that kid years ago and softened him up a bit."

"Simon doesn't soften under the strap. His hide only grows thicker. You should recognize that."

"I recognize lots of things. Oh, God," she had suddenly pleaded, looking up and raising her arms suppliant-like toward the stars, "please let Malcolm come home safely from over there. He's such a good son. He deserves every possible consideration. Just compare him to Simon." She rasped anew, lowering her arms from God and turning on Farragan. "I've never had a bit of trouble with him. He's never crossed me nor been anything less than a perfect gentleman with me. He went to school in business administration, stayed in the Church, and always had good, clean-cut friends you'd be proud to have as guests in your house. Now he's in Viet Nam fighting for his country, and when he comes back he'll find a nice girl and marry her and come into the business where he's needed. Compare that to that long-haired bum of a son of yours, Arthur."

Farragan was silent out of charity. Instead he gazed out on the Atlantic where the lights of a liner inched slowly up the coast toward New York. Malcolm was a sot, in his opinion. And incredibly stupid besides, with what Farragan had always envisioned as a layer of gummed-up cells on the exterior of his brain that patently resisted the bombardment of anything like a new idea. Apparently he simply preferred the universe as he had found it on that first awakening day of full consciousness (though doubtless late in his young life, in the case of Malcolm). For his own part, Farragan despised his nephew nearly as much as he hated Malcolm's mother. They were truly two of a kind: Mother Righteous and Son Righteous. Only Anna, from thirty additional years of fevered practice, was by far the worse. Often, of a peaceful summer's night, Farragan had sat quietly for hours sipping Scotch on the darkened sun deck and watching Anna at the surf's edge below staring relentlessly over the heaving waters like a Gatsby at her own green dock light. On occasion, she too had reached out trembling arms as if to touch it. Who knew what her light symbolized? More and Better Righteousness, perhaps. The fascist dictatorships of Portugal and Spain that Farragan guessed lay due east across the Atlantic from New Jersey. There, but for the language, she would be perfectly at home.

In any event, his fervent hope had always been that she would wade into the foam and try swimming for the light. Farragan would not have called out to stop her. That plunge would have meant an end to her fouling of his waters, of which she had always been so capable: the closest he had ever come to rejecting his beloved Church was the day he learned she kept her rosary wrapped about the revolver she carried in her purse, the better to insure accuracy when her inevitable rapist Negro made his grab for her foundation garments.

But any comparison of Malcolm and Simon, his cousin, was ridiculous. He had wanted to tell her this often. Simon, the son of Farragan, was a genius. In truth, Farragan had a special passion for the superbly intelligent. The greatest pleasure of his mid-forties was to sit with bowels whirling on the edge of his chair, sipping at his Scotch, and listening to Simon analyze the causes and results of events through which Farragan had lived—a participant along with the masses of other participants—but only rarely thought about. During one memorable night until the first light of dawn he was made to understand the 1929 stock-market crash from the viewpoint of social injustice. The mystery unraveled at last, then. A good thing to know. Until that time, for Farragan's purposes, the high-flying biplane of American corporate finance had merely taken a nose dive into the cornfields of Iowa, or wherever it was that the Republican Hoover had come from. . . .

"Simon will be a Phi Beta Kappa next year," Farragan told his sister above the roar of surf.

"He may live to eat that distinction, Arthur. People in this country are getting sick and tired of these permissive intellectuals. When Malcolm gets back from Viet Nam I'm going to have him give your Simon a dressing down for what he did to me tonight, since you don't seem capable of doing it. That's one little engagement you can count on about five months from now."

In that instant Farragan might have lopped off Anna's head and gleefully watched it bob in a bloody broth on the waves. Instead, he wished for Malcolm's death. But then he retracted, feeling ashamed: he loved his country far too much, had served it too devotedly in the war of Farragan's generation, to hope for the destruction of one of its soldiers. A compromise was in order, then. A moment after his discharge from service, when he passed, stripped of his uniform, through the gates of the Marine base to the freer air outside, let him be struck and killed instantly by a car, O Lord.

"You're going to have to decide who stays this weekend, Arthur. Your son and his friend, or me. There's not enough room in your house for the three of us."

"You'd better go then, Anna," he said evenly, not looking at her. "I see you seven days a week sometimes. This is the first occasion I've been able to get him home for a few days since last Thanksgiving. I can't afford to lose him."

"You mollycoddling unpatriotic bastard! I always knew there was something wrong with you, the way you took so many of your vacations over there in France. And spending all that money to have those cases of wine sent home when we have such wonderful wines here in America!"

"What the hell does that have to do with anything?"

"Everything, Arthur. It's symptomatic in your case. That's why you've got a twenty-one-year-old son in the shape Simon's in now!"

"For Christ's sake, Anna, drive down to Jim's place in Cape May and stay there for the weekend, will you? Give me a few days of peace."

"I'm going right now. Get my bags from the guest room and bring them out to me. I won't go in your house while they're still here, Arthur."

Then she had turned and recrossed the beach in furious slashes toward her car while Farragan had thought of braining her from behind with a shell. Instead, he had climbed the stairs to the sun deck again, wordlessly passed by Simon and Rollins, found Anna's luggage in the guest room, carried it to the railing of the deck and thrown it over the side into the sand at her feet.

"You pinko bastard, you! You hippie lover!" she had raged, bending to seize handfuls of sand and hurl them up at him. In response, Farragan had picked up an ice bucket, whose cubes were mostly melted by then, and rained the contents directly down upon her. Her hair had instantly collapsed into a sodden fluff, and from shock, the next two handfuls of sand had merely trickled impotently through her fingers. She had picked up the two suitcases, thrown them into the back seat of her car and lurched backward out of the driveway.

"You're going to hear from Jim about this tonight!" she had screamed out in parting.

"I suppose so," was all Farragan had had in him to answer. He watched for a time as her taillights flew up the road away from his house, then disappeared. In another moment he picked up his drink again and sat down opposite Simon and Rollins. He trembled with rage. Muriel, a black shawl drawn about her head and shoulders, had appeared timidly at the door. "Has she gone away yet, Arthur?"

"Yes, Muriel, it's all right to come out now."

"She was terribly angry, Arthur. She frightened me."

"Don't worry, Muriel, she won't be back for a while. With luck, she'll burst some of her plumbing from the strain and bleed to death."

"Here's hoping," Simon had said, raising his unfinished glass in expectation. Farragan had stared a long moment at his son. "The thing I don't understand, Simon, is why you can't take a haircut every once in a while, and be a little more discreet with people about that protest-literature business when you know it riles them up so much. It would make things easier all the way around."

"I'm not going to be dishonest with myself for the sake of someone like Anna, Father," Simon had said.

"We ought to eat now, Arthur," Muriel had interrupted. "Dinner has been ready for over an hour."

Grateful for the interval of dinner, Farragan had gone inside to eat two huge helpings of *paella,* which the cook—a woman who lived with her husband and five children in the scrub-pine forest on the mainland and who had not ever stirred farther from home than Philadelphia—made unaccountably better than any Farragan had tasted anywhere in Spain. In memory of Anna, there had been lots of French wine, too. Later, to his father's delight (though he had not believed a word of it), Simon had left off criticizing Johnson's war and shifted to Roosevelt's, explaining how the late President had engineered the Pearl Harbor attack. Rollins was generally in agreement.

At one-thirty, satiated with his son's instruction, Farragan had gone to bed to wait for Jim's telephone call from Cape May. When it had come, after twenty peaceful minutes spent listening to the roar of surf, he had lifted the receiver after the second ring. "Yes, Jim?"

"Arthur, what the hell happened up there? We just now got Anna calmed down and put to bed. She picked up two speeding tickets on the parkway and sideswiped some guy coming off the exit. She took a swing at the second cop with her purse, and now she has to go to court for assaulting an officer."

"Anna always did have a bad temper," Farragan said quietly.

"I might, too, if I knew my nephew was carrying around a bunch of subversive literature in his car when my son was in Viet Nam."

"It was only a gag," Farragan lied. "They told her that just to get her goat because they know she's so excitable."

"Excitable? She's over fifty, you know. You're damn lucky she didn't have a heart attack on you. Who's this Rollins character she threw the drink at? Is he that long-haired queer that Simon roomed with out in Chicago?"

"Yes, the same one."

"Well, I wouldn't let him in my house, Arthur. That kid smelled like a pile of shit the last time I met him. How do you know they don't have a bunch of subversive material with them in that car? He's just the type."

"I don't," Farragan conceded weakly. Through the receiver he could hear the rising intensity of Jim's breathing and knew the relentless pursuit had begun. Naked beneath the sheets of his own bed, he pictured his brother, fully pajamed from the soles of his feet to his ears, lying propped up on one elbow (agressively, if possible) in preparation for the firing of his next salvo. Beside him would be Margaret, his wife, sweet and kind and totally intimidated, the lone woman in the universe to whom Farragan's instinct toward chivalry stretched out furthest. On occasion, Jim had even terrorized her in public. Farragan had an instant vision of her reaching into the drawer of her bedside table, removing a pair of scissors, and stabbing it into the area of his brother's liver. But Jim's voice growled on.

"Why don't you go downstairs into that garage and check and see what they've got with them, Arthur?"

"What the hell am I supposed to do?" Farragan said. "Rip up the floor boards?"

"If it seems necessary, yes. And look for marijuana, too. All those hippie types use the stuff. If you find it, destroy it. You'll be doing those two bums a favor. They'll be in for a lot of trouble if the cops find it on them."

"What does it look like?" Farragan asked, suddenly alive with curiosity and sitting up in bed. He sensed the instinctive lowering of his voice. For no reason known to himself, he had never thought of Simon as partaking of this vice.

"Charlie Douglass told me last week that it's brown-colored and looks like those little bouillon cubes Mother used to make stew," Jim had whispered, as if Edward, his son, were hiding beneath the bed. "What these hippies do is put it in a saucer and light it, then they all sit in a circle and pass it around and sniff up the smoke. It's supposed to have the same effect as a fifth of bourbon, though I can't for the Christ see how it's more fun than drinking. Does Simon drink?"

"No, not really. He rarely ever finishes what you give him."

"Then you'd better go downstairs and check that car, Arthur. I'll wait on the line till you get back."

Dutifully Farragan had risen from bed, slipped on a robe and crept downstairs, through the darkened kitchen, and into the garage, where he flipped on a light to illuminate the three cars. Simon's was in the middle, with the keys in the ignition. Farragan had first opened the trunk to probe through the boxes of protest pamphlets, looking uncertainly for a small packet or perhaps an envelope that contained the marijuana-flavored bouillon cubes. But there had been only the annoying revelation that Simon had chosen to somewhere discard his spare tire, the better to make room for his literature.

In minutes more Farragan had checked out the glove compartment, beneath the seats, and in the depths of the convertible-top storage well, and pulled up the carpeting on the transmission train to learn to his satisfaction that Simon had not yet discovered and destroyed the Christopher medal that Farragan had taped there for his safety before handing the gift car over to his son. But there were no bouillon cubes to be seen, and he had returned, vengeance-minded, to Jim, still waiting on the phone.

"Nothing!" he spat all the way down the coastal darkness to Cape May.

"That doesn't mean a thing, Arthur. There are a thousand places to hide something on a car. He could have it taped to the inside of the rocker panels or under the hub caps. Lots of possibilities. Did you find any of that subversive stuff?"

"No."

"Why don't you take a look in their suitcases tomorrow when they're not in their room?"

"Why don't you go to hell?" Farragan had said. "I'm not working for the FBI. Simon's my son. Just because he wears his hair a little longer than the rest of us and has a friend with body odor doesn't put him on the ten-most-wanted list."

"That kid of yours is so damn un-American, Arthur, it makes me just want to strangle him. My Edward wanted to drive up to Beach Haven tomorrow to see Simon, but I'm not going to permit it. He's a big-eyed innocent one, and the likes of those two weekend guests of yours would take a real pleasure in contaminating him.

They'd give him some of that marijuana and stuff his pockets with that subversive shit, and he'd think it was fashionable. I'm going to find something for him to do around here."

"That seems unreasonable, Jim," Farragan said with extra earnestness, the better to contain the string of obscenities that lay waiting to be hurled. The notion of nineteen-year-old Edward unable to visit because of Simon pained him. No, rather, infuriated him. Of all the Farragans alive on the earth, Edward was certainly the most congenial. The wonder of it was that he came from Jim. But then he had inherited the essential good nature of his mother, Margaret, and paid but a shrewd and winking lip service to the spartan huffings and puffings of his old man. Farragan was certain of this: he met with Edward often, used him selfishly as a son by proxy to fill the void that came from not seeing Simon for months on end or hardly ever knowing where he was. Edward was then a junior at Villanova, attending summer school. Often in the lonely Philadelphia evenings, with Muriel at the shore and Marie not available to him, it was Farragan's delight to take his nephew to dinner for the sheer pleasure of watching his prodigious eating. Then off to a show or over to the race track at Garden State. Edward was a considerable companion. Less brainy than Simon, he was nevertheless the compleat young man in his own way: a nifty balance of ballet and baseball, girls and golf; he spoke a credible though accented French. The only laughter Farragan ever heard out of his Muriel these days came from watching Edward's antics on a surfboard before their home when they could borrow him for a weekend. The other nephew, Malcolm, could disintegrate, for all Farragan cared. Edward he had already generously provided for in his will. But he could not bear to lose this substitute son.

"Listen, Jim," he had said, trying to conceal his pleading, "you know how much Simon likes Edward. Why not let him drive up tomorrow so Simon can see how the other half lives? Edward's a good, clean-cut kid. He'd set a fine example for Simon."

"You're damn right he's a good clean-cut kid, Arthur. That's the way I raised him. And that's the way I want him to stay. I don't need for that superbly intelligent war-protestor son of yours to go putting lumps in his mind. No, he won't be going up to Beach Haven tomorrow, and Simon better not try coming down here until he gets rid of that friend of his and cuts off some of that hair and starts looking like a college boy again instead of some hippie freak."

"Aw, go fuck yourself, you narrow-minded bastard!" Farragan had shouted into the phone. Then he had slammed the receiver into its cradle and risen swiftly from the bed to prance about the room like a boxer, punching with all his might at vague, bobbing, and essentially mocking images of Jim and Anna. In another moment, predictably, the phone rang.

"I'm going to forget what you just said to me, Arthur," Jim screamed at him up from Cape May. "I'm going to forget because we're partners together in a business, and our business will be in sad shape if I can't speak to my partner next Monday morning."

"Thank God Mother's not alive to hear this." Anna spoke her disgust into the wire from an extension.

"Mother! Mother! Always Mother!" Farragan had shrieked back. He believed the hair on his neck was bristling by then. "What about our father? Do you remember him? That sweet, good man? Remember how kind he was? He was better than Mother. Once they took me to Grant's Tomb in New York and she ranted for half an hour about how Grant was a great general and saved the Union and how many Confederates he had killed, and when she went away for a minute, father just turned to me and said, 'Grant was a drunken bum.' Wasn't that a refreshing bit of honesty for a change?"

"No," Jim had said testily, "it was just typical of the old man.

Never having gotten anywhere in life, he was a real muckraker when it came to anyone who had made a name for himself. Everybody knows Grant was a lush. Abe Lincoln used to send him whisky by the barrel to keep him happy. But his personal life doesn't detract one iota from his usefulness as a soldier."

"Think of all the battles he won, Arthur," Anna had said, enthusiasm rushing into her voice.

Oh, God, what use? Farragan had thought, lying down and drawing himself up into a self-protecting fetal position. Over the wire, in an alternate rhythm like a badly timed car, he could hear the raspings of their breathing. The eternal teammates: Jim and Anna. The point of his Grant's Tomb story had been so excessively clear, that he thought of telling it over again—in monosyllables—lest the example be lost. But to what purpose, finally? He was already prejudged: the other Farragan, the family's border-line case.

"Arthur?"

"Yes, Anna?" he had answered, preparing himself anew.

"No, Arthur, this is Muriel. It's late, Arthur. Why don't you sleep? We've all had such a tiring day."

"Muriel, dearest," Jim had said, "I hope we haven't kept you awake with our little tiff tonight?"

"Yes, Arthur has been very excited. It's not often his son comes home to visit. You should all stop fighting until Monday."

"Muriel, darling, I hope you'll forgive me for dumping that drink on you," Anna had said, purring. "I intended it for that boy, Rollins."

"Yes, I understood, Anna. It's been a trying day. Your aim was poor. Everyone needs to rest."

"You're right. Good night, Muriel dear," Anna said.

"Good night, Muriel. Sleep late so you'll be rested in the morning for the Independence Day parade," Jim had added.

"Good night, Jim and Anna. Happy Independence Day to both of you," Muriel had said in her specially timid voice.

Farragan had listened in disbelief as the three hung up simultaneously and wondered how long his wife had been on the extension in her bedroom. Long enough to hear the invectives that had raged across the wires in judgment of her only son? Or Farragan's spirited defense of his father? But he guessed sadly that her failed mind had merely recognized that anger charged the atmosphere, and she had acted instinctively to quell it. In any case, he was grateful to her: the wide-eyed mien of her retreat from reality was the only power he knew of in the universe to keep Jim and Anna at bay for any length of time.

Only it was a flimsy enough guarantee: nothing to be depended on to protect him forever.

# CHAPTER 9

## Independence Day

But happy Independence Day indeed!

In his cell at Saint Blaise, Farragan recalled bitterly the events of that next day of wakening, which was July Fourth. At breakfast on the sun deck, before he had finished his first cup of coffee, he was into another round of battle with Simon and Rollins over their proposal to distribute antiwar literature at the Independence Day parade later in the morning. Farragan could not retreat from this. By choice, he knew a limited number of their summer neighbors, had never tested the extent of their political tolerances; in the same way, he believed, they refrained from inquiring after his own. They were tennis friends and fishing friends, and if he should ever have occasion to pass by one of them pale-faced in winter on the Philadelphia streets, Farragan guessed he might not recognize the man, so strongly would he be identified with the summer shore and the cult of sunshine and the place of escape. Farragan's son, in one vicarious weekend of visiting, was not going to wreck the unworded code his father had maintained with his neighbors for these twenty summers running. His plan was that they should go to the parade, taste of tightened chests and palominos and majorette's thighs, then go home for a drink and a long lunch.

"No, Simon, that's absolutely out of the question," Farragan said.

"Then we'll go to another part of the island, Father. We can't afford to let an opportunity like this, when there will be so many available, slip by."

"Some of those available people might take it into their minds to pound the hell out of you for your trouble."

"I've been beaten up before, Mr. Farragan," Rollins said.

Good, Farragan had thought, barely able to contain his pleasure. But something, evidently, had shone through. Rollins had stared at him narrowly for a long moment, then announced, "So has Simon been beaten up."

"Simon? My Simon? Where?"

"In Concord, Massachusetts, last July Fourth."

"Holy Mother of God!" Farragan had chanted into the face of his son. "You are a stupid son of a bitch! What do you expect is going to happen to you handing out that subversive crap at a national shrine on Independence Day?"

"Today, by comparison, ought to be a cinch, then," Rollins had joked, and Simon laughed appreciatively. From love, Farragan had thought of pulling out his son's long hair by the roots in great handfuls. Anything to keep him at home. But Muriel, as in the phone conversation of the night before, had muted the confrontation.

"Simon, Rollins, are those pamphlets you have against the United States of America?" she asked. She had been staring over the deck railing out to sea, seemingly oblivious of their argument behind her.

"Yes, Mother, they are," Simon said.

"You may not take them to the Independence Day parade, nor hand them out anywhere on this island."

Incredibly, there had been no protest, Farragan recalled. The command (?), suggestion (?), directive (?) had come forth in her special voice of the oracle behind the temple curtain. In response, Simon and Rollins had merely exchanged conceding shrugs and returned the literature to the garage.

Later, the baby sitter came by to guard their twin daughters, and they had all gotten into Muriel's car and driven to the parade route, where Farragan stood, paranoid and apprehensive of trouble, among his summer neighbors, who alternately tipped their hats to his goddess wife (the custom was not dead, Farragan knew: it only waited for the proper woman to revive it) and stared openly at his long-haired son and companion. But more from curiosity than menace, Farragan decided in time. The shore was a casual enough place, after all. It also occurred to him that, having seen so little of Simon about during the last few years, most people probably did not even know he was Farragan's son. That both pained and comforted Farragan but put him at ease enough to enjoy, with Muriel at his side, the predicted waves of majorettes and palominos and the new addition of a bagpipe band that nearly set Farragan to peeing, as bagpipe bands always did.

In time Muriel's special friend and protector, Binky Applebaum, the lifeguard captain marched stiffly past, leading his troupe of bronzed young lifesavers. He waved shyly to Farragan and Muriel, and Farragan clenched his fist and smiled and nodded emphatically to Binky to indicate that his efforts as captain had produced a tough and well-disciplined bunch this year. In response, Binky seemed grateful. Farragan considered it duty to give encouragement to Applebaum for whatever possible reason since he had first learned that Binky had suffered the ultimate war wound to his sex in Korea. Beside him, Muriel smiled and waved also after her fashion. Without Binky's innocent willingness to look in on her at least once a day, there would be no possibility of Muriel's spending the summer weekdays at the shore with the twins. Farragan was specially indebted to Binky and glad for the calm that three months on the edge of the Atlantic's vastness brought Muriel. In another moment the captain and his guards had passed, disappearing into a shimmering heat mirage.

When five minutes later, the colors approached and the crowd opposite him arose from folding chairs and curbstone seats, Farragan first heard the chorus of angry mutterings behind him.

"Stand up!" Someone finally spoke the words, and Farragan, turning, knew instinctively what he would find: while the American flag, flapping at right angles toward the bay on the breeze that blew in from the ocean was borne near by a girl astride a black horse, Simon and Rollins sat resolutely on the curb in protest.

"Stand up, for God's sake!" Farragan whispered to his son. His intensity, he believed, prompted a man who had his hand on Simon's shoulder to remove it.

"No, Father, I won't. Not while murders are being committed every day in Viet Nam in the shadow of that flag."

"That's not the flag's fault. Now get on your feet."

"Simon, Rollins, stand up." Muriel addressed them in the same voice as earlier that morning. "The American flag is going past."

It had worked for Simon, Farragan recalled. He had spent a short uncertain moment looking at his mother as if she had just betrayed him, then come to his feet. But not Rollins. The friend of Simon had continued to sit, and for good measure began to chant a litany of purported American abuses in Viet Nam. Farragan, in what he believed was his life's single greatest act of rage to that date, had kicked Rollins fiercely in the shin, then reached down into the tangle of his hair to yank him to his feet. "You stand when your flag goes past, you goddam bum!"

"Good! Good for you!" a man had praised him, and others had nodded approvingly. One woman had reached up from beside him to pat the contour of his shoulder. But the touch had hardly been comforting. Farragan, from the effort of his fury and the heat of the day, was suddenly close to fainting. Before him, the parade had trickled to a halt, and he could see with microscopic clarity that the flag-bearing girl on the black horse had bad teeth and whole ranges of bristling acne across her face. The horse had raised his tail and defecated copiously on the street. Farragan thought weakly of having another shoulder to lean on, but he must never presume to touch upon Muriel's. . . .

"Muriel, I feel ill. I've got to go."

"Yes, Arthur. I'll come with you."

They had turned to find Simon and Rollins had already departed. Once through the spectators (who were solicitous and eager to help), Farragan had caught sight of his son and friend walking swiftly away toward the house about a block ahead of them. With Muriel, he had gone to sit in the open Cadillac, whose leather seats were roasting. After a moment, he opened the door and vomited gratefully into the gutter.

"I can't remember ever having been so angry in my life, Muriel," he said, not knowing if the thought would register, but needing to say it anyhow.

"Yes, Arthur. Patriotism can be a dangerous emotion."

"Everything is so confused these days. I can't even talk to my own son. Where does he take his ideas from, Muriel? I've always tried to keep an open mind. I want my politics to be fair and middle-of-the-road. I want the minority groups to have a decent shake. God knows I've tried to hire as many Negroes as possible at the terminal without Jim or Anna nailing the door closed. I wish the war in Viet Nam would just stop, too. But not standing to salute the flag . . . I've never heard of such a thing."

"America has many problems, Arthur. But they'll pass. The new order will be one of love and peace. Repression and violence will be unknown."

Farragan had turned to stare at his wife. Today she spoke like Simon: the incessant malarky about universal loving kindness, the new order of politics. In that instant he wished fervently she would expend her limited energies on the business of beatifying violated women and leave politics to the pragmatists: it was safer that way.

"Where did you learn about such things, Muriel?"

"I know them from inside me, Arthur. When the new order comes, no woman will ever need be afraid of being raped or violated."

"That's certainly to be hoped for, Muriel."

But that was all. Her talk of women and violations had given him an idea. He had driven her to the house, then, desperate and sweating and grasping at straws with the need to contain his son, he had rushed off to the palace of Emilio Serafina to invite that gangster's twin daughters to lunch with Simon and Rollins.

Near the house, even on the Fourth of July, was the nondescript black sedan of the FBI or the SIC or the Treasury Department or whoever it was that stalked Serafina night and day as if they expected him eventually to nail up public notice of his guilt on his doorpost. Since meeting him one Sunday morning after Mass, Farragan had tasted of Serafina's hospitality, fished from the deck of his lavish yacht that was forever tailed by the same innocuous cabin cruiser as it left the bay, long before he understood the reason for the trailing cruiser and the nondescript car. The two men sweltering in that vehicle already had his name and photograph; Farragan had long since been cleared.

He had parked the Cadillac and ascended the front steps to lift the bottom of a huge American flag that hung like a curtain over the entrance. Inside, in the dark well of the vast front porch, Serafina sat obesely beside his mother, eating one of the oil-soaked tunafish hero sandwiches that he devoured almost incessantly. The old lady was praying a rosary.

"*Buon giorno,* Arturo."

"*Buon giorno,* Emilio. Hello, Mrs. Serafina."

"Hello, Arthur. Have a seat, please."

Farragan, trying to mask his nervousness, had taken a chair beside Serafina's mother and stared through the porch screens at the black car shimmering in the heat on the outside.

"They never go away, do they, Emilio? You'd think they'd take a day off on July Fourth," he tried making a joke.

"Fuck them. Excuse me, Mama." Serafina had patted his mother's hand. "They make lousy gentlemen, those two. Day before yesterday when I left the house their battery was dead, so I went back and gave them a push to get them started so they could follow me, and they didn't even say thanks."

"*Basta!*" the old lady said. "I'm saying a rosary, Arthur, so the temperature goes up to a hundred forty degrees and broils them alive inside that black car. You'd think the government would spend a few dollars extra to air condition the thing with all the money they take for taxes."

"Want a drink, Arturo? A little gin and tonic?"

"No, Emilio, I need a favor instead."

"Anything you need. Just ask, Arturo."

"How about lending me your daughters for the afternoon," he said.

"About that I'm not so sure. What's up?"

"My son and his friend are in for the weekend, and I thought, since they don't know any girls locally, they'd enjoy meeting the twins. I could take the girls over for lunch and have them back this evening."

"Is the other boy Catholic, Arturo?" Serafina had asked. The gangster-mogul did not permit his daughters to date non-Catholics. They were entering seniors at Immaculata in the city, and Serafina knew the name of every boy who came to visit them at school. Also, they were to marry Italians, apparently.

"No, the other kid isn't Catholic."

"What is he?"

"Some kind of Protestant. Episcopal or Presbyterian probably."

"A Jew would be better," Serafina's mother said. "At least they believe in something. The Protestant doesn't believe in anything except the opposite of what us Catholics believe. That's how their church got started."

Serafina nodded his head in agreement. "Those two out in the car are Protestants. You can tell by their haircuts."

Farragan had looked through the screens at the Federal Protestants, each of whose young blond head was trimmed into a neat flat top. This kind of talk was dangerous, he decided on the instant. The luxury of being a Catholic racist was too tempting: every word, every phrase of collusion was a bit more offal dumped into a river of sewage whose smell was not altogether unpleasant. The three of them might stay happily seated on this front porch for the rest of their lives talking just so, and let Simon and Rollins fend for themselves. Farragan thought of Serafina's yacht, the *Stella Maris,* with its five-foot figurehead of the Virgin on its prow, running majestically out of the bay, far ahead of the government cruiser.

"How about it, Emilio? For just a few hours?"

"Well, all right, Arturo. But no hanky-panky. Keep your eye on that other kid, O.K.? The girls are on the beach. Let's walk up and get them."

They had left the house, passing beneath the American-flag curtain, and started along the road to the beach.

"I'm surprised they don't follow us to the water," Farragan had said, looking back to see one agent removing binoculars from a case.

"They tried that once. The one in the driver's seat is from Nebraska. The first time he ever saw the ocean was when they dumped him on this island. Once I went up to the beach and he decided to follow in the car. He drove right off the road into the sand up to his axles. His next mistake was leaving the car and going for a tow truck. By the time he got back, the neighborhood kids had dumped about twenty pounds of sand into his engine. Now he stays put right where he is."

"There's no reason, then, why you can't get away just by walking over the dunes and swimming for it, Emilio."

"Impossible, *paisan*. They've got a submarine out there. Shhh. Don't make noise, Arturo. I want to see what they're doing."

With their father, Farragan had crept to the top of the dune, preparing to spy over the edge, hoping beyond hope that the Twins Serafina were sunning naked on that usually deserted stretch of beach. Instead, they sat talking with their aunt, Serafina's sister, who was a nun.

"Giulietta! Claudia! Come here, darlings!" the mogul commanded. The two sprang up from their towels, leaving the nun behind. As always, even on this morning of ultimate concern for the future of his son, Farragan had felt the familiar levity overcome him at the sight of today's oil-coated bodies that overcame him no matter where he had occasion to see them: at Mass on Sundays when they winked naughtily across the aisle at him while Serafina prayed for victory over the Feds with his head in his hands; or on board the *Stella Maris,* where their father permitted topless sun bathing outside the three-mile limit. Farragan believed his sustained fantasy of lying naked abed with the two of them, deliriously kissing the ranges of their breasts and running his fingers through their moist underparts, would keep him potent until the moment of his death. Once, thinking of it, he had ploughed, from a lack of caution, into the back of a delivery truck stopped for a light. . . .

"Hello, Mr. Farragan. What's wrong, Daddy?" they sang in unison. Golden crosses hung round their necks and trickled into the clefts of their bosoms.

"You're going to lunch at Mr. Farragan's house with his son, who's the same age as you two, and his son's friend, who's a Protestant. Watch out for the friend."

"Yes, Daddy," Giulietta answered, a grim look, like fear, replacing the eager smile on her face.

"Go to the house and shower, then dress modestly," their father told them.

"Yes, Daddy."

"Bring along your bathing suits, girls. You may want to take a swim with the boys after lunch," Farragan said.

"Take one-piece suits, girls," Serafina ordered. "There's less chance of hanky-panky that way."

"Yes, Daddy."

Oh, shit on you and your hanky-panky, thought Farragan. But still, two Serafinas in one-piece suits were miles ahead of anything else he could muster on short notice. Farragan stood beside their father and their aunt, the nun, who had wordlessly joined the two men, and intently watched the beauties descend the dune toward the road that led to the house. Please be the proper intermediaries, O Serafina sisters, he petitioned silently, closing his eyes and barely restraining himself from lifting hands to heaven. A plaintive litany had poured out of him: make my son Simon a slave to one of your luscious Italian Catholic bodies: bring him back to the logical comforts of society and Holy Mother the Church where he belongs:

make him believe you refuse to marry him unless he cuts his hair and thinks daily about the need to change his underwear: lay down the law of womankind about where Rollins has to go: take Simon to Capri with you until the war in Viet Nam is ended. . . .

Please. Please. Please. . . .

Farragan opened his eyes to see Serafina regarding him narrowly. "What are you thinking about, Arturo?"

"I was only wishing, Emilio, that they might stay forever as perfect as we see them today."

"Impossible, Arturo. And it's their own fault. I have them on strict diets—yogurt and figs and stuff like that—but they sneak Italian food on the side. Children are so ungrateful, Arturo. Do they want to grow fat like me? I always ask them. I'm beyond repair, but they still have a chance. But you can't give kids today a lesson for nothing."

"You're absolutely right, Emilio," Farragan had agreed unctuously. But that was all: in ten minutes he pulled away from the house with the twins in the front seat beside him, laughing delightedly while swerving along the road at their revelation that they had brought along their bikinis after all.

At home, he knew almost instantly he had made a mistake. Simon and Rollins were sullen and still chaffing at Farragan's having dared to reach into Rollins' hair and yank him to his feet at the parade. They had greeted his gift of the Serafinas as if his arms encircled two wriggling pythons instead of the curvaceous flesh of young girls. For their part, the twins stared unabashedly at Rollins' long mane, and Farragan, whom they trusted, felt them impulsively burrow deeper into the protective sweep of his arms: in addition to Protestants, their father also did not permit them the company of boys, even Catholics, whose hair was in excess. In that short, pained moment of mumbled introductions and terse nods of recognition, it came to Farragan that the daughters of Serafina were somehow more

nearly like himself—in taste and style and the capacity for hope—
than the young men he counted on them to save.

"I'll leave you young people together and tell the cook to
bring lunch out here for you," he had nearly shrieked, in his anxiety
that they at least talk with each other, then made his bumbling retreat toward the kitchen, banging into a sudden gauntlet of knee-
high tables and the arms of chairs on the way.

Later, as he ate a nervous lunch with Muriel in the dining
room, he listened for the sounds of youthful laughter outside. But
there was nothing beyond the soft moan of wind on the rise and the
occasional clank of a fork. Once, no longer able to picture the four
of them together, he crept to a window and slyly eased back the curtain's edge. Simon looked relentlessly out toward sea; Rollins, just
as relentlessly, toward the houses of Farragan's neighbors; the Serafina twins read the label on a bottle of rosé, most of which evidently they themselves had consumed, and giggled intermittently
from its power.

"Christ, what's wrong with that kid!" Farragan had said, releasing the curtain and stamping his foot into the floor.

"Those are not Simon's kind of girl, Arthur," Muriel had said
softly.

"What is Simon's kind of girl, Muriel? Can you tell me that?
I'd bring a truckload of whores down from Philadelphia if I thought
he'd talk to just one of them. What kind of woman does he like?"
he had asked, advancing on the table with suppliant arms extended
toward her, forgetting that she had been feeble-minded already for
four years since the twins. In alarm, she had sprung up from her
chair. "Not whores, Arthur. Simon doesn't like those kind of
women. They're women who want to be violated. . . ."

Then, fearful yet another time of her own husband, she had
rushed from the room.

Farragan had sat down again, close to crying from frustration, and settled for a cup of coffee instead. In time, he stood up and went outside, where the sisters, who seemed drunk, greeted him with effusive relief. He understood it was the moment for another directive.

"Maybe you young people would like to change into your suits and walk off lunch on the beach. You might go for a swim later, too."

There had been a kind of garbled agreement, and the foursome had dragged themselves unenthusiastically into the house to change for the beach. Five minutes later Farragan had presided over their departure with a wan smile, only slightly comforted by the knowledge that the Serafina sisters, flushed and giddy from their wine, would a thousand times have preferred to stay behind with Farragan, who was nearly as old as their father. He had watched for a time as they moved gradually out of sight along the beach: Simon and Rollins, fish-belly white and clad in baggy surfer suits with their hair streaming behind them in the wind, were followed by the sun-blackened twins, who wore the merest of mere bikinis, and whose hair, unaccountably, seemed oblivious of the wind. Like nymphs, the Serafinas had gamboled to keep up with their uncaring dates. Miserable, Farragan had gone inside to nap.

Only to be awakened in forty-five minutes by the wrath of Emilio Serafina.

Ironically, he remembered this night in his cell, he had been enjoying a dream about his son enjoying a candlelit dinner with Giulietta Serafina when the cook knocked on his bedroom door to tell him her father was cursing the name of Farragan and his progeny over the phone. Apprehensive, he had switched on the bedside extension.

"Farragan . . . ?"

"Yes, Emilio?"

"Don't call me by my first name any longer, Farragan. Call me Serafina and cross to the other side of the street when you see me coming!" the mogul had raged in a voice whole octaves higher than anything Farragan had believed him capable of.

"Emilio, what's wrong?"

"You don't know what happened today, Farragan?"

"No. For Christ's sake, what happened?"

"Those two boys aren't back at your place yet?"

"No."

"Well, my daughters are here, Farragan, and it's three miles farther along the beach, you bastard! Somebody in a dune buggy picked them up and brought them right to the door to me, otherwise they might have collapsed from the exhaustion of running. As it was, they were crying their heads off and shaking from terror!"

"Emilio, please tell me what happened." Farragan had thought instantly of rape and an eternal vendetta with the Serafinas that the law would be powerless to avert until every Farragan anywhere was dead.

"They went into the dunes, Farragan, and first off the two boys took off their suits."

"Oh, God, no, not with the twins. . . ."

"Which doesn't bother me so much, Farragan. I send the girls to the nuns' school and try to help them live clean, upstanding lives, but it's a naked age and I can't protect them from everything. It's in all the magazines on the newsstands, and I read them too. I can't go on hoping they'll be spared from seeing some guy's cock until their wedding night when all they have to do is open a book on anatomy in the library. That's not what it's all about. My Giulietta and Claudia, they told me the truth: they thought the boys wanted to play, so they took off the tops of their suits."

"What happened then? They tried to rape the girls? I'll kill them!" Farragan raged. "I promise you, Emilio, I'll beat them sense-less!"

"You won't believe what happened then, Farragan! Your son and that long-haired freak of a friend of his threw clam shells and handfuls of sand at my daughters' bare breasts and called them stupid and said they were the most unattractive girls they had ever seen!"

"Oh no, not that. What the hell is wrong with them?" Farragan had sunk weakly onto the bed. Vaguely, from the other end of the wire, he heard the din of arguing Serafinas that raged beyond the periphery of his numbing shock. Then there was a new voice.

"Mr. Farragan . . . ?"

"Yes?"

"Mr. Farragan, this is Claudia. Oh, Mr. Farragan, we like you so much. You were always so good and we loved the way you took care of Mrs. Farragan after she got sick. We don't blame you for what happened. We're so sorry this had to happen to you of all people. It's a terrible thing for you to find out about your only son that he doesn't like girls so much."

"But are you sure, Claudia? Are you sure you're not exaggerating this business?" Farragan had begged, wanting to disbelieve.

"I blame you, Farragan!" Her father had cut back in. "I blame you for it all! I send you my daughters, who are watched over by nuns nearly three hundred sixty-five days a year, for just one afternoon, and two bums throw clam shells and sand at them! My daughters, Farragan, who've been on special diets for years and have never had skin blemishes or braces on their teeth like other kids, and for whom I always carry a gun when I'm with them to keep evil-intentioned men away, and look at the insult to their character and beauty they have to suffer! If you see me after Mass for the rest of the summer, don't you dare try to talk with me, Farragan!" Serafina had slammed down the receiver.

The need to know quickly the ordered part of his family had been the second wave of response to Serafina's ugly disclosure, and he had gotten up to splash water on his face and dry it in the bathroom, then gone to the kitchen where the cook, her head shoved far into the dark cavern of the wall oven, had not turned around to acknowledge him. He looked for Muriel in her bedroom and the living room, then quietly opened the door to the nursery, where he found her seated on the floor playing with the twins. The three had smiled toward him simultaneously, and his daughters raised their arms to be lifted, and Farragan, immeasurably comforted, had blown them a kiss, then withdrawn swiftly to look after the unordered part of his world.

His rage over Simon's defilement of the sisters Serafina grew apace.

He had returned to his room and taken binoculars from his closet, then snatched up his tennis racket as a weapon and hurried from the house onto the beach in the direction of the dunes. Once there, it had taken him fifteen minutes of climbing the highest sandy peaks and looking into the valleys and lesser ranges of hills that surrounded them to find the pair: they stood in the shallow and calm waters of the bay clothed in their suits once more and picking clams from the mud. Farragan had thrown down the binoculars and stumbled across the dune hills, determined then that if he never did another thing in life, he meant to clobber Simon at least once with the tennis racket he flailed in the air in revenge for the twenty-one years he had never laid a hand on him.

But Simon was agile as a gazelle, even two feet deep in water, and Rollins more so, and the two had split in opposite directions and headed for the shore, so that when Farragan crashed into the bay after his headlong rush down the side of a dune, he fell upon empty waters.

"Stand still, Simon! Stand still, goddam you! I'm going to hit you!" Farragan had raged, pulling himself out of the water.

"No! What the hell for, Father? Because of those two stupid girls you lined up for us? They deserved what they got."

"Those girls are beautiful, you queer! Their father has armed guards to watch over them because so many men find them desirable! Any red-blooded American boy with his mind in the right place would have been trying to get the bottoms of those bikinis off instead of throwing clam shells at their tits! You've disgraced me, Simon!"

"You've disgraced yourself by pimping for us, Mr. Farragan!" Rollins had said. "Those two girls were born and bred to be Establishment prostitutes, if I ever saw any!"

"Pimping! So that's what you call it? I was trying to help you! Those two girls were your last chance to save yourselves!"

Their laughter had enraged him out of all proportion. Impulsively, the three had started racing along the edge of the bay then, with Simon and Rollins loping easily in front and Farragan in furious pursuit, brandishing the tennis racket weapon over his head.

"Simon! Simon!" Farragan screamed after them. "I've got to know something from you!"

"What, Father?" Simon had stopped for an instant to ask the question, then made a near right-angle turn and headed into the dunes, with Rollins beside him. Desperate to reach his son with the racket, Farragan had cut around the edge of the hill the two ascended, hoping to catch up with them on the other side. But the way was blocked by yet another dune, and he had climbed it, knee-deep in sand and ranting after them, "Are you still a virgin, Simon?"

"Are you kidding? I lost that when I was fourteen!"

"Fourteen? Fourteen years old? You were only a freshman in prep school then!"

"There was a kind woman in the near-by town, Father, who didn't charge too much money."

"Jesus Christ! Am I going to clobber you! Fourteen years old! No wonder you're in the mess you are today! After that, there was nothing left to be curious about!"

By then they were running and howling with laughter up the middle of a long canyon, and topping the ridge beside it, Farragan had stumbled and rolled end over end down the hill, striking himself twice in the head with his own weapon. When he got to his feet and scrambled after them, they were already far ahead. At the end of the canyon, he followed their tracks up one side of the last dune before the ocean and halted at the top: they had made the beach and were jogging easily along toward the house.

"Simon Farragan! Simon Farragan!" he had called after his son. "You go straight to the garage and get into your car and get the hell off this island! Don't dare stop to talk to your mother! Do you hear me? Get out and never come back!"

For good measure, he had flung the tennis racket after them, and though it fell far short, both Simon and Rollins had stood a long moment to watch its flight, turning head over handle, until it landed harmlessly in the sand.

"Father, why are you doing this?" Simon had called to him. "Just because of those girls? They were shit! Haven't you got any taste? Those girls were really shit! They were like two kewpie dolls! They're not enough reason to try to hit me with a tennis racket!"

"I'm doing it because of those girls and everything else!" Farragan had ranted from the top of his dune. "You've defiled your manhood! You know how much I love your mother! She's not ever going to find out about this! How do you think she'd feel if she knew that the little boy we sent away to the Jesuits when he was fourteen was consorting with a prostitute as soon as he got there?"

"I'm surprised she couldn't tell from the changed look on his face, Mr. Farragan," Rollins had said.

"You shut up, you big smelly turd! I'm talking about your mother, Simon! Do you hear me? I couldn't stand for her to know! Get in your car and get out! You've got one more year of college coming from me, and after that you're on your own. But don't try coming home again!"

"How long was I supposed to have waited, Father? Will you tell me that?"

"Until you were twenty-one," Farragan said automatically. But Simon and Rollins had merely shrugged at the intensity of his tirade, then set off again at a trot while Farragan sat down from exhaustion atop the hill of sand. Fourteen. The notion of his son's knowing woman already at that tender age swept over him in a wave of anguish; yet he was at least honest enough to admit that the better part of his rage was prompted by sheer vile jealousy. Though for the moment, for public information, he might lay the cause of the anger on the insult suffered by the sisters Serafina and their father who had been his friend. But fourteen: Farragan had absolutely no idea how it might have seemed. His own time had finally come at twenty-one, in the back seat of his mother's Dusenberg parked in the garage on a night of shared fear and elation that was the inevitable and thankful end of five or six years of incessant masturbation and shy lurkings in the environs of Camden whorehouses since the idea of having a woman had come strongly upon him. That night of the first time—with its desperate fumblings, the rough smelly undergarments of their cleaning girl, and the discomfort of conscience caused by the relentless staring of the luminous statue of the Virgin iron-glued to the Dusenberg's dash—he could remember with insistent clarity. The fear. The fear: Jesus! Where had it all come from? The thought that Simon, child of a more secular age who had early disowned the images of favorite Philadelphia saints that Farragan and his Muriel used as part of the stage props of their lives, had simply gone to a bordello and paid his money and come at the age of fourteen with presumed artfulness and no particular psychic malaise between the hireling's thighs only served to increase the pangs of jealousy. He continued to sit atop the sand dune, bristling with his fury. Even now the favorite saints still came back to haunt him: In this, his middle adult life, impotence was not an unknown thing. It was only slightly less frequent than it had been when he was a younger man. And he still covered the bedroom statues whenever he had occasion to make love.

Far up the beach, the two had disappeared in the wide lake of a liquid mirage. The last time Farragan had ever seen his son in America. . . .

But now, in his cell at Saint Blaise, Farragan decided there were certain consolations to knowing that Simon had lost his cherry and enjoyed conjoining with women of his own choosing, though his father would still have chosen the sisters Serifina for him if given the option. For the precedent set by the Farragans' mother— and so revered by Jim and Anna—of forcing Stephen off to fight the Nazis was an altar astride an earthquake fault. It had nothing at all to do with Simon.

Farragan remembered there was a coffin picture of his mother in Edmund's room. He stole along the hallway toward the sound of his brother's snoring and past the small moans of one of the others, who proved to be El Greco. Edmund's door was open, and the cleric lay fully clothed in his hunting jacket and jeans atop his bed, the sweat still shining on his face.

On his dresser, in a gold frame identical to Anna's, was the coffin picture. Farragan quietly took it and returned along the hallway to his room. There, in the first hint of dawn, he gazed at the Farragans' mother in her casket, her face wreathed in the beatific smile of the mortician's handiwork and softened by the glow of tall funeral candles on her polished skin. When she had died so suddenly on them, the Farragans were frantic with the need for remembrances and decided to have her photographed at the viewing. Farragan kept one picture in his bedroom at home, as did the others—except for Anna, who carried hers with her in her purse at all times.

It was this way—calm with the infinite calm—that he preferred best to recall his mother: then she was most harmless. For if the old lady had sent Stephen to his duty, she had also sent him to his death, Farragan reflected sadly. And by now he was absolutely certain she had wished for it. The story had come out some two years after the war when Farragan and Muriel had been joined in an American cemetery in Normandy by his parents to visit Stephen's grave. There the old man had weepingly accused his wife of Stephen's death and reminded her of how meaningless the notion of duty had proven when most of their own drivers and many others they knew had unaccountably stayed home.

"Maybe I did send him out to die," she had screeched at her husband in the forest of small white crosses. "Maybe I did. But I had my reasons. It was me and not you who walked up on the beach down at Cape May one night the summer before the war started and found him lying stark naked on a blanket kissing another stark-naked boy. Wasn't that a fine sight for his mother to see? Kissing and buggering each other like some kind of animals. I didn't even dare to tell you about it. Let him be dead rather than trying to have us live with that for the rest of our days. There was something wrong with his mind. He was sick. God knows I didn't raise him to be like that."

No one had said anything as she stomped back to the rented car and climbed inside. But for the others, the truth had been omnipresent: Stephen was dead, then, not for any price of duty, but because, for his mother's purposes, he was not fit to live. The old man had never spoken of it again.

Farragan, holding up his mother's picture to the dawn, tried to remember something of Stephen. But beyond the fact of his incredible good looks and continued addiction to the Roosevelts and the liberal causes of the thirties, much of the past was blotted out. His older brother had been an enigma, Farragan decided, distant and melancholy, rarely approachable except for a few brief, unsolicited flings like the time he had taught Farragan to drive a car. Beyond that, nothing. It was from Jim, mainly, that Farragan had had to take all his dogma for life.

But one thing was certain, Farragan decided as he undressed and prepared to sleep: some time in the future, before he might perhaps ultimately have to turn the liquidator's .38 upon the two super-Americans of his family to protect the life of his son, Jim and Anna were going to learn that there was not one fucking iota of patriotic fervor in the old lady on the day she turned Stephen over to the military at the induction center.

# CHAPTER 10

# The Need for Days
# of Prayer and Fasting

From Tuesday noon, when he awoke, to bedtime that night, Farragan played retreat master of Saint Blaise in the absence of Edmund, who refused to leave his cell until the first possible hour of return to the Sportsman's Club for a drink.

But it seemed to matter little to the two retreatants. The El Greco youth—who still could not be persuaded to leave—was content enough to pursue the winding paths once designed for solitary contemplation in the company of the real retreat master's brother, who was at least a Catholic. From early afternoon until well into sunset, Farragan was plied with a list of baffling questions on the theological intricacies of the religion that was by now more a part of his marrow than his mind, so much did he take it for granted. Given to him by his parents, it coursed through the blood, for his purposes, much like the integralness of the Rh factor he had also inherited from them. To hell with proselytizing and the casting of nets after the likes of this ardent seeker beside him: the True

Church was better extended through the blood, he thought. Then he was caused to remember Simon: receiving the gift of faith from his father, he had not even bothered to open the package before Farragan got it back in his face.

But in the main Farragan gave good advice, telling him to trust in certain shadowy elusives as prayer and faith, and wondered if the drunkard Edmund might have done any better. To old Bowen he maintained his original protestation—that the business of his daughter was a frame-up—each of the four times that day he was made to hear the story. And during the last telling, in the TV room when he wearily peered at the Late Late Show and held the weeping ancient's head to his chest for comfort, some instinct told him that this laying on of hands was far more correct than the presumptuous discourse on the inevitable moral lassitude of womankind that Farragan had been forced to make three times already that day while not really believing it.

By bedtime, then, he was milked: he lay back, preparing for sleep, and immediately deplored the necessary cloak-and-dagger complexity of the three days before him. The beautiful plan of the Farragans, worthy of an enclave of logical businessmen who had a bit of incidental killing to do on a particular day in another country, was almost completely fouled up by now. And Farragan desperately needed that plan to provide cover for his own particular mission. Only one thing seemed certain, and that was the absolute necessity of confronting Simon in Montreal according to schedule on Thursday, so as to present the wavering Edmund with a *fait accompli*. After that, Farragan guessed his brother the priest would fall meekly into line and serve up the proper alibi to the police if events ever arrived at that stage, though it seemed highly doubtful. Come Thursday, he would be traveling to and from Montreal with false identification papers provided by one of Anna's shooting-range cronies, and, all things considered, Farragan had not the remotest intention of ever squeezing a trigger in Canada.

But one could not be too cautious. Farragan, once having saved the bud of his own bad seed, still had a life of widespread responsibilities to live out. In the event that some overly diligent work for whatever reason brought the police to the gates of Saint Blaise, it was important that El Greco and old Bowen be able to concur with Edmund that he had never left the place. Thus the plan for two days of solitary prayer and fasting in the guest house that he had hit upon that afternoon while walking about with the prospective convert. El Greco, all afire with his current spiritual lusting, would be an intense respecter of that special Catholic prerogative and not come anywhere near. Beyond knowing that he was in the compound, Bowen would hardly care about what he was up to: robbed of Farragan's ear and the small comfort of his breast, the old one would doubtless shift his plaint to Marie when she arrived sometime the next afternoon. Ruefully, Farragan pitied his woman that prospect, for she would be doubly put upon. Once as confidant; then, with her blue eyes, blond hair, and unaccountable propensity for summer white dresses, as the obvious symbol-at-hand of Bowen's fled virginal daughter. Or anybody's, for that matter. Sweet God, if he only knew, Farragan thought, delightedly touching himself beneath the sheet. Marie made love like a tigress in the sack, contesting (he guessed) invisible rivals of legend, Catholic or otherwise.

But time later for the pleasures of the flesh, though Farragan longed for her arrival. Marie was his single great consolation in the midst of all this intrigue: two feet firmly planted on the earth, the reasonableness and certainty of someone twice her twenty-three years, she possessed what Farragan earnestly considered was a calculated decadence bred into her by her stay at French boarding schools. He saw her as absolutely amoral. But blessedly so, for the condition suited Farragan's purposes exactly. He was not yet done with worshiping at Muriel's shrine, even though five years had elapsed since her retreat into the mists. Marie, because she was Marie, dealt in half-commitments to her lover, and Farragan responded in kind, grateful at not being forced to assume any inevitable responsibility for her that would call for the unseating of Muriel. Muriel was his Catholic wife and would be so forever. Marie, his mistress, albeit Catholic, he repaid for her trouble with the goods of commerce—her car and clothes and the checking account he kept generously supplied. For Farragan, then, the distinction was easy. And it appeased any possible doubts of his own to remember that Marie had preferred it that way from the very beginning.

Outside, far beyond the bars of his cell, Farragan heard the dull sound of scraping and guessed last night's herd of deer had returned to the fence. In moments, though, a sudden rash of warning snorts was followed by the high whine of the Land Rover's transmission breasting the final hill, and he listened as the deer galloped off in fright. But at least Edmund, no matter what his condition, was back inside the gates. Farragan would rest easier with that knowledge.

The engine was switched off, and impulsively Farragan rose from his bed to peer through the window in time for the sight of his brother vomiting against the side of the jeep, each outrush of his bilge punctuated by an incredible moan that Farragan decided was but one part sickness to nine parts absolute despair. Thank God their parents were dead and not able to see this spectacle, for some final reckoning of the Farragans with the problem of their brother the cleric was fast approaching. Edmund was finished as a priest, his sacred ministry kaput. Only Farragan had no idea where he went from here: opportunities were doubtless limited for near-fifty-year-old men whose chief occupation for twenty-five previous years had been the saying of Mass and absolving of sins.

He watched as Edmund started jerkily up the steps into the house and wondered how his brother might respond to the real presence of Marie later in the day. Farragan was unable, he decided, to bear any more problems on top of the already existing complexity, and he thought on the instant of calling Marie in Philadelphia and telling her to cancel out. But no, that was impossible also: the marvelously contrived assassination plot of the Farragans had need both of Marie and Marie's car, but especially the latter, for without it there was no way of getting back to Philadelphia unseen to catch the flight for Montreal on Thursday. Farragan could only hope for the best from his brother, then.

He climbed back into bed and listened as Edmund entered the hallway outside his door and lurched the length of it to his own room. Then Farragan heard the loud creak of springs being settled upon, and almost instantly afterward a crescendo of snoring that told his brother was out for the night, and probably well into the late afternoon, too.

But at noon, when he awoke, he looked outside to see Marie standing beside the convertible Farragan had given her, with Edmund graciously collecting her bags. The El Greco youth came shyly down the steps, and she was introduced to him as Farragan's ward, though Farragan winced with the memory that El Greco and the old one had heard her called his mistress. Bowen hobbled across the lawn from the fence and proclaimed loudly that she looked like an angel, then informed her that he was the one who had given her the story of his prostitute daughter over the telephone two nights before. Marie assured him that she did not believe a word of it. Without greeting her, Farragan closed his window and hastened to shower and shave.

Ten minutes later as he crossed the expanse of lawn toward

the guest house where she had been installed, Farragan caught sight of the El Greco youth peering through one of the back windows to the inside. Circling the place, he came up behind him through the tall grass and stood for a moment trying to decide whether to kick him in the small of the back where it might do excessive harm to the likes of his kidneys, or attempt some sort of karate chop on the exposed stem of his neck. In the end, he flung himself rudely on El Greco's back and began beating his head with his fists. Beneath him, the Peeping Tom dropped flat to the earth, then twisted about under Farragan to identify his assailant, shielding his face with both arms from the rain of punches, and calling for mercy in the name of Christ.

When he switched his plea to the justice of God, Farragan jumped to his feet. "And you wanted to convert to Catholicism!"

"I can't help being a man, Mr. Farragan, in the same way Father Edmund can't help it. We're not infallible. He says there's no place in the Church for those who would have unswerving antisexual attitudes. He says . . ."

"That's bullshit! He's just telling you that to compensate for his guilt over the terrible condition he's gotten himself into these days. I hope to God you were asleep last night and not around to see your spiritual mentor coming home from town at three a.m. with the load he had on."

"Father Edmund is a good priest, Mr. Farragan," the other said defiantly. "He hates the ultrarighteous. Without flexibility, the Church would strangle and die. He told me that himself. People can't help being horny, after all."

"Nuts to you, Farrow! Does Catholic fallibility give you the right to go peeking into windows where a young girl is undressing? Especially when she's my ward?"

"I knew I was being watched, Arthur," Marie called through the window screen. "I could feel those intense, dark eyes of Mr.

Farrow's burning into my flesh. There was a fine blush all over me."

"Jesus Christ, Marie, . . ." Farragan pleaded.

"Hello, Mr. Farrow. What are you doing down there on the ground?" she said, opening the screen and thrusting her head to the outside. At the same time she reached out her hand to pat a kiss on Farragan's cheek. In the midst of the twin blond curtains of hair that fell long to her shoulders, her face was alive with impish humor.

"I'm being fallible, Miss Glennis," El Greco said with unexpected wit and smiled sheepishly back at her. Then he rose to his feet, asinine with embarrassment, keeping two hands before the rude admission in his trousers that evidently refused to recede.

"Mr. Farrow is here at Saint Blaise in consideration of converting to our religion," Farragan said. "You could at least be a little disapproving."

"I would be, Arthur, but I'm anxious to convince Mr. Farrow that ours is a happy religion."

"I'm absolutely convinced of it, Miss Glennis," El Greco told her. "Mr. Farragan, may I have permission to escort your ward to the Sportsman's Club tonight for a drink or two?"

"Out of the question!" Farragan advanced toward the other, whose pointed, dark features hung with a beard now recalled the stock lusting look of a satyr. Incredibly, yesterday's great neurotic eyes of religion had become tiny live coals in the mask of his face. Short of actual rape, Farragan could not conceive of such an overt display of intent.

"Absolutely out of the question!" Farragan said again, barely restraining himself from hitting El Greco.

"It's easy to see that she's a little bit more to you than just your ward, Mr. Farragan."

"Get the hell out of here, Farrow! This is outrageous! You're here on retreat. Do you think I'm going to stand for this kind of lewd suggestiveness from you in front of a young woman?"

"I guess not, Mr. Farragan, in view of what it seems to imply about you. You have your nerve to call Father Edmund corrupt."

"You son of a bitch!" Farragan lumbered into full gallop after El Greco, who turned and sprinted through the waving high grass. But the younger man was faster and charged round the one-armed Jesus statue and onto the cinder driveway that led to the entrance of the main house. Behind him, Farragan heard Marie urgently calling his name. Grateful for any excuse, he drew to a halt before coming out of the grass onto the drive. In front of the house, El Greco stared defiantly back at him: Simon all over again, Farragan thought miserably. Breathing heavily from his rush and already arun with sweat, he relinquished the last word as futile and returned slowly to his woman. By now she stood outside before the door in the white blouse and blue culottes she favored for golfing. Farragan winced inwardly at the sad smile on her face; a little like pity, he thought.

"I'm forty-six years old," he told her savagely. "Twice as old as that one, I'll bet."

"So what, Arthur? You're being silly to let him goad you the way he was able to."

"You weren't exactly helpful. You seemed to enjoy him quite a bit."

"Who wouldn't, Farragan dear? The notion of a young man running around a retreat house with an unrelenting erection is pretty comical if you've got any kind of a sense of humor. What's happened to your own lately? You were about ready to explode on the phone the other night when Edmund and the hunters called up to serenade me."

"It's nothing. I'm sorry. I guess I have been a bit irritable lately. I've had a lot of things on my mind."

"Simon mainly, I'll bet. You ought to change your thinking

about him, Arthur. Going off to make a new life in Canada instead of slinging lead in Viet Nam for Johnson's war machine isn't the worst thing he might have done."

"Simon is a traitorous, draft-dodging bastard, Marie. I'm not going to change my opinion on that."

"Then at least conceal it, or I'll go back to Philadelphia this afternoon. I'm about the same age as your son, if you care to remember. That blood-and-guts last-war patriotism of yours wears just as thin with me as with Simon, Arthur. Save it for when you get together with your sister, Anna, and your brother Jim. That's their kind of language."

"I notice you pointedly leave Edmund out of this, Marie."

"Edmund's more like you, Arthur. He's better than those two. They're fascists."

"Your Edmund has turned into the Whisky Priest of late. He goes down to the village bar and drinks his ass under a table nearly every night. Make that compatible with your ideals about people."

"It's not difficult, Arthur. You haven't got the right to expect any more from him after the way he's been kept up on this mountain top for the last twenty years. You ought to consider yourself lucky he hasn't hanged himself already. Now relax, if you can, Arthur. We've got two free weeks to spend together."

"Two weeks with the exception of tomorrow, unfortunately," he sighed, hating himself for the deceit. "I found out yesterday that I've got to be in Philadelphia for a little secret dickering with the union before we go into negotiations on a new contract. I'll take your car and leave early in the morning. I should be back sometime early the next morning. But to avoid complications I don't want either of those two retreatants to know I've left the place. This business is smelly enough as is. It might end up in a grand-jury investigation if I were found out. I've told Farrow and Bowen I intend to hole up here in the guest house for two solitary days of prayer and fasting. You'll just have to move into the main house for those two days and pretend I'm out here wasting away in an earnest purge of the spirit. Make sure they don't have a reason to disturb me, all right? I really need your help with this. Edmund knows I'm going and will play along. I'll try not to eat very much while I'm away so I'll look properly debilitated."

"Dear God, Arthur, talk about the intrigues of a Philadelphia businessman. How are you going to explain away the fact that the car is gone?"

"Tell them that we took it down the hill and left it at a garage for a lube and oil change. Neither of them leaves the place except at night to go to the club with Edmund for a drink. They're not likely to be looking for it."

"All of this is so annoying, Arthur."

"Doubly so for me. But, in the end, it helps to raise the cash that pays the bills. Yours included, if I have to put it on that level to enlist your support."

"Ow. Low blow. I like the idea of being subsidized, Arthur. It's a nice, civilized custom that I happened upon during those long lonely years in Europe. I just don't like being reminded of it. That's not quite like you."

"Forgive me. You're really being put upon. It's unfair for me to leave you here by yourself, especially with the old man, who's obviously going to see you as his daughter the hooker of old, and that nutty Protestant satyr. Watch out for him."

"He's harmless, Arthur. Merely horny. I'll lock the door to my cell whenever I'm inside. Just look at how comical he is standing up there on the steps."

Farragan turned to regard the El Greco youth, who, rather than comic, seemed to him more audacious now than ever. Beside him, Marie had begun laughing again. He resisted the urge to smash her for her own variety of corruption.

"Why don't we go inside and pull the blinds, Marie? I think I'd like to be able to touch you and make love to you without that freak looking in the window."

"No, not now. Let's go for a walk, Arthur. You've really let him get to you. Any love-making you do now would only be a test, and I don't like the idea of serving as the proof. You'll be over it by tonight. Let's cut through the fence over there and go into the woods. The exercise will be good for us."

Farragan took her hand and they walked quickly through the high grass to an opening in the fence and then into the first line of trees. Turning, they saw that El Greco had left the steps and was following them. Marie began to run through the trees, pulling Farragan behind her.

"How far are we supposed to run?" Farragan asked, panting. "It would be much easier for me just to go back and punch him if he'd stand still."

"Be adventurous, Arthur. We'll lead him into the woods and lose him. Then you'll regain your sense of superiority and make wonderful love to me."

Ten minutes later, scratched and bruised from climbing over rocks and fallen trees for the lack of a path, they came unexpectedly to a vast kind of box canyon, full of scrub pine and underbrush and surrounded by sheer rock walls topped by a thick growth of white-flowered mountain laurel bushes. Farragan, always leery of snakes in the environs of so many fallen trees, saw the natural bowl as a perfect resting place for rattlers and refused to enter. But accordingly, he thought of sending El Greco therein. Behind them, their tracker crashed through the brush in furious pursuit. Following Marie's directive, Farragan raked the leaf cover with a tree branch to indicate falsely that they had entered the place, then, while Marie took the other, scrambled up one side of the cliff and arced along the canyon rim to a proposed meeting place beyond some laurel bushes at the opposite end.

Only moments after they were settled in hiding, El Greco rushed into the box. Farragan was instantly disappointed that an advance guard of six-foot rattlers did not rise up to assault their pursuer. With Marie beside him, he looked on as El Greco began cautiously moving through the underbrush. His shirt was torn and his face smudged with dirt and running with sweat. In time he began calling out to Marie. "Miss Glennis! Miss Glennis! I know you're in here. Won't you come out and talk with me?"

Cached above, a grinning Farragan clasped his hand over Marie's mouth to stifle her laughter.

"Miss Glennis, I know you're Mr. Farragan's ward, but surely he doesn't resent my advances, in view of the pure and essentially spiritual way I intend to make love to you. . . . The physical aspect, Miss Glennis, will be incidental. You won't even feel it. Don't be afraid of me, Miss Glennis. I'm not a base and blindly lusting person. Father Edmund has explained the evil of this condition to me. Won't you come out now?"

After a long silence, during which the exquisite smile of the satyr's anticipation receded from El Greco's face, he began moving again into the brush, fearless, evidently, of meeting either Farragan or a rattler in his course. Minutes later he stood atop a small mound of rock and tried again. "Miss Glennis, I saw you naked in the guest house. You said you knew I was watching and you liked it. Remember, Miss Glennis?"

"Remember, Miss Glennis," came the muted echo from the canyon, and Farragan on high checked the inclination to leap into the pit and smash the look of unbridled lechery from El Greco's face. Beside him, Marie dug her teeth into his shoulder to keep from laughing out loud, so that Farragan nearly yelped with the pain. Farrow stepped off his mound of rocks and began probing the brush now with a stick. They saw that his eyes had become rheumy with frustration, wide again as yesterday's great neurotic eyes of religion. After a time, he jabbed at the bushes with the end of his stick as if he wished to puncture Farragan for his efforts, and Farragan above winced with the instinct of what he was up to.

In time, El Greco pleaded again for a hearing. "Miss Glennis, I have rarely tasted of any woman. I confess it now. I've never known love from a woman freely given. I've only consorted with prostitutes the like of Mr. Bowen's daughter, and never for less than twenty dollars each time. Somewhere a woman must love me for myself. Will you please be the one? I'm beginning to have strange feelings about women. Sometimes I think I hate them. Will you help me?"

Farragan looked at his woman and saw something like sadness in her eyes and knew that, for all her European-bred persuasions, she was as close to servicing the plight of the El Greco youth as she ever would be. But blessedly, the look of incredible self-pity and suffering on the face of the tracker below turned suddenly to cold defiance as he began flailing the brush with his stick and banging furiously about through the crotch-high scrub pine so that Farragan anticipated the result of it all might be self-castration.

"Miss Glennis! Miss Glennis!" El Greco called. "If you don't make love with me I won't convert to Catholicism as I intended! Do you want to be responsible for my staying outside the True Church? Do you want to go to your deathbed with that responsibility on your Catholic soul?"

"Yes, you dumb bastard! It would be a pleasure!" The voice of Farragan boomed from on high: somehow not unlike the voice of God, all things considered. In lieu of thunderbolts, Farragan hurled rocks. Big ones. Though at forty-six he no longer had the arm of a young man in his twenties, and the El Greco youth, fleeing like a frightened greyhound from the canyon, easily eluded them.

# CHAPTER 11

## Farragan's Ward

Before he was made aware of her one July Sunday morning at Mass two years ago, Farragan had been earnestly praying for the appearance of a Marie Glennis since Muriel had gone out into the fog after the birth of the twins. And ever since, he could never rid himself of the notion that the answer to his prayers was a special gift of Muriel, and not of God at all.

On that particular day, however, between the concealed frenzy of his pleading and roguish winking at the daughters of Serafina, he had failed to notice the long-haired blonde in a lace mantilla and white summer dress when she glided up the aisle past him to the altar railing for Communion. Somewhere in the midst of his begging the Almighty to deliver him from the need for the motherly young prostitute he consorted with once a week in a West Chester motel, Muriel had touched him timidly on the arm and whispered in her special voice that came from wherever she lived beyond the core of Reason, "That girl is quite beautiful, Arthur."

Wringing his rosary, Farragan had concurred silently, watching the blonde return down the aisle to take a seat behind them. He considered that she must be the recently bloomed daughter of some summer friends of theirs, but he could not remember who exactly.

"She's the niece of the two sisters Glennis, who've invited us to their party this afternoon, Arthur," Muriel had whispered loudly to him. "She's just come back from France, where she's spent about four years in school. Her parents are dead. You knew her mother—she was Agnes Graham—from that time at Saint Monica College before the war. This girl is going to live with her aunts. She speaks French."

On the instant Farragan changed his mind about going up to the huge old weatherbeaten house of the sisters Glennis for a drink that afternoon. Normally he despised them, for they placed too much emphasis on the solidarity of summer fellow parishoners at the church, and were always after him for favors like drain-pipe repairs, or a special intercession with the shore-town mayor whose name Farragan could never recall. Impulsively, he had turned about in his seat to seek her out: between the guardian aunts, her head was bowed reverently over clenched hands and the folds of her mantilla swung lightly to either side. Farragan was frankly incredulous that anyone like her might be even remotely connected with the Glennis clan.

Nevertheless, that day after Mass he sought them eagerly outside the church, not knowing quite what he was up to, in view of the presence of a ring of lifeguards already surrounding the girl. While he made a frantic kind of small talk with the aunts, Muriel unexpectedly descended the steps and approached the youthful circle. As always, there was the certain reaction of men to the closeness of Farragan's wife: they drew apart; in lieu of hats to tip, the guards shyly nodded their heads.

"I am Muriel Farragan, a friend of your aunts'," he heard his black-clad wife tell the blonde. "Would you like to meet my husband? I knew your mother years ago when she was at Saint Monica College. My husband knew her also."

Life was indeed cyclic, Farragan thought at that instant. Twenty-five or more years before he had climbed over the spiked ten-foot fence into impregnable Saint Monica's one late-spring evening for a rendezvous in the shrubbery with this girl's mother. Naked and trembling as much from the chill of nighttime dew as passion, they had been caught making love by a campus guard, who had smacked Farragan's buttocks with his night stick and later handed him over to the police.

Agnes Graham had been expelled on the spot, and charges were filed against Farragan and a date set for a hearing. All this, until the Farragans' mother, viewing the event as a lusty good joke and a feather in the cap of one of her sons, got the wheels of her far-flung Catholic associations rolling. The charges against Farragan were dropped, Agnes Graham was reinstated, and a check for one thousand dollars deposited with the college president for the express purpose of strengthening defenses against the possibility of another intrusion in the night by a sex fiend.

Later, for no reason Farragan could remember—except, perhaps, that she had already been spoiled—he had drifted away from Agnes Graham, who had married a career diplomat named Glennis. This girl, their only child, had been born in France right after the war. Her parents were both drowned in a sailing accident on the Chesapeake Bay just three years before, and their daughter given over to the sisters Glennis for custody, though she remained at school in France.

Farragan shook hands with her while Muriel spoke softly to the ancient aunts of one of her beatification candidates. "I'm Arthur Farragan."

"I know who you are. I've been wanting to meet you for years.

My mother told me all about that night at Saint Monica's back before the war. It was the single great event of her life. She later went out and marked the spot with a stone X. It's still there, or at least it was the last time I heard about it."

"You're kidding me!" Farragan said. "Your mother actually told you that story?"

"She was always telling it. She thought it was marvelous fun. It nearly cost my father his job one time because she got tipsy and told it at the wrong party."

"And it never angered your father to hear her tell it? To hear about me?"

"No, not after he decided it was your one great moment of glory also. He heard you'd become a kind of dowdy Philadelphia businessman and was satisfied with the knowledge that your days of breasting the walls of girls' colleges were over."

"I could do it now if I had to," Farragan said.

"Hah. All of this before the doors of a church, Mr. Farragan! Are you coming to my aunts' party this afternoon? It seems like a better place to reminisce over old sins than right here."

"I was planning to head back to the city this afternoon, but I'll put it off until evening just to hear more of my past. It's refreshing, considering the state of my affairs these days."

"I knew there was something dark and sad in you. I could tell from behind you in Mass by the bend of your back. See you this afternoon, Mr. Farragan," she said, retreating hastily up the steps to join her aunts.

Concurring then, in the late afternoon Farragan and Muriel and her friend Binky Applebaum, the lifeguard captain, walked slowly from Farragan's house on pilings amid the sand dunes to the rotting monstrosity of the sisters Glennis for the party Farragan had been anxiously awaiting since Mass that morning. Listening closely, he thought he could just discern above the sea noises the rustle of folded newspaper in Binky's shorts that compensated for his Korean War wound, and as often before, clucked sadly to himself over the unfair parcelings of the Fates. Though he never failed to give thanks for his own condition: Farragan, a man of forty-four, was going this day to sip martinis with the reincarnation of a woman whom, in the fullest tradition of the great rogue lover, he had scaled a convent wall to make love to more than twenty years before. The rest of the summer then, and perhaps years beyond, was full of promise. Instinctively he knew he would succeed with her daughter, for the daughter wanted him to succeed.

But alas for the plaything of vengeful Fates on the opposite side of Muriel: tall and handsome and only in his mid-thirties, he would never make love to a woman again in his life and had not for many years already. Farragan, were he compassionate enough, might have wept for what Binky would never know. Applebaum, his great blue eyes watered through with suffering, could scarcely look another man in the face with the knowledge of his self-limitation. Now he dragged his feet wearily in the dust. Tiny clouds of it exploded behind him.

At the gate of the sisters Glennis, the eldest of the two ancients immediately petitioned Farragan to make the uninvited cluster of lifeguards that had followed Marie home from the beach leave the party. They stood drinkless and apart from the other guests and the small, sad combo in one corner of the vast enclosure of sandblasted lawn, still dressed in bathing suits and sweatshirts. Marie turned coquettishly in their midst. Farragan's first enraged instinct was to grab up the heavy pronged garden rake he saw near by and charge the ring, shredding the exposed flesh of their thighs and calves with its teeth, but Applebaum usurped that pleasure and left Muriel's side, walking swiftly over the grass to the guards. Within a minute, they had all quietly left, thanking the sisters Glennis for their hospitality. Marie came gliding up to Farragan in their wake.

"Who was that tall, handsome one who made all the swimmers go home, Mr. Farragan?"

"His name is Applebaum. He's a Jewish fellow who pulled my cousin's niece Stephanie out of a bad surf a few years ago. He watches after Muriel down here during the week when I'm in Philadelphia."

"How liberal you are, Mr. Farragan."

"Binky has a wound from Korea, Marie. Like the Hemingway character, he doesn't have all his equipment down there," Farragan said, properly suppressing, he hoped, the notion that anything about Muriel was a cause for levity.

"Oh, I'm sorry. . . ." The tough fiber of her supreme self-assurance was parted for the first and last time ever in Farragan's memory. Together, they had looked to where Binky stood in the midst of the muted revelers sipping a drink, Muriel holding quietly to his arm. He had stared for a long second at Marie, then turned shyly away as if he knew he was being spoken about.

"Everyone among our friends down here at the shore knows the situation. Binky has never really made any secret of it, God bless him. And he's very gentle with Muriel since her illness. For her to spend the summer at the shore with the twins would be impossible if Binky didn't look after her."

"It must be a comfort for you to know he's here," Marie said, just as her two aunts shuffled up, carrying drinks for Farragan and their niece. Behind them, the combo ground out the "Tea for Two" cha-cha. Farragan thought of dancing to get away from the sisters Glennis before any more petitions came his way.

"Have you met Mr. Applebaum, Marie?" the elder asked, handing her a drink.

"No, not yet."

"He's safe to know," the younger proposed, taking a lei from a shopping bag and putting it around Farragan's neck. "He lost most of his plumbing over in Korea."

"Miss Glennis, . . ." Farragan said. Some instinct—like loyalty to Applebaum—crept out of him and he resisted the urge to stomp on the toes of her little-old-lady shoes. "Binky has been a good friend to Muriel and myself. He saved my cousin's niece from drowning once, if you remember."

"That's just what I was about to say, Mr. Farragan. He makes up for it in so many ways. And he's a Jew, too. It's nice to have people about for a change who aren't exactly like oneself."

"I'm not like you," Farragan said fiercely.

"Well, not exactly, Mr. Farragan. But you're a lot less romantic and interesting than Mr. Applebaum with his Jewishness and his impotence, if you see what I mean."

"He has good connections, too," the elder chimed in again. "He has often interceded with the mayor for us."

"Speaking of favors, Mr. Farragan," said the younger, "we wonder if we might prevail upon you to do something for us?"

"What?" Farragan asked warily. He felt the dig of Marie's finger in his back.

"We wondered, since you're returning to the city tonight, if it would be too much trouble to take Marie to our home in Cynwyd so she can pick up her car and drive back down in the morning?"

"Of course it's not too much trouble, Miss Glennis."

"She also wants to see the X," the elder told him.

"What . . . ?"

"At Saint Monica College. Where you made love to Agnes in 1940 in the shrubbery."

"Jesus, Mary, and Joseph!" Farragan exclaimed. He grew instantly red with embarrassment, then began howling with laughter in union with Marie and her two aunts. Heads turned, startled perhaps by the unexpectancy of ever finding any real gaiety at a party of the Glennis sisters'. On the instant, the band left off discordantly from the "Zhivago Waltz" and lurched again into its Latin repertoire. The younger aunt pummeled Farragan's arm with her fist, then took another lei from the shopping bag she carried and slipped it over his head. "Oh, you're such a definite rogue, Mr. Farragan. It will probably be dark when you get there tonight, but we'll lend you a flashlight to help you find it."

Then they skipped away, dispensing more leis from their bags and leaving Farragan, nondancer, to shuffle back and forth with their sleek blond niece in the unaccustomed paramilitary joggle of sound-alike cha-chas. All this against the background of a fiery sunset. Obliging them, the band played continuously for more than an hour. Hordes of shrieking children hung out the windows of neighboring houses and relays of party guests came by to applaud his prowess, and Farragan was sweated and exultant in response. When the combo broke, he said good-by to Muriel and the sisters and their guests and left with Marie to return the long distance through the Jersey pinelands to Philadelphia.

At Saint Monica College the gatekeeper waved them through with a commendation to the driver for returning his daughter early to the dormitory. Farragan winced at his surmise but kept silent, following the twisting lanes that wound through the acres of park to the main buildings, then beyond to descend a long slope toward the spiked fence that now kept a new housing development from encroaching on the college, instead of the wooded tract of Farragan's day.

They parked the car and, taking the flashlight, walked slowly down the hill, Farragan almost certain he knew the spot after so many years. He poked about in the shrubbery for a few moments and was interrupted by a surprise voice behind them that caused Marie to grab his arm in fright.

"Are you lookin' for the X?"

They turned swiftly to see an aged nun bent over a cane; she was almost the oldest woman Farragan had ever seen.

"Yes, Sister, that's what we're looking for," he said.

"It's right here. I'm standin' on the very spot. Most people have a hard time findin' it because the shrub beside it has grown so big."

"Do lots of people look for it, Sister?" he asked.

"Oh, yes. It's the site of a moral lesson. Every year our freshman class is led down in groups of ten to learn about the place of the X. Some of them vomit when they hear what happened here. How did you come to learn about it?"

"A girl who has long since graduated told us about it, Sister," Marie said.

"I can't blame your father for bringin' you here to see it, young lady."

"What happened exactly, Sister? The details are a little obscure," Farragan said, digging his fingers into the palm of Marie's hand in hopes of suppressing her laughter.

"One spring night just before the war one of our girls became a victim of concupiscence and invited the attention of a non-Catholic workman who climbed over the fence to meet with her in these same shrubs. When he had taken his pleasure with her, he strangled her and left her here, covered with nothing more than a mocking sign of the cross made of leaves down the naked front of her."

"Sweet Jesus, mercy! And he was never caught?" Farragan asked.

"Never. Though I trust his soul has found its proper place in hell."

"God willing," Farragan chanted.

"God willing," Marie echoed, then broke into peals of laughter. She collapsed onto Farragan, who, barely able to contain his own mirth, could feel her shudderings against him.

"Is she laughin' or cryin'?" the nun asked.

"Crying, Sister, of course. It's not every day a young girl has to hear the particulars of a rape."

But then Marie slid to her knees, clasping Farragan about one leg and howling openly now so there was no confusing her laughter.

"Cryin' indeed! What kind of girl is your daughter to succumb from humor after hearin' a story like that?"

"A bitch, Sister. Nothing less. Given to concupiscence herself. It's obviously been pointless for me to bring her here."

"Moral lessons are lost on some," the nun said to Farragan. "Take her home and take some of this ivy with you." She bent painfully to snip off a piece of it. "Plant it in a black flowerpot and keep it in a prominent place and you'll always recall the rape of that sweet virgin when you look at it."

"Oh cripes, Farragan, take me out of here before I die of laughter," said Marie, still on her knees. He reached over to take the sprig of ivy from the nun and dropped it into his pocket, then hauled Marie to her feet and hastened her up the hill to the car. By now the tears were streaming down his face.

At the car door they heard the voice of the nun raging through the darkness: "Farragan? Are you the one? Are you the Arthur Farragan who did this terrible thing twenty years ago?"

"It's him, Sister! He's the one!" Marie shrieked back while Farragan tried to muffle her sounds. He bundled her into the front seat and sprinted around to the opposite side as the white wimple of the old nun began rushing up the hill at them at a surprising speed. Farragan started the Cadillac and lurched out of the parking space, but not before she made a vicious swing at the car with her cane. Glass rained down on the asphalt of the drive, and Farragan guessed immediately she had connected with one of his taillights.

"It's him! Farragan's returned to rape again!" the nun howled into the night.

"He'll never rape again! He's only returned to remember!" Marie called.

"I could rape again if I had to," Farragan said, but quietly, for his triumph was already incalculable as far as he was concerned: blessed be the mad nun, then. May she live forever to spread his young rogue's fame to the farthest limits of Philadelphia. He drove slowly out of the compound and past the night watchman, who appeared startled to see Marie also exiting but did not call after them.

Later, in the deserted summer quiet of his home in Wynnewood, Farragan searched the basement for a clay flowerpot and a can of black paint while Marie prepared dinner in the kitchen. They ate with the planted ivy between them on the table: force-fed with Vigoro and spring water, the horticultural desperation somehow equal to Farragan's own frenzied hope that this girl might choose to switch-hit for the motherly West Chester prostitute, whom he decided on the instant he was not up to seeing ever again. She obliged him; they made love afterwards in his bedroom. But mirthfully so, Farragan half-conscious of playing the near-middle-aged voyeur run riot in a dormitory full of young virgins, while Marie responded in kind. He had only ever made serious, desperate love to Muriel (after covering the bedroom statues), had even awakened, on occasion, to weep shamelessly in the middle of the night at the thought of her death. But this girl was a safe bet, he reasoned in the smoke-filled peace of after-climax: operating easily within her own strict set of limits that he surmised were absolutely commercial and not likely ever to make a raid on that hallowed shrine within him where Muriel dwelt.

A marriage of convenient passion, then, was what he was ordering up with the daughter of Agnes Graham. A continuous and exultant breasting of convent-college fences, designed, as in the case of this girl's mother, not to tax his emotional goods in any particular way, especially when Farragan had none to give.

Accordingly, he put off going to the Zephyr terminal the next morning and instead drove with her into center city, where he had helped choose, then paid for, a new twelve-hundred-dollar wardrobe. That for a start: at the Bellevue Stratford for lunch, they discussed her proposal for a limited checking account while Farragan basked in the inquisitive, and occasionally frankly admiring, stares of other dowdy Philadelphia businessmen.

On a bench in Independence Mall that Farragan had not visited since the day he had participated in the memorial service right after John Kennedy's assassination, they made pragmatic plans for twice-weekly meetings at Farragan's home until after Labor Day, when Muriel and the twins would return from the shore. Until then, they would play weekends at Beach Haven by ear, hoping for earnest and distant conferences on the beatification candidates between Muriel and the sisters Glennis, or a renewal of Muriel's side trips with Binky Applebaum for Sunday brunch to Atlantic City, where Binky's brother managed a hotel. Their cook might be depended upon to take care of the twins.

Privately, Farragan was amazed at the very deliberateness of himself. In the shadow of Independence Hall, where long lines of Girl Scouts unloaded from chartered busses to file past the Liberty Bell, which he had once been held up by his father to kiss as a child, Farragan was in the process of buying himself the ongoing use of a woman to fill the vast gap between Muriel and the West Chester prostitute. Not that the idea of keeping Marie was especially un-American. It was only that his giddiness at the incredible ease of acquiring her seemed irreverent in the presence of that ponderous heritage, and, more conscious than not, he tipped his summer straw hat toward the edifice in a muted parody of a religious act. But little matter. Every so often—every twenty years or so, perhaps—there had to be a completely winning day, regardless of where you were when the finish line was crossed. He considered that all that remained after he returned Marie to her car at her aunt's house in Cynwyd was to call Eileen in West Chester from the terminal office and tell her he was done with her services.

But Eileen, sounding at three-thirty in the afternoon as if she had just awakened from ten hours of a drugged sleep, broke for a time Farragan's thread of easy compliances. By six o'clock he was on his way to the State College at West Chester with a hundred dollars cash in his pocket to meet with her. She sat alone on a bench opposite the library and overlooking the playing fields, where young men, clad only in shorts and track shoes, jogged monotonous circles in the face of the beginning sunset. From a distance, as he walked toward her, Farragan suddenly decided she was his ultimate romantic concept of a high-priced whore, and it pleased another part of his vanity to recall his involvement with her. It also occurred to him that, given the regimen of their relationship, he had only rarely seen her wearing clothes in the past. Today she was clad in a blue sheath dress and her rhinestone sunglasses and the mink stole that Farragan had given her in the second grateful year of their union, when Christmas fell exactly on their regular weekly meeting day. She drank coffee from a paper container.

"Sit down, Arthur," she said without looking up.

"Do you come here often, Eileen?"

"Nearly every day when the weather permits. It's exciting to watch young men sweat. Sometimes I have fantasies about going down to their locker room with them."

"That must be pleasant for you." Instinctively, he moved closer and put his arm about her shoulders. The touch of her mink at the end of a blazing day was unexpectedly cool.

"It compensates for certain things. Why are we breaking off, Arthur, dear? Have you found someone better than your Eileen to

listen to your problem with Muriel? Though I can't imagine anyone
better after the three years' experience I've had."

"Not better, Eileen. Just different. It's time for a change."

"Tell me one thing, Arthur. Am I losing out to a nigger?"

"No, Eileen, she's a white girl."

"Thank Christ. I don't think I could take that. I feel a little
better already." She sniffled, then removed her sunglasses to wipe
away two tears that were beginning a slow descent through her
mascara. Impulsively, Farragan drew her to himself and kissed her
forehead. She settled in against his chest and began sobbing openly.

"I loved the way you loved Muriel, Arthur. I thought it was
the most romantic thing I'd ever heard. I used to cry every Wednesday night after you left. And I loved Muriel, too. I thought she was
the most beautiful woman I'd ever seen."

"You got a look at Muriel, Eileen?"

"Yes, Arthur. About a year ago I couldn't stand it any longer
and I borrowed my sister's Revlon house-call kit and went to your
place in Wynnewood one afternoon. Your housekeeper answered
and told me nobody needed anything, but your wife said to let me
in anyhow. I stayed for an hour and a half."

"You talked with Muriel? In my house?" Farragan believed
his tone was incredulous. He felt tears flashing to his own eyes at
some notion of absolute defilement.

"I gave her a manicure beside the swimming pool."

"You weren't supposed to go anywhere near Muriel, Eileen!"
Farragan had shouted at her.

"No, but I was supposed to hold your head in my arms every
Wednesday night and listen to you talk about how much you loved
this goddess. I think it was a miracle that I didn't try to see her before I did. I'll bet the new one doesn't hold out as long."

"The new one already knows her, Eileen."

"Oh ho, the plot thickens. Doubtless she won't be confined to Wednesday-night working hours."

"No, Eileen, she won't. She's one of us."

In the instant that he said it, Farragan might have bitten off his tongue. But Eileen seemed oblivious of the slap, or at least pretended to be. Farragan followed her eyes. They traveled with one runner on the field below: a big kid, deeply tanned and firm, who had done the circuit at least ten times since Farragan's arrival.

"That one's a junior," Eileen said. "Or at least he's been here three years. I think tonight I'll walk down there and talk with him."

"You'll frighten him," Farragan said, kidding her, the anger receding.

"I think I'll invite him for a ride in my convertible to cool off. He might enjoy dinner at my place."

"That would be nice. I should go, Eileen. Here's something for you."

He handed her the envelope with the hundred dollars inside, and she took it, mechanically dropping it into her purse. He kissed her swiftly on the forehead and stood up.

"The new one won't work out, Arthur, if you keep talking about Muriel all the time," she had said softly.

"Yes, she will. I believe she has absolutely no capacity to love anyone. That makes her safer even than you."

"Then hang on to her. But I still bet it doesn't work out the way you think it will. Your conditions are absolutely the most special I've ever heard of. You're in love with an illusion."

Then she stood and descended the grass incline toward the playing fields in her great, shambling, professional walk, while Farragan grew momentarily excited himself at the possible response from the unwary runner.

He returned to his car, and drove past the library on his way off the campus, and around the rim of the track. Below, Eileen had halted her man and walked slowly about him, admiring, obviously, the mink stole that she had somehow already persuaded him to wrap about his sweated loins.

But Marie had worked out, Farragan recalled, despite Eileen's best instincts and her geisha-like adeptness with palmistry and a tarot deck that she insisted in later urgent phone calls to him was abysmally pessimistic.

For by the end of August, a month after he first met Marie, she was already his ward. On a Sunday morning after Mass the elder of her aunts had drawn him away from Muriel on the church steps and asked him to meet her, strangely enough, in a bay-side bar late in the afternoon. Farragan, trembling through a prenoon swim and a hardly eaten lunch with the possibility that the aunts might have found out about Marie and himself, was put instantly at ease when he entered the bar and saw the old one smiling softly to herself in a booth over a long-stemmed glass of some liqueur. He sat down opposite her and ordered a beer.

"Mr. Farragan," she had begun, "I wonder if I might ask you a deep personal favor?"

"I'm sure almost anything would be possible, Miss Glennis," he said eagerly, relief surging into him in great warming clouds like many glasses of beer.

"Well, what I wanted to ask was this: both my sister and I have noticed how fond Marie has become of you lately. I'm quite sure she views you as a replacement for her dead father, according to the psychologist's view. And our pastor, Father Smiley, is also of this persuasion. We wonder, quite simply, since we're both becoming so old ourselves, if we couldn't prevail upon you to act as if she were your ward—unofficially, of course—in the event anything happened to either of us. I mean, not monetarily, or anything like that,

Mr. Farragan, since she's well provided for. But just to direct her, so to speak, so that she'll be able to find a good Catholic young man to settle down with eventually. You are an upstanding member of our parish, after all, and we wouldn't dare have asked you if we hadn't seen you at Mass so often."

Darts thudded into a board on the wall behind them, and Farragan, pausing to give weight to his response, enjoyed a momentary vision of Marie absolutely naked lying coyly about the head of her aunt in the smoke the old lady blew in furious puffs from a reeking cigarillo. The ancient's face grew progressively more creased with anxiety, until Farragan decided it was time to play at being magnanimous. In the instant before he spoke, her nervous fingers snapped the cigarillo in two.

"Well, yes, Miss Glennis, I believe this can be arranged for. The thought of your deaths is repugnant to me, of course, but at the same time I'm saddened to think of poor Marie alone by herself without a living relative in the world."

"You're such a good man, Mr. Farragan!" the old one shrieked. She had taken both his hands fiercely into her own and immediately knocked over his glass of beer. Faces turned toward them from the bar, and a drunk had raised his head from a corner table and shouted in earnest imitation, "You're such a good man, Mr. Farragan!" then fell instantly back to dozing. The bartender automatically brought him another beer, calling him by name now. In the end, they had stayed until well after sundown, Farragan eight beers to the good while the ancient matched him with her long-stemmed glasses of urine-colored liqueur, toasting Farragan's Christian excellence, Marie's new safety, and the advent of a happy and painless death for the sisters Glennis. Farragan had drunk exuberantly to that last proposal.

And a week later he enjoyed the same kind of ease with his own family, though until that time it had never occurred to him that he might have to justify Marie to them in any way. But the shedding of a few tears had been worth it in the long run.

The event was precipitated by meeting Anna and two of her cronies while Farragan dined with his ward of only a few days' duration in a center-city restaurant. The candlelit darkness was instantly pregnant with the unspoken question: where was Muriel?—and Anna had immediately made the situation worse by introducing Marie, whom she did not know, as Farragan's secretary.

The very next night he was called up to the round table in Anna's garden, where his two brothers and sister were already convened when Farragan arrived. Even the softness of gaslight could not belie the purposefulness of Jim's and Anna's faces: he had obviously been prejudged. Edmund, the weak link in the chain, sat blessedly uncertain between them. Farragan had looked up to see J. Worthington Duffey, fully clothed, staring perplexedly down at the group. As ever, the flowers suffocated inside Anna's midget greenhouse. Farragan took the remaining seat at the table. Instantly, Jim propped up the coffin picture of their mother: the flickering gaslight flame, reflected, danced like a tongue of fire above her head.

"We won't need this," Farragan said, laying the picture face down on the table in what he guessed on the instant was his life's single most deliberate act.

"What would she think, Arthur, if she knew you were running around town with some blonde?" Jim had demanded.

"She'd probably think it was pretty funny if she knew who the blonde was," Farragan said.

"Who is she?"

"Agnes Graham's daughter. You know, that girl from before the war when mother paid out the thousand bucks to save me from those nuns at Saint Monica College."

"Holy God, you're kidding me!" Jim had roared, pounding the

table with one great fist. He broke into gales of laughter. "The daughter! I don't believe it! How did you ever find her?"

"I met her after Mass one Sunday down at Beach Haven."

"Oh, good Christ, what a tiger!" It was Anna's turn now. She grabbed up the coffin picture and held it tightly to her, convulsing with mirth. "Remember how proud mother was of Arthur that time? She kept calling him Valentino and pinching his cheek. She would have had it read from the altar if she were able to. Arthur was twenty-one, and Agnes Graham was his first girl."

"I was eighteen and I'd already lost count," Farragan declared unctuously. "It just happened that that particular one broke into headlines." Privately, it came to him for the first time that it had occurred only months after their mother's discovery about Stephen.

"I was told to look angry," Edmund had joked to Jim. "How shall I look now?"

"We'll know in a minute, Edmund," Jim said. "Arthur, what about Muriel?"

"That girl was quite lovely, Arthur, but she doesn't hold a candle to Muriel," Anna said.

"This isn't a beauty contest, Anna. I haven't made love to Muriel since that trouble she had when the twins were born. Certainly you must have guessed it. She's like a six-year-old child."

The words "six-year-old child" had come out of him in a muffled sob and he pressed a handkerchief to his instantly liquid eyes and cried more from real sorrow than the need to dupe them. When he lowered the cloth, he saw his two brothers and sister staring at him with frank pity.

"Oh, Arthur, we had no idea," Anna wailed. "I mean, you just don't think about things like that. And you never said anything to us."

"What was there to say? Muriel is my wife. The idea of annulment or a divorce outside the church is out of the question, as far as I'm concerned."

"Yes, definitely that," the others mumbled, somewhat in unison.

"What do you think, Father Edmund?" Jim had asked, the incredible deference filling his voice as it always did when he had occasion to make use of Edmund in his priestly office. On cue, Edmund's eyes lost their wavering uncertainty and he gazed absorbedly at his finger tips. Impulsively looking upward, Farragan saw that J. Worthington Duffey had removed his shirt. He fumbled tentatively with his belt, until Farragan frowned in annoyance, shaking his head. Then he drew the curtain closed and switched off the lights.

"Arthur is not the kind of man who can be without a woman," Edmund said, and the others nodded agreement. "God, in his infinite wisdom, has seen fit to cloud over our beloved Muriel's mind, and we can only guess why. But I feel certain God would not begrudge Arthur the consolation of this young woman in view of his great loss, and also his dedication in sticking by Muriel when another man might have petitioned for annulment."

"I agree," Jim said. "The point is, Arthur, not to ever let Muriel find out what's going on, so that neither she nor her people can file for divorce. It's messy socially and bad for the business if the word gets around."

"Yes," Anna said, "have your fun with the young one, Arthur, until you get tired of her. But by all means don't let Muriel find out. Are you sure she doesn't suspect anything?"

"I'm not certain she has the capacity to suspect anything," Farragan said. "Some days she doesn't even seem to remember who Marie is."

"Anyhow, keep them apart as much as you're able to," Jim advised. "No use running the risk of Muriel's marbles coming back one day in a keen burst of insight and fouling up the program."

But sadly, though it was the thing he desired most, Muriel's marbles had not returned. And that year especially, even with the entrance of blonde Marie into his life, he suffered through the final days of summer at the shore, the fleeting time before fall that he had always enjoyed best with Muriel, his true wife. Only that season she preferred to spend nights sitting on the deck with Binky Applebaum, her friend, who had sustained the ultimate horrible wound in Korea. Neither touching nor speaking, they stared out over the waters at the lights of distant ships.

Behind them, Farragan wondered earnestly about the Creator's plan of substitution. His heart ached also for the thing he wanted most and could not have.

## CHAPTER 12

# A Happening in Montreal

The day of the mercy mission.

Farragan rose in darkness at four a.m. on Thursday morning, softly kissed Marie, who did not waken, silently begged forgiveness for his deceitfulness, then shaved and dressed and carried his bag out to the convertible.

He turned over the engine, which came quietly to life, and was preparing to leave when the front door of the main house suddenly opened and Edmund appeared on the steps, barefooted in his cassock. Silently the retreat master made the sign of the cross over his brother, and Farragan solemnly received the benediction, then stood out of the car to deliver a stern warning: "Make sure you keep your mouth shut down in that bar, Edmund."

But Edmund only scowled and returned to the house, and moments later Farragan eased through the gates and down the hill.

By seven o'clock he was at the airport in Philadelphia. He parked the Oldsmobile in the extended-time lot, and went immediately to the Air Canada desk to confirm his eight-thirty flight and pick up the envelope containing the baggage-locker key that Anna had left there for him the day before.

When he found the locker, Farragan took out the gift-wrapped box it contained and went into a men's-room cubicle, where he sat on the lid of a toilet to remove the .38 in its shoulder holster and to strap it to himself.

Then he deposited the silencer attachment in an inside jacket pocket and leafed through his new set of identification. In accordance with the name on the plane ticket, he was Arthur Franklin Cowley on his Pennsylvania driver's license, Social Security card, gasoline-company and Diner's Club credit cards, and his automobile insurance forms. There was also a permit for that same Cowley to carry a .38 revolver—in the event of any problem with the Canadian customs on the way in. There would be no trouble on the way out: he was to drop the gun into a Montreal sewer before the time of his return and tear up the permit as well.

At the bottom of the box was a sealed envelope with instructions from Anna to open it only on the flight to Canada, and Farragan dutifully tucked it in a jacket pocket, then removed his own cards from his wallet and deposited them in the box, replacing them with the fake set. A moment later he was in the process of tying up the gift wrappings once more when, impulsively, engaged in some unspecified revolution of his own, he reached for Anna's letter and tore it open.

Inside—as he had half-expected—was a reprint of their mother's coffin picture and a copy of a Stephen Crane poem called "War Is Kind," with Anna's penciled note that he read it for courage and inspiration stapled to the bottom. Farragan, giddy with a sudden fatigue at the remembrance of being up and about for nearly four hours without any food, continued to sit on the lid and scanned the neatly typed lines:

WAR IS KIND

Do not weep, maiden, for war is kind.
Because your lover threw wild hands toward the sky
And the affrighted steed ran on alone,
Do not weep.
War is kind.

Hoarse, booming drums of the regiment,
Little souls who thirst for fight—
These men were born to drill and die.
The unexplained glory flies above them;
Great is the battle-god, great—and his kingdom
A field where a thousand corpses lie.

Farragan read on, disbelieving, then suddenly choked with laughter at the realization that Anna, borne blindly on by the excessive currents that made of her a modern-day Brünnhilde of Philadelphia, had completely missed the intended irony of the poem. To her, obviously, war *was* kind. And Crane the great martial poet, approved for club-night readings to her inner council of gun-toting, right-wing widows. She had even enforced the judgment by adding a commentary—*Remember our own dear mother, Arthur*—in the margin beside the last stanza:

Mother, whose heart hung humble as a button
On the bright splendid shroud of your son,
Do not weep.
War is kind.

On the instant Farragan thought of quitting his toilet seat to call Anna and inform her that, in the midst of her precise plannings to get the Farragan family executioner safely in and out of Canada, she had made one bad fumble. But what use? It was only a question

of semantics. Instead, remembering that he himself had written po-
etry at Georgetown after his return from the war (some of it love
poems to Muriel), he pulled out a pen and sloppily parodied the
Crane verses on the back of the typed sheet:

> Do not weep, Farragan, for war is kind.
> Because it happens to be going on when your son
> Needs exterminating for his peaceable attitudes,
> You can use it as a justification for killing him.
> That cowardly, draft-dodging bastard.

Somehow, detached from all consideration that this was the
actual day that Jim and Anna meant for his son to be done in, Farragan was delighted with the ease of composition. But then, all the
truth that was in him this particular morning had obviously leaped
out onto the paper. For another few minutes he indulged himself
with revising, but succeeded only in changing the word "son" (a
stumble word these days) to the French *"fils,"* and "peaceable attitudes" to "honesty," since more and more Farragan dared to believe
that that one word held the key to the estrangement between Simon
and Farragan's America.

In time, he put the poem and coffin picture in his pocket and
finished tying up the cache box, then left the men's room to look
for an empty baggage locker in the lobby outside. When he had
found one and placed the gift package within, he drew back and
warily scanned the crowd about him before depositing his quarter
and taking the key. Privately, Farragan was amazed at his own reaction, even with not at all intending to execute the crime that all the
paraphernalia he bore was meant to facilitate. This was truly the
spectacular age of man, he thought ruefully. The spy vogue has
made apprentice sleuths of us all; master sleuths, if you went at it
with the earnestness of someone like Anna. Anyhow, the word

"paranoia" was by now firmly cemented into the jargon of the kitchen psychologists. What Farragan believed he was searching for in that instant was a hidden camera or someone who had the look of being able to read minds. A police medium, perhaps, a type stationed in airports and train stations and bus terminals for the psychic detection of crimes before they were committed and who had misinterpreted by now that Arthur Farragan, businessman and American, Catholic and war veteran, secret Democrat, father of three children, husband of one woman and illicit lover of another, was on his way to assassinate his son for refusing to face up to his duty to his country, and that Farragan was equipped also with false identification and a .38 revolver strapped to his side beneath his jacket.

But there was no one—neither standing about nor sitting in the files of waiting-room chairs—who looked intent enough to be deciphering his duplicity or purpose in taking a plane, so he gave up the quarter and took his key, then slipped into a restaurant for toast and coffee to calm his ongoing lightheadedness.

On the flight to Montreal he ordered the earliest drink of his life and dreamed the killer poses again. Then turned them out of his mind forever. Over the rounded green peaks of what he presumed were the Catskills in New York State, he abruptly decided the best course of action would be to simply barge in on his son, dramatically waving the gun in his face and demanding, "Do you see what I've been sent here to do?" That should shake up even Simon the Inscrutable, who had thought his father insane during the two secret trips of warning Farragan had made to Montreal previously. Only make sure the blinds were drawn during all of this drama.

In Montreal he deplaned and walked easily through customs as Arthur Franklin Cowley. Outside the terminal, carrying his bag, he picked up the airport bus to begin the elaborate system of change-offs he had worked out with Jim and Anna the week before.

He meant to follow through with it—ludicrous as it seemed in light of today's real purpose—because he had a certain instinct that his brother and sister viewed Simon's assassination as a ritual killing that must needs be performed by his father alone, to insure its total justice, and consequently might have sent someone to Montreal from Philadelphia to shadow him. The idea annoyed and frightened him at the same time, and he spent most of the trip into the city to lower Saint Catherine Street scrutinizing the other passengers in the rearview mirror from his vantage point in the first seat behind the driver.

But there was no one in particular who appealed even to his heightened suspicions, and when he left the bus he walked several blocks north and took a taxi past McGill University and the base of Mount Royal to the west side of La Fontaine Park, where one day, years before, Farragan's father had been lost for over ten hours until the police found him sleeping off an afternoon drunk under a tree while his wife petitioned for favors at the Shrine of Saint Joseph. But Farragan had no time for that remembrance of happier years: now, he had difficulty finding his second cab and in desperation thought of suspending the change-offs and walking directly to Simon's apartment when an old and clanking Mercedes diesel that he did not at first recognize as a taxi hove into view.

It bore him sagaciously—despite his new emphasis on speed rather than wearisome tourism—to the Jacques Cartier Bridge to Nun's Island, where he waited a still longer time for the third and last cab to take him to Dorian Street, within a block of where Simon lived. By then, though, he was almost assured that no one was tailing him.

Twenty yards from Simon's apartment building he was hungry with the hunger of a nervous stomach and ducked into a sleazy-looking restaurant with an elaborate French menu to quiet that organ. He ordered a mushroom omelet and onion soup and countered his sweating palms with the thought that he might wait until dark to plead with his son to save his own life. Something seemed wrong with the full light of day: darkness should better enhance the dramatic necessity. But at the same time he cautioned himself not to stay too long: there was still Marie atop the mountain at Saint Blaise, confined within the same gates as the horny El Greco youth.

When he remembered that he should not eat too much, since at that very moment he was supposed to be a fasting penitent in the monastery's guest house, Farragan put down some money, left the restaurant, and entered Simon's building immediately because he was too nervous to wait any longer. He hauled his bag up the five flights to his son's apartment, set it in the hallway beside the door, and took out the .38 with its silencer attachment to assist his terrifying theatrical intrusion. The door opened suddenly before him.

It was Rollins.

"Oh, shit," Farragan said quietly.

"Are you still pissed off about those two girls, Mr. Farragan?" He extended one long, thin finger to touch the end of the silencer and push it away at right angles to himself.

"No, about something else. Where's Simon? What are you doing here?"

"Simon's at his girl's apartment. I'm here about a week now. I finally decided to come over."

"I'll bet that was a soul-wrenching decision for you. I thought you were going to law school to be a civil-rights lawyer and change the course of American history."

"I was in law school. But there was too much prejudice about the length of my hair and the cut of my clothes. I simply failed to look like everyone else. It's somehow important, except for obvious racial distinctions, that everyone look alike in law school. It has to do with professionalism."

"Well, you're certainly different, all right. But I wasn't betting on you to change history. Now, how do I get to Simon's girl friend's place?"

"Do you really expect me to tell you with that gun in your hand? What did you come here to do, kill him?"

"No, to warn him," Farragan said, holstering the revolver again. "His aunt and uncle are out to assassinate him for trying to beat the draft."

"*Très Américain.* He told me you were in Montreal twice already to tell him that. He doesn't believe it."

"He's got to believe it. They sent me here today with this gun to bump him off. You know how fucked-up his aunt is. Remember how she tried to beat your brains out last summer for hauling around that antiwar protest literature with you? His uncle's the same way, if not worse. Now take me to him. If nothing else, I'm going to make him take the gun so he'll have something to protect himself with when they come after him."

"I'll take you to him, Mr. Farragan, but Simon won't take that gun from you. He loves peace and would naturally view a gun as an instrument of war."

"How would he feel about martyrdom?" Farragan asked ruefully. But that was all: by now they were moving down the steps of the foul-smelling building, Rollins barefooted and alive with jingling ringlets and Farragan carrying his suitcase heavily against his leg.

It was two blocks to the apartment of Alouette, Simon's girl friend. As ever, Farragan was amazed by and cursed the intensity of summer heat in far northern Montreal that seemed much more oppressive than Philadelphia's, six hundred miles to the south. He was also amazed by the working proximity of himself and Rollins, and not without a tinge of ironic humor even on this desperate day, he turned slyly several times to watch the reflected images of the generation gap moving past storefront windows. Farragan gliding and

Rollins bobbing. That's what it was all about, Farragan supposed: merely a difference in rhythms. At the same time, he was pleased that none of the other pedestrians paid them any particular heed. In Philadelphia, his native city, Farragan would not have felt comfortable walking the streets with a hippie.

"Rollins, this girl Alouette, what's her religion?" Farragan asked after a time.

"Like us, Mr. Farragan. Honesty and love of beauty. She's really a beautiful chick."

"I mean, what ancient idols was she accustomed to worship before she converted to honesty and beauty?"

"Oh, that. Catholic probably. She's French-Canadian."

"Oh, that's nice," Farragan said quietly, thinking how pleased Muriel would be if she could be made to understand that Simon was finally safe in Montreal and married to a French-Canadian girl of a good Catholic family. An acceptable end point to all the hopes, so many times already dashed, that Farragan had ever had for his son.

At the girl's apartment building, he bade Rollins good-by.

"If you kill Simon, you're going to have to kill Alouette too, Mr. Farragan. That'll be two murders of former Catholics on your currently Catholic conscience," Rollins said.

"I'm not going to kill him. I've come to save him. I've told you that already."

"Just the same, I'm going to be standing out here while you're in there. When you get ready to leave, tell Simon to signal me from the window so I'll know he's O.K. Otherwise, I'm going for the Mounties before you have a chance to get back here and shoot me."

Farragan said nothing, merely handing his bag over to Rollins to guard until he returned. He went into the building and up the stairs to the third story, drew out the revolver, gritted his teeth, and prepared again to make his dramatic, convincing entrance.

Farragan knocked savagely on the door.

"Come in, Rollins. It's open."

Farragan the Assassin rushed wildly into the room, brandishing the gun—and promptly withered from embarrassment at the sight of Simon and his Alouette, clothed only in a sheet, smoking cigarettes, on a mattress on the floor. Simon sat up abruptly. The girl clung to him in a fright.

"Father, where have you come from?"

"From America."

"I guess you have. Where else do people carry guns when they come to visit?"

"Oh, can that crap! Simon, you've got to believe me this time! They're out to kill you! They think I'm here today to do exactly that!"

Both Simon and his Alouette sat up on the mattress now. The sheet covered only their bottom halves. Despite his frenzy of pleading, Farragan was moved to instant aggravation over the even greater length of Simon's hair. Like John the beloved Apostle or the Christ himself, it fell to the shoulders of Farragan's son, snarled, tawny and unwashed. Again, the father thought of tearing it out by the roots in great handfuls. Then Farragan saw the girl: her breasts were round and firm with the porcelain look of nippled egg cups; they did not sag. Her hair, like Simon's, hung long and dark and framed a face of great doelike eyes that reminded him of Muriel's own. In the noontime sunlight that filtered through the tattered curtain and down a column of living dust, her skin glistened incredibly from some coat of moisture.

"Are you all sweated up, miss, or is that just some kind of oil on your body?" Farragan asked timidly.

"It's oil, Mr. Farragan. Simon thinks it's more erotic to make love this way."

Her answer triggered the first flutterings of an erection in Farragan. He closed his eyes for an instant, remembering the early days of his marriage when he and Muriel had rubbed each other with lavish handfuls of Johnson's Baby Oil, then made slow love to the pock! sound rhythm of the vacuum between their bodies breaking and sealing. Coyly they suggested the pleasure to each other by the code name: The Oil Depletion Allowance. Usually it occurred on Wednesday evenings. . . .

"Father, do you actually mean they sent you here to kill me?" Simon asked. Aggressively disbelieving now: perhaps he had come up with his own interpretation of the closed-eyed moment of Farragan's remembering.

"Yes. That's what I'm trying to tell you."

"Are you going to do it?"

"Of course not. But I've got to be able to convince you of your danger this time! You've got to believe me!"

"I believe him, Simon," the girl said, her accent obvious now. "Why else would he come here looking like this?"

"But, Father, nobody does anything like that any more. This is the twentieth century and we're Americans, not Sicilians or anything like that."

"I know. I know all that. But their kind of moral code is tribal and, in terms of their most reasonable fantasy, they may think they live in the Papal States or some place like that. I'm not willing to judge. All I know is you're in danger."

"Simon, you've got to listen to him!" The girl pleaded now, throwing her arms about Farragan's son and rising out of the sheet so that she was plainly naked. "He's your father and he loves you. Look how he's trembling."

"Come here, Father. Sit down with us. You're shaking like a leaf," Simon said. Farragan edged toward the mattress, still embarrassed, despite his pleadings, at their communal nakedness, which seemed, by now, not to embarrass them at all. This evidently had something to do with that much-touted generation gap. He sat tentatively on the mattress edge and was seized immediately by the girl, who planted a fervent and presumably grateful kiss on his cheek. Farragan's shoulder fitted neatly into the cleft between the egg-cup breasts. On the instant it occurred to him that he dare not begin moving his arm in cautious exploration because he wanted to so badly. Thus he kept the shoulder rigid: this was his son's Muriel, after all, and one man's meat was another man's poison, as Farragan's father had always so aptly put it. To calm himself, he thought of the shame he might feel at having the only hard-on in the communal ring of a nude psychotherapy session if ever he came to participate in one.

In another moment Simon had thrust his arms about his father also, and Farragan, giving way, wept copiously into his long hair, oblivious of its stink.

"Simon! Simon!" Farragan begged, "please take the gun, at least, if you won't leave the country! Take it and use it to defend yourself! If your Aunt Anna or your Uncle Jim come looking for you, shoot first and ask questions later!"

"No, Father, I don't want your gun. Under the circumstances, if Anna or Jim do come gunning for me, I think the best thing would be to submit to them. The movement has need of martyrs. I'm worth more to them dead than alive."

"Look, you fucking asshole," Farragan ranted at his son, "cut the cheap romantics! Your only responsibility in this day and age is to yourself! And if you won't think about your mother and me, think about her! How would you feel, Alouette, if they came up here from Philadelphia and shot him?"

"I'd be proud, Mr. Farragan, to be known as the girl friend of Simon Farragan, who died for the cause of peace."

"Oh, I've got to go, Simon," Farragan said wearily. There was no alternative. He could not indefinitely stand the lack of pragmatism in anyone. His son was too very much the romantic idealist, and the girl a French-Canadian flower child. He would have to go back to Philadelphia and work at preserving Simon's life from that end: assassinate Anna, perhaps, before the next dawn. That should throw some sort of wrench into the mercilessly turning gears of their plan to murder his son. Now he stood up, covertly rearranging the front of himself. The beginning of erection was returning from his proximity to their nakedness, and Farragan thought it best to draw the line on one's voyeuristic tendencies when it came to one's own son.

"Go to the window, Simon, and signal to Rollins that you're O.K. so he doesn't call the police on me," Farragan said.

"No problem, Father. Rollins wouldn't call the police. He hates them. He probably just told you that because he was afraid you might shoot me."

"I don't understand a lot of things about young people these days, Simon. I used to presume I did."

"What will you do now, Father?"

"Go back to Philadelphia and try to prevent those two super-patriots from taking your life, since you don't particularly seem to care about it. Only do me a favor: don't commit suicide for the cause of peace. That would be the last straw. There's a difference between that and martyrdom. It doesn't make much sense for me to try saving your life back in the States if you intend taking it up here anyhow."

"I won't let him commit suicide, Mr. Farragan," Alouette said. "You can count on me for that."

"That's very good of you. I must go then," Farragan said. He waved a wan good-by, which they responded to with dim, perhaps pitying smiles, then exited through the door and walked slowly down the steps and out of the building, thinking for an instant of the two of them coming together in a passionate embrace beneath the sheets, then erasing the image from his mind. Outside, Rollins stood beside Farragan's bag, balanced on one foot like a crane and scratching at the sole of his other foot.

"Did you kill them, Mr. Farragan?"

"No. Of course not. Simon merely said that you would never go for the police anyhow because you hated them so much, so it wasn't necessary to signal you in that case."

"He shouldn't have told you that. It was my last defense against people like you who do fear the police. What will you do now?"

For the immediate moment Farragan was uncertain. The day was incomplete, abysmally incomplete: he was getting improper reactions everywhere. He had stored up for this day for so long a time that he needed a cathartic response to achieve balance again, and thought on the instant of going to Saint Joseph's Basilica. Perhaps he would witness a miracle.

"I think I'll walk to Saint Joseph's and stay there for the rest of the day," Farragan said.

"Maybe you'll see a miracle, Mr. Farragan." Rollins nudged him, the devil's smile coming on to his face.

"Yes, that's exactly what I was hoping for, Rollins," Farragan said, not smiling.

"I'm going over to McGill. I'll walk you that far."

They set off: Rollins bobbing and Farragan gliding, as before, though the younger man carried Farragan's bag now. At Saint Catherine Street they turned into heavy pedestrian traffic, and Farragan began suffering all the more acutely from the heat. Unable to open his jacket because of the revolver strapped to his side, his misery in the ninety-five-degree heat was compounded by the exhaust fumes of cars and busses and the screeching of the multitiered tourist trolleys which ranged up and down the wide streets, and he looked increasingly into the air-conditioned chill of restaurants where, to him, a whole race of stout afternoon matrons appeared to be picking at frosted green salads.

Rollins, who seemed oblivious of the heat, led him eventually into the campus of McGill University, and Farragan clung closer for fear of losing his guide in the press of students—most of whom seemed to him almost completely homogeneous to the eye. But in the main that was no real surprise to Farragan: except for their accents (and even that not a certitude), he had always had difficulty telling Canadian and American young people apart during previous trips to this country. Only now it dawned on him that most of the accents he was hearing today on campus were those of Americans. He looked more warily about and suffered a sudden tinge of weakening fear, despite the wearing of a gun, at the notion that he must have blundered exhausted and sweating into the very center of the enemy encampment ridden with border-hopping draft dodgers: there had to be a physical center to their universe, and this, obviously, was it. All about him students were grouped and arguing—doubtless in preparation for protests. He saw that they observed his middle-aged intrusion with thinly veiled hostility.

Farragan was so intent upon the numberless enemy that he realized only after a long moment that a paper thrust before him and apparently needing his signature was a petition to Lyndon Johnson to halt the war in Viet Nam immediately, withdraw the troops, and fire Lewis B. Hershey, the Selective Service director. All at once. The petition bearer was a long-haired hippie with an American flag sewn to the sleeve of his jacket (sacrilege! sacrilege!), who was seated on the edge of a fountain that Farragan had been in the unconscious process of skirting.

"No, I'd rather not," Farragan said politely. A small fear was growing apace in him like a kindling flame.

"Why not, Mr. Farragan?" Rollins asked. "These are all the things you've come to Montreal to save Simon from anyhow. Johnson's a fascist and Hershey's a pig. Thousands of American troops are killed every year trying to uphold a government in Saigon that has virtually no popular support. Why not sign it?"

"No. I don't want a test made out of this. Johnson's your President and Hershey has a lousy job. I've never been to Saigon, so I'm not qualified to say how much popular support the government has," Farragan said, thinking at the same time that the righteousness of the Left was in its own way as noxious as the righteousness of the Right. But he was also prepared to admit to himself the truth about the petition: there were vile considerations of status at work. Farragan would gladly attach his name to a plea of dowdy Philadelphia businessmen intended for Johnson's desk. But he would not be the only dowdy Philadelphia businessman on the list of long-haired expatriates, most of whom he assumed, were, like Simon, on the dole from their businessmen fathers. Bad enough to have a son in that condition already. It was not Farragan's intention to embrace the whole dismal lot of them with the kiss of his signature. He had come to save but one. And that for reasons of kinship rather than ideology.

"No, Rollins, I'm not going to sign it."

"You're a snob, Mr. Farragan."

"Why's he wearing a gun?" the petition holder abruptly demanded of Rollins. "Is he CIA or something like that?"

"No, I'm Arthur Farragan of Philadelphia," he told the American-flag hippie desperately. The kindling fear inside him had blazed out into the open by now: unwittingly his jacket had flopped open. The word "gun" traveled through the stand of young people near by in a kind of breathless rush. An army of eyes turned to regard him in response.

"I've come to Canada to warn my son who's the same age as you that his life is in danger if he doesn't leave and go to Europe to get away from the people who want to kill him," Farragan said in a rush. "That's why I'm here."

"Who are the people who want to kill him?" the petitioner asked.

"His aunt and uncle."

"Are you kidding?"

"He's not kidding one bit," Rollins assured him and the other eager listeners. "I know them. The kid's aunt is the most fucked-up woman I ever met. She practically sleeps with an American flag wrapped around her at night. They sent him here with the gun to kill his own son."

"Very ritualistic shit. Even for America," the flag hip pie said. "What did the kid say when you gave him the word?"

"He's unimpressed," Farragan told them. "He's toying with the notion of becoming a martyr for the cause. His girl friend approves of the idea also."

"That's brave and very beautiful," a girl said. "I can understand how she feels. The cause has need of martyrs."

"Then why not offer yourself up? Douse yourself with some hi-test gas and make a nice clean job of it," Farragan said angrily. His fear had instantly subsided when he heard her say "beautiful." That word grated on his ears of late. Before him, her eyes had the glazed-over look of a five-cocktail afternoon, and since she was not of Farragan's generation, he presumed it was due to drugs rather than booze.

"I'm going, Rollins. I want to light a candle at Saint Joseph's before I return to Philadelphia."

"That should end the war in Viet Nam, Mr. Farragan. Why did you have to yell at her, anyhow? She's being sincere."

"Just because she's being so sincere. I can't stand that type of sincerity. And because she gives me a pain in the ass. That's why. The same way Simon does. All of you sitting up here on the dole from your parents without a realistic thought in your heads. I come here to warn my son he's slated to be bumped off and he informs me he'd enjoy becoming a martyr, then this lady proposes that it's all of it a beautiful sentiment."

"You sound just like my father," the flag hippie said. "A narrow-minded, uncompromising bastard!"

"Probably so. All fathers must sound like that after a time. There's no recourse with the generation of idiots we've unleashed."

"I ought to knock you on your ass for that, Farragan of Philadelphia!"

"How would you like a bullet through your head for your trouble?"

"You'd better go, Mr. Farragan. This is no place for you," Rollins urged. "The mentality is different. You're older. But I still think you're O.K. You've got all the wrong ideas, but basically the right instincts."

Farragan regarded his son's friend narrowly for a long minute. "I have the feeling I've been supporting you also for some years now. Didn't you once tell me that your family had disowned you? We Catholics are much too generous."

"Yes, Mr. Farragan, you're a generous people. But I'll keep my eye on Simon to help earn my keep."

"See that you do." But that was all: Farragan lifted his bag and began walking swiftly away from Rollins and the others toward the west gate of the university, saddened in the extreme that he had not had sufficient legal cover for shooting the American-flag hippie in the head. That would have sufficed admirably for the cathartic response he was so desperately seeking: a sense of completeness to the so far fruitless day.

Ahead of him, past the university laboratories, he could just discern the last rise of ascending street that swelled up against the palisades of Mount Royal and dead-ended there, then turned right into the road that ran along the cliff base and eventually wound into the park itself where the basilica was located. Long minutes later, when he himself crossed that same rise, Farragan sat down exhausted on the curb, half-consciously watching the combination of a bald-headed hunchback and his woman who stood a full head taller beside him receding out of sight around a bend in the road. Farragan mopped his brow with a handkerchief, thinking about the real possibility of a heart attack if he had to walk very much farther, until he saw an empty park-tour horse and carriage clopping toward him from around the bend where the walking twosome had disappeared.

He hailed the driver, who turned the carriage about. When he was aboard and had given directions for the park, the man started the horse off at a fast trot until they came within sight of the hunchback and the woman still walking along the road. Abruptly, the horse was reined to a slow walk.

*"Elle est votre fille?"* the driver, turning, asked him in French, though Farragan had spoken to him in English. For the second time since he had strapped on the gun that morning he actually thought of using it on someone.

"No, she's not my daughter. Of course not. Just drive, please."

Seated before him, the man merely shrugged his shoulders and clucked to the horse. But Farragan saw he kept it lightly reined just the same. They followed the walkers for more than a mile, past the point where the steep promontory gave out and the actual park above was accessible by walking up the wooded slope. In time, the hunchback and his woman suddenly left the road and headed into the trees.

*"Ils vont faire l'amour,"* the driver said excitedly to Farragan.

"Where? . . . Up there?" Farragan asked.

*"Oui. Toute cette colline c'est une grande bordelle."*

"What? Speak English."

"That whole hill is just one big whorehouse."

Farragan told the man to stop, dropped five dollars into his hand, and hurried out of the carriage and along the roadway as the driver swung the horse about again. When he came to the swath of rumpled grass they had trod on, he looked up and saw them passing through a fringe of trees about three hundred yards ahead. Then they were gone from sight.

Farragan crept up the incline, avoiding the brittle patches of unraked leaves and whiplash of low branches to guard against noise. He peered about, and seeing no one, stopped to attach the silencer to the nose of the .38. Then he inched forward again, dragging the bag after him, and squinted against the sunlight through a line of shrubbery at the sudden apparition of the dome of Saint Joseph's in the distance.

Then he looked down. Ahead of him, not more than forty feet away, the hunchback and his girl lay on the grassy slope of a small gully. Covering his mouth lest they hear the intensity of his breathing, Farragan watched as they smoked and talked and he thought of a substitute killing to achieve his worthy catharsis: he might shoot Quasimodo then and there and leave the girl to take care of his body while the assassin fled back to America. But the man stubbed out his cigarette and unexpectedly began kissing the girl, then rolled over on top of her in the grass. He went for the zipper on her slacks while she seemed to resist mightily, and Farragan, holstering the revolver, considered yelling down to the hunchback to put his tongue in her ear since they all loved that. But he kept quiet and watched the other deftly pull up her sweater and slide it over her head and loosen her bra, which gave with a loud and thrilling snap.

Quasimodo eased off the girl's slacks and the pants with them, and Farragan, from his position, observed with disappointment that her crotch was shaven. He looked on as the man kicked off his shoes and slid out of his pants, and saw with absolute shock the Creator's attempt at balance in the universe: Quasimodo's erection —more proboscis than phallus, as must needs be to compensate for the unnatural half-moon curve of his body—that he wet with saliva and slid into his victim, who now roiled and trembled yet smiled incessantly beneath him.

Above, in double ecstasy, Farragan recalled also the two blacks of that night years ago at the Rodin Museum. But this was at least twice as good. Below, the hunchback's naked buttocks pumped up and down, and Farragan saw with approval that he varied his rhythm with an expertise that told he was obviously not an initiate. Then the woman climaxed for the first time in an ongoing trill of moans and small shrieks while clasping and unclasping her legs around the Quasimodo's back. During the long subsequent minute when her lover—perhaps out of reverence—halted the rhythm of his assault to watch closely the benign vision of her face, and she herself was content to merely beat her heels into the turf beneath her, Farragan came gradually to realize that he was erect and protruding desperately against the cloth of his pants.

Then came the voyeur Farragan's undoing:

Quasimodo swung over onto his back with his partner atop him and began rocking back and forth along the arc of his curved spine like a rocking horse gone mad to the limit of its runners, the woman a hapless victim of the insanity who was merely caught on board. Farragan could not believe in the possibility of such fucking: like some machination of the burlesque, grotesque as all the writings of the black humorists he had ever read, worse even than the woman and donkey he and Muriel had once witnessed copulating on stage in Havana before Castro's revolution had done away with such filth. . . . But the grotesque shall grotesquely fuck, evidently. There was a look of mutual loving in their eyes, and in the end, when Quasimodo and his woman, anchored on the end of the phallus-proboscis, climaxed together in a chorus of more moans and small shrieks, Farragan felt the same eye-flashing exultation go through him and, lightheaded, he clutched at the trunk of a small tree while taking a fix on the distant statue of Saint Joseph atop the basilica and realized without any particular annoyance that he had just come in his shorts.

What greater sharing, after all?

Sweet Mother of God! his mind praised over and over again. How proud he was of Quasimodo! Now, below, the hunchback and his love lay parted and side by side, laughing and smoking again. On high, Farragan giggled mirthfully through clenched teeth, trying to imagine what they were saying to each other. His total instinct was to burst through the brush and run downhill to thank them for providing this day's badly needed invitation to catharsis.

Instead, he wiped himself as carefully as he was able with a handkerchief and sneaked back down the incline through the trees. Or skipped rather: for Farragan was delightedly happy. When he gained the road again, he was not overly surprised that the horse carriage stood waiting for him only a small distance off.

*"Ils ont bien fait l'amour?"* the driver asked Farragan, excited with the expectation of a good story.

*"Oui. Très bien,"* he replied, swinging aboard. *"Fantastique.* On his back. Like this," Farragan demonstrated, lying across the seat. "With the girl on top of him."

"Oh, *mon Dieu.* On his back? With the hump like he had it?" the driver asked, at the same time returning Farragan his five dollars.

"Exactly so."

"Oh, God. And the girl? *Elle n'était pas votre fille?* She was not your daughter?"

"Are you kidding? She wasn't a very pretty girl. She wouldn't be a daughter of mine," Farragan said, anxious to set the record straight.

"Perhaps she was a prostitute, then. Someone the hunchback procured for his initiation."

"No, he's done it plenty of times already. It was easy to see that."

"It's just as well it was not the first time then," the driver said. "The first time is always tentative and uncertain. The suspense might have been too much for your heart. The tendency is to identify."

"Yes, but I was sure he was O.K. all the time. Drive around for a bit, will you?"

They set off, stopping once for Farragan to buy a fifth of chilled rosé that he opened and cached in a paper sack and sipped along the way while the driver turned around continually and related episodes to Farragan from his apparently endless collection of tales about voyeurs who came to the park. When he had heard three different versions of what he decided was the same sixtyish man watching his wife and her boy lover on Saturday and Sunday afternoons, Farragan called for a halt, bade the driver good-by, and switched to a cab that carried him out to the airport. On the way he flipped the empty wine bottle out the window into a cane-grass field.

At the terminal he had to wait only forty-five minutes for his flight back to Philadelphia. Once on board (having paid extra to sit in first class) and away from Montreal, where the sun was setting in earnest, he ordered dinner and a half-bottle of French rosé.

"Usually one takes red wine with steak," the hostess said in English, not fooled by the precision of his affectation about wine and French foods.

"*Au diable ces anciennes coutumes! Donnez-moi du rosé,*" Farragan told her in the flawless French he had never spoken before in his life.

*"Vous avez raison, monsieur,"* said a fat French-Canadian who sat beside him. *"Enfin, je suis fatigué par la tradition, vous savez."*

Farragan was also tired of tradition and a few other things, he decided, looking out on the fantastic shades of the declining sun. After the events of today, it was beginning to bear down on him like a colossal weight. And it would still have to be reckoned with when he arrived in Philadelphia and would have to begin explaining to Jim and Anna that Simon would not be coming home within a week boxed up in a coffin.

Farragan sipped another glass of wine and returned to a previous consideration: trained by his family to be the killer of his own son, he might instead turn the skill upon Jim and Anna. But Anna first. For all the rancor he bore his sister suddenly surfaced. A bitch, a shrew, more righteous than anyone he knew, the very type to kill for a variable like patriotism. Farragan prayed silently for courage. He would get off this plane and fire the muffled pistol yet today. Accordingly, he ordered more wine, and the fat French-Canadian helped him polish it off before Philadelphia was reached.

They landed a little after nine, and it was finally dark. The plane taxied in near the terminal, and above the roar of idling jets, Farragan heard someone calling his name as he descended from the aircraft.

"Arthur! Arthur Farragan!"

Farragan looked up to the lighted observation platform and saw Edmund, in jeans and hunting jacket, waving his arms madly at him while a curious knot of people looked on. Fearing for Marie, Farragan rushed away from the carpeted walk to the fence below the platform.

"Arthur . . . Arthur . . . Jesus, Mary, and Joseph! You won't believe what happened!"

"What happened? Is Marie all right? Did that guy do something to her?"

"No, Arthur, it's Anna," Edmund screamed, tears streaming down his face by now. "She's been blown to smithereens by a bomb!"

# CHAPTER 13

## *Anna Goes to Meet Her Jesus*

"Arthur! Arthur! There wasn't a single piece of her left as big as your hand!"

Along with the other flight passengers, Farragan had entered the terminal through the customs area and winced at the sight of Edmund rushing along the corridor toward him like a demented elephant, leaving crowds of startled travelers in his wake. In the long minute since his brother the priest disappeared from the observation platform above, Farragan had recovered from his initial shock and decided that, all in all, he was rather pleased Anna had been blown to bits by a bomb.

"Calm yourself, Edmund. How did it happen?"

Farragan had taken the other's arm and steered him toward a near-by men's room that was blessedly vacant. He splashed water on his face over a sink to drive away the wine while Edmund did a little dance beside him. In the wall mirror Farragan saw that the cleric's face was somehow a combination of horror and excitement, possibly over being afoot in the real world where something was actually happening for a change.

"The woman who lives next door says Anna opened the door to her little greenhouse and a bomb went off. Christ and Mary, Arthur, I got there almost as soon as the police! She was spread all over the walls and in the shrubbery! The back of the house was almost completely blown inward! It doesn't seem possible she's dead!"

"Why were you in Philadelphia, Edmund?"

"Oh, first because of Marie. Mr. Farrow started making passes at her right after breakfast, and we decided it would be best if she returned to the city, since she was proving too much of a distraction for him in the midst of his conversion attempt. And also because I wanted to beg Anna to send a telegram to Simon and tell him to get out of Montreal for the time being. Did you . . . ?"

"No."

"Oh, thank God !" Edmund threw his arms about Farragan. "He was always so kind to me, Arthur."

"Yes, I understand. Who do the police think killed her?"

"They have no idea. Do you think it might have been the Negroes, Arthur?"

They were outside the men's room now, walking along a corridor toward the baggage claim. At least half the faces they passed were black.

"It wasn't the Negroes," Farragan said quietly.

"Who, then?"

"I have no idea."

"Arthur, why didn't you shoot Simon like you were supposed to?"

"I changed my mind. What we were going to do was stupid."

"Yes, it was horrible. But Jim isn't going to like it one bit. Especially with Anna dead. He's going to tie up all this antiwar dissidence with Anna's killing and Simon's defecting to Canada. It's all of the same kettle of stew, you know, as far as he's concerned. I'm sure Anna was murdered for her politics."

"That's not hard to believe," Farragan said disgustedly. "Even I didn't like her politics very much, and I'm her brother."

"We shouldn't talk this way, Arthur."

"Don't play priest with me, Edmund. You didn't like her either."

"No, I guess I didn't."

But still Edmund began blubbering again, and Farragan left him leaning against a pillar in the main lobby and went up to the baggage claim to retrieve his small suitcase. From a distance, the cleric's weepings appeared equal to Peter's legendary own after the threefold denial of the Christ. A knot of people gathered round him. When Farragan drew near him again, bag in hand, an old black woman had laid a kindly hand upon his hunting jacket. "Are you lost, young man? Are you lookin' for your people?"

Wordlessly Farragan steered Edmund out of the lobby and through the front doors of the terminal, where he decided to leave Marie's Oldsmobile in the extended-time lot and instead shoved Edmund into the Saint Blaise Land Rover. Farragan's brother stopped crying and drove out of the airport and through the darkened meadowland ugliness at the bottom of the Schuylkill, then into the Expressway going north.

"Did Anna at least get the conditional last rites?" Farragan asked after a time.

"Yes. But in Christ's name it was conditional in the extreme," Edmund said, sobbing again. "There wasn't a single bit of her about to lay the holy oils on. Two of the policemen who came ended up by vomiting. I vomited myself. I've never seen such a mess. They put her together in a plastic bag. Arthur, really, who do you think could have done it?"

"Is it possible that some of those gadgets she had in that igloo of a greenhouse might have gone off?"

"No. It was dynamite. The police found a trip wire and detonating caps. Do you think it might be some of those union people you're always sparring with?"

"No."

"Then who, Arthur?"

"Oh, Edmund, I don't know," Farragan said, exasperated. He did not care either, he decided, except perhaps as a curiosity. In the last analysis, the kinship of families was never as much as people like their mother always made it out to be: Anna was better off dead, in Farragan's estimation.

"The police are really hung up for a motive then, beyond Jim's insistence that it's someone on the far Left."

"They ought to turn the case over to Jim, then. What funeral arrangements have been made?"

"She's to be waked in a closed coffin at Jim's house after the police are finished with her. She'll be buried from the cathedral with a solemn high Mass in four days. Mrs. Crow has called all the women from the auxiliary organizations that Anna belonged to, and they'll all be represented."

"That's fine," Farragan said. "That's what Anna would have loved. Too bad she couldn't be around for it."

"Yes," Edmund agreed. But that was all. Farragan remembered to stash the .38 under the Rover's front seat before they pulled up in front of Anna's house on Panama Street, where neighbors stood looking at the eerie turnings of dome lights atop several police cars parked near by. Jim's Lincoln was on the opposite side of the street, a few doors away.

A policeman checked them out, then admitted them, and they passed quickly through the living room, where a detective still questioned Crow, the housekeeper, who threw up her arms plaintively to indicate her ignorance, then began sobbing anew when she caught sight of Farragan. Jim sat in the remnant of Anna's kitchen, staring at the mangled copper fixtures that had been blown inward with the wall. Broken glass and plaster littered the room. Outside, in the glare of portable lighting, a police photographer took pictures of a crater in the garden that approximated the dimensions of Anna's greenhouse. Some of the flowers it had contained were incredibly still intact and hung like blossoms on the four evergreen trees that filled each corner of the garden. Above was the starry sky of an August night. Farragan saw that most of the studio window of J. Worthington Duffey's apartment was blown out, and Duffey himself and a workman were in the process of boarding it up with plywood sheets. Farragan turned his attention to Jim: the eldest of Jedda Farragan's children had obviously been copiously crying.

"Did you get him?" Jim asked in a whisper, putting a powerful hand on Farragan's arm.

"No, I couldn't find him."

"He wasn't there? In Montreal?"

"No one has seen him for a week."

"He did it then!" Jim gnashed out. "That dirty draft-dodging motherfucker killed his own Aunt Anna!"

"Don't be ridiculous, Jim. In the first place, he wouldn't have as much reason for killing any of us as we decided we had for killing him. And in the second place, he couldn't risk coming back to the States to attempt anything like that. Don't waste your energy speculating in the wrong direction."

Farragan read in his silence that Jim had begun to see the logic of that argument. "Who could have done it, Arthur?" He was pleading now. "Do you think it could have been some of those niggers on relief Anna was always writing to the newspapers about?"

"No. With all the police around here normally, it would be almost impossible for a nigger on or off relief to get into the house."

"How about that guy Rollins, the long-haired one that Anna had the trouble with last year at the shore?"

"No," Farragan said, after a long moment of trying to decide whether or not to throw Rollins to the lions. "He'd have even less reason to kill here than Simon, and the same risk getting into the country and out again."

"Then who, Arthur? It's got to have been somebody on the Left. But who? There are so many possibilities."

"I absolutely don't know, Jim," Farragan said, looking through the debris of Anna's kitchen into the star-filled sky above. To himself, he was ready to concede that he was grateful enough to whoever it was that had taken the trouble.

Anna would have loved her own leavetaking.

Farragan's judgment was echoed by more than one person during the three-day archaic ritual of her wake that took place at Jim's home, where Fagan the mortician had dumped the embalmed remnant of her into a closed-top coffin, while also getting sick in the process.

For most of the first evening, Farragan sat before the casket and tried to picture the carnage it contained. But the image was beyond him and he turned instead to trying to recall the scrap-laden floor of an old-fashioned butcher shop before the advent of supermarket packaging, with which he had more success. All about him, in the flagging air conditioning, the place was packed with close friends of the family, and some of the dead souls and large delegations—fully uniformed in the face of the late-August night humidity—from the various organizations to which Anna and Farragan himself and Jim belonged.

Not without irony, the first night of Anna's wake was the third night of the Democratic convention in Chicago, and Farragan

could not help thinking there was an immensely appropriate crescendo of background music being provided for his sister's parting.
Speculation was rampant as to who had ordained that parting and
much of it, inevitably, found its way to the Windy City. Farragan
walked once into a side parlor where there was food and drink and
a television set available to the mourners and heard a mammoth-
busted crony of Anna's, all dolled up in the full regalia of the Catholic War Veterans Ladies' Auxiliary and bursting with sweat beneath her mascara, opine that the bombing was done by some of the
same people being herded off the screen by Daley's police, or others
just like them. Other regaled women unctiously agreed: it was well
known, after all, that Anna was a Communist-hater. It was either
the Communists or the hippies, then. Everyone in the room seemed
willing enough to give the Negroes the benefit of the doubt.
Framed in the doorway, Farragan nodded in polite, sad agreement to
their conjecture. Privately, it came to him for the first time that if
Simon were not hiding out in Montreal, he would probably be
fighting cops that night in Chicago.

In time, nearly prostrate with the heat and the odors of a forest of flowers and dripping candle wax, Farragan went outside to the
garden. There, before the house and in the drive between the soft
islands of light that illuminated Jim's acreage, which had once been
their father's own, were nearly a hundred cars, and Farragan, as always, whenever there was a wedding or funeral, wondered where
they all came from. He sat down heavily on a railing at the edge of
the terrace, thinking how much more agreeable was the soft outside
night. Whole choirs of crickets chirped in the darkness. After a moment he was aware that Margaret, Jim's wife, had come out behind
him.

"Hello, Arthur."

"Hello, Margaret. I was just marveling at the numbers of cars
out here."

"Yes, I am too. She had so many friends. It makes me frightened to think there are so many people about who could like your sister, Anna, Arthur."

"Did you do it, Margaret?" Farragan asked mutedly. There was a bemused smile on his face, he believed. He decided on the instant that if she answered yes, her secret would be eternally safe with him.

"No, Arthur. I don't know anything about explosives. That's probably the only reason I hadn't gotten round to it before now."

"You've really kept this under wraps for a time, Margaret."

"I wonder if they'll try to take a coffin picture of her, Arthur, like that one of your mother that stands guard in my bedroom every night. I hear dear old Anna looks like a bunch of reject scraps from a dog-food factory."

On the same impulse, both Farragan and his sister-in-law began laughing uncontrollably, and Farragan stuffed a handkerchief into his mouth to stifle the noise. In another moment someone came to the door through which they had just exited and stuck a disbelieving head outside. Farragan squeezed Margaret's arm in an effort to make her stop. "We'd better not let Jim see us laughing, Margaret."

"I guess not," she said ruefully. "What with his other problems, this is liable to put him over the brink. He's close to the end of his rope now."

"He and Anna were great friends. He'll miss her."

"That's not all that's wrong. Our Edward was married three days ago by a justice of the peace down in Maryland. I don't suppose he told you anything about that?"

"No, he didn't. My God, you're kidding! Whom did he marry?"

"The girl next door down at Cape May. Dr. Carter's daughter, Susan."

"They're Protestants, aren't they?"

"Yes. Which is most of the reason Jim hasn't accepted the fact yet and isn't bothering to tell anyone. He still thinks he can convince Edward his marriage needs annuling. But he won't do it now. Edward has changed his thinking since the day he threw the letter at you in the car on the way home from the airport. He sat around for a good part of the summer trading war stories with that old buddy of a father of his until he just got sick of it. Now he's in open revolt."

Both looked through the French windows and across two rooms to where Jim sat, obese and confused-looking, on a gilded chair beside Anna's coffin, a rosary playing between his fingers like an Arab's worry beads. His clothes appeared to Farragan to be several sizes too small for him, and he had the aspect of someone slowly choking to death from the unrelenting tightness of his necktie. They watched silently for a long moment, then saw his interest aroused by Edmund. Farragan's brother the priest, released from his haunted monastery for the days of Anna's wake and burial, sat talking animatedly in a circle of cloaked War Veterans ladies, the happy smile on his face miles distant from the sorrowing Jim expected. Jim stood up and walked across the room to correct his brother. The ladies fell instantly to sorrowing. In their midst, Edmund was meek and chastened now.

"He's such a turd, my husband is," said Margaret fiercely. "He'd die if he knew that I drove his son and new daughter-in-law down to Maryland to the J.P. to get married."

"My God, you did?"

"Yes, I did. Jim was going to have him married in the cathedral, one-armed and in his soldier suit as soon as he got the girl to sign an agreement that any children would be baptized and raised as Catholics. He even spent three long-winded evenings in a row trying to convince her that she ought to convert to Catholicism because it was the one True Church and she'd feel better afterward for having made the choice. On the fourth night I piled them into a car and drove them down to Ocean City. Now, ironically, they're living with Dr. Carter right next door, and there's not a damn thing Jim can do about it. He tried once to get into the house to plead with Edward, and the police chief threatened to arrest him."

"Are you sure you didn't kill Anna, Margaret? I won't tell anyone," Farragan assured her earnestly.

"I'd like to ease your mind, Arthur, but I didn't kill her."

"Alas, it doesn't matter that much. It would merely have been comforting to know."

"I'd better go back inside, Arthur, and look like the stricken sister-in-law."

She stood up and walked back into the death rooms, while Farragan marveled at this night's proving of all the certain instincts he had ever had about her. But in a moment he conceded to himself he was far more intrigued by the case of Jim: Which, he wondered, was the greater pain of loss for his brother? His Anna or his Edward? To know that Jim was carrying the weight of both disasters at the same time was little to gloat over in Farragan's estimation. For when the time inevitably came to begin shrugging off that oppressive burden, Simon, now safely abed with his Alouette in Montreal, would be in for a new round of trouble from America: Jim could be counted on to react against his nephew's impunity with a superrage. Farragan thought that now that Anna was dead, he might avail himself of the target range in her basement several times a week until he understood more clearly which course events were going to take.

In time, Muriel, dressed all in black and carrying a drink in one hand, came unexpectedly out on the terrace. She appeared to Farragan to be weaving slightly.

"Muriel, I have some happy news," he called to her.

"What is it, Arthur?"

"Edward was married to Dr. Carter's daughter a few days ago."

"Who is Edward?"

"Edward, Jim's son. Your nephew."

"Oh, him. Yes, it was a lovely wedding." But that was all. Sadly Farragan recalled that her dimness increased whenever she had too much to drink. He stood, thinking to touch her once while she might be too insensible to protest, but she evidently understood his motive and shied away into the house. Farragan followed her miserably inside, wondering distantly who was winning the street war in Chicago.

On the second night, when all the funerary stage props—ladies' auxiliaries, Knights of Columbus delegations, union representatives, occasional friends, and most of the dead souls—were already in place, and Farragan was seated beside Anna's coffin with Muriel, his wife, Marie, his mistress, walked in with the sisters Glennis. It was the first time he had seen her since Saint Blaise and Farragan thought she was covertly scowling at him. His instinct was to rise and kiss her ardently on the spot, begging forgiveness, and telling her that he had gone to Montreal merely to warn Simon rather than to liquidate him, until he recalled ashamedly she had not even known he had made the trip to Canada. Instead, he held himself in check and shook hands with the two old women. Then Marie, who dug a row of talonlike fingernails into the palm of his hand to punish him.

When he sat down again, rubbing the wound she had inflicted, he scrutinized her more closely as she crossed herself and stood a moment in a parody of prayer before the coffin. If she were praying at all, he guessed hers would be a prayer of thanksgiving rather than any hope for the comfortable eternity of Anna's soul. Marie wore a black-belted dress and black heels, and her hair fell, incredibly blond, to the level of her shoulders. At the sight of her, Farragan had noticed, two of the War Vets' ladies, sitting like cloaked, bemedaled walruses at the end of a row of chairs opposite him, had gone stiff with resentment. Ah, but Farragan was suddenly proud of this woman of his: she was incredibly feminine, a whole universe away from that rack of paramilitary amazons who he always considered wished openly for continuous wars. Looking at the soul sisters of his own dead sister, it surprised him suddenly to recall how many of them, like Anna herself, had outlived their own husbands.

Marie and the two ancients passed on to the next room, and Farragan rose wearily and almost continuously to greet more legions of the many people they knew. One thing about Anna, he thought vexedly, despising their numbers: she had exactly the same latent sentimental nature as the Farragans' mother herself. The dead souls had merely passed into her care when the old lady died. Like a ward boss, Farragan imagined, she kept a few out of the poorhouse, and everybody got at least a Christmas card. Now they came in droves to see their Anna, the way they had come to see her mother, Jedda, before her. They shuffled past Farragan and crossed themselves before the coffin and perhaps wondered at the arrangement of bloodied meat therein, then went into the rooms of the food and drink. Each and every one of them had decried Anna's death and the events of Chicago in the same breath.

At ten-thirty, Edmund began the rosary. On the second night of Anna's wake, it appeared to Farragan, about three hundred hot and sweated people had stayed to kneel in the downstairs rooms of Jim's house to pray for Anna's immortal soul. Death is the true poetic muse of our cult, Farragan decided, nearly lulled to sleep by the chant-suggesting rhythm of many Hail Marys in a string. Only he wondered earnestly on the moment how many more years this poetic form might survive, for the young people refused to learn it. In the slight breeze that wafted in from outdoors, the plumes of the Knights of Columbus fluttered slowly back and forth; also the fringed edges of four American flags behind the coffin; also the nearly identical cloaks of the various ladies' auxiliaries heaved to and fro on the draft, except for one—badly out of timing—who fanned herself violently with the flapping edge of her cape, and whom Farragan thought of shooting to restore the universal cadence. But all bodies (the fanning woman included) seemed to adhere to a relentless tempo of shifting weight: from left knee to right knee, and return. Then he saw Marie, in a corner, who did not. Farragan watched her closely: she knelt rigidly erect and unflinching, and did not bother to pray. At twenty-three, she was the only person in the entire house under forty, as nearly as he could discern. A slight smile, like satisfaction, spread across her face, and Farragan, who felt the lust rising up inside him, wondered at the same time if she had somehow made arrangements herself to have Anna bombed while she was out of the city. How ironic then: Farragan, her lover and fellow retreatant at the Monastery of Saint Blaise, was also her alibi.

When the mourners left, things fell neatly into place for Farragan, who badly wanted to see his mistress. Muriel was adamant about returning for the night to their daughters at Beach Haven, and Farragan, conceding that she drove a car better than anyone he knew, saw her off into the August darkness immediately after the rosary. Marie, who had first to escort her aunts home, promised to come later to Farragan's house. Forty minutes later, while he swam naked in the enclosed pool, she let herself in with her own key and walked onto the deck beside the water.

"Nice job you did on my sister," he said quietly but not reproachfully. He floated on his back, sucking his breath in sharply to better conceal the flabby folds of his waist.

"Screw yourself, Arthur darling. Flattery will get you nowhere.

I was sure *you'd* done it. It's all too coincidental. I, after all, was up at Saint Blaise with Edmund and those two screwball retreatants of his. You were in Philadelphia at some meeting that was so secret that you had to sneak out while still pretending you were at the retreat house to get to it."

"You think I did it?"

"You're the likely suspect, I'd say. Where was the meeting?"

"In Atlantic City."

"You're lying. But I don't care. Mankind is better off for having Anna Farragan blown to pieces. Maybe if you find time in the next few weeks you'll go after Jim. Then you and I and Muriel and Edmund and my aunts and Binky Applebaum can live happily ever after."

"Wouldn't that be nice," Farragan said. He meant it. Like a whale, he blew streams of the lightly chlorinated water out of his mouth and watched Marie as she slid out of her clothes and left them piled neatly on the diving board, then climbed down the ladder into the pool and swam toward him, the blond hair trailing behind on the flood. On the instant, he decided there would never be any means of erasing the image of that immoral night in the midst of Anna's wake when Farragan, a suspected killer, swam naked with his mistress, also a suspected killer, in the closed-in pool of his Wynnewood home: such things, happily, can be expected to live on in dreams.

"I want to make love to you," he said when she was within grappling distance.

"Only on one condition, Arthur. You have to swear that Mayor Daley is a fascist pig."

"Mayor Daley is a fascist pig," he said perfunctorily, though he did not believe it. While he deplored the violence of Chicago, something deep inside him that he rarely admitted to was taking great pleasure at the firm-handed response of the mayor's cops to the howlings of rebellious youth. Also, he meant to cast the seventh secret vote of his life for a Democratic President in November and rather hoped the man would be Hubert instead of Gene. Even though he was supposed to look like Gene.

On the third and last night—as per Jim's arrangement with the union bosses—their drivers came en masse. Farragan decided there were a lot of younger ones he did not know by name and he was sure they were probably feeling quite put upon in having to come to the wake of Anna, whom he assumed they knew better by the legend of her ferocious temper than by any real dealings with her. He found it ironic also that nearly half their drivers were black and that they should end up sharing the duty of being part of her honor guard, after all was said and done. Farragan felt embarrassed for them as they ranged themselves self-consciously on either side of the coffin. But it was all Jim's fault: he was such a stickler for form. No consideration at all that nearly half of them were patently despised by Anna merely for the color of their skin, and the remaining whites—if a reason need be given—for as little as the fact that they belonged to a labor union.

Later, when they had served their time and were released into the warm night (with audible sighs of relief), the first to enter after their departure was Binky Applebaum, walking shyly in his inevitable way into the charnel house of Christians to stand before the coffin of Anna, whom Farragan decided instinctively Applebaum would have hated had he known her better. Farragan, after a long moment of imagining him saying a Hebrew prayer, rose to greet him, the man who lacked his plumbing, and introduced him to Jim, who seemed only vaguely interested in shaking hands. Then Applebaum was steered to a seat, and Farragan noticed for the first time that all the Beach Haven friends sat together: Marie and Muriel, the sisters Glennis, Binky and himself. Only the estranged Serafina and his daughters were lacking. In time the rosary was recited, and Applebaum knelt down with the Catholics to pray for Anna's immortal soul.

"How many did you count, Arthur?" Jim asked him the following morning at the cemetery. They stood with Margaret, Edmund, and Muriel in the shade of a large tent that had been erected over the Farragan family plot for the burial service and watched the last of the mourners' cars drive off. Behind them, Anna's coffin was slowly lowered into the hole.

"I got one hundred and twenty," Farragan replied. Jim scribbled furiously on a small pad, then checked his calculations a long moment.

"I read one thirty-one," Jim told him.

"One hundred and twenty, Jim," Margaret said.

"One hundred and twenty, Jim," Muriel said in support.

"I lost count," Edmund confessed.

"My God, there were one hundred and twelve in mother's cortege and we dared to think that was a Philadelphia record. But then it's Anna's turn and there's one hundred and twenty. Jesus! If only she could have been here to see it! Think how proud she'd be, Arthur!"

"I can't help feeling she's here with us now at this very moment and delightedly observing," Edmund said, casting his eyes convincingly upward—toward Heaven, perhaps. Jim, as always, paying full heed to the possibilities of the spiritual, looked piously into the sun, then began blubbering again into his handkerchief. Margaret and Muriel merely bowed their heads. Farragan, for his part, thought of kicking his brother the priest in the ass and throwing him into the hole with Anna for good measure. For the cleric had made the Solemn High Requiem Mass in the cathedral, where he as celebrant was assisted by two bishops, into an absolute life triumph for their sister, Anna. Before the final prayers he had preached a gratuitous eulogy of more majestic proportions than he had ever employed in all the previous years of his ministry: lauding Anna's charity and patriotism; her self-sacrifice and loving kindness; her hope for universal peace and spirited defense of the one True Church.

The amazons of Anna's women's clubs who sat behind the family in unceasing cloaked and colorful rows had belched and sobbed in response. Their occasional loud shouts of agreement gave the stately old cathedral the instant flavor of somebody else's low-brow evangelical religion, rather than Farragan's preferred brand of formal chant-ridden Catholicism.

Across from the immediate family, the dead souls had also belched and wept. In the first pew of that side had sat Marie, Farragan's woman, the sisters Glennis, and Binky Applebaum. Once, Marie had turned her head toward him and smiled ruefully past the edge of her mourning veil at the judgment of Edmund on Anna's generosity: Jesus Christ, Farragan thought in that instant, how conveniently one lays aside the truth at a time like this. Anna hated more than she could possibly love: Negroes and the Viet Cong, the unions and the Democrats; everything except her church, the Republican far Right, and Malcolm, her son, beside whom she had minutes before been laid to rest.

"We ought to go quickly to the house. The guests will be arriving already," Jim said, urging them toward the limousine. Farragan winced as he recalled that the funeral supper this time was to be a garden party held on Jim's lawn in a humid heat for more than eight hundred guests. He decided he would work hard at getting drunk. That way he would have a reasonable excuse for not comprehending when Jim climbed on his back again sometime later in the day about the necessity for killing Simon.

# CHAPTER 14

## Serafina Guards
## the Liberty Bell

On the Monday after Anna's funeral Farragan was signing checks in the terminal office when the restless urge to be outside and walking the streets overcame him. Little would be placed in jeopardy by his absence, he decided. More and more, through coteries of long-time employees, the place seemed to run itself. He looked out a window into the terminal yard and watched a black driver skillfully ease the back end of a trailer up to a loading platform and realized, as on the last night of Anna's wake, that he still did not know the man's name—or, from this distance, even the make of the tractor he commanded. But that was only a measure of his near indifference. With Anna dead and buried, Farragan guessed that Zephyr Motor Freight had reached the height of its expansion. Beyond replacing some of the older stock and bettering hauling times to their customers in the South, Farragan had no particular ambitions for the line. Except that he meant to have the Zephyr trademark on the trucks redesigned if he could get Jim drunk enough to agree to it. The fey smiling leprechaun holding a banner that read ZEPHYR MOTOR FREIGHT against the broad green background of a four-leaf clover had always incensed him. Now, with Anna dead and gone, they might, God willing, advance to a more American motif.

In time he was finished with the checks and left the office to drive into center city. He parked the car in a lot and stood a long moment trying to decide whether to walk west toward the Penn campus or east to Independence Hall and Society Hill. In the end, he decided on the Liberty Bell. The Penn kids all looked like Simon to him, and he considered he had failed there, and the sight of each of their individual concerned faces was a painful reminder to him.

He marched down Walnut Street, past the Jefferson Hospital, and came to Independence Mall, where he took up a seat for a time to watch the eternal busloads of Girl Scouts and fat patriotic ladies unloading before the shrine. Already, though it was a scant few days after the end of the Chicago convention, cars plied the street before him with Humphrey-Muskie stickers on their bumpers. In a way, Farragan decided, he was pleased that the assassin had chosen to bomb Anna out of existence the week of the convention. One happy result had been to keep Jim's head away from the TV screen and silence the inevitable foul-mouthed denunciations of the demonstrators he might be counted on to make. Great thanks for that bit of peace and quiet, then.

But some certain instinct told Farragan he would not be hearing any unbearable loud mumbling from Jim for some time to come. His brother had arrived at the terminal that morning ashenfaced and shattered-looking with the twitchings of a bad hangover and admitted to Farragan for the first time the unsolicited news that Edward, his son, had indeed been married to Dr. Carter's daughter by a J.P. and was living in Dr. Carter's home next door to his in Cape May. Watching him, Farragan's instinct had been to deliver up an enthusiastic congratulations, pouring quarts of salt into the wound while it stood open, but instead he had merely said, "I'm sorry," and gone into his office.

There had been no mention of Simon, though Farragan had lived in heightened anticipation of his son's necessarily being the first subject of discussion come Monday morning.

After perhaps fifteen minutes, Farragan stood up and walked across the street to Independence Hall to see the Liberty Bell. It was always a singular pleasure. He entered with a troop of Girl Scouts marching in single file and saw immediately the ponderous bulk of Emilio Serafina, to whom he had not spoken in more than a year, leaning against a wall and intently watching the bell through a line of tourists. Automatically, Farragan searched for Serafina's trackers. One stood in a corner watching the mogul over that morning's *Daily News*. The other, the blond Nebraskan, Farragan now remembered passing on his way up the front steps of the building.

"Arturo. . . ."

"Hello, Emilio. How have you been?"

"Can't complain, Arturo. I heard about your sister. Any idea who did it?"

"Any number of possibilities. The police are working on it now. What are you doing here? Touring?"

"No, I'm guarding the Liberty Bell."

"What are you talking about?"

"No, I mean it, Arturo. I watched the Democrats out there in Chicago and I started thinkin' what if some of those boogies from the ghetto or some of those peace demonstrators wanted to make trouble here in Philly? What gesture of greater defiance could they make than to come down here and knock over the Liberty Bell? It's cracked, Arturo. If it falls over, it would probably break in half and that would be the end of it. I couldn't stand for that, Arturo. Mama brought me here many times when I was just a little boy. I've often brought my own children here on a Saturday morning."

"There are guards here, Emilio. Nobody's going to knock over the Liberty Bell."

"I think somebody will. I come here every day now around the peak period at noon to give them a hand. I'm carryin' a gun. With my two bloodhounds, that makes three extra guards, although those two don't know yet why they're here."

"All this seems very patriotic of you, Emilio," Farragan said wryly.

"I know, Arturo, and besides, I hope it will put me in better standing with the Feds when my case comes to court. I've been indicted. A judge would have to do a lot of thinkin' before he slapped a heavy sentence on the man who saved the Liberty Bell, right?"

"Right, Emilio," Farragan answered distantly. Inside, he decided nothing was pure. His total impulse was to rush across the room and kiss the curve of the beloved bell before it grew a definitive moss coating in rejection of Serafina's defilement. Instead he turned irritably to watch the gangster's near-by tracker watching him.

"My name is Arthur Farragan. You know me from Beach Haven," he called across to the agent, furious that on certain days a slit-eyed sleuth hiding behind his *Daily News* was the best the government had to offer you in return for the incessant paying of high taxes.

"How are your daughters, Emilio?" he asked after a long moment, during which the agent failed to acknowledge him.

"Gone. The both of them. Two weddings in one month. Both were pregnant. Didn't even bother to finish school. Both married guys that if you ask me are just fortune hunters. What the hell good does it do to send them to the nuns' school that has a ten-foot-high fence around it when two guys like those can get in at them anyhow?"

"Maybe they broke out and found the guys."

"Not my daughters, Arturo. That's not the way I raised them. You should see the one Giulietta landed. He wears French suits and has hair almost all the way down to his ass. They come to the house to show me my granddaughter and Giulietta sits there for hours and plays with his hair. She combs it for him and kisses it and even puts it in her mouth. And he's a practicing Catholic, just like me, to boot. That's the part I can't figure out. Sweet Christ, you'd think he'd at least have another religion so you could blame it all on something you don't understand. Arturo, you should see it when they go outside on the lawn. My neighbors come and take pictures. After all the money I've spent partying it up with people in my block, I now get sly, unsolicited photographs of my daughter and son-in-law in the mail. A lot of good it ever did me, all those nuns and special diets."

"You can never tell how they're going to turn out," Farragan said. But that was all. He stood for a long moment beside Serafina, who closely scrutinized the shuffling line of tourists, looking, Farragan supposed, for his inevitable group of blacks or long-haired dissenters who meant to knock over the Liberty Bell. But none showed face—at least in that interval—and Farragan prepared to leave.

"Arturo, wait. You look sad. The news about my daughters upset you pretty much, huh? I know how you used to like them. Listen, I know it's a bad thing to suggest just a few days after your sister is in the hole, but how would you like to go to the track? Like we used to. We could have drinks and lunch at Garden State, maybe even win a little money. I've got two secretaries out in the car. They're funny, Arturo. I chose them myself for their sense of humor. What do you say? You need a little cheerin' up."

"O.K., Emilo, let's go."

They bade the bell a reverent good-by and left Independence Hall to walk to the old Customs House, where Serafina's Bentley convertible sat outside in the sun with the engine running to keep the two comic secretaries properly air conditioned. Serafina yanked open the door and dove into the back seat between the two girls, who were almost exactly what Farragan might have expected: young and stupid, the age of the mogul's departed daughters whom he had once locked up behind tall convent fences with nuns. Farragan sat up front with the driver.

"Arthur, this is Naomi. Her friend here is Geraldine."

Naomi was evidently for Farragan. Geraldine was already taken: she was barely able to acknowledge Farragan from behind the bent crook prison of her boss's vast arm.

"Did any niggers come today to bother the bell, Emilio?" Naomi asked.

"None today, honey. But I got a feelin' there's trouble comin' one of these days. We won't worry about that any more today, though. Put down the top, George. We're goin' over to the track at Garden State to cheer Arthur up. His sister was just buried a couple of days ago."

"What did she die from, Arthur?" Naomi asked. "A heart attack?"

They were moving then into the cobbled approach to the Ben Franklin Bridge, and, half-turned, Farragan saw the driver race into the express lane that Muriel always favored and, like her, hurtle across toward New Jersey at twenty miles above the limit. Behind them, the Federal Ford was in close pursuit.

"She was blown to bits by a bomb," Farragan said evenly. At the same instant he felt the car swerve into the oncoming lane as the driver turned his head sharply, then regained control.

"Oh, my God! Who could have done such a thing?" Geraldine asked.

"It's too bad your sister is dead, Arturo," Serafina said, leaning forward, "but a lady like that had to have lots of enemies. Those times I met her down at Beach Haven she had a righteous or outraged opinion about nearly every damn thing. She's the only one of your family that ever put up a beef about those colored guys the union was taking in. Gubbiatti the union man told me that. She used to call him up and give him hell all the time. Once he went over to her house on Panama Street and she was downstairs in the basement with a revolver shootin' at a cardboard mockup of a boogie. Did you know about that, Arthur?"

"Yes," Farragan said mutedly, "I knew."

"If you ask me, Arturo, some of those boogies got wise to that shootin'-gallery stiff and rigged that greenhouse of hers."

"I don't want to talk about it any longer, Emilio."

There was a long silence while Farragan felt the two girls staring into his back, fearful, he supposed, but at least fascinated by his proximity to such an event. To Farragan, the situation was delightfully ironic: in his most romantic presumption, he had always imagined that Serafina lived in a world where bomb murders were daily fare. Now to find that he, one of the righteously Catholic Farragans, was an object of someone else's romantic illusion was almost unbearable comedy. Seated in the brilliant Bentley, anointed by the bright sunlight of a late-summer day that was broken intermittently by the great towers of the bridge, Farragan gave way to his own years-long ongoing personal fantasy:

He was Gatsby, isolated in his own bucket seat, in the casual company of two hoods and two comic secretaries, crossing the bridge into Manhattan in the 1920s: the height of his romantic self-vision. Farragan had read *The Great Gatsby* thirty-one times in the five years since the twins were born and Muriel had fled frightened into the mental mists. The characters and situation were hardly analogous, but he conveniently equated the end point of his own and Gatsby's ultimate quest. They shared the cup of incredible hope: as Gatsby should have his Daisy, so Farragan might return his arms about his beloved Muriel, and he had spent many lonely evenings in his Wynnewood home with Muriel away at the shore weeping bitterly (when he had enough Scotch in him) that Fitzgerald had not thought better to put a happy ending in the book. Now he closed his eyes and thought of being young and clad in knickers and appropriately golden, and imagined the Manhattan towers coming up to meet them.

When he opened his eyes they were already at the toll booths on the Jersey side of the Delaware. Beyond was the squalidness of Camden, Philadelphia's sister city.

They crept with the traffic into the track, then went up to the pavilion restaurant, where Serafina had already reserved them a table. Naomi fell conveniently into place beside Farragan, and in the elevator he took the liberty of reaching to touch the outline of her bikini panties that he had seen through her billowing dress, as she had intended. In response, she looked gratified.

"I got good tips, Arturo, today," Serafina told him when they were seated. "Play Kit Karson to win in the first race. He can't miss. Do you want to order some lunch?"

"I could use a drink first, Emilio."

"I'm hungry, Arthur," Naomi said. "I left home at seven this morning and didn't have time even for a cup of coffee."

"Then we'll have to feed you," Farragan said.

He called a waiter and they ordered. Then he sent down a bet to the windows: twenty dollars on Kit Karson. They waited for the first race to begin, and Naomi talked quietly with Farragan about her hunger.

"I can't understand what's wrong with me, Arthur. I'm always so hungry. I tried dieting with one of those plans but had to give it up because I was so edgy and irritable."

Farragan looked closely at the girl: she was only slightly over-
weight, and he wanted to tell her she was unnecessarily concerned.
But the dumbness of her face that told she would be accidentally
pregnant before the year's end and her allegiance to Serafina rankled
him. So he told her, "You probably have a tapeworm, Naomi."

"Do you think so, really, Arthur?"

"It sounds like it to me."

"Arturo, what the hell are you tellin' her that for?" Serafina interrupted. "She doesn't have a worm. And she worries too much as
is without havin' somethin' like that on her mind. You don't have
a worm, Naomi honey."

"Why tell her that, Emilio, if she actually does have a worm?
She should have it looked after. You know those damn things can
get to be twenty feet long. I believe you can actually die of malnu-
trition because of them."

"You mean he eats everything I put into me?" Naomi said.

"That's how he grows so big. In the end, he gets ninety per
cent and you get ten per cent. Do you ever feel irritable and tired?"

"Lots of times. Look at the circles under my eyes. I often can't
sleep at nights either."

"Jesus Christ, Arturo, there's about forty seconds till the first
race. How can she enjoy it if she's imagining she's got a tapeworm?"

"I'm not imagining it, Emilio. I really do have it," Naomi
said.

"You didn't even know you could have one until Arturo here
suggested it. It was only a suggestion after all."

"Do you have loose bowel movements, Naomi?" Farragan
asked. Below them, beyond the glass, the crowd rose with a roar as
the horses burst from the starting gate. At their table, three pairs of
eyes waited on Naomi's admission.

"Yes," she said simply, then burst into tears.

"What should we do with her, Arturo?" Serafina asked submissively.

"I don't think there's any reason to ruin our day, Emilio. We'll just buy Naomi a few drinks to put the thing under the weather, then take her to a clinic for an X ray after the race."

"But how can I sit here for nine races when I know I have that thing inside me?"

"You might not think about it," Serafina said angrily. "You might've been carryin' the thing around inside you for years. Is two more hours goin' to hurt?"

"Calm yourself, Naomi," Farragan urged. "Have a drink. That will slow him down for a few hours."

Below, from the corner of his eye, Farragan saw the horses rounding the far turn. Number six, Kit Karson, was in second place at the rail. Across from him, Naomi wolfed down the killer drink and called for another. Serafina looked at her with a kind of reverence as if she bore the Holy Spirit rather than a tapeworm. The other girl, Geraldine, looked at her as if she were unclean. Kit Karson had slipped into third place coming into the stretch.

"Kit Karson isn't going to win, Emilio," Farragan said.

"It's only one race, Arturo. There's eight more. Listen, tell me somethin'. If she has the worm, like you think, how do they get rid of it?"

"It depends on how long it is, Emilio," Farragan said knowledgeably. "If it's shorter than six feet, she takes some pills and defecates the segments. If it's longer, they often have to operate because it doubles back on itself and starts to strangle the small intestine. Unless they operate, it's almost impossible to get all the segments out."

Below, at the finish, Kit Karson came in fourth. Above, Serafina held a weeping Naomi against his chest.

"Holy Christ, Arturo, is there any way to catch it? I mean, is it contagious?"

"You can pick up the eggs through sexual intercourse," Farragan explained in what he guessed was the neatest one-liner of his life.

"Emilio . . ." Naomi suddenly raised her head to stare at her boss.

"Holy Mother of God!" Serafina cried, turning instantly pale and crossing himself.

"You bastard!" Geraldine, the other secretary, hissed at him.

"Kit Karson came in fourth," Farragan informed the three of them.

"I gotta go, Arturo," Serafina said. "I gotta take Naomi to the doctor. I'll leave Geraldine here to keep you company. Just get her back to Philly afterward and put her in a cab, O.K.?"

"You better take Geraldine, too, Emilio," Farragan said, winking.

"Yeah, you're right, Arturo," the mogul said, rising, his face suddenly becoming a great wreath of a smile. There was conspiracy here. He walked round to Farragan and whispered in his ear. "Personally, I don't think I have it, since I never have runny shits. But it's good to be on the safe side."

"You're absolutely right, Emilio."

"Arturo, do me a favor. Here's my bet money in this envelope with a list of the horses I picked for each race and how much I want to lay on them. Play it for me, O.K., and I'll pick up the winnings next week in the city from you?"

Farragan smiled wanly as Serafina began retreating.

"Good-by, Mr. Farragan," Geraldine said.

"Good-by, Geraldine. Good-by, Naomi."

"Good-by," Naomi said miserably. Then they were gone, with Serafina shepherding the worm-bearing one solicitously.

Farragan continued to sit at the table. On the second race he bet a hundred dollars of Serafina's money on a horse called Raintree to win. He bet twenty dollars of his own on Flamingo, the favorite. Raintree came in sixth and Flamingo first. Farragan began to see the pattern: there was twelve hundred dollars left in the envelope, all of it slated for horses with middling-high odds. Even if as many as three of Serafina's choices came in, Farragan decided he might cover any winnings out of Serafina's own money. But he sensed that none of the mogul's nags were going to come in. He put the twelve hundred into his pocket, declined sending down a bet for himself, called for another drink, and watched the third race. He had already made his money today, then, and it pleased him, especially since it came from the purse of Serafina, where one absolutely got nothing for nothing.

During the fourth race he asked for a telephone and called Marie to tell her he was quite sure that Anna's killer was not Emilio Serafina.

"That's too bad," she said. "It would have been convenient to have him to blame it on. He's part of a convincing tradition, after all. As it stands, I still think you did it. What were you really doing that day you went into the city for contract talks?"

"I was involved in contract talks."

"If you say so, Arthur. . . ."

"You really don't care if I killed her or not, do you?"

"Not especially. If you did, I think it would have been a nice, deliberate act on your part for a change. You're weak in that way, Arthur. But otherwise it might have been one of those women she was always competing against for high office in her organizations."

"Those dames are all so fat they couldn't possibly bend over far enough to connect the wires."

"Then who did it?"

"Nobody did it. We imagined it. Just be thankful it's done. I haven't had a gram of remorse over it. Listen, can you drive over here to the track? You might get here for the last two races, then we can sit and have something to drink and watch the crowds file out and try to figure out who did it. There's nothing so beautiful as the sunset at Garden State when the crowds are filing out and you've managed to steal a few bucks from the likes of Emilio Serafina."

"One of my young men is coming to pick me up for dinner, Arthur."

"Call him and tell him you're ill."

"That seems too indulgent, Arthur. There have got to be a few young men coming around here for my aunts to remain appeased. We've discussed all that. Remember?"

"Yes, but for this once couldn't you just call and explain that you're sick? Otherwise we might never get a chance to sit down again and figure out who killed Anna."

"All right. You win. I think I actually love you a bit. But it will take me at least half an hour to get there."

"In the pavilion restaurant. I'll wait for you there." He was about to tell her he loved her a bit too, but decided he could not take the risk.

In half an hour, in the middle of the seventh race, Farragan looked up to see her coming across the room. Heads turned inquisitively at the sight of her, and Farragan for the first time felt a curious panglike terror over growing old and losing her pass through him. For the instant—but merely for the instant—he permitted himself to think that she was even more beautiful than Muriel.

She sat down wordlessly, and Farragan ordered her a drink. They watched quietly through the eighth and ninth races, and sat for an hour afterward while the great crowd dissipated, but did not speak of Anna. Later they went to Wynnewood, where they swam another time in the pool and made love in Farragan's bed.

# CHAPTER 15

## *Jim Also Goes to Meet His Jesus*

On the Wednesday after his winning Monday at the track Farragan was committed to be part of the Knights of Columbus guard of honor for the auxiliary bishop at evening confirmation ceremonies in Saint Theresa's Church. His daughters were not old enough to be confirmed, so there was no need for Muriel to come up from the shore, and Farragan contented himself in that direction by phoning her before he left the office to deliver the weather report of an impending gale and remind her, as always, to get in touch with Binky Applebaum in the event of any trouble. Then he rose wearily from his desk, girding himself for the prospect of driving home and facing up to Mrs. Crow for yet another tear-drenched meal.

Crow had been cooking and crying by day in Farragan's deserted home since Anna's funeral, enjoying a therapeutic working layover until the hopeful advent of another position as housekeeper for people who must needs be of Irish descent and rigidly Catholic.

"I'd want them to be just as good and Catholic as the Farragans themselves," she had told him on each of the five days since Anna was covered over, forgetting after the first that she had said it only the day before.

"I don't think you're going to find any other people quite as good or Catholic as the Farragans, Crow," he responded ruefully each time.

"Well, yes, Arthur, you're right about that," she conceded. But that was all. Desperately, since her arrival, Farragan had prayed for the existence of another family of Farragans and racked his memory for the name of any kin or associates with an elderly unattached lady in their ranks who might help fulfill Crow's aspiration of live-in companion slave. He needed to get her the hell out of his house. This evening he entered and found himself confronted inevitably at the end of a blazing September day with one of her special starch-and-potato dinners that Anna had favored over her doctor's advice, and which might have been counted on to do her in eventually anyhow if a bomb had not.

He ate his meal at the kitchen table, while Crow, finished weeping, sat in a corner and deftly polished his K. of C. sword from her past experience with Anna's three husbands and let him in on the neighborhood dirt that some young man four houses away whom Farragan did not know had recently gotten a girl pregnant and was about to marry her.

"I wouldn't go to that wedding, Arthur. Wild horses couldn't drag me there."

"Have you received an invitation, Mrs. Crow?"

"No, but I still wouldn't go. I'd want them to know I disapproved. Young people these days think premarital sex is theirs for the asking. Anna's Malcolm never did anything like that. He died a virgin. It's upsetting, her dead and your neighbor getting married for that reason all in the same week."

"I don't know my neighbor, Crow," Farragan said.

"Thank God for that blessing, Arthur. You're spared that trial of conscience."

Grateful for being spared any trial of conscience, Farragan finished dinner, dressed in his tux and plumed hat, retrieved his sword from Crow, and drove to Saint Theresa's, where a man from his chapter directed him to go to the sacristy behind the church. Inside were about thirty other Knights, standing and talking in little groups. In a corner, near the portable baptismal font, Farragan spied Mahoney, who always asked after Simon, and determined to stay away from him. He eased into a circle and was immediately aware of his polite, reserved acceptance: they all still had Anna's death on their minds. He imagined that the particular horror of that leave-taking and the seeming lack of any solution had kept the telephone wires sizzling all week.

"Arthur," one called Fitzpatrick, who was born in Ireland and whom Farragan always got the urge to kick in the crotch, addressed him in brogue, "have you heard anything else about poor Anna's killin'?"

"Absolutely nothing. The police have no idea who it was. Neither have we, the family."

"If ya ask me, it was Vietniks or Communists who done it. Ya all know how she felt about the war, what with her Malcolm gettin' killed over there. Here, Arthur, have a little nip of this. It'll make ya feel better."

The flask of rye was half full, and Farragan knew from the ring of suddenly sheepish faces that it had already made a round within yards of the church's main altar.

"To the Knights for helping me in my bereavement," Farragan proposed, taking a long sip.

"A little of this and you'll forget her, though God knows she was a fine woman," Fitzpatrick said, taking another swig. Farragan saw the fire leap into his eyes. His nose seemed to grow distended and bulbous on the instant.

"It wouldn't surprise me if it was one of those women she was always locked in a power struggle with in some of those organizations she belonged to," another called Welsh surmised.

"That's a possibility," Farragan easily conceded, out to wreck the system. "My sister had a credible number of enemies."

"There were a lot of things that were pretty damn brutal about your Anna, Arthur," Welsh said. "I remember once at the parish picnic when she threw a drink, glass and all, against the wall because the bartender hadn't mixed it right for the second time. I mean, cripes, it was only a church picnic and not the Hilton bar."

"I don't know if you can imagine the possibility," Farragan muttered to Welsh, whom he liked, "but it's a blessing she's dead and taken all her hatreds with her."

"Amen to that, in Christ's name," Welsh replied.

"Well I, for one, won't agree to that, Arthur," said Fitzpatrick, who had overheard. "She was a fine and generous woman all her life, and if I hadn't married my Catherine, I certainly would have chosen Anna Farragan."

"You deserve each other," Welsh pronounced after another swig from Fitzpatrick's bottle. On the instant, Fitzpatrick drew his sword and held it against Welsh's chest.

"Let me draw mine, Fitzpatrick," Welsh begged. "I'll kill you with it."

"Go ahead," Fitzpatrick offered gallantly. They all watched, forming a circle, as Welsh yanked out his sword and lunged at his milkman opponent. Drink was the better part of the thrust, Farragan guessed. Through the sacristy door, beyond which hundreds waited in the church for the bishop to show, came the low rumble of warm-up organ music. Inside the sacristy, Fitzpatrick reeled and flung himself at the diminutive Welsh. The latter, like Errol Flynn, dodged and parried and slapped at Fitzpatrick's buttocks with the flat of his blade. There were guffaws of laughter, until a burly priest whom Farragan had never seen before walked in from the altar and demanded, "What the hell's going on here?"

"It's a duel, Father," Farragan told him. "The sacred stuff of antiquity lives on still."

"Well, save it until after the ceremony," the cleric said, grabbing Fitzpatrick's free arm. "His Eminence is waiting out front in his car. You guys are supposed to be lined up along the main aisle by now."

Welsh and Fitzpatrick were quieted down by several men each and fitted back into their plumed hats. Farragan, along with the rest of the Knights, hastened out the sacristy's rear door behind the gruff-spoken priest, who trotted through the long garden in the darkness, following the meandering path that led toward the front of the church. The Knights, by twos, trotted behind him, their plumes bobbing and swords clanking. Beside Farragan, Fitzpatrick drew his cape close about him and flailed his hip as with a crop, and Farragan was caused to remember the other's proposal during one meeting that they buy up all the old black police horses for the Knights to ride in parade: Fitzpatrick, evidently, was mounted astride one of them now.

In front, they dodged through the lines of confirmation candidates dressed tentatively like angels in robes of white and surged up the steps to range themselves by twos along the main aisle. Fitzpatrick stood opposite him, his sword, like Farragan's own, held rigidly before his face. In moments, to the martial whirrings of the organ, the file of candidates and their sponsors began entering the church from the soft September night. Some of the young ones Farragan knew, but only a few, and it occurred to him that, except for the payment of tithes and attendance at Sunday Mass, his activities in the parish had gone into a real slump since Muriel's retreat into the mists.

The presence of numbers of adults near the end of the line surprised Farragan, until he recalled that converts were confirmed also after their baptism into the faith. He thought distastefully of El Greco and wondered if he were still at Saint Blaise with Edmund, searching for the proper entry portal to Catholicism: Let him be denied knowledge of that special avenue, O Lord. Keep the club membership select.

In another moment a black man passed before them, and Fitzpatrick opposite tried to meet Farragan's eyes with a look of visible rage. Fuck you, Fitzpatrick, Farragan thought, I wouldn't give you the satisfaction. The milkman's fury only served to bolster an abiding heresy in himself: there were days you could leave the Church and take your wife and progeny with you because people like Fitzpatrick were your fellow communicants. For Farragan's purposes, Fitzpatrick, except for the fact that he delivered milk, was a Feverer, the mountain bus driver of Philadelphia—a person Farragan unhappily had few defenses against. Part of the problem was the fault of their mutual religion, he reasoned. One trouble with Catholicism was that it encompassed a welter of vertical ethnic divisions. No high church–low church to keep Farragan and his Muriel apart from Fitzpatrick and his fat Catherine and their ten carotene-looking children: the shit and the gold lumped together in dubious cohesion, as Farragan saw it.

The bishop was coming. The music boomed and swelled with the suggestion of triumphant entry as he swept close to Farragan's post along the aisle. Across from him, Fitzpatrick turned his head behind the upheld sword and smiled obsequiously at the prelate. Incredibly, the latter reached out and touched Fitzpatrick's arm, smiling also. Then he swished past Farragan, a rich man, whom he did not notice.

"Arthur," Fitzpatrick whispered joyfully through the ranks of priests who came behind the bishop, "did you see how he touched me?"

"Yes," Farragan said out loud, so that heads turned all about him. "Yes, that was very nice," he added. Fitzpatrick, for his part, looked a trifle uncertain.

Oh, Jesus, Farragan thought, if there were only a way to bring down the sword he held in his hands and cleave Fitzpatrick's skull in two and still call it an accident. If only. But there were too many witnesses. A whole church full of them. Even now a child on the pew beside him—the prosecution's perfect innocent and emotional testifier—pulled mischievously at his cape.

In moments more the bishop was seated on the main altar, and at a click sound from the Knights' leader, Farragan advanced to the middle of the aisle to gravely touch swords with Fitzpatrick, then turned to begin the measured filing out of the church until their services were needed on the prelate's exit. Outside, after the heavy scent of candle wax and incense, Farragan gratefully drew in the warm night air, then made a beeline for Welsh and Mahoney, who were taking up seats on the church steps. Once beside them, Farragan, who did not smoke, asked Welsh for a cigarette. He lit it and leaned back to blow amateur puffs into the atmosphere as Fitzpatrick tumbled into place next to him.

"We should've bought them horses that time I proposed it at the meetin'," Fitzpatrick said to no one in particular.

"What the Christ for? Who'd take care of them?" Mahoney asked.

"Oh, somebody would. We'd find a way. But that's not the important part. It's the romance I'm thinkin' of. Wouldn't it thrill you, Arthur, to come out here and see a line of black horses tied up to the rectory fence, snortin' and clompin' in the darkness and waitin' to bear us off when the bishop was gone?"

"No," Farragan answered.

"Well, it would me. Cripes, just thinkin' about it is the only thing that keeps me goin'. All I've got in the world otherwise is the wife and ten kids and my mortgage and the insurances and a friggin' milk route. If I didn't have the Knights and my horse dream, I don't know what I'd do. Most of the time when I'm peddlin' milk in Kensington I pretend we're ridin' through Society Hill to old Saint Joseph's Church. It'd be a real nice sound with a lot of horses clatterin' over that cobblestone in the churchyard all at once, wouldn't it?"

Farragan, witlessly clutching his amateur cigarette, stared like Mahoney and Welsh beside him past the place of the waiting horses to the long files of parked cars in the street. It was for the other's incredible honesty that he so despised Fitzpatrick, he decided on the instant. No man should leave himself so vulnerable to his fellows. Somehow, the milkman's horse fantasy, with its hint of pain, was equal to Farragan's own fevered wish that he might know Muriel again before it was too late. Not a thing he would ever divulge to a line of plumed and cape-covered men seated on a rise of church steps in a Philadelphia September night. One also had to take into consideration the listener's capacity for embarrassment.

Beyond the cars, in a park across the boulevard, crickets chirped and frogs croaked in a lily pond. Inside the church, the bishop had already begun sparring with the confirmation candidates, the special lilt of his voice forcing the rhythmic cadence of question-and-answer that Farragan knew by heart from the many years of serving in Knights of Columbus honor guards. All told, it was a boring ritual. In response to the prelate's query: How can we be saved? Welsh broke the silence of long minutes.

"If I had to do it all over again, I think I would have raised the lot of my kids Quakers and let it go with that."

"It's always the educated ones like you, Welsh, that heresy's rash breaks out on," Fitzpatrick said. "I don't see what the hell good it did you and Arthur to get graduated from Georgetown if you end up talkin' like that."

"Shut up, Fitzy," Farragan said. "You don't understand what we're talking about."

"Arthur, why are you always talkin' to me like that?" Fitzpatrick asked, whining. But he never finished.

At that instant a police cruiser pulled up before the church and discharged Mrs. Crow, who rushed toward him through the darkness, flailing her arms. "Arthur! Arthur!"

"What is it, Mrs. Crow?"

"Arthur, it's Jim, your brother!" she said breathlessly. "He's been blown to pieces by a bomb, just like Anna!"

"What in the name of God are you talking about?" Farragan demanded, seizing her arm.

"He turned the key in his car tonight at the terminal and a bomb went off under his seat! About twenty of your drivers saw it happen. The police telephoned, then they sent a car to the house to take you to the terminal for identification. Arthur, one officer told me it was so bad that there was a hole blown right through the roof of his Lincoln!"

"Arthur!" Fitzpatrick thrust in front of him. "There's somebody after your whole family. It must be Communists or somebody like that. We'll all go home with you, Arthur, and stand watch tonight to protect you."

"That'll be good, Arthur," Crow said. "What with the police, that'll make about forty armed men."

"Don't let him get into his car, for God's sake. It's liable to be wired," somebody said.

"The police are checking it out now," Crow told them. "There's a big bomb-squad truck around the corner. They're going

to make sure there's no bomb attached to the motor. I showed them
which one it was."

"They don't have the key," Farragan said softly, vaguely aware
that his stomach had contracted to a fist, and he thought that whenever it should open he was going to vomit.

"Don't you know they have the key to everything? They
looked at the car, Arthur, and found a key to it within minutes."

He let the news sink in with dumb resignation. At the entrance to the church a crowd had gathered from curiosity over the
noise and the eerie whirling of the police cruiser's dome light that
the cop inside had flipped on after Crow's arrival. Farragan found
himself being led away toward his own car by his fellow Knights.
Approaching, they heard the engine running.

"It's all clean," a cop said to Crow.

"This is Mr. Farragan, officer. The brother of the dead man."

"Is there anything left of him to identify?" Farragan asked the
cop weakly.

"Not much, sir. He went right through the roof of that
buggy."

"Oh, my God," Farragan cried. Then he turned to one side
and vomited, distantly aware that some of it was going to have to
land on someone's pants legs. When he lifted a handkerchief to his
mouth to wipe away the residue, Fitzpatrick was already steering
him into the car. Crow and Welsh sat in back. The plumed milkman took the steering wheel and eased onto the boulevard to follow
after a police car.

They drove to Farragan's home with a trail of cars behind
them, the bishop and his thunderous exiting instantly forgotten. At
the house, unmarked police cruisers were parked in the street and
Farragan's driveway also, and another bomb squad poked through
the shrubbery near the enclosed swimming pool. The inside of the
house, Crow informed him, had already been given the all-clear.

Once inside, Farragan asked to be left alone, and he went up-stairs to lie face down across his bed, shivering with spasms of his newly discovered terror: Anna's leavetaking, despite the pleasure it had brought him, was no mere gesture on the part of some kind soul who understood that the Farragans' sister would be better off dead. Someone—from either the inside or the outside—was after the clan Farragan. And after Jim, there remained but two others to be disposed of: Edmund and himself. On the instant he remembered Muriel and his twin daughters and wondered after their safety. He reached for the phone to dial his house in Beach Haven, then thought better of upsetting Muriel and phoned Binky Applebaum instead. There was an agonizingly long minute of no response until the receiver was lifted and Farragan heard a breathless panting on the other end.

"Binky, this is Arthur Farragan."

"Oh, hello, Mr. Farragan. I'm all out of breath from running in from the beach."

"Binky, a terrible thing has happened. My brother Jim has just been blown up by a bomb, just like our sister, Anna."

"Oh, that's terrible, Mr. Farragan."

"Binky, do you own a gun?"

"No, of course not. Why do you ask?"

"Because I'm afraid for Muriel, Binky. Some crazy person is after our family. It would be a perfect time for them to harm her down in Beach Haven while everyone's attention is focused here in Philadelphia. Binky, there are two rifles on the wall of my bedroom down there. The ammunition for the Winchester is on the left-hand side of the top shelf in my closet. Please sleep over there tonight and keep the gun ready. Just make some excuse to Muriel about your need to stay there."

"Mr. Farragan, I don't know anything about guns. I wouldn't even know how to load it."

"But you were in the Army in Korea. You were wounded there. You must know something about a gun."

"I was a payroll clerk in Finance, Mr. Farragan. My wound is from having the misfortune to sit down on the wrong seat of a jeep. It was booby-trapped."

"Oh, I see. I'm sorry it happened that way, Binky," Farragan said dimly. "Perhaps I'd better phone the police chief and have him check on Muriel."

"Don't worry, Mr. Farragan. I make up for it in other ways. I'm deadly with a bowie knife. I've brought down sea gulls on the wing at thirty feet with it. There's no need for alarm. I'll go there with my knives and stay over until morning."

"Are you sure it's O.K., Binky? I mean, if someone tries to get into the house with a gun . . ."

"I'll kill them, Mr. Farragan. Don't worry about anything. Muriel will be safe."

"Thank you, Binky. I must hang up now. I'll phone you to-morrow."

"Call me at your place, Mr. Farragan. I'll stay there all day to make sure everything is O.K."

"Yes, all right. Good-by, Binky."

It was a kind of relief anyhow, Farragan decided as he replaced the receiver in its cradle. He sat up to unbuckle the scabbard that was pinching his leg and listened for the downstairs noises: Crow, weeping anew, was passing out sandwiches and coffee to the Knights and the cops; Fitzpatrick assigned guard posts for the night to his sword-bearing brothers. Impulsively, despite the fresh horror of Jim's death, Farragan thought of ordering everyone out of his house. This, until he realized that under no circumstances did he intend to spend the night alone, or with only the additional company of Mrs. Crow, who would be too spooked to stay over anyhow. He listened to the heavy tread of feet mounting the steps and hoped desperately it would not be Fitzpatrick, whom he both despised and needed.

Granahan, the detective, a long-time friend of Jim's and of his, he supposed, lumbered slowly into the room without knocking. Farragan saw from the redness of his eyes that he had somewhere been crying this evening. He sat down heavily on a chair opposite the bed. Instinctively, Farragan sensed that his voice would be phlegm-coated.

"Who hates the Farragans so much, Arthur?" the cop asked after a long moment of staring into the carpeting.

"You tell me. I may be next in line. Or second choice as an alternative."

"I'm up against a wall. There doesn't seem to be a motive. We've checked out the union and all the crazy colored who might've hated Anna for her letters to the *Daily News* editor and all left-wing grenade-throwers who might not have taken kindly to her patriotism, and all the potential rival gun clubs to the one she belonged to. Nothing anywhere."

"If it's not an outside job then it's an inside job, Granny."

"We've thought of that. Your Muriel is sick, Edmund's a priest, and Margaret I've never seen on the street without Jim at her side. She's that helpless alone. Then, Malcolm is dead, Edward hasn't left his father-in-law's house in Cape May since he got married, and your Simon is studying in Montreal."

"He's dodging the draft in Montreal."

"Even less reason to try coming back into the States, then. And he hasn't tried, by the way. So that leaves only you."

"You think I did it?" Farragan asked incredulously.

"No, you didn't do it. I've had a tail on you all week long. But you were the only one who seemed to have a plausible motive. Who gets your trucking line with Jim and Anna gone, after all?"

"Me," said Farragan, realizing miserably for the first time that he now had the whole of something he had not even wanted a third share of formerly.

"But, like I said, you didn't do it. How do you know a character like Emilio Serafina, Arthur?"

"We were once the two chief contributors to the summer parish down at Beach Haven," Farragan said.

"Stay away from him. The Federals have a tail on him. You're liable to end up being subpoenaed when they get round to trying him."

"If I'm still alive. . . ."

"God willing," Granahan pronounced. "I mean that, Arthur. I'll do everything I can. I'm going to put a two-car watch on you, and I'll sleep with you myself at night if I have to. Jim wasn't a ᵔretty sight to look at. Arthur . . . how long has this thing with the Glennis girl been going on?"

"I wondered when you'd ask that."

"You met her at the track on Monday. She was in the house all alone with you last night until six this morning."

"I've been seeing her for about two years now, Granny. As discreetly as possible."

"Your secret is safe with the Philly police, Arthur. I gather, then, that Muriel is very sick."

"I'm afraid so, Granny."

"It's a strange life, Arthur. Your family always looked like pure gold from the outside, what with the money and the houses and big cars and the trips to Rome to see the Pope whenever the fancy overtook you. Now that I get closer to the inside, it starts to seem like a lot of tarnished copper."

"The fault is our mother's, Granny, if it needs to be explained. She somehow managed to convince the world that we were part of the papal nobility when we were merely Farragans."

"She was a great woman, Arthur."

"No, she wasn't, Granny. She was as deceitful as the day was long. Our father was the honest one. I guess that's why no one cared for him very much."

"Yes, well, getting back to the Glennis girl, Arthur, I want you to know she looks like the prime suspect so far. I shouldn't be telling you something like this, but you'd better prepare yourself emotionally in case it becomes necessary to book her."

"What the hell do you imagine Marie Glennis knows about explosives, Granny?"

"Don't be naïve, Arthur. She could've gotten hold of someone to do the job for her. Any bright young physics or chemistry major of her acquaintance might have done it competently enough."

"But why? What motive could she have? She didn't much care for Jim's or Anna's variety of politics, but with millions of other people in the country possessing the same mentality, I'm sure she would consider it a futile gesture to retaliate by starting with them."

"The motive is Zephyr Motor Freight, Arthur. I think we've seen the last of these killings. Now that she's made certain you've got the whole pie instead of only a third share, it's my guess she's about to go after the money."

"How ironic. Now that it's all mine, I intend selling it. I never particularly cared for it anyhow."

"So what? What will the terms of sale be? A dollar a year for the rest of your life? No matter what you decide, she can't lose. It's either money in the bank or money on the road. Tell me, Arthur, do you love her?"

"I don't want to continue this conversation, Granny. You're grasping at straws now. I thought police work was supposed to be methodical. This is too much theorizing."

"Would you like to go down to the morgue, Arthur, and see what is left of Jim?"

"No, not that."

"Then permit me the liberty of grasping at straws for a bit. What about those two old aunts of hers, the Glennis sisters? How well do you know them?"

"As well as anyone might who's been trying to keep away from them for the last twenty years. They're both nearly around the bend, as far as I'm concerned."

"So much so that you couldn't envision the possibility of their working in cahoots with the girl to make sure she was nicely settled with a wealthy husband when it came time for them to kick off?"

"Granahan, you are really crazy!"

"Am I, Arthur? People talk a lot about you and Muriel. I'll be blunt: all the people that you or I or Jim or Anna ever knew think you're a living saint for taking care of her these four or five years the way you have. But how long is a man supposed to remain emotionally involved with a sick woman? You've been seeing the other one for two years now. She's young and beautiful and apparently intelligent. Are you going to try to tell me that she hasn't gotten to you somehow?"

"She's gotten to me," Farragan confessed mutedly. On the instant he thought he might vomit again if he had not already lost all of his bilge near the church. The terror he had felt at the prospect of being next or alternative second in an unknown demon's plan to exterminate the clan Farragan was replaced by a greater terror at the notion the killings were part of the sinister machinations of someone in whom, despite his frenzied self, he had invested emotional goods. Not Marie! Not someone from their crowd in Philadelphia who lived in another suburb like Farragan's own, voted Democratic like himself and partook of identical Communion at the identical universal Mass on any given Sunday. His total impulse was to rush to his car and hasten into town to determine whether the beloved city of Marie and himself was still ordered this night as he had seen it that morning: that the art museum kept the same distance from the Cathedral, and the Academy of Music from City Hall. . . .

"Guard yourself, Arthur," Granahan said. "I shouldn't have told you what I did, but if it turns out she's the one, you're liable to be in a strait jacket after Jim and Anna from the shock."

"Yes, I'll be careful, Granny." He listened again to the tread of heavy feet mounting the stairs and heard the clinking of ice cubes in a glass besides. "You'd better go now," he told the cop. "That must be Edmund."

Granahan rose silently to open the door to the sight of Edmund, ashen-faced and shaking and glistening with sweat from the effort of his fear and the weight of his hunting jacket on a September night. He clutched a newly made drink in his fat hand.

"Someone is trying to murder our whole family, Arthur," he whined, then began to weep openly.

"Control yourself," Farragan said as Granahan eased out the door and closed it behind him. "Where's the strength of your priestly vocation now?"

"Don't make such poor jokes, Arthur. I choose to think of reality now. First Anna, then Jim. Both by the same means. It's obviously the same party. You say it's not the union or the colored people. Then it has to be Simon. You didn't do what you were supposed to do when you took that trip to Montreal. Was it because you couldn't find him, Arthur? If he wasn't there, I'll bet he was here in Philadelphia with false identification papers rigging up a bomb in Anna's greenhouse."

"You traitor bastard, you!" Farragan shouted at his brother. "You were supposed to be the great friend and drinking buddy of Simon's! No, it couldn't have been him. I saw him in Montreal. He was happily abed with some flower child named Alouette. Philadelphia was the furthest thing from his mind."

"If it wasn't Simon, who was it, Arthur?" Edmund begged, pouring down half his drink.

"I don't know. Neither do the police. I think we had both just better resign ourselves to the fact that the next time either of us opens a door or turns the ignition switch of a car we might be blown to pieces."

"But I don't want to die, Arthur. Not now. Now that Jim and Anna are gone, I can come down off that hill and find myself a woman. I can get married and live a whole life just like anybody else. I don't want to die when I can be free for the first time in my life."

"You're still a priest, Edmund," Farragan said evenly. "Don't forget that. Now why don't you finish your drink and go comfort Margaret, if she needs comforting, as a priest should."

"No, Arthur. I'm not leaving this room tonight. I'm not going anywhere in Philadelphia by myself."

"You're going to have to sleep on the floor, then," Farragan said savagely. "I'm not sharing my bed with you."

"I don't care. I'm just not leaving tonight."

Moments later, when Farragan had undressed and turned out the lights, Edmund lay down on the carpeting and covered himself with his hunting jacket. But Farragan, listening to his brother's small moans and tossings, could not sleep—until about three a.m., when the fat priest climbed into his bed and held him tightly about the chest the rest of the night until Crow wakened the two at eight in the morning to begin preparations for Jim's wake.

# CHAPTER 16

# Death of a Grand Tradition

The word was out, Farragan decided as he sat through the first naked evening of Jim's wake: somebody was after the Farragans, and the friends and retainers were afraid to show. Instead, they made up for their absences with floral tributes, and the first-story rooms of Jim's house were filled with wreaths and baskets. Now, in the soft pink lighting, two bees spun across the top of Jim's closed coffin on their way to another flower.

To himself, Farragan was vexed at Margaret and her plan for a three-day viewing. Under the circumstances, it was plainly absurd. But there was no changing her mind: incredibly, on hearing of Jim's death, she had completely rejected her ironist's conspiracy with Farragan and reverted to the infatuated time before her marriage, proclaiming that three days was hardly enough for such a great man, and vilifying Rome for failing to make her husband a Maltese Knight before his end had come. Farragan could scarcely fathom her new-found capacity for self-delusion, but he felt it would be pitiable in the extreme if no one came at all. Now there were only Edmund, Muriel, Margaret, and himself, and two plain-clothes policemen outside on the porch, who checked the constantly arriving floral wreaths for bombs. More police, Granahan's concession to the possibility of a mistake about Marie Glennis, ranged about the house in unmarked cars.

"We ought to have had a High Mass and buried him immediately afterward," Farragan said, breaking the unbearable silence after a time.

"We couldn't bury him just like that, Arthur," Margaret protested. "What might he say from up there now where he's looking down at us?"

"He might not be up there, Margaret," Muriel said suddenly. "He might have died with a mortal sin on his soul. Then he'd go straight to Hell. Remember what the Church teaches."

"Muriel, for Christ's sake!" Farragan assailed his wife for the first time ever. "That's not the sort of thing you say to a dead man's wife at his wake."

"But, Arthur, that's what we've always been taught. Weren't you taught that, Margaret?"

"In these special cases, Muriel dearest," Edmund said, scrambling frantically, "one always presumes the best for the deceased. Jim died so abruptly. Almighty God will certainly take this into consideration when making his judgment on our poor brother's soul. Also there's the fact of all the wonderful good he's done for the community and the Church. Margaret has no reason to fear about where Jim is now."

"But Arthur," Muriel went right on, "don't you remember that Benedictine priest who used to come to Saint Theresa's parish to give the mission? I can't remember his name. But each time he preached about dying unprepared in mortal sin. Remember that story he used to tell us about the locomotive engineer in the nine-

teen thirties who beat his wife, then went to work and drove his
engine straight into another one that was on the same track at sixty-
five miles per hour? Oh, Margaret," she turned to grasp the arm of
her sister-in-law, who looked as if she were about to topple over in
faint, "I was terrified. I can still hear the Benedictine standing on
the altar screaming like the engineer when the boilers burst and he
was being scalded to death. He tasted the punishment of his Eternity even in the last few seconds of his life, the priest used to say.
Don't you remember, Arthur?"

"No!" Farragan shouted. "And you don't either, Muriel! You
never heard a story like that in Saint Theresa's church!"

He glared at his wife for a long moment that Margaret, piti-
fully distressed, could not have failed to notice. But apparently the
barb finally penetrated Muriel's feeble-mindedness: the earnest question mark of her eyes receded into her normally childlike mien and
she was silent. Spent, Farragan buried his face in his hands rather
than have to look again at Margaret. But indeed he did remember
the Benedictine's story, and on the instant resolved the very next
morning to begin making daily confession in preparation for the
possibility of his own death. This was the merciless part of their
communal religion: there might be a Hell. There had to be something. No Farragan anywhere had ever been raised to believe one
could get off in life absolutely scot-free—their mother had seen to
that.

"Arturo, *paisan,* hello."

"Mr. Serafina!" Edmund leaped to his feet at the sight of the
gangster. "Welcome!"

The others stood up in absolute relief to shake hands with Serafina.

"A tragic happening. A truly tragic happening, Arthur."

"Yes, it certainly was. Do you know my sister-in-law, Margaret?"

"We've met before at Beach Haven," Margaret said. "It's kind of you to come here."

"It looks like you could use the company, Mrs. Farragan. These first nights are always still as death."

"Yes," agreed Muriel.

"Yes, indeed," said Margaret. There was an uncomfortable silence, then Serafina strode to the coffin and blessed himself. He lowered his head, closed his eyes, and apparently prayed deeply. After a minute, he turned to Farragan.

"By the way, Arturo, that girl Naomi didn't have a tapeworm like you thought she did."

"Didn't she, Emilio?" Farragan asked weakly.

"No, she was just a little run-down. You know how they get with too much work and worry."

"I'm glad she's in good health, then. Won't you have a little drink?"

"Just a small one is O.K. Have one with me, Arturo."

They left the others and went to the paneled dining room, where Crow sat weepy-eyed in a newly rented maid's uniform looking at the sea of food that Farragan feared was on its way to spoiling.

"I hear there's a lot of guys afraid to come to your brother's viewing, Arturo. Gubiatti the union man tells me he got calls from important people seriously worried. That is, they want to live. That's why you got so many flowers, I guess. He's also havin' some problems with your drivers. I heard a little story today that about thirty guys paid some suicidal nigger you got workin' for you down there five bucks apiece to turn over their truck engines for them this morning. They all figure somebody else's management is trying to run you out of business."

"It's not that. I'm sure of it. We don't have any direct competition in that sense. We purposely went after the long-distance

Southern routes so we wouldn't have to waste energy bidding against everybody else on local contracts. Those drivers aren't thinking about a walkout, are they, Emilio?"

In the instant he asked the question it came to Farragan that Serafina was indeed a man of many parts. To the buffoon who guarded the Liberty Bell on his lunch hour, Farragan must beg to know what his own drivers were about to do. Otherwise, no one was entirely certain what the mogul did for a living, or where he did it, though obviously it was highly remunerative. Farragan's notion had always been that Serafina held immense, unpublicized powers in multitudes of personal fiefs connected to him like spokes to the hub of a big, hairy wheel.

"I won't let them pull a walkout, Arturo. But they won't send up a delegation either. They're afraid. And it occurs to me that you can't run this viewing for three days by flowers alone."

"Can you get me some people, Emilio? His wife despised him until the instant he was blown up. Then she changed tack. She's going to be pretty badly off if someone doesn't show."

"I might get you some for tomorrow night. But they'll have to come in from Jersey. It's got to be somebody who hasn't heard too much about the bombings. The Philly papers are really playing it up big."

"How many can you raise?" The moment he asked the question Farragan thought with fury of the family's dead souls up in Kensington and decided there was no hard and fast rule on loyalties.

"Let's say fifty, Arturo. Twenty-five couples. The president of an Italian artistic society in Perth Amboy owes me a favor, and he ought to come through on this. They can all drive down here by themselves, but you're gonna have to stand them to some food and a drink. O.K., Arturo?"

"O.K. Just instruct them to tell Margaret that they're Zephyr drivers. She won't know the difference. She doesn't know any of them anyhow."

"There won't be any slip-ups, Arturo. Don't worry about anything."

Farragan believed him. In time, Serafina finished his drink, and a cigar besides, and made ready to leave. He proffered his condolences to Margaret a second time, and Farragan saw him outside. The gangster-mogul's gray Bentley convertible was the only car in the driveway, and they stood for a long moment in the well of the front porch watching the driver raise the top in deference to the sprinkles of rain that began inevitably at the end of that day's fierce humidity. In the street at the end of the drive Serafina's Federal police were exchanging police pleasantries with Farragan's city police.

"Tell me, Emilio," Farragan said, "why did you come? You didn't know Jim that well at all. Was it because you figured no one would show and you didn't want Margaret to be so badly disappointed?" Something in Farragan was responding warmly to the notion that Serafina, like himself, was a man who could stand to see no woman suffer pain of any kind. This, despite any vehement judgment Farragan had made of the mogul's crassness in the past.

"No, Arturo, *paisan,* it was because of that son of a bitch of a tail the Feds have on me. I mean the one from Nebraska who got his car stuck in the sand that time down at Beach Haven. I hate him. Almost two years he's been followin' me around, Arturo, and he still pretends I'm not there. He's drivin' me crazy. Last week I was goin' up the Jersey Turnpike to New York, and I stopped in a Howard Johnson's for something to eat. He comes in right behind me, sits down beside me at the counter, and orders the exact same thing. But I'm beef sirloin rare and he's well-done, right? When the waitress brings the orders she gives him the rare and me the well done. So I turn to him, Arturo, and say, 'I think we've each got the other's platter there, crime buster!'

"But he keeps lookin' straight ahead, Arturo, and he doesn't say anything, so I jabbed him in the arm and I said, 'You've got my meat there, pal.' And then he spoke for the first time ever, Arturo. He said, 'I don't know what you're talking about, sir. I ordered well-done sirloin, and I'm eating well-done sirloin.' This, Arturo, with the fucking blood from the rare meat comin' down over his lips onto his chin and a look of nausea on his Midwestern puss like he's about to vomit on a second. I didn't know what to do, Arturo. I just fell apart. Me, Emilio Serafina, I fell apart. I pushed back the food and put my head down on Howard Johnson's counter and started to bawl like a baby. I mean, how much is one man supposed to take? Those Feds knew what they were doing when they put that guy on me."

"All this seems very sad, Emilio. But it still doesn't answer why you showed up here tonight."

"Because of him, Arturo. Because of my robot from Nebraska. I figured, if a bomb did go off around here, it'd be good cover for a few slugs to go winging their way in his direction. Who's to blame his accident on the likes of me, what with the reign of terror that's going on in your family?"

Farragan was mute on response. Beyond the porch, in the lighted darkness, the rain fell more heavily now, and his impulse was to throw off his clothes and descend the steps naked for a cleansing. Serafina could find shit in the heart of a lily. Some primitive instinct—like defense of clan—that Farragan did not often indulge, rose rapidly to his lips: "I don't think you should be so opportunistic about my family's bad luck, Serafina."

"Arturo, *paison,* don't be holier than thou with me, O.K.? I'm supposed to be the disreputable gangland figure. But what's happening in your very reputable family has got Lucrezia Borgia beat. You just ain't sacred any more. So don't be mad at me if I use your tribe for running cover. It's convenient. I'm trying to make up for it, after all. Let me know how many more people come to this wake besides the fifty I send over tomorrow night. You couldn't get a squadron of kamikaze pilots to march across the lawn of this place the way things are now."

"Yes, thank you, Emilio," Farragan said distantly. He shook hands with the new ally of the remaining Farragans.

As he drove off, Serafina graciously had his driver pause a long moment before turning into the street to permit his tail from Nebraska to slip unobtrusively back to the Federal Ford in order to follow him. Despite himself, Farragan stood laughing at that example of professional courtesy.

Then he went inside to pray a rosary with Margaret, Muriel, Crow, and Edmund for the repose of Jim Farragan's soul.

Serafina the gangster was the only mourner to show that first night.

The next night fifty-three members of the Fra Filippo Lippi Artistic Society of Perth Amboy, New Jersey, dutifully wished Margaret their deepest condolences over Big Jim's death. Serafina, on the outside, kept them coming in staggered groups of six and eight so it would not seem conclusively like conspiracy. But for Farragan's purposes they were all wrong. They looked and talked like polyglot literati rather than truck drivers, and drank far too little, and he waited for the moment that Margaret would turn around and demand to know who they really were.

But she did not, and, talking with a number of them later, Farragan learned that Serafina had told them Jim resided in a closed coffin because the length of him had been run over unwittingly by a ten-ton truck after he collapsed and died behind it at the Zephyr Terminal from a heart attack. There was, therefore, little of him left that was appropriate for viewing. No one seemed to know anything about a bomb, except for their leader, a tall cadaverous man with a goatee and otherwise impressively demonic features who sipped interminably from the same night-long glass of sherry and stared at the burnished planes of the coffin.

"Papa Satan, Papa Satan, *aleppe*," he said of the whole business to Farragan while shrugging his shoulders. "Dante. Seventh canto, fourth circle. The indecipherable gibberish of Plutus."

"Yes," Farragan agreed, also shrugging. He knew the words. At Georgetown in his sophomore year he had come home from class one December afternoon to find that his roommate, Abel McGraw, had just left to participate in the newly declared war. The same words, with a question mark appended, were written in soap across his dresser mirror, and Farragan had that day long ago given them the instinctually perfect translation of: who can tell what the future will bring? McGraw, he had heard, died from a clunk in the head while safely crash landing his bomber in an English pasture. The rest of the crew escaped unharmed. It made about as much sense, he speculated, as Jim's going through the roof of his Lincoln.

When the literati had sat for an hour more, then helped themselves again to food and drink, prayed a rosary with Edmund and delivered final condolences to Margaret, they took leave for Perth Amboy. On the way out, Farragan pressed a new bottle of sherry into the leader's hands. Inside, seated by the casket that held her husband's remains, Margaret seemed properly appeased.

The following afternoon, in the midst of a high ninety-degree heat, Marie and her aunts showed up. Farragan watched them cross the room to stand before the coffin, and could not, despite himself, erase from his mind the new thought of Granahan's prompting that Marie, who despised Jim and Anna to excess for their politics, might just be responsible for their deaths for reasons of profit. Part of it at least made sense: why else would she (and the old ladies, for that matter) be unafraid to come there?

"We are so sorry again, Mr. Farragan," the elder of the aunts told him. "Tragedy seems to be stalking your family."

"It's truly a pity that their deaths have happened in this fashion," the other one said. "People are afraid to come to the wake, and there was never a man who deserved a grand wake more than your brother."

"He was almost a Knight of Malta," said Jim's widow.

"Yes, we know that. Everyone did. But they're still afraid to come. People called us and warned us that someone might put a bomb in a floral basket."

"I don't think that's possible," the older said. "I have a theory that it's an inside job. It's probably safest for us to be here, since the mad bomber is probably here with us."

"Yes," Farragan agreed. It seemed logical: including Crow, who sought ways in the paneled dining room to keep the trays of hors d'oeuvres from spoiling, there were eight of them present. A goodly number to pick from. But if he entertained the possibility of the three Glennises being the killers, did that mean they thought Farragan might be also suspect?

"Many people feel that you are responsible for this, Mr. Farragan," the younger Glennis told him. "They think you may have coveted your entire business for yourself and decided to eliminate your partners, so to speak."

"But I didn't," Farragan protested. "They were my brother and sister. I loved them."

"That's exactly what we told everyone who called."

"Who called?"

"All the summer people from the island and lots of others that we know from Saint Theresa's parish," the elder said. "But we also told them that, even if you were the killer, there was absolutely no danger in showing up here since you obviously weren't going to plant a bomb wherever you chanced to be."

Sweet God! Farragan thought to himself. Absolved of the possibility of guilt by Granahan the detective, he had not even considered that he might be universally suspected outside the Police Department.

"I didn't kill my brother and sister, Rachel," he said solemnly to the old lady.

"If the truth be known, Mr. Farragan, we really didn't think so. We've seen you praying too often and too earnestly at Mass, after all. It's just that no one can figure it out. There just doesn't seem to be a motive other than for you to want control of your entire business."

"Or someone else to want control of it for me," Farragan said meaningfully, the instant after both old ladies had fallen into conversation with Margaret and Muriel.

"Drop dead, Mr. Farragan," came the low retort from Marie. Farragan was pleased to see that only Edmund, mystified, appeared to have noticed the tense exchange.

The evening of the third and last day before the funeral, one-armed Edward, the son of Jim, and his new wife entered early into the quiet of what promised to be the most dismal session yet and stayed only five minutes near the body of his father. But it was the best to be hoped for under the circumstances, Farragan thought ruefully. Just one moment inside the door, and he was already drawing flak from his mother with her insistence that he honor his father's memory and be married in the Church. Privately, Farragan might have smashed his brother's widow. He was reminded of his own mother with her sudden midstream changes and recalled with annoyance that she had done greater service to the crumbly earth of her husband's grave than she had ever done to his person. Farragan had been wrong to befriend Margaret, the fellow sufferer, and keep their quiet conspiracy all these years until now.

During her pleadings and weepings beside the coffin, Edmund had left the room, and Farragan himself had looked distressedly away toward the gathering darkness outside and thought about being abed with Marie. He was relieved after a time to realize that Edward and his wife were standing expectantly before him. Across the room, Muriel laid comforting hands on the rejected mother.

"Thank you, Uncle Arthur, for the wedding gift," he said, extending his one good arm for a handshake that Farragan embarrassedly clasped with the wrong hand.

"It will pay our apartment rent for a whole year," the girl said. Farragan observed her closely for a brief moment and decided she was somewhat prettier than he remembered her from meetings in the past. And plainly happier. But her calves and ankles impressed him with their heaviness, as before. He recalled that she was a nurse. Many nurses seemed to him to be exactly that way.

"Where is your apartment, Edward? What will you do now?"

"The apartment is in West Philly. I start Penn this semester as an English grad student."

"Will you be an English professor? In college, Edward?"

"I hope so."

"That's what I always wanted to be," Farragan said distantly. It came to him once again in that instant—perhaps for the last time in his life—that if he had not fallen heir to Zephyr Motor Freight after the war, he might have gone on for an advanced degree. Then he would have returned to Georgetown to subtly confound the students of the Jesuits with his personal notes on *Ulysses* and *Finnegans Wake*. Also, he would teach *Madame Bovary* and, of course, *The Great Gatsby*. And Joyce's *Portrait of the Artist as a Young Man,* because he had delightedly read it by flashlight under the covers in his dorm room when Joyce was anathema to the Jesuits and considered it an experience that no undergraduate of any generation should miss. Even if there was no longer any defiance to take pleasure in.

When he looked up he saw Edward and his wife staring at him as if from a great distance and somewhat pityingly. It was the same look he remembered on Marie's face the time he had chased El Greco at the retreat house, and Farragan decided in that moment that he knew what the much-prattled generation gap was all about. It was that look. Plain and simple. And it did no good to rage against it. . . . That look would end up consuming you.

In time they exited, and Binky Applebaum was next to break the long silence that followed their parting. It occurred to Farragan as Binky plodded across the room that he had somewhere divested himself of much of his previous shyness at being in the death house of gentiles. A confidence born of repetition, evidently. Only the eternal suggestion of deep personal anguish was still strong in his eyes. That was one misery that would never go away.

"I think it's terrible what's happening, Mr. Farragan," Binky said after presumably praying again in Hebrew over the coffin of Jim.

"Yes, it is, Binky. Why weren't you afraid to come? I hear all the people on the island think it's an inside job. They think I did it." Farragan was conscious of a more than mildly anguished question mark at the end of his voice. But he could afford it. He had always talked easily with Binky.

"Some do. Others just keep it to themselves. I talked with some people last night, Mr. Farragan, and we all agreed that if it was you, then it was obviously perfectly safe to come here."

"Thank you," Farragan said miserably. "The Glennis sisters said exactly the same thing."

"But then somebody else said it might be an outside job instead of an inside job, and it wasn't worth taking the risk. So nobody's coming."

"Why did you come, Binky?" Farragan asked, prepared to suspect the lifeguard captain.

"With my condition, it doesn't particularly matter whether or not I get blown up. I really don't have too much to look forward to, if you know what I mean."

"Yes." It made sense to Farragan somehow.

That last night for the rosary there were but Farragan, his Muriel, Margaret, Edmund, Applebaum, and Fitzpatrick the milkman.

Fitzpatrick stayed on in the quiet house after the others had left and had three drinks to Farragan's one.

"Why weren't you afraid to come, Fitzy? None of the other Knights showed up."

"They're scared, Arthur, and who can blame them? For me it doesn't matter. I've been tryin' to find an agreeable way to commit suicide for years now. It would take care of a lot of things. I'm sick to death of the wife 'n' the ten kids 'n' all the yellin' 'n' screamin'. I've tried gettin' up enough guts for years now to walk into the front of a truck down on Broad Street, but I just can't bring myself to do it 'cause it's a mortal sin to take your own life 'n' I'd end up in Hell for all my trouble. But if I come here where there was a bomb, somebody would take my life for me, 'n' it wouldn't be my responsibility."

"Yes, it would, Fitzy. Because the hope was there, if not the certainty. And that counts just as much. You still wanted to die, after all."

"Yes, well, I still do. Arthur, let's go over to Kensington for a drink at Ginty's Shamrock Bar 'n' try to put the death wish under the weather for tonight. That's where your mother used to go for her monthly bender. A lot of the old people will be there. They'll be glad to see you."

"No, I'm not going. If they're so eager to see me, why the hell didn't they come to Jim's viewing? They all think I did it, anyhow."

"No, they don't Arthur. None of them think you did it. They're your mother's people. If they thought you did it, they'd all be here since you're not about to blow yourself up. They think it's an outside job. The cops think so, too."

Ah me, thought Farragan, the wonder of it all. Arthur, a prince of the house of Farragan living on his Wynnewood Acres was more isolated from his own fate than his mother's old drinking gang. It was comforting to know, though, that the police really had absolved him. The idea of going to Kensington was suddenly greatly appealing, since he knew he could expect a full bushel of honest sympathy from anyone he met there.

"O.K., Fitzy, let's go to Ginty's."

"Can we go in your Cadillac, Arthur? The old people would be impressed if they saw me come up in that."

"You can drive it if you like."

"Oh, that would be nice, Arthur."

They left the house and the casket that contained Jim's pieces and Fitzpatrick began delightedly to drive across the city to Kensington.

"I once had a dream about dyin' in a Cadillac convertible on the Expressway at two a.m. in the morning, Arthur. It was a very romantic dream about just breakin' up with a beautiful girl. And I was young 'n' rich 'cause I was a mutual-fund salesman. And I didn't have the red hair like now. It was black like Italian hair 'n' straight like Valentino used to wear it. And anyhow, Arthur, I was killed 'n' my picture was in the *Inquirer* 'n' everybody said, 'Didn't Fitzpatrick go out in style, now?' "

At first Farragan had to resist the urge to laugh out loud at the recounting of the dream. Then he thought he might cry. For a moment he guessed that, though he had not been able to kill for patriotism, he might indeed kill for mercy. For Fitzpatrick was badly needing to be dead. He might take the milkman back to Jim's house and its den full of guns, fire one into his heart as he had been taught to do by Anna, then dump him on the front lawn of his house, where his fat Catherine would find him in the morning.

In time, they drove up to Ginty's Bar and Fitzpatrick sounded the horn to bring out the patrons so they might see him in Farragan's Cadillac.

But the horn sounds fell impotently on apparently deaf ears, and Fitzpatrick relinquished the keys to Farragan and they went inside.

Fitzpatrick, as if he were a nurse, steered Farragan to a table and sat him down before the expected deluge of sympathizers were upon them. Within five minutes, after they had all apologized for not showing at the wake, they had all returned to the bar to watch the television news coverage of the bizarre Farragan deaths. Only Theresa Ginty, his mother's friend, stayed behind.

She was clearly dying, Farragan judged, reflecting that death or the nearness of it pervaded everything these days. She was still as corpulent as ever, but the flesh was no longer corpulent firm and hung from her arms and cheeks in great pouches. Her hair hung long and snarled to her shoulders, and she wore a night gown because she had been called from her bed by her brother when Farragan entered.

"It's good your mother is gone, Arthur, and not around to see this happenin'." She looked far across the room to where Anna's smiling picture appeared on the screen above the bar. The announcer explained that she was widely known in the city for her participation in charitable organizations.

"Yes," Farragan murmured. It came to him for the first time that, with the direction the killings were taking, his mother might well have been a recent victim by now if she were still alive. The Ginty seemed to read his thoughts: "She'd probably have been blown up by now herself, though."

"Why do you say that?"

"I don't know, Arthur. Just a hunch, I guess. Jim and Anna and your mother, Jedda, was pretty much alike. You're like your father, Arthur. There was a man that always made me uneasy. He walked about for his whole life like he had a little secret inside him that nobody was ever goin' to find out about. It used to drive me mad tryin' to figure out what he knew that I didn't."

"He kept a lot to himself, Arthur," Fitzpatrick said. "That's how he was. With Jim and Anna, you knew exactly what they were thinkin' the instant after they thought it. Many thought he was a snob of a man with all his money 'n' everything. But not me. One time in January, the year before he died, I was comin' back from my route with the milk truck past the art museum, 'n' it was snowin' 'n' he was crouched down behind a fountain havin' a snowball fight with nigger kids. Cripes, he looked like he was havin' the time of his life. . . ."

"Arthur, are you afraid somebody's goin' to try for you next?" the Ginty asked.

"Yes, either myself or Edmund," he confessed. Then he began to cry. But not for himself. He realized he had already assumed an un-Christian kind of fatalism toward the prospect of being bombed. Every Vietnamese, apparently, lived with that selfsame fear each day. But it was for Muriel or the condition of Muriel that he wept: the thought that he might be blown to pieces without ever knowing her again the way she had been before the birth of the twins cut him to the quick one more time. But how could he tell that to Theresa Ginty who was actually dying, or Fitzpatrick who prayed earnestly for his own death?

"Oh, Arthur, for Jesus's sake, don't cry," Fitzpatrick said. "If I only could trade places with you! If only I could go out some fine mornin', start the motor of your Cadillac 'n' get blown right through the canvas of the roof. What wish fulfillment, Arthur! That would be wonderful. I can just see me archin' through the air 'n' maybe gettin' hung up in some tree branches for good measure."

O Christ! thought Farragan, the shanty Irish! They were poetical enough about death. But to be poetic in the very act of dying—that was too much.

"But I wouldn't want to be too badly disfigured," Fitzpatrick said.

"Why?" the Ginty asked. "You can't have it both ways. The easy dyin' and the sweet, angelic set of your puss in the coffin."

"It's not for that. My body's already promised to science. They expect it to come in in pretty good shape, after all."

"That's very altruistic of you, Fitzpatrick," Farragan said reservedly, trying desperately now to climb out of this lush womb of sentimentality. He distrusted his nearness to his "roots" when he was drinking and with people like these.

"It's not anything like that, Arthur. I can barely afford to keep livin', so how the hell is anyone I know expected to put up the money to bury me? This way seems saner. The medical school'll come for the body, 'n' the wife'll tell the kids I was dedicated to the advancement of research. That way I'll be immortal."

"I'll give you the money for your funeral, Fitzy," Farragan said, the tears rushing from his eyes.

"When my kids could better use it for their schooling? Or a new roof on the house? Don't waste your money, Arthur. Besides, I'm promised. Look here, I've already got the possession stamp tatooed on my foot."

Farragan and the Ginty watched as Fitzpatrick pulled off his shoe and the inevitable woolly stinking sock. On the bottom of the foot that he twisted upward for them better to see was the visible sign of Fitzpatrick's immortality: a tatoo that Farragan could not believe existed though he saw it before him. Fitzpatrick, whom he had despised more often than not, was a signed and sealed package destined for the knives of medical students, then. The tears flashed forth copiously. The Ginty cried also into the great hams of her arms. Then she begged Fitzpatrick to let her kiss the foot. But instead it was Farragan who slid to his knees before the milkman.

"Let me kiss it, Fitzy."

"Go ahead, Arthur. The humility'll do you some good."

Farragan, reveling suddenly in the awesome stink, placed his lips ardently on the tatoo and kept them there for a long moment. From above he felt Fitzpatrick's great hand lay benignly on his head. *Mea culpa, mea culpa, mea maxima culpa:* Forgive me my distance from these great people, O Lord. I have truly been a snob. Very un-Catholic. He continued to cling to Fitzpatrick's foot, thinking it better even than a thousand six-a.m. stops in a confessional, until the milkman began to wriggle the foot and giggle. "Arthur, stop it for Jesus's sake."

Farragan got up abruptly, wolfing down another drink to wash away the horrible taste in his mouth.

"That was good what you done, Arthur," the Ginty said. "It was for the selfsame reason your poor dear mother came here once a month on a bender. Though Christ knows it would've been easier on her liver if she'd 'a' had Fitzpatrick's foot to kiss instead."

"Yes, she always looked like hell for a few days afterward," Farragan said. He slammed down another drink, then cried some more. There was no getting round it, Ginty had said the truth: a resolute lifetime of trying to call himself the child of his father had been mere false perception, an elaborate self-cuckoldry. He was the child of his mother. All Farragans everywhere were the children of their mother. For a long moment he lay his head on the sleeve of his jacket and sniffled consolingly. Then he rose from his seat to check out his image in the blue-tinted bar mirror and saw with approval that he was truly his mother's son. The vision prompted another bout of crying. The Ginty joined in, and Ginty's brother, who was weeping also now from the habit of complicity with his sister, brought them another round. Across from Farragan, Fitzpatrick, bent double and flushed red from the struggle to return his shoe to his foot, looked up beseechingly. "Arthur, I can't tie my laces."

"Fuck it," Farragan said.

Hours later, with Fitzpatrick barefooted and carrying his shoes in a paper bag, they went outside, where the milkman demanded the right to start up the Cadillac in case there was a bomb wired to it. Farragan complied. It might as well be now as ever. He staggered to the corner of Ginty's building and stood at the end for protection, while Ginty's patrons crouched down behind parked cars nearby. Farragan watched as Fitzpatrick crossed himself and called to old Theresa to tell his wife he had always loved her and to say good-by. Then he turned the key in the ignition. But there was only the soft purr of the Cadillac's power coming to life in response. Disappointed, the onlookers rose up from behind the protecting cars and trooped dejectedly back into the bar. To Farragan's eyes, Fitzpatrick looked decidedly ashamed for having put such hopefulness into the lot of them, then failed to come through with an explosion.

In the morning, while Farragan suffered acutely from a hangover, Edmund read the funeral Mass over Jim's pieces in the cathedral. There were nearly fifteen hundred people present: all their fearing friends, the veterans' organizations, civic and church groups that had been unwilling to chance coming to the viewing. Concurring with medieval precedent, perhaps, they had evidently decided a cathedral was off limits for a bombing.

Later, however, in the cemetery, it was apparently considered a real possibility again: there were only about twenty hardy souls to see the great Jim Farragan's coffin covered into the earth.

# CHAPTER 17

# In Which Much Happens

If there were to be any more funerals, Farragan decided, the weather at least would be bearable enough after the end of September. Along with the habit of daily confession, he had taken to driving each morning to the cemetery—thankful for still being alive—to contemplate his designated spot for eternal resting and enjoy the postdawn-nature freshness and the singing of birds while he was still able. These things counted heavily now.

In the Farragan family plot their parents were buried side by side in the middle, with Anna next to their mother on the right, and Jim next to Anna on the extreme right. On the far left was Stephen's marker, though Stephen was buried in Normandy. Farragan himself had chosen to be placed next to their father, a prospect that no one else particularly coveted, and Edmund was to go also on the left between Farragan and Stephen's marker. Muriel, when she died, would be buried with her people in Virginia, a point she had insisted upon almost since the first days of her marriage.

It occurred to Farragan that the burial positions were properly chosen. He would get down there with his father, and if dialogue were possible, it would be peaceable in the extreme: reminiscence and half-boozed moralizing. Jim and Anna would doubtless be into righteous causes with their mother, but the possibility of sound carrying seemed minimal, and since she was to the other side of his father, Farragan guessed he might safely ignore her.

But he found he could not persist a long time in the being-dead fantasy. Besides, no one had been blown up in two weeks, since Jim, and he began to feel self-conscious about driving to the cemetery each day, trailed by the same protecting unmarked police car that sat in a lane several acres of tombstone away and probably puzzled over Farragan's morbidity.

This, until the sixteenth day after Jim's funeral, when the trailing car suddenly left off watching and puzzling and came up behind him to tell him that he must telephone his brother Edmund immediately at Saint Blaise.

Farragan raced out of the cemetery, with the police car behind, and made for a phone booth, assuming that someone had made an attempt on Edmund's life. But when he heard the whimperings of the priest's voice, Farragan was hardly prepared for the cause of sorrow.

"Arthur, Father General is dead," Edmund wailed into his ear.

"Father General who?"

"Father Mahaffey, the general of my order."

"Oh, him."

"He was the smallest, holiest man I ever knew, Arthur. He was only four feet eleven inches tall. His cassock had to be specially ordered. He died at our mother house in Cimson, New York, and he's being brought here for burial. Please come up, Arthur. I need to have you here."

"But why, Edmund? What can I do? I'm sorry Father General

is dead, but I just can't take the prospect of another funeral for its own sake these days."

"We don't have enough men to bury him, Arthur. There are only four of us left alive now, and we need seven. That's you and Mr. Bowen and Mr. Farrow."

"Oh, God. Can I at least bring Marie along?"

"Yes, if you like. Though discreetly, of course. Some of the ladies from the Sportsman's Club auxiliary down in the village will prepare food for us. Perhaps she can help them."

"She'd just love that," Farragan said sarcastically, startled to note at the same time how incredibly animated Edmund became at these times of death.

Farragan placed the receiver on the hook for a long moment, then retrieved it to dial Marie, shaking his head for the benefit of the cop outside to indicate that no one was dead by bombing, at least.

The first to answer was the elder of the Glennis sisters. She quizzed him for an interminable minute on the progress of the investigation into the bombings, then assured him she did not consider he was responsible. Farragan thanked her profusely and urged her to work hard in his behalf at turning the tide of public opinion. Then he asked for Marie.

"My aunts think you're clean," she said instantly on taking the phone from the old lady.

"God bless them. Who can it be, then? Listen, will you run up to Saint Blaise with me for a few days? Edmund's Father General is dead and needs burying. There aren't enough people left according to the rules of his order, so he's drafting myself, El Greco, and old Bowen for the job."

"I'm so sick of other people's dying, Arthur. Did he get it with a bomb, too?"

"No, just old age. A very peaceful death, I'm sure. Why don't we go? The change would be pleasant."

"Not so pleasant for me if someone makes a bombing raid on you or Edmund while I'm along. How would I explain the loss of something like my head and an arm to my aunts?"

"Your instinct toward self-preservation is commendable, dear," he said dryly. You are also Granahan's chief suspect, he might have included. On the instant he understood what he was really about in telephoning this invitation and he sighed despite himself at the notion of yet another occasion of duplicity. In the weeks since Jim's burial, though he had made love twice against all the ragings of his reason to the girl who might be the killer of his brother and sister, he had come to view the detective's proposal as at least plausible. There seemed to Farragan to be no other motive. And he had thought before of getting her out of the city into neutral territory to discuss the possibility. If she admitted her guilt, they would call it a draw. Make a truce: Jim and Anna were merely two mounds of manure blown off the pleasanter landscape of Farragan's existence, for his purposes. His son's safety had also been assured. There was much actually to be grateful for. And to his mind there was no danger in exposing Edmund at Saint Blaise to the killer: his brother the priest was ultimately harmless, and had no claim at all on the Zephyr Motor Freight that she coveted. Marie knew that.

But if, as she proposed, someone made a bombing raid on Farragan himself, then the killer was not Marie, and she was generously enough provided for in his will.

"All right, Arthur. I was planning to go to the shore for a few days just to get out of the city. But Saint Blaise will do nicely."

"What will you tell your aunts?"

"No need to tell them anything. It appears they know everything."

"You're kidding."

"Not at all. I guess we just haven't been the careful sophisticates we thought we were. Anyhow, they think it appropriate that I'm breaking in with an older man. It's a noble French tradition, they maintain, and my aunts have always enjoyed their fantasies in French."

"God love them for it. Anybody else would have sent the gendarmes after me. How would they respond if I asked you to run away and marry me?"

"Don't be absurd, Arthur. They'd say no and I'd concur. Even the French nobility of Bala Cynwyd is not without its own applied set of rules. You're married and I'm as young as your son. Besides, they figure you're the target of the mad bomber, whoever he is."

"Thank them for their optimism. That makes me a bit weak in the knees even though right now there's a cop outside this telephone booth keeping an eye on me."

"Do we have to take them along, too?"

"No, we go alone. Outside Philadelphia, I'm on my own. I'll pick you up at two this afternoon."

Chastened, Farragan drove to the Zephyr terminal to arrange for a two-day absence and sat long minutes behind his desk watching out the window and speculating on his eagerness to sell the whole works. This, before those cadres of trusted office employees, effectively terrorized for years by Jim, sensed the real extent of his lack of interest and began a nightmare of accounting abuses to make up for the years of their servitude. In time, Quinn, the yard supervisor, came to tell him that the first of the newly painted trailers had arrived back at the terminal. Farragan went to check out the fresh nonethnic symbol and decided he liked immeasurably better the simple blue lettered word ZEPHYR trailing fast upon a blazing comet. He was about to leave for his car when two black drivers came toward him from around the cab of a near-by rig.

"Mr. Farragan? . . ."

"Yes?"

They were Stilson and Noble. Noble, into his sixties, had worked for the old man in the thirties and was close now to retirement. If Farragan were ever asked for his idea of an Uncle Tom, he would have instantly proffered Noble. In accordance, the old man removed his hat. Stilson, who was thirtyish, and drove a Cadillac like Farragan's own, did not.

"What's up, Noble?"

"Are you gettin' rid of all them little Irish guys on the trucks now, Mr. Farragan?"

"Yes. I think the simple lettering is more attractive, don't you?"

"That's for you to decide, Mr. Farragan," Stilson said. "What we'd like to know is if you'd agree to quietly move Little Black Sambo out of the garden patch over there since Charlie Irish is comin' off the trucks?"

"I don't understand, Stilson."

"We mean that little statue of the nigger kid over there."

Farragan stared for a long moment. In the middle of the terminal yard was Anna's flower garden, annoyingly placed so that trucks often had to swing full circle about it for two tries before they might properly maneuver into the loading stalls. In its center was the small black figure of a naked Negro child taken from Jim's front lawn and placed there years ago. Farragan was so accustomed to seeing it that he actually never saw it any more. Like the flowers, when they were in bloom, it was perpetually covered with dust, nearly to the extent of being totally camouflaged. To realize suddenly that its continued existence depended on a counterbalance provided by what Stilson called Charlie Irish was saddening: the blacks had used the leprechaun as a derisive racial symbol, then, because the whites had obviously used the statue.

"I think I'll have the whole flower bed removed. It will make things more convenient here in the yard, anyhow," Farragan said distantly.

"I think your black employees would appreciate it, Mr. Farragan, if you would take away the statue in your car with you now," Stilson said.

"That statue's been there twenty-one years, Mr. Farragan," Noble said. "It's time he went away now. The country's in a bad mess. People ain't kiddin' no more when they makes Little Black Sambo jokes."

"Or Charlie Irish jokes, either," Farragan, a white, reminded him. But he resolved to take the statue away, considering that if he were meant to be the target of a mad bomber, he might at least accomplish a single last act toward equitable justice in his life. Even if it were merely symbolic. He walked to the flower bed, lifted Black Sambo at arm's length to guard against the dust, and walked with it to his car. He was aware of something like a momentary work stoppage among his employees on the loading platforms that ended when he chose to stare hard at one fat-assed white named Rawlins, whom he had always catalogued as a redneck and whom he instinctively disliked. But Rawlins had merely bent his back again to his work, and any possible confrontation was avoided.

Farragan put the statue in the Cadillac and drove, followed by the trailing police car, to his own home to store it in the garage and pick up the two-day bag he had requested Crow to pack. Then to the sisters Glennis. On pulling into the driveway, he was halted by Corinda, the younger of Marie's aunts, clipping at a hedge. In the near distance, the other, Rachel, played a little-old-lady's game of putting at a golf ball.

"We're very sorry about Father Edmund's general dying, Mr. Farragan," she said. "It seems death either stalks your family outright or is never very far away."

"Yes, it does seem that way, doesn't it, Miss Glennis?" Privately, he wondered when she would begin speaking of himself and Marie.

"Marie is preparing to leave for two days to aid Father Edmund at his monastery, Mr. Farragan—despite the danger of a bomb threat that she chooses to ignore. It seems one of the finest duties that can be performed by a Christian gentlewoman, don't you think?"

"Yes, of course."

"She is a Christian gentlewoman, of course, Mr. Farragan. The fact that she's sleeping with you is only a complication that has arisen because of all that time she spent in France. The French are like that. There they have a tradition among the nobility of—"

"I know what the tradition is, Miss Glennis," he interrupted.

"I hope you do, Mr. Farragan, and the limits it implies. We consider that any prospect of marriage to you is absolutely out of the question. Marie deserves a better chance in life than to marry a man twice her age. You won't be a good horse forever, you know."

Farragan might have fainted at that rebuff. She was no longer the doddering ancient. He saw it in an instant. He had been stupid to account her merely Miss Glennis of summers at the shore. She was hard with the truth when it was necessary to speak it.

"You're right, of course, Miss Glennis."

"We're very sorry about Mrs. Farragan and her condition. But you can't have your cake and eat it, after all. Your life has not been altogether desolate. You have children and a comfortable income."

"Yes, Miss Glennis. I'd better pick up Marie now."

"When does Mrs. Farragan return from Beach Haven?"

"Soon, I suppose. I thought it best for her to stay there with the girls until we see which way events are going here in Philadelphia."

"That's wise but unwise at the same time, Mr. Farragan. You ought to recall her and set about establishing a new relationship with her after whatever fashion you can. You've become entirely too dependent on Marie during these horrible events of the last few weeks. Please don't think of doing anything so ambitious up at Saint Blaise as trying to entice Marie to run away with you. My sister and I calculate that you've got little to actually hold you in Philadelphia right now beyond the prospect of a quick sale of your business, in which you've professed to be uninterested. And the bottomless well of your devotion to Mrs. Farragan may begin to seem to you only an entrenched habit of many years if you actually come to think about it. As a liability, she could be left behind and be well provided for monetarily to assuage your conscience. So, therefore, do all you can to avoid the occasion of candlelight and wine up at the monastery, Mr. Farragan."

The convertible's top was down, and she stood squarely opposite him at the passenger's door, and he fully expected her to turn and snip off the radio antenna with her hedge clippers by way of emphasis. Ahead of him, Rachel, the elder, came forward armed with her putter, and laid it carefully on the Cadillac's hood.

"Have you been told, Mr. Farragan?" she asked him.

"Yes, Miss Glennis. The message has been conveyed."

"All of this is so sad, Mr. Farragan. We had studied you so earnestly all those Sundays at Mass and thought you the perfect guardian for our niece in the event of any calamity overtaking us. We were very naïve not to foresee this possibility."

"And I'm correct in assuming that guardianship was your only consideration, Miss Glennis? You were not the least attracted to Arthur Farragan by the knowledge that he had money and could have more and a wife who might be legally locked up in an asylum because of her condition?"

"What are you saying, Mr. Farragan?" the younger asked.

"I'm asking if the three Glennis girls had anything to do with the deaths of my brother and sister, dear Rachel and Corinda?"

"Of course not, Mr. Farragan!" they exclaimed in unison.

"I don't believe you. Now get out of my way, please." His fury had risen at being told he was an old man and at being so desperately on the defensive as he had been these past weeks: they were the mad bombers. He was sure of it now. These two Catholic relics who had fallen heir to a centuries-upon-centuries tradition of ecclesiastic intriguing and put it to damn good use. They were out to make sure their niece made a pile on her first marriage, and maybe even cut themselves in for a share. It made sense: as long as he had known them, they had kept three houses on an independent income; they might be very well scraping the bottom of that barrel now. Ahead of him, ancient Rachel dodged out of his path onto the lawn and Farragan floored the accelerator to race up the driveway to the front steps, where Marie sat waiting with her bag. The old lady's putter clattered off the hood onto the asphalt when he slammed on the brakes before her.

"They did it," he told Marie fiercely. "They killed my brother and sister and they're using reverse psychology on me to get me to marry you."

"They didn't do it. I wouldn't marry you. And stop playing outraged hypocrite. It's general knowledge that nobody saw a single tear in your eye during the last two funerals we participated in. If you could find the bomber, you'd probably reward him. Now I don't want to hear anything else about it, or I'm staying home."

She climbed into the car without a further word, and they returned down the driveway past her aunts, who made multiple signs of the cross over the twosome, though they obviously intended to exorcise the devil in Farragan alone. In twenty minutes more they bade good-by to the trailing police car at the end of the Expressway and were happily free of the city.

They arrived, after more than two hours of never mentioning Jim or Anna, at Saint Blaise as Father General's body was being unloaded from a battered old station wagon. Farragan helped carry him inside, only slightly disconcerted by the fact that the General's remains were not enclosed in a coffin. He lay clad in his cassock, looking like a dead young altar boy, atop a wide plank of wood that Farragan assumed was a rough-hewn door or perhaps the top of a retreat-house table. His carrying partner was the El Greco youth, who rambled on somewhat incoherently about the fact that truck drivers must have been startled to look down from their cabs and see Father General just lying there dead on the rear of the station wagon.

Inside, they prepared for what Edmund called the first watch. The tables in the dining room had been removed and two rows of tall funereal candles were arranged on either side of twin sawhorses, on which they placed the dead priest's pallet. Almost as soon as Father General was located, three other priests, like specters, drew near from out of the room's shadows. Farragan, who had never seen all five Tirungians together at one time, even with one of them dead, was frankly pitying. They were all somewhat like Edmund, though none so fat. Sad, timid men with the implacable look of being Jesuit or Franciscan rejects. But their response to Father General's death was clearly different from that of Edmund who had become something of the handmaiden of death. He actually enjoyed the occasion because it brought people and activity near him. Each of the three watched the wizened form of their general apprehensively, as if they were reminded of their own proximate mortality for the first time in a long time.

"There must be seven of us for the watch," Edmund pronounced. "So Arthur and Mr. Farrow and Mr. Bowen will have to dress up in Tirungian cassocks."

"But we aren't priests, Edmund," Farragan protested.

"That's not the point, Arthur. The substance means little in this case. It's the form that counts. You'll have to help us with the election of a new Father General also."

As he said that, Edmund winked at him, and Farragan knew resignedly how he must vote. As apparently did Farrow and Bowen, who jabbed him simultaneously with an elbow from either side. When Marie went down to the dungeon kitchen to aid the Sportsman's Club ladies in their task of preparing food for the watchers, Edmund brought out their robes, the special black-hooded habit of the Tirungians' times of mourning which the nonpriests struggled into, then directed them to their positions with the priests on the appointed stools. Predictably, the funeral chanting of many monks soon rose out of the hidden P.A. system.

In time, sweet contentment swept over Farragan, and he began to think he might sit so forever, swaying slightly to the mournful ebb and flow of voices, wrapped in the great folds of the Tirungian cassock with his face hidden in its shadows from the world. Old Bowen sat across from him, a bony white mask in the midst of his cowl, and beside the ancient was El Greco, the glazed eyes of his mystic persuasion shining fiercely in the dimness. Between them, Father General lay in slightly smiling peacefulness on his plank. Farragan was reminded at one and the same time of his own father and the tombs of the Spanish kings that he and Muriel had once seen in the Burgos cathedral. Tiny men, evidently, shorter than five feet, were buried there. Part of the historical joke, the guide had told them, about midget warriors, the ilk of the legendary El Cid, who were armored in portable sardine cans.

After two soporific hours during which no one had stirred and Farragan's bladder was near to bursting despite the calm, Edmund picked up a staff, tapped it three times on the ground, then spoke. "The first watch is ended."

Outside it was quickly darkening, and Farragan rose from his stool to look behind him in the gloom and see Marie watching him from a seat and calmly puffing a cigarette.

"You look very well in your cassock, Arthur. You really ought to have been a priest. Though on second thought, celibacy isn't exactly your bag."

"I feel very comfortable, thank you."

"Father General's preparations are almost like a vacation compared to the last two viewings I've been to."

"They are rather peaceful. He was a good man, from all accounts. I suppose that's why there are so few of us here to honor him. Let's hope this is the end of other people's dying for a long time to come. As far as funerals go, it will be my preferred memory."

"You say that so meaningfully, Arthur. I almost hope for both our sakes that someone goes after Edmund. Because you know that I know he doesn't own a dime's worth of Zephyr Motor Freight. And anyone that takes the trouble to kill him isn't after the golden egg, so to speak."

"It's a marvelous theory, Marie. Now all you and your aunts have to do is bump off Edmund to shift the suspicion away from the fortune-hunting motive."

"Fuck yourself, Arthur dear. You really are getting to be a difficult old man. I wonder what it was I saw in you in the first place, anyhow."

"My money?"

"Hardly. I suppose it was your redeeming honesty despite yourself. Don't try laying a lustful hand on me while we're in this monastery, or I'm liable to castrate you for your trouble. I think I'd be doing myself an immense disservice to permit my chief accuser to make love to me in the same breath that he calls me a murderess."

"You don't understand, Marie," Farragan said, sitting beside her now and half-covering her with the folds of his habit. "I'm not asking you to pay for your crime. It's a blessing they're gone, as far as I'm concerned. I'm just asking you to admit it to me and remove the uncertainty. I'll never tell the police."

"Oh, Arthur, drop dead. Let's go to the kitchen to eat."

Farragan was silent. Following Edmund, they navigated the tortuous stairs to the kitchen. Everyone sat about the great table on which Farragan had once smashed his hand and ate stew from bowls and pieces of buttered Italian bread and drank glasses of sweet Manischewitz wine that normally did service on the altar of the chapel. The simplicity of their communal meal appealed to Farragan despite his ranking out by Marie, and he began to think of the entire proceedings as happily medieval.

"Arthur, will you volunteer to help dig the grave?" Edmund asked when Farragan had put away his last pewter spoonful and carefully wiped his mouth.

"He's to be buried here?" The medieval bubble had burst at the suggestion that Father General's leavetaking was not to be all monkish meditation and communal meals with wine and crusty bread.

"He'll be buried on the hill behind the Virgin's grotto, Arthur. The grave has to be six feet deep, but it only has to be four feet eleven inches long."

"I'll help you, Mr. Farragan," the El Greco youth said. "Burying the dead is a corporal work of mercy."

"I'll hold the lantern," Marie said. "That way I'll be sure neither of you hits the other with a shovel and pushes the victim into the hole."

"I'm not capable of that any more, Miss Glennis," El Greco said. "The satyr inside me is dead. Father Edmund has shown me the way. Besides, I've got a favor to ask of both of you. In the afternoon, after Father General's burial, I'm to be baptized. I don't hesi-

tate to ask you or Mr. Farragan to be my godparents because Father
Edmund has explained the special nature of your illicit relationship.
Would it be all right?"

"Yes, of course," said Farragan instantly to cover up his reluc-
tance. In truth, he was still not excited about having El Greco in
the faith. But being a godparent every two years or so was something he had grown used to in adult life, and it might as well be
Farrow as anyone else this time.

In another hour, when it was fully dark, though moonlit, they
went outside to dig the grave. Farragan had not done anything more
strenuous than play tennis in years and wondered frankly how he
would stand up to the ordeal of digging. But the El Greco youth
had the certain fanatical look of a professional performer of corporal
works of mercy, and Farragan guessed he might be counted on to do
the lion's share of shoveling.

They found the place Edmund had marked off atop the hill
and Marie lit two lanterns against the night and graveyard spirits. El
Greco began to attack the covering sod with the frenzied, unfamiliar
strokes of a pick, then soon collapsed out of breath on the damp
grass to tell them about the possibility of arousing one of his attacks
of asthma. Farragan resigned himself to digging most of the hole
alone.

It took three hours to complete. Marie and El Greco called out
encouragement and old Bowen hobbled back and forth from the
main house with pots of coffee. Farragan found the digging arduous
in the extreme and more than once thought of killing El Greco,
who held forth—despite threats—for nearly the whole time on the
depth of his sorrow over the deaths of Jim and Anna and even the
Farragans' sainted mother, none of whom he had ever known. Near
the end, when he approached the six-foot depth, it was especially
difficult since the hole was but four feet eleven inches long and
made for awkward bending and heaving of the dirt. At last, Marie

and El Greco and old Bowen and Edmund pulled him from the pit, and Farragan was barely able to stand up straight.

Covering the grave with a tarp against the possibility of rain, they went in to the second watch. Farragan, aching in a thousand places, sat bundled in his robe another time across from El Greco, whom he decided he hated all over again. Father General, as small as before and presumedly as saintly, lay smiling at the ceiling between them. Farragan saw after an hour that El Greco, who stared unceasingly at the dead man, was crying now; long, incredible streams of tears that merely rolled down his cheeks without any accompanying rack of sobs. Before the watch was over, the new convert was snoringly fast asleep, though the tears still coursed down, and Farragan wondered with considerable awe and much change in perception how he might be even the smallest part worthy to be the godfather of a man who contained such rivers of incredible sorrow.

After the second watch was completed, they went gratefully to bed (Farragan by himself), only to be awakened for third watch at six a.m. At nine a.m. began Father General's Requiem Mass. At eleven he was carried on his plank up to the fresh grave atop the hill and gently lowered in by ropes, with only a black cloth across his face to protect it from the dirt that Farragan and El Greco rained in upon it. After all the elaborate flower-trimmed stupidity he had recently seen, Farragan decided he would like to be buried exactly so: thrust rudely into a hole in the ground and compactly covered over with dirt.

In the afternoon of that same day El Greco was baptized and received into the Church. Farragan was his godfather, Marie was his godmother, and Edmund administered the sacrament. Farragan decided that as long as he lived he would never forget the sight of the new convert standing naked to his waist in an illuminating shaft of light with the holy water straining through his beard, looking for all of his intense neurotic new Catholicism as if he were posing for the Master, El Greco himself. Somehow, Farragan felt, the new communicant belonged definitely to another, earlier century. Marie judged so too, apparently: "I can just imagine him receiving Communion," she whispered meaningfully. "He'll probably slither up the aisle on his belly to feel worthy of the privilege."

It came as no particular surprise, an instant later, when Farrow announced his desire to be ordained a Tirungian as soon as possible. The news was also welcome to Farragan, since it seemed to diminish the possibilities of godparent responsibility on his part in the future.

For a gift Farragan gave El Greco twenty dollars in an envelope on which he had written: *To our new convert, Mr. Farrow.* Marie gave him twenty dollars also and a luminous Saint Christopher medal that Farragan realized uneasily had been attached magnetically to the dashboard of his convertible only a short time before.

At six o'clock they ate dinner once more with the Sportsman's ladies in the kitchen dungeon, Farragan annoyed that he had to stay at Saint Blaise still another night to participate in the election of a new Father General. The whole thing was a blatant fix, though none of the timid monks was up to actually calling it that. There were but four bona fide Tirungians left in the world, and the rules called for the seven it had taken to bury the old leader as the minimum number to elect a new leader. Thus El Greco, old Bowen, and Farragan himself were to dress up in Tirungian habits again, presumably to vote for Edmund. Farragan's brother wanted the job badly, for whatever reason: he sat chewing his nails instead of eating, and the small, ratty gleam had returned to his eyes.

After dinner, when it was growing dark, they went into the great hall of the Crusader shields, where Father General had lain in state on his plank, to prepare for the election. Father Alphonse, the eldest, handed out the five-foot staves they were to use to tamp the stone floor to show affirmation of their choice of candidate for next ruler of the Tirungians. He intoned a loud prayer in behalf of honesty and impartiality. Then they sat in a circle, all properly habited, and waited while Father Alphonse called out the list of names.

"Father Alphonse."

There was one knock as Father Alphonse struck his own stave on the floor while the others sat in silent judgment of his chances.

"Father James Gerrity."

There were two knocks this time: Father James Gerrity for himself and Father Alphonse, who, it seemed to Farragan, was glaring openly at Edmund.

"Father James Sloan."

Predictably, there were three knocks: Father James Sloan for himself, Father James Gerrity, and Father Alphonse, all three of whom were now clearly glaring at Edmund.

"Father Edmund," Father Alphonse gnashed out. There were four knocks in response, the first clear majority of the voting: Father Edmund for himself, Old Bowen, El Greco, and Farragan.

"This doesn't seem right," Father James Gerrity said. "None of Father Edmund's supporters are ordained priests, after all."

"But I will be in time," the El Greco youth told them.

"And I've lived my life each day as if I were a priest myself," old Bowen said.

"I'm Father Edmund's brother," Farragan said, apologetically shrugging his shoulders to show there was little he could do under the circumstances.

"That, at least, is true," Father Alphonse said, sighing. "I guess Father Edmund is our new general."

While Farragan, El Greco, and Bowen stood by, the three losers knelt in turn before Edmund to kiss his hands in homage, though Farragan half-expected one of them to take a bite out of his brother instead. Afterward they trooped back to the kitchen for a drink of celebration, where Edmund spoke the singularly inappropriate words that caused Farragan to drink more than he ought to have: "If only mother were here to see me now."

In the morning, dizzy with a hangover, he went up the hill to level the earth on Father General's grave in some token last affinity for that small, holy man and stood about for a long moment thinking inexplicably of Mahatma Gandhi. Then he bade good-by and congratulations again to Edmund, who asked his brother to prepare a news release about his ascendancy for the Philadelphia papers when he returned to the city.

# CHAPTER 18

# *Alas, Edmund Also . . .*

When at eleven o'clock two nights later Edmund tearfully phoned Farragan, who was abed with Marie, to inform his brother that someone was shooting at him with silenced rifles, Farragan urged him to ring the state police before the telephone wires were cut, then hung up to call (within the limits of conscience) just as many people as possible, including Granahan the detective, to establish an alibi. Then he phoned the State Police to reinforce Edmund's plea for help and begged them to send a car to the retreat house immediately. Marie, who had gotten dressed and watched the entire proceedings with frank disbelief, stood up after a time and wordlessly left the room. Fleetingly, from his bedroom window, Farragan saw her march resolutely down the driveway to the street.

In another minute Edmund phoned back to say that Farrow was dead and that if Farragan called off his hired killers they might still call the convert's death an accident. Edmund stressed tearfully that he had still not called the police. Behind his brother's breath-

ing, Farragan heard the noise of shattering glass and tried to guess
how many people were firing at once. He ordered Edmund to call
the police, since he had already done so.

"Then it isn't you, Arthur?"

"Of course not!"

"Who in God's name can it be? You were the only one left to
suspect."

"I don't know, Edmund. Honestly I don't."

"Look to yourself, Arthur, for they'll be after you next. Do
you hear them firing?"

"Yes."

"Arthur, I'm so frightened. I've always tried to live by the
laws of Holy Mother the Church, and now this is happening to me.
They'll kill me. They've already killed Farrow, Arthur. He looked
over a window sill to try to see who they were, and they shot a bullet right through his forehead. I don't have a gun, even. Arthur . . ."

"What is it?" One hundred and fifty miles away in Philadelphia, Farragan felt himself convulsed with a nameless terror. He sat
on the floor now with his back to the side of his bed, his legs drawn
up before him, and one arm cupped tightly about his knees. Edmund's breathing came raspily into the wire. From his own heart,
Farragan had a clear suggestion of how his brother's must needs be
pounding.

"They've come into the house, Arthur," Edmund whimpered.
"They've broken the glass at the front door and let themselves in. I
can hear two sets of footsteps. Oh, Arthur . . . listen! Arthur, it's
the police! Arthur, I'm not going to die! I can see their flasher
lights coming up the mountain! There's four whole cars full of
them!"

"Don't cry, Edmund! Don't worry any more!" Farragan found
himself screaming like a participant in the end of a good Western.

"It won't take them more than a minute to get up that hill! They'll catch whoever it is! There's no other way on or off that mountain!"

This was it, Farragan decided: the payoff for the incessant dole to the Police Benevolent Association that every Farragan, while living, had belonged to. In life there had to be one brilliant, crystal-line-clear time for everyone when the cops came crashing through the barricades to restore order and purpose and haul the anarchists off to their punishment. This was it for what was left of the clan Farragan, then. After this night, Farragan judged, he would have at least one weapon in hand to bludgeon the arguments of Simon his son who hated the police so aggressively.

"Arthur . . . oh, Arthur, they're stuck!"

"What the fuck are you talking about?"

"There's something across the road about halfway up. They can't get past it. Oh, Arthur, I'm still going to die."

"Sweet Mother of God . . . Edmund, where are you now?"

"In the sacristy."

"Edmund, hide behind the altar! If they find you, implore the protection of the Church. It was always done in medieval times. They might be Catholics!"

"Oh, Arthur, don't be such an ass! The whole place is a church. Arthur . . . I can hear them coming up the stairs. Arthur, I have no defense. I'm going to be killed. Say quickly an Act of Contrition so I can listen to it."

"O, my God, I am heartily sorry for having offended Thee, . . ." Farragan began. On the other end of the line, Edmund cried softly now. As Farragan ended the prayer, his brother spoke with an incredible calm. "Arthur, I must go now and hide behind the altar. I have always loved you dearly as a brother. Much more so than Jim. That's all I want to tell you. They're in the hallway on this floor now. I'll drag the phone around the corner with me and perhaps you'll hear who it is."

Farragan heard the swish of Edmund's cassock as he moved out of the sacristy to the altar, and then a small clunk as the priest presumably set the phone on the floor beside him. After a long moment, horrific with its depth a silence, there was a muffled sob, then the words, "Good-by, brother Arthur." In response, Farragan cried bitterly, halting when he heard with unbelievable clarity the first fall of the killer's footsteps: light and tentative, cautiously rounding the corner before the chapel doors to start up the center aisle. Farragan, hearing the gate to the altar railing swing open, began shouting through the phone, "Stop! Stop in the name of God. You're killing an innocent man!"

But there was no response. Seconds later Farragan heard Edmund scream out, "Arthur! Oh, my God, you won't believe who it is!"

"Who is it? Who is it, Edmund?"

"No, I can't tell you! You'll never believe it!"

The words were chopped off by the whizz of a silenced revolver, and Farragan, weeping alone in Philadelphia, listened as his brother screamed and thrashed a moment in the space behind the marble altar, then apparently died.

The phone was hung up with a soft click that sounded in the listener's ear.

Granahan the detective was in Farragan's driveway less than a minute after the killer had replaced the receiver in its cradle at the monastery. He urged Farragan into some clothes, pushed him into a police car, then drove faster than Farragan had ever traveled over land before to the International Airport, where they boarded someone's private helicopter on loan for the trip to Saint Blaise. Leaving the lights of the city behind and churning northward along the Delaware past the smaller illuminated clusters of what he assumed was Washington's Crossing or Yardley, Farragan thought se-

riously for a time of knocking out the pilot with the heavy wrench
he fingered beneath his seat; braining the man and crashing them to
their deaths into the vast dark spaces of woodsy Pennsylvania before
the killer or killers saw fit to do in the last Farragan of his generation. Better to die now than endure the merciless expectancy: Farragan was not a good enough Catholic for that kind of resignation.
Only he saw in the glow of instrument illumination the look of
pained dismay on Granahan's face and remembered the detective
had five children. Impulsively, he asked the pilot, who wore no
ring, if he were married.

"Yes, sir," the man spoke, "I have three kids, too."

"Don't get any funny ideas, Arthur," Granahan warned. "I
don't have any jurisdiction down in that forest."

"What the hell am I going to do, Granny? I think I'm going
to pieces right now."

"Save it, Arthur. You'll need your wits about you. They're
smart, whoever they are. They got on and off that mountain without using a car and the Staties never even got near them. They
threw a couple of big trees across the narrowest part of that road to
force them to leave the cars, then set up a trip-wire farther up the
road that let go with a fusillade of thirty-thirty blanks that kept
twenty or so troopers on their bellies for about fifteen minutes.
They've got to be hired hit men. They haven't done an amateur
thing in three tries."

"It wasn't the girl. I told you it wasn't. She was with me when
it was happening."

"I said they were professionals. The girl isn't, but all it takes is
money. And what better place for her to be than with you in the
hay when all this is going on? She should already have been picked
up for questioning by my men by now."

"Granny, we're from Philadelphia! From the suburban par-
ishes. My family ran a trucking company. It was an honest business.

We went to church and lived in peace with our neighbors. We weren't racketeers. And the girl is one of us. How can any of this be happening? I'm trying to tell you what our life is like!"

He had both hands on Granahan now, pleading, until his fingers recognized the outline of the gun in the cop's shoulder holster. Then he eased, stunned by the remembrance that only a short time in the past, before the Democrats' convention, he himself had worn just such a revolver in pretended service to two patriot-killers in a mission of mercy to save his son. Thence had it all begun. Granahan seized his arm, pinning it tightly across his chest.

"You're trying to tell me what your life is supposed to be like, and I'm sorry it's gotten all fucked up on you. Now calm yourself, Arthur, or I'll have to throw the cuffs on you. This is the first time I've ever been off the ground in anything higher than a ten-story building, and I'm scared shitless. I'm getting set to vomit the instant I touch down."

For his part, Farragan merely wept. He had lost control now. Some combination of fear and horror had convinced him it was useless to gobble another breath of air. No one had the answer. Not Granahan the wise cop or Marie the inscrutable, who even now was being interrogated by the police. And certainly not the Church, that manure pile of platitudes that Farragan saw on the instant he had never considered leaving, since he had never in his lifetime dared to put it to the same test of honesty that Simon, his son, had already done and ended with. In the dark sky over the Pennsylvania Poconos, vibrating to the whump-whump beating of the copter's rotors, Farragan decided on the instant he rather felt more like quietly laughing than crying, as was expected of him. Implore the protection of the Church, he had actually advised his brother in the moment of his danger. Sweet funny Christ! What a stupid thing to say. . . .

In ten minutes more they touched down on the floodlit overgrown lawn of Saint Blaise and found three state-police cars before the front steps and another at the gates holding back the few curious. Inside they were still taking pictures, and Farragan and Granahan were led through one of the carpeted and paneled reception rooms, where El Greco lay in a blood-soaked Tirungian cassock, the top of his head almost lifted off by a bullet.

"Whoever hit him was a Deadeye Dick," a state-police captain told Granahan. "Lifted his hairpiece with one bullet from a thirty-thirty. The old man died from heart failure in the ambulance on the way to Stroudsburg. They didn't even need to touch him. He was hiding up a fireplace and in shock from fear when we got here. It took four of us to haul him down from there."

"Christ Jesus," Granahan whispered. "How about the priest?"

"He's behind the altar in the church. Two bullets right through the heart. It doesn't look like he had a chance to save himself. This is the third one in the same family, isn't it?"

"Yes. This is the priest's brother, Mr. Farragan."

"What's up, Mr. Farragan?" the state cop asked.

"We don't know, captain, and down in Philly we're two murders ahead of you," Granahan said.

"Where's my brother?" Farragan asked. They sounded like two cops on a TV serial. He needed to view the reality of a dead, fat priest.

"Still behind the altar. Are you sure you want to see him, Mr. Farragan?"

"Yes."

They marched through another paneled and carpeted room and down the long hallway to the chapel, where the captain and two troopers who had joined them removed their hats. Automatically, Farragan genuflected before the tabernacle and noted that all but one of the policemen did also. He edged around behind the altar, dreading to see the presumed mask of frozen terror on dead

Edmund's face. But there was no suggestion of that emotion, or pain either. Edmund had died sitting up against a stack of small benches and blood still oozed down the front of his cassock, which was completely stained. His chin hung down on his chest but turned slightly to one side, so that his mien, if anything, was somewhat ironically comic, and perhaps even grateful. Uncontrolled, Farragan began crying bitterly. Granahan, also, wept into a handkerchief.

"Jesus Christ, a priest!" the detective raged. "They couldn't even leave a priest alone! Who the hell is it, Arthur?"

"It's not Marie. She loved Edmund. You ought to call Philadelphia and tell them to let her go, Granny. She'd never be responsible for a thing like this."

"I'm impotent!" Granahan nearly screamed. "Before God's altar, I don't know how to help you, Arthur. I'll double the cops tailing you now, but you might as well prepare yourself for the fact that some number of professional killers is going to try a hit at you sometime in the near future. I only hope one of my boys is close enough to get a shot at them and at least prove they're flesh and blood, because I'm starting to think they're otherworldly."

"Yes, perhaps they are," Farragan said softly. But it occurred to him that, except for the fact of Muriel and the twins, it really did not much concern him now whether he was bumped off or not. The will to live had gone out of him.

"Do you think they'll go for Muriel or Margaret, Granny?"

"No, I don't think so, though I've guessed wrong before. They're working their way down the main tree of the Farragans, and you're all that's left. It seems the worst thing I've ever done, Arthur, to have to stand here and tell you I think you're just as good as dead."

"Well, I've made my Easter Duty, as the Church would have it. I just hope that when it comes it's painless. I hate pain."

Then, impulsively, he bent down over Edmund and kissed his brother's forehead. He was kissing the dumb sweetness, he knew.

In two days Edmund was buried in the family plot with a protective policeman standing on either side of Farragan and Muriel. Father James Sloan—the new head of Edmund's order because he had received the next highest number of votes—read the departing prayers. Privately, to Farragan and Muriel, he lamented the passing of Edmund and consequently Saint Blaise, and wondered out loud where the money had come from to keep it running. Farragan did not think it necessary to tell him.

Otherwise, there was only a wrathful yet sorrowing Marie and her aunts and four of the men from Somerton Pines and their wives, who lamented Edmund's passing and the closing of Saint Blaise also, but could not really determine—especially in the case of El Greco and old Bowen—what function it had ever served.

As ever, even flat up against the prospect of his own death, Farragan still had no defense against the salt-of-the-earth types. He could not, for the life of him, imagine how Edmund had stuck it out on the mountaintop as long as he had.

# CHAPTER 19

# Farragan's Retreat

Within a month of Edmund's burial, in mid-November, Zephyr Motor Freight was sold outright to a syndicate, conveniently formed within the tortuous empire of Emilio Serafina. The sale agreement stipulated, in return for a reduction in sale price, that all the Zephyr drivers on the job under present contract agreement stay until the next scheduled bargaining session. But even after the reduction, Farragan was still a wealthy man.

Only he considered his money of little use since he expected to die a hundred times each day.

He stayed at home now with Muriel and the twins, who had returned from the shore, and Mrs. Crow and thought after a time he might go daft. Crow could not be gotten rid of, and he supposed she would simply hang about until she died, babytalking to Muriel and their daughters and cooking interminable Irish stews in the same large pot that she never washed, the better to preserve the hereditary flavor. But Muriel seemed to enjoy Crow's incessant gossiping—if Farragan did not—and he often found his wife in the kitchen, seated primly on a work stool, nodding her head in rhythm to and smiling myopically in the same eternal way at the house-keeper's onrushing monologue, whether it be good, bad, or indifferent. In the last analysis, he supposed, it was Muriel's appreciation of Crow's prodigious effort to fill the smallest silence with noise that kept her coming back for more. Farragan decided that, at such speed, his wife could be counted on to understand actually very little of the dirt the housekeeper peddled. And just as well. . . .

Each morning, in deference to some ritual, Farragan (over his brief spate of heresy, since he had nothing to reinforce it with) and Muriel went together to early Mass. Farragan lit dollar votive candles daily and prayed for the protection of Muriel and their daughters, Marie his mistress, and Simon his son, the repose of Edmund's soul, and his own painless death in the event of an attack by the killers, though he felt more venially self-indulgent each day since they had not stirred in seven weeks, and even Granahan was growing skeptical of their intentions. Muriel, for her part, prayed for Farragan's safety from the killers, Simon, and their daughters, the departed souls of Edmund, Jim, and Anna, and the happiness of their friend Binky Applebaum, who had so little to look forward to in life. All in that order of importance, she told her husband.

One morning the seventh week after Edmund's burial, when the first light snow had fallen in Wynnewood, Granahan waited for Farragan and Muriel outside the church after Mass and told Farragan his tail was being removed for lack of any action on the part of the killers.

"It'll probably happen the day after you take those cops away, Granny," Farragan said dully.

"You seem remarkably calm, anyhow, Arthur," Granahan said.

"I always am for a few hours every morning after Mass and

Communion. It's starting into the afternoon that my hands begin trembling from fright and I find myself peeking out the windows and thinking about a drink. I always hope I'll get it walking down the church steps in the morning. If I were badly wounded and meant to die, I might be a bit more stoic about my pain, then."

"Shush, Arthur, don't talk that way with Muriel here," Granahan said. "You know how to use a gun. I'll get you a permit to carry that .38 you told me you have. The only reason I'm doing it is that I don't think you're one-tenth as spooky as you were a month ago. Then, you would've started throwing lead at anything that came near you."

"I'll carry the gun, Granny, but I don't think I'll bother to use it on anyone. If they do come after me and I beat them off, it would only mean they'd try again. I'd rather get it over with."

"I don't think they're going to try for you, Arthur," Granahan pronounced slowly, looking a far distance past Muriel, who stood apart from the two men, and into the church's brick side as if the certain knowledge were written on a tableau hung in the sanctuary. Snow melted into the thin fibers of his gray hair. His breath smoked tiny clouds in the cold air. "I think they're finished, whoever they are. It has nothing to do with methodical police work. Just a hunch and something like woman's intuition, I guess. But their pattern is broken. Six weeks is a long wait when they moved so quickly on Jim, Anna, and Edmund. They've chosen to spare you for some reason, I think."

"Call me tomorrow at midnight and see if I've managed to live through my first full day without my four watchdogs. If I don't answer, you'll know what happened."

"If you don't answer, it'll just mean you're sleeping soundly. If you get it anytime during the day, I should know within five minutes at most."

"That's comforting. At least one part of my fate won't be to end up in the Philadelphia papers as a rotting, unclaimed corpse. A wealth of family pride and tradition of lavish funerals couldn't stand for that possibility."

But when Granahan called at midnight of the first full unprotected day, Farragan was alive to answer him. As happened the following six days at midnight, until the detective protested he was tired of his morbid task, promised to continue his investigation into the deaths of Jim, Anna, and Edmund, and urged Farragan, for sanity, out of his house and into the world.

Complying, with the .38 strapped to his shoulder despite his subsiding fear, Farragan groped about to try reordering the splintered pieces of his old existence. But he found immediately that if he were not hiding in his home, then he had no real working occupation—what with Zephyr Frieght gone to Serafina and the people of his syndicate—and consequently time lay heavy on his hands. Since it was nearly December there were no longer any summery days at Beach Haven to spend walking on the sand, and no golf or tennis matches to be had either. He took up the slack in exercise by swimming in the enclosed pool at his home (alone, since Muriel did not go into the water) and marching defiantly about the city, perhaps in full view of the killers, visiting the art museum, trudging the lanes of Society Hill and photographing all that was historic and available in the city for an album collection for his daughters. Also he indulged his re-emerging voyeuristic flame by sneaking into the smaller, shadowy theaters along Market Street for the nudist-colony skin-flick matinees, praying all the while that no one had seen him enter or would see him exit.

People, whose presence in life he had formerly taken for granted, he now began to seek out voraciously. But it was difficult: Philadelphia was a small town, after all, and the name of Farragan was now synonymous with plague. In the two months since Edmund's death he had made love but twice to Marie, both because it was once again necessary to arrange motel meetings now that Muriel was back home, and because Farragan had been fearful to venture out of his house more often than that. But now, somewhat more assured of his continued existence, he rushed to her desperately, even promising to unseat Muriel, only to find her engaged in a calculated retreat from his life. He could not say when it began exactly. It was not because she bore him any particular malice: somehow Granahan the Sensible had managed to convince her that Farragan's accusations about her complicity in the murders were merely a tool (that lovers were wont to use) and that, in fact, he had been her chief supporter and acting character witness.

Instead, Marie, who had at one time loved him hard in the face of overwhelming competition from Muriel, a spiritual quality with a deranged mind, was now frankly pitying. Farragan sensed it miserably when he went several afternoons each week, full of hope, to sit on the same cushioned marble bench and watch her at work in the interior-decorating salon she had opened in early November on Spruce Street (in a location obtained through Serafina, who may merely have evicted the former tenants in her behalf) with a good-looking, well-spoken young designer, also named Arthur, whom Farragan thought of shooting with the .38 from vile jealousy, until Marie persuaded him her business partner was a homosexual. In time, Farragan, aware that he had no absolute prerogative here and unnerved by Arthur's knowing and superior smile, left off visiting her at work and had to be content of occasional evenings with seeing her for a drink and dinner. These days, he was impotent in bed with her, on the average, fifty per cent of the time.

He tried lunching at their country club. But he was in purdah there because of Jim, Anna, and Edmund, and he realized with horror after two or three visits that the physical distance the other members maintained from him at the bar or in the dining room must equal their naïve calculations of the space needed to dissipate the power of a bomb blast at center Farragan. Outside that circle, whose radius appeared to be variously thirty to thirty-five feet, one apparently had a substantial chance of survival: a theory—formulated since Hiroshima—not unlike the second concentric ring of punishment that occurred after the dropping of an atomic bomb.

Only the priests indulged him. Adventurous men, close to God, and saddled with no immediate family, they either believed in Christ's command to minister unto the sick and bury the dead or were just plain suicidal. Anyhow, they sat at lunch with Farragan, who did his level best to keep a conversation afloat and wondered at the same time who was pitying whom. The talk was predictably of Jim, Anna, Edmund, Salvation, the Afterlife, and Seeing Jesus, and each time the tingling heresy rose up in him and he was tempted to admonish the cleric to can the shit and shove the platitudes. But he was too lonely to be that brazen. Instead, he entertained the sad and equally heretical thought that his son, Simon—who had neither Church, nor country even now, nor political-party affiliation, was a much more highly moral person—despite living with his girl friend—than Farragan the father had ever dared to be. For Farragan, that notion injected a kind of balance into the proceedings. Especially on the day of his final visit, when Farragan lunched with three ancient priests who said a separate round of prayers for Jim, Anna, and Edmund in turn among them.

After that, beginning the second week of December, and through Christmas, he saw a lot of Fitzpatrick and Binky Applebaum, neither of whom much cared if he unwittingly carried a bomb into their presence. Binky was holed up for the winter in his A-frame house at Beach Haven, working on his interminable novel about the Korean War and Israel, and Farragan, needing his company, bore cases of Binky's favorite San Miguel beer down to the shore and sat long hours before the lifeguard's fireplace, demolishing six-packs, listening to a passionless reading of the panoramic saga of Americans, Koreans, and Israelis and, between chapters, gleefully urinating the beer into the wind from Binky's sundeck since there was no one to take him to task for his impropriety in December.

With Fitzpatrick, it was even better. As often as three evenings a week they met, either in Ginty's Bar or Fitzpatrick's Christmas kitchen, with its uneradicable smells and great coal-burning stove, where they reminisced at the oil-cloth table and wept over the deaths of Jim and Anna and Edmund and the Farragans' own mother, and sang (after Fitzpatrick had taught him the words) howling, back-slapping renditions of the old Irish songs that Farragan had not been permitted to know as a child. This while Fitzpatrick's ten snotty-nosed, carotene children cringed together in the corners in visible fright at the intensity with which their father and his friend Farragan took their pleasure, and the milkman's fat and stoic wife, Catherine, measured out the rounds of rye with the eye-squinting care of a bartender who has been entrusted with the universal-standard shot glass.

In time, Farragan agreed to accompany Fitzpatrick on his milk route for a few hours of one early-morning delivery shortly after the New Year began. Though he was uncertain about protocol here: should a man who had recently owned a two-hundred-unit freight line of his own consent to serve as delivery boy to the hireling driver of a small local dairy, one of whose trucks might have been accommodated four times over in a single one of the Zephyr rigs? But there was no demeaning money involved, he told himself. It was only a lark and an occasion for exercise, and he pictured an agreeable participation at last in one of his romantic childhood fantasies about the milkman cleaving the early-morning darkness in his snub-nosed truck, running bouncily over the cobblestones with the side doors open, drawing in great draughts of the frigid air while the racks of bottles clattered and chimed behind him, then stopping to sprint to the doorsteps of customers' houses with the goods. All of which came true on his first day on the job, except for the dismaying revelation that milk now came packaged in plastic cartons and no longer clattered and chimed.

By the end of the first week Fitzpatrick was well pleased with his assistant and told him so: "You've become like a lamb, Arthur, compared to how you was. You're the easiest man I ever worked with."

"I've missed a lot in life, Fitzy, not to know what pleasure good, honest labor can bring. It's a special kind of service, too, delivering milk."

They kept a flask of brandy in the glove compartment against the early cold and passed it for a round again for perhaps the fifth time that morning. They were in Port Richmond, near the docks, and the temperature was about five degrees above zero.

"You're good, Arthur, 'n' so easy to talk to after all these years of seemin' like a snob bastard. You remind me of your father when he was still alive 'n' livin' with your mother in the old place in Wynnewyd. Many's the summer mornin' I'd come to deliver the milk 'n' find him asleep in the grass behind the house 'n' covered over with the dew because your poor mother hadn't bothered to take him inside the night before when he passed out from the drink. I'd wake him up 'n' give him a little milk for nourishment, 'n' we'd sing 'Toora-Loora-Loora' or somethin' like that till your mother started screamin' out the window, then I'd help him into his hammock so he'd be warmed by the sun, 'n' he'd be off to sleep again first thing. He was so peaceful, Arthur. The old people are like that when they're goin' back. I never saw a man enjoy the trip as much as your father. He musta drunk a case a day before the end. And so meek, like a little livin' lamb. You remind me of him yourself, Arthur, what with your kindness 'n' willingness to help, 'n' the ever-sweet word on your lips these days."

A mortal terror crept into Farragan: worse even than his dread
of the unknown killers who might still come after him or his fear of
ultimately losing Marie with whom he was hopelessly in love now
that she was no longer accessible. Fitzpatrick had as much as told
him he was going back: acceding to the inner dyings and crum-
blings, embracing the lush grayness of senility that the Farragans'
mother—if she had never done another thing—had taught all her
children to rage against. Bouncing dangerously over the cobblestones in Fitzpatrick's milk truck, Farragan took a vise grip on the
handle bar before him and fought to stomach the terror. Beside
him, the driver, whose eyes, he could see in the instrument lighting,
were glazed with brandy and sentiment, lifted the flask to his lips
again. Farragan seized it and hurled it out the open door. It shattered on the hood of a parked car.

"Arthur, what the Christ did you do that for?"

"I'm not going back, Fitzpatrick! My father was eighty-five
when he died! I'm not even fifty! I'm only forty-six years old!"

"But, Arthur, you seem that way to me now. Can I help it if
that's the way you seem to me? There's no hard 'n' fast rule. Some
men give up the tough grip early in life 'n' others, like your father,
hang on for ages. There's no rule. Lookit Feeley who was in the
Knights with us, Arthur. He was gone at forty-one."

"You stupid bastard! Feeley died of cirrhosis of the liver! He
drank himself to death!"

"Sure, Arthur, that's what it said on the certificate that went
up to Harrisburg. You have to put somethin' down. 'Wanted to die'
ain't a legitimate reason."

Fitzpatrick stopped the milk truck for a light and Farragan
leaped out, screaming that the other was never to contact him again,
and raced up the middle of the streetcar tracks after a PTC trolley
that sat at another light a block away. He made it aboard and collapsed into a seat behind the driver as Fitzpatrick, who had run his

light and come up behind the car, pounded on the window beside
him.

"Arthur! Arthur! What did I do wrong?"

"Get out of here, you milkman fucker! People like you are the
quicksand traps in life! The death angels! You're a big Irish spider
who tangles the unsuspecting up in his web for the pleasure of
watching the slow sap ooze out of them, even if it takes thirty years.
Now I understand for the first time why our mother had only two
days a month of the likes of you and used the other twenty-eight for
putting hard money in the bank. Get away from me!"

Cowed, Fitzpatrick receded behind him as the trolley crossed
the intersection and surged up the street. Farragan fished in his
pocket for a quarter, dropped it into the token box, then noticed for
the first time that he was the only passenger in the car. The driver,
who said he was Irish, evidently noticed also. At the next red light
he stood up from his seat and smashed Farragan neatly across the
mouth for his treachery to the race. Farragan, who had thought
Fitzpatrick was the last of his tribe, decided not to press charges.

He determined to return to business to save himself.

Serafina was helpful here, obliging him with a confidential
prospectus on three retirement-home developments that had need of
capital like Farragan's. For the next few weeks, until the end of January, he was kept blessedly busy flying about the country. The first,
in Arizona near Phoenix, had the best possibilities, it seemed to
him, except that a partnership would require him to spend much of
the forthcoming year in that dry furnace of a state and little at all in
Philadelphia. The second, in southern California, was vetoed by
Marie, whom he begged to go along for the trip, because it meant
to cater to retired Middle Western white Protestants, and by 1969,
she argued, the country had endured quite enough of that bullshit.

It seemed best to comply with her, though it would have been a safe return on investment.

The third, in mid-Florida, was intended to be built on a drained swamp. The first day out, sloshing in hip boots through several feet of water with his proposed partners, Farragan, who hated snakes, saw two water moccasins entwined blissfully about each other and a length of fallen tree and decided the place, once built, would be a ghost town if word ever got out that such creatures existed in its environs. In the end, nothing was adequate, and he returned to Philadelphia to consider buying a commercial building in center city or going in with Serafina's mob on a super nightclub near one of the Jersey tracks. And other schemes that filled his days with at least the necessity to contemplate them. But before his conscience forced a decision, Farragan and Muriel received a telegram from Canada informing them of Simon's impending actual marriage to Alouette. Joyous at that distraction, Farragan found sufficient honesty in himself to admit that re-entering business for the sake of fending off senility would only invite disaster. He had no real enthusiasm now: better to wait out the summer and see how he felt about it then. There was still time.

Simon was to be married on the fifth day of February. His telegram to his parents had ended with an unexpected submissiveness: DO WE HAVE YOUR BLESSING. In response Farragan had wired: OF COURSE YOU HAVE OUR BLESSING. PLEASE SEND PARTICULARS ON ALOUETTE FOR INQUIRER WEDDING ANNOUNCEMENT. YOUR ROOTS ARE STILL IN PHILADELPHIA AFTER ALL.

The announcement information, when it arrived, was faultlessly composed and included a high-gloss photo of their future daughter-in-law clad stunningly in an evening gown: she was no longer a free-loving Canadian flower child. She was Alouette Marie Saint-Beuve of Sainte-Ephrime Province of Quebec and the graduate of not one but two Notre Dame academies and McGill University.

Both her parents were medical doctors and staff members of a Quebec City hospital. She taught secondary school in Montreal, where Simon, a graduate of Brandeis University in Waltham, Massachusetts, was a doctoral candidate in political science at McGill. He was the son of Arthur and Muriel O'Hara Farragan of Philadelphia and Beach Haven, New Jersey. His father had been, until his recent retirement, owner-director of Zephyr Motor Freight, Inc., of Philadelphia. The couple was to be married in L'Eglise Saint-Jean Baptiste at Miss Saint-Beuve's home in Sainte-Ephrime.

Not daring to change a word lest the whole of the beautiful litany of parental pride dissolve before his eyes, Farragan rushed it off to the *Inquirer* and joyfully withstood the onslaught (by telephone and telegram because of the lingering bomb threat) of congratulations from friends and acquaintances who had seen the news and who had been accustomed formerly to sending floral tributes and morbid cards of condolence.

"They always turn out all right if they have good stuff in them," Crow dispensed so unctuously about his house that Farragan, despite his happiness, actually thought of clobbering her when he remembered that the housekeeper had formerly taken her dogma from Anna, who had meant to kill Simon.

"It's good that she's a Catholic girl, Arthur," Muriel said. "It will be easier for them when it comes time to raise the children. Because Simon is also a Catholic. The mixing of religions is complicated and dangerous. It demands more compromise than either party is often able to give. Divorce occurs and the children suffer."

"She's the very best we could have hoped for, Muriel," Farragan told his wife exuberantly, wondering as ever how her fogged-in mind managed such elaborate theoretical clarities when she often did not seem to recall who Simon was.

The day before the wedding Farragan and Muriel flew to Montreal, rented a car, and drove through the February snows to

Sainte-Ephrime, where Simon had booked them into the best and only hotel the town had to offer. There, where first off in the lobby the ancient fear rose to Muriel's eyes at the prospect of having to spend the night in a double bed with her husband, the real end of Farragan began.

The wedding announcement had been a fraud. An act of charity on the part of Simon to appease the customs of distant Philadelphia and restore his father to a kind of respectability. Blessedly, no other Philadelphians beside Farragan and his Muriel had come to witness the truth. Alouette was not of the town of Sainte-Ephrime. There was no church of Saint-Jean Baptiste. Her parents, medical professionals that Farragan had imagined gliding up to meet him in a black and sighing Citröen, were in reality dirt farmers in far north Quebec, whom Alouette despised and had not even bothered to inform about her marriage.

The wedding was to be held in a hippie commune about ten miles from the town where Simon and Alouette were the honored guests for the occasion. Solicitous, the hotelkeeper and lobby fossils assured Farragan that the place was morally degenerate and physically unclean. "They try to live like the Krajakois, the Indians who lived there a hundred years ago. They share their women and do not bathe. Even the Krajakois bathed more frequently, legend has it. You should kidnap your son back to America, *monsieur,* cut his hair, and cause him to take a bath."

"That's impossible," Farragan told them stonily. "Simon could never be made to take a bath."

The next morning, dressed in his tuxedo and favorite cashmere overcoat, Farragan rammed the rented Chevrolet through three-foot-high unplowed drifts to reach the place. When he saw it, a low-lying and smoking collection of sodded huts like the hogans of Comanches or Sioux, replete with yelping dogs and children, he went nearly rigid with accumulated shock.

"I think I'm losing my mind, Muriel."

"It looks like an Indian village, Arthur. I once saw a picture of the inside of a house like that. The mother and father and all the children and the dogs and even the horses lived there during the winter. It looked very warm and comfortable except that it had a dirt floor."

Farragan merely rolled his head from side to side. He closed his eyes and swept away the scene of snow buried and smoking hogans. They could not have come to this: from expectant Philadelphia of the *Inquirer* wedding announcement to a hippie commune in the arctic of Canada that was meaner than the meanest American Indian reservation Farragan could imagine. He enjoyed an instant vision of Simon and the girl of the announcement picture descending the cathedral steps back home through a blizzard of rice toward the long file of bunting-draped Cadillacs that would bear them away to married life. As it was meant to be! When he opened his eyes, he saw that Simon and his bride had emerged from one of the huts to stand against a backdrop of others like themselves: long-haired, many with headbands and crude sheepskin jackets, the men resembled warriors. The women, who seemed, except for Alouette, to huddle all together, held children or baskets in their arms. One of them bore a papoose on her back.

"Don't be afraid, Arthur," Muriel said. "These are good people. I can sense it. Otherwise our son, Simon, would not be with them. Oh, Arthur, I prayed he wouldn't die when you told me he was sick last summer, and my prayers were answered."

She stood out of the car, smiling radiantly now. Farragan watched her through a haze: she wore her mink coat against the cold air, with her head uncovered. Beneath her coat was the new Schiaparelli dress that she and Crow and Marie had spent a whole day shopping for in center city a week before they were to leave for Montreal. It occurred to him distantly that they were absurdly overdressed. He hoped none of the hippies would laugh at them. Before him, Simon rushed up to Muriel. "Mother, I haven't seen you in such a long time!"

"Simon! My darling Simon!"

Farragan was jolted anew by her intensity: she literally broke down sobbing. In years he had rarely heard her speak above an exalted whisper, except when she was frightened. Now he reacted with instant jealousy to the sight of her laying hands on the long hair of her son and holding him to her, when she would not suffer the touch of her husband. Alouette and the members of the commune looked on approvingly. Farragan heard that most grating of all words—"beautiful"—repeated many times.

There was no priest of the Roman Church to marry them. They were joined together, in the largest of the hogans, which was a communal meeting hall and specially decorated with fir boughs and dried corn for the occasion, by one whose claim to spiritual excellence was apparently his membership in a California sun cult. Also he stood taller than any of the others. Rollins was best man. Drums beat softly and two women chanted in a corner. Farragan, in his tuxedo, stood beside Muriel in her Schiaparelli dress and wept bitterly. Muriel, who held a smoking incense stick in her hands (Farragan had refused to accept it) smiled benignly on the scene.

"Oh, Arthur, this is very beautiful."

"No, it isn't, Muriel," he whispered fiercely to her. "No it isn't at all." He wiped his liquid eyes on the sleeve of his jacket. In the name of peace, love, and more grating beauty, the hippie priest called down a blessing on the son of Farragan and Alouette. Farragan, for his part, walked outside, pushing through the skin-covered door to sit down on a convenient seat-high snowbank that was stained with traces of urine—animal or human. Above, low-lying clouds were pregnant with tons of snow. His most fervent wish was that it drop all at once, encapsulating him in an instant glacier forever, saving him from the necessity of returning to Philadelphia and having to provide the wedding details. In moments Muriel came outside, still holding the remnant of her incense stick. Her eyes were wide again with earnest puzzlement. "Arthur, are you ill. Please come inside or we'll miss Simon's marriage."

"A marriage, Muriel? Is that what you call it? Muriel, we're Irish Roman Catholics! What kind of fucking shit is that?"

In his intensity he sprang from his seat to beseech her with open arms. The familiar fear returned to her eyes and she dropped the incense stick and rushed inside. In time Farragan followed, because of the cold, and heard his son pronounced married before mankind. For Muriel's sake, he congratulated Simon, who did not realize apparently that his father had walked out in the middle of the shaman's benediction. He also placed a facetious kiss upon his new daughter-in-law and privately deplored her smell. He shook hands graciously with Rollins. If the hippie movement had indeed peaked and was declining, as he had heard, then he meant to have them all on his side when it came time to persuade Simon to return home and be properly married. For now, he hoped the depth of his desperation did not show through.

As they drove off, Farragan's son and Alouette were being led by the shaman to their own private honeymoon hogan. At Sainte-Ephrime, they checked out of the hotel, disdaining to relay any information to the expectant hotelkeeper, and began the drive back to Montreal and the airport. Farragan used the silence to construct the series of graphic lies he meant to tell anyone in Philadelphia who inquired after the particulars of Simon's wedding.

In another month, in March, Farragan took himself unhappily back to Canada. There was some of the Zephyr sale money to be settled on Simon, and Farragan proposed (after an exchange of letters that were shocking with their suggestion of indifference on Simon's part) meeting him in Montreal and helping him set up an investment plan that would provide an income for Simon and important security for Alouette and their children in the event of a calamity overtaking Simon. Surprising to Farragan, his son did consider himself properly married and meant to have children.

But it was no good: Simon, born of proper Philadelphians, cared as little about money and its applications as he did about conformity and bathing. In the end, he proposed most of it be used for correct charitable purposes.

"Don't give it to the Catholic Church, Father," Simon said. "If it's my money, then that's something I absolutely insist upon."

"Whom can we give it to, then?" They ate in a greasy spoon near Simon's apartment. He could not be persuaded to enter one of the better French restaurants along Saint Catherine Street.

"Are there any Reform Democrats lurking about down in Philadelphia?"

"Not with an organization treasury that I know about. Why don't we give it to the regular Democrats, Simon? Your mother and I always vote that way."

"No, Reform Democrats or nothing, Father. You said it was my choice."

In the end, only cancer research was pure enough. The steam had run out of Farragan's hope to make his son solvent despite himself, and he bade good-by to his son and daughter-in-law at the airport and returned, on the day he had intended, to Philadelphia.

The plane touched down at eight in the evening, in darkness and a thick ground fog that said the land was warming up in preparation for spring, even if the night air was not. Farragan found his car in the lot and drove slowly home, thinking how tired he was of winter. It had oppressed him especially this year, probably because he had had so much time to reflect upon it: he hoped it was for that reason, and not the price of approaching near to fifty years of age.

Before his house, he parked in the street since there was an unknown car blocking the driveway. Farragan tried to remember whose it was, then grew apprehensive of a visit from the killers when he could not: Muriel only rarely had callers and never at all in the evening. He closed the Cadillac door softly, taking with him the revolver he now kept under the front seat instead of strapped to his shoulder.

Only the pool lights were on, and he crept across the lawn to peer through the window above the rim of the black-out curtain. Inside, Muriel and Binky Applebaum swam naked in the aquamarine water, kissing and cavorting, chasing each other across the lanes while Muriel called out to her friend the lifeguard captain in the most lucid fashion possible. Farragan, the husband, stared wide-eyed as Binky climbed out of the water in preparation for diving in on top of his wife. War wound, bullshit! He arched through the air and Farragan gasped at the sight. Instead of an inch of it, he had nearly a foot hanging between his legs, like the blunt pendulum of a grandfather clock. He must have kept it severely taped to himself so it wouldn't show through his clothes; the rustle of paper in his shorts could have been the merest thinness of cellophane, then. For what else was there room enough? Dazed at the notion of so awesome a cuckolding, Farragan nevertheless managed an aggressive tapping on the window glass: the bare bones of his pride needed to let them know they had not gotten off with it completely. He had no hope, however, that the wrong would ever be redressed.

Inside, Binky and Muriel traded frightened looks. Then Binky shrugged his shoulders resignedly and hoisted himself out of the water. Muriel clambered up a ladder behind him. Together, they advanced to the window and stared out at Farragan.

"Come inside, Arthur," Binky said, inviting Farragan into his own house—and calling him by his Christian name for the first time in memory.

"Thank you," Farragan mumbled and went to the double-curtained door on the other side of the pool, where Muriel, still naked and unabashed, admitted him. The eternal myopic gaze of her eyes that he had known for these six years past was gone. The old intelligence was returned.

"How was Simon, Arthur?" she asked him.

"On his way to becoming a Canadian citizen. He wasn't much interested in money, I'm afraid. He's given the lion's share to cancer research," Farragan said. He felt himself on the verge of hysterical tears.

"It's the best thing under the circumstances, Arthur. I hope the entire problem is at a close."

"It was you, Muriel, of course, who got Jim and Anna and Edmund and young Farrow?"

"Yes. Binky was a demolitions expert in Korea with the Army. He's a crack shot with a rifle, too."

"I wish you could see all my marksmanship awards, Arthur," Applebaum said.

"You've killed four people outright and frightened another into a fatal heart attack. How can you stand there and talk about your goddam marksmanship awards?"

"It's too bad about the young man at the retreat house, Arthur," Muriel spoke. "We tried to warn him to leave, but he had the faith and wouldn't go. And Edmund was a mercy killing, for want of a better way to put it. But the other two had it coming. They were going to kill my son, the odious bastards."

"They were the worst kind of people, Arthur," Binky said. "Fascists. They were ridden with prejudices and warped principles from the past. America isn't like that. This is the Age of Aquarius, Arthur."

"They were also two brothers and a sister of mine. Why didn't you kill me, since I was supposed to finish off Simon?" Farragan

wept openly now. He sat on the edge of the diving board for support.

"We decided you'd never kill your own son, Arthur," Muriel
said. "I was your wife for many years, after all. I knew how much
you loved Simon. You were the best of the best of the Farragan
bunch, along with Edmund too, of course. But that was another
problem."

"You still are my wife, Muriel."

"Yes, legally. But that's the extent of it, as far as I'm concerned. About six years back, when the twins were born, I decided
that was as neat a time as any to pull a strategic retreat from that
damn family of yours, Arthur. And from you too, by the way. I had
certain primitive lusts as a woman that weren't being satisfied on
that altar of a marriage bed of ours. It was boring. I'd encourage you
now not to be a hypocrite about any of this, Arthur. We've known
about and tolerated your situation with Marie Glennis for two years
or so."

"You have?"

"Yes," Binky said, "but nobody minds. Let's go into the den
for a drink, Arthur. Muriel and I would like to propose a new order
of things to you."

"What new order of things?"

"Come inside, Arthur."

They walked toward the door, wrapping their nakedness in expanses of beach towel. Muriel, dripping slightly, entered first, then
Farragan, followed by Binky Applebaum, who resembled a Roman
in his toga. Muriel picked up a cigarette and lit it, then sat on the
arm of the sofa Farragan had collapsed onto. Despite himself, he
marveled at how she remained eternally young. Her breasts, incredibly, were high and pointed of themselves; her skin was the same
ivory smoothness he remembered from the days when he had apparently failed to please her on the altar of their marriage bed. About

her waist, when she had stood naked, was only the merest suggestion of a woman who had had three children. In another minute
Binky had served them their drinks.

"How did you find out that Jim and Anna were going to assassinate Simon, Muriel?" Farragan asked, warmed instantly by the
Scotch.

"Crow told me, Arthur. Her method was particularly touching. She apparently overheard one of your target-practice sessions
and needed to get what she knew off her conscience. She chose to
tell me because she figured I was somewhat daft and might not understand enough to do anything about it, but at least the knowledge
had been delivered to someone."

"Good old Crow. Are you sure she won't make any trouble
with the police for you? She must've figured out you're at least par-
tially responsible for all this killing. And she was awfully tight with
Anna, after all."

"She despised your sister, Arthur. Anna was always relegating
her to minor committee work in the War Veterans Ladies' Auxiliary, when Crow had visions of grander office. Anna was the chief
competition. Crow's away at a convention now, and she called earlier this evening to tell us she was just elected some kind of vice-
president. If Anna were still alive, Crow would be rolling bandages
or doing something like that."

There was a long sighing silence while Farragan cried some
more, wiping his eyes occasionally on the end of Muriel's towel, and
greedily finished his drink. To himself, so universally cuckolded, he
began to seem like the purest person he knew. Truly the pearl
among the swine that inhabited the once lush landscape of Farragan's Philadelphia. Binky fixed another drink for him, then sat beside him on the sofa. "Do you want to hear about the new order of
things, Arthur?"

"What's the new order of things, Binky?"

"The old believers have been destroyed, Arthur. Let's carry on as we find ourselves now. We're liberated. You have your thing with Marie Glennis, and we'll have ours. No more sneaking around. It's annoying, and deceitful besides."

"Do you love her, Arthur?" Muriel asked simply.

"Not as much as I love you."

"It's just as well. You'll enjoy her more sexually from being able to think of her as a bit of a slut. As you do. You've inherited too many confining notions about women from that bitch of a mother of yours and her eternal vomiting about the Virgin Mary. That business of covering the statues in the bedroom when we wanted to fuck, then uncovering them when we were finished, was maddening. Now I think we all ought to drink to Binky's proposal."

"Why don't you call Marie tonight, Arthur?" Binky suggested. "She'd be glad to see you. We'll be downstairs in the guest room, and you can use your room upstairs. If she feels like it, we can all have breakfast together in the morning. We'll wear clothes."

"There doesn't seem to be anything I can say about morality or the lack of it, does there, since I carried on my own little subterfuge for these last few years?"

"No, Arthur, there really isn't much to say," Binky agreed. "Especially, if I may be indelicate, since you went along on a plan to murder your own son."

"I never planned to murder him. I only went along with Jim and Anna so I might warn him properly. I used to send him letters begging him to go to France or Sweden or someplace like that, but he always thought they were funny. I was desperate to convince him."

"Was he ever really convinced?" Muriel asked.

"I think so the last time I saw him."

"Thank God for that, then. He'll be all that more decisive

about sawing off his roots, which in this particular case is the best possible solution. He'll make a good life up there in Canada with his new wife."

"One hopes for that, Muriel," Farragan said. "He's our son, after all."

Then he drained his second glass.

"Another, Arthur?"

"No, thank you, Binky. Enjoy yourselves. I'll go upstairs and call Marie now."

Farragan stood up to leave the room and climb the steps, dimly amazed that he was complying with all this: but so much had been taken from his control. He removed his clothes, showered, then climbed into bed naked and telephoned Marie. Almost predictably, the receiver was lifted by one of her aunts. Marie's voice came over the wire moments later.

"You'll never guess what happened," he said, anxious to establish the new order of things immediately. He attempted an elaborately blasé tone.

"What happened, Arthur?"

"I've just discovered that Muriel has been playing an ingenious game all these years. She isn't sick at all. She's been having an affair with Binky Applebaum, the lifeguard captain. They've invited me to invite you over for the night, since they're sleeping together downstairs right now."

He had lost the blasé tone. His voice now contained a hysterical edge that he was trying desperately to modulate with humor: it had all the proportions of a funny, sick joke, after all.

"I'm afraid I won't be coming over, Arthur."

"Why not?"

"Because of a little story Muriel told me a few days ago about what you were doing that day I was stuck up at Saint Blaise and you were supposed to be in Philadelphia for secret talks with your union. You were in Montreal, weren't you, Arthur?"

· "Yes, I was. But Muriel didn't understand, Marie. I only played along with them, with Jim and Anna, to have an excuse to go to Montreal to warn him firsthand that they were gunning for him. I sent him letters before that and he thought they were funny."

"I don't believe you, Arthur. You probably just ran short on guts that day and couldn't go through with the job. I'm going to hang up now. Please don't try to get in touch with me again."

"It was Muriel and Binky who killed the others. I thought you'd at least want to know that," he blurted out.

"That's comforting to know. As I remember, you almost physically terrorized me to admit that I was the killer. And if not me, then certainly my aunts."

"But I never really suspected you, Marie."

"Yes, you did, Arthur. You suspected me primarily. Now I've got to hang up. My aunts will have instructions to hang up also when they hear your voice. And don't try coming around the house. There was some talk of hiring an armed guard and a police dog to watch the place."

"But, Marie . . ."

"Good-by, Arthur."

"But, Marie, I'll never see you again."

"Yes, that's what I hope for. . . . Good-by, Arthur."

She put down the phone, and with the soft click in his ear Farragan knew she was gone.

"She's gone." He said it out loud to no one in particular: perhaps to the cursed statues with vigils burning before them on the top of his bureau and a corner table; perhaps to his mother's coffin picture on the bedside table.

"Yes, she certainly is gone, Arthur," came the echoing judgment through his ear. It was Muriel; she had listened in on an extension.

"Muriel, why did you tell her I went to kill Simon, when you know I went to warn him? There'll be no way to convince her otherwise, now that you've told her that. Why did you do it?" He was sobbing now, racked with coughs, watching the tears drip onto the violet sheets and make tiny islands of a deeper-purple moistness.

"To punish you, Arthur," came the incredible voice of a Medea. "To punish you, you cocksucker! You dirty rat shit fuck of a turdeater! You prick! You queer! You despicable asshole! To punish you for not taking that .38 revolver the first time they put it in your hands and killing them both on the spot! They wanted to murder your son! Our son! Do you understand, you lily-livered, mothersucking faggot! To punish you for making me have to do what you, his father, should have done! How dare you let them think you were going to kill your son for them and their shiteating outraged principles! Fuck them! And fuck you, Arthur Farragan! I'll have Binky drill you right between the eyes, and he's a lot better with his .38 than you are with yours, I'll bet!"

"Muriel! Muriel! In the name of God, where will I go? What will I do?"

"Go to hell, Arthur Farragan. That's where to go. I've put extra statues in your bedroom tonight and lit extra vigil candles. There are three rosaries ready to go on your dresser top and not one but two coffin pictures of your goddam mother. With that awesome combination about you, see if you can't figure out where to go."

He replaced the receiver after her surprisingly soft click-off and got out of bed, deciding to put on some pajamas for the first time in years. He slid into them, astounded, when he looked down, at the shrunkenness of his sex, then picked up one of the coffin pictures and the large Franciscan rosary that Muriel had bought for him in Italy, and climbed back under the covers, holding the coffin picture to his chest. He tried praying the rosary but could not get more than a few Hail Marys into the first decade and gave up on the attempt. He switched off the lights and watched the vigils flicker for a time and thought of the coming spring and the seasonal return of Philadelphians to the shore, where he would be a leper and an outcast and decided he could not face that prospect.

His was the consummate loneliness: estranged even from God, he reasoned as he dropped the rosary listlessly to the floor. Then the metaphor of his life came to him in a blinding flash. He still enjoyed that kind of romantics, no matter how down and out he was: he had been all this time rushing toward the tiny pinpoint of light at the end of an ever-narrowing funnel. Beyond the pinpoint, once squeezed through, lay the universe of souls, where he must seek the wandering shade of his father. The search was on.

He rose from bed again to find the .38 he had hung in the closet. He thought it best to use the silencer also, since he did not want to disturb Muriel and Binky. There would be time enough for that in the morning.

He got in beneath the bed covers again, put the gun to his temple, and got up some guts. The instant before the bullet whizzed into his brain he discovered what target Jim and Anna and he had actually been shooting at down in Anna's basement gallery so many months before.